The man's voice was breathless and strained—little surprise, since Maggie still lay atop him, her back to his chest. Poor guy. She was not, Maggie readily acknowledged, a petite wisp of a woman.

"I'm all right, I think. You?"

"Great. I think."

Maggie chuckled—overwhelmed by a sense of the ridiculous. "We're stuck here forever, tangled in a ladder."

"Nope. I've got my arm free. From here it looks as if maybe your right leg . . ."

"Ow!"

"Sorry. Elbow. What was that I hit?"

"You don't want to know."

"Here we go." She ended up still on top, but she faced down instead of up, and her arms were free, along with one of her legs. "Less like a pretzel."

As their eyes met, they both grew still, suddenly aware of the intimacy of their entangled position.

"Hi," he said, his smile entirely too charming for a man in such an undignified position. He had his leg between her knees and his face six inches from hers. Somehow a friendly, breezy hello didn't seem quite appropriate.

"What are you doing?" She demanded as he started to squirm beneath her.

"I think I can get my other arm free if . . . all right!"

Maggie jumped as his just-liberated hand brushed her breast. The passing touch was a shock through the thin cotton of her shirt.

He grimaced. "Sorry."

"Right."

"All groping is strictly unintentional."

"I'll try to remember that," she replied caustically.

Are you all right?

Bantam Books by Emily Carmichael

FINDING MR. RIGHT
A GHOST FOR MAGGIE

A Ghost for Maggie

EMILY CARMICHAEL

BANTAM BOOKS

New York   Toronto   London   Sydney   Auckland

A GHOST FOR MAGGIE

A Bantam Book / August 1999

ISBN 0-553-57875-8

Published simultaneously in the United States and Canada

Bantam Books are published by Bantam Books, a division of
Random House, Inc. Its trademark, consisting of the words "Bantam
Books" and the portrayal of a rooster, is Registered in U.S. Patent
and Trademark Office and in other countries. Marca Registrada.
Bantam Books, 1540 Broadway, New York, New York 10036.

PRINTED IN THE UNITED STATES OF AMERICA

OPM   10   9   8   7   6   5   4   3   2   1

I would like to express a special thanks to Andrea Prince, proprietor of the Surgeon's House bed and breakfast in Jerome, Arizona, for taking time to talk to me about the day-to-day workings of her lovely inn. Thanks also go to the hospitable residents of Jerome for their patience in answering my questions about life in their unique town.

A Ghost for Maggie

Prologue

Being dead isn't all it's cracked up to be. Take my word for it. The afterlife is about as dull as one of Sadie Johnson's tea parties. Not that I was ever invited to one of Sadie's stupid parties. Sadie would have turned up her toes in a dead faint if I'd come within fifty feet of her house, especially when she had her lady friends visiting. Still, her parties had to be dull as kicking dirt—all those stiff-necked, dried-up hens cackling about the weather, their lumbago, and whose cross-stitch wasn't quite up to snuff. You can't get more boring than that.

Or maybe you can. Like I said, the afterlife is pretty damned ho-hum. At least mine has been, so far. You've heard those hellfire-spouting preachers shouting that you've got to be good? That the folks who pray in church every Sunday are getting a harp when they cash in, and the folks who have a bit too much fun are getting a pitchfork? Horseshit! All of it. I'm here to tell you it's a lie. If anyone should have been pitching brimstone when she checked out, it would have been me, *because I'm about as wicked as you can get. Or at least I was a hundred years ago, before Jackass Jake Schmidt shot me dead in the outhouse. Being wicked isn't as easy once you're planted six feet under.*

Let me introduce myself, folks. Robin Rowe's the name—or Roberta Rowe, if you want to get fancy. Red Robin, the fellows called me, and the name brought a smile to their faces. It surely did. With my red hair, sultry smiles, and the curviest shape God ever gave a woman, I was the hottest thing in Jerome, Arizona. Hell, I was the hottest thing in the whole Wild West. I could knock a man off his feet with a twitch of my hips and send him to heaven with a smile. I could make a man forget his troubles with a touch of my lips and a soft whisper in his ear. As I said, I was wicked. And I was very, very good at being wicked. My girls were good, too. They weren't in the same class as me, of course. But damned close. I didn't hire cheap strumpets to work in my house. Only the classiest ladies, ladies who knew how to please a man and send him on his way smiling. Fellas always got their money's worth at Robin's Nest.

But that was a hundred years ago. Things are different now. Jerome's mines aren't cranking out copper, silver, and gold these days. The shafts and tunnels are boarded up tight. The miners who flocked to Robin's Nest are long gone, replaced by busloads of gray-headed folks from New Jersey and curious sorts looking for the Old West. And the kinds of places that get flocked to are the T-shirt shops and ice-cream joints, the stores that sell jewelry, artwork, and the pitiful clothes that pass for fashion nowadays. I could give these modern gals a hint or two about how a woman should dress. But then, nobody cares what I think anymore.

That's what I get for being a ghost. It took a good while for me to get used to that. I wasn't happy about getting shot, as I'd been counting on a lot longer life than a measly thirty-eight years. It doesn't seem fair, somehow. I worked hard all my life—and if you don't think we sporting ladies work, why don't you try it for a while? Lying down on the job doesn't mean you're slacking off when you're a strumpet. I started out as a lumberman's daughter with only two dresses to my name: my workaday dress and my Sunday-go-to-meeting dress. But when Jake Schmidt shot me, I had a mansion in Jerome, a closet full of fancy gowns, two dresser drawers full of jewelry, and a pile of money that made the town's bankers my very good friends.

But more important than all of that—I had a seventeen-year-old daughter in school in South Carolina. Seventeen is such a fragile age, and she was so sheltered. Too sheltered. My fault, I reckon, but what was I supposed to do? Let her lead the same hardscrabble life I'd put up with? She didn't even know how her mother made a living. I told her I owned a hotel—just a wee stretch of the truth.

Understandably, my Laura was a tad put out when she learned the truth about her mother. Embarrassed, too. I can't blame her. Still, she carried resentment too far when she ripped my name from the family Bible and vowed not to speak it ever again. Disrespectful is what that was. Fancy woman or not, I was still the mother who carried her inside me for nine long months. And her marrying that Homer Pilford was plain stupid. He just wanted her money—my money it was, really. I would have given her hell if I'd been alive at the time. But I was new at being a ghost, and I hadn't gotten the knack of getting people to listen to me. Now, if I say boo, you'll hear me—if I want you to. But that was a hundred years ago, and even ghosts need time to learn their trade.

Well, Laura was unhappy with that gold digger Homer, as I could have told her she would be. Her two daughters screwed up their lives as well, and their daughters, too. I watched it all, helpless, till I was sick and tired of the sorry lot of them. Finally, as the new century came in, there was only one little gal left who carried my blood, and she was continuing the family tradition of trashing her love life. Her natural urges weren't the problem. Her heart was the problem. She was headed for spinsterhood, sure as hell. And there went the glorious legacy of Robin Rowe. Not only did the family pedigree lack my name in its proper place, thanks to Laura, but the whole family was about to peter out like dust blown away by the wind.

Then something happened. Someone up there who pulls the strings dumped my great-great-granddaughter, Maggie Potter, right smack on my doorstep. It was spring of the year 2000, a day of blue skies and blazing sunshine, and she stood like a lost child in the middle of the lane in front of Robin's Nest. I recognized her right off. Blood calls to blood, you know, even when you no longer have any.

Pretty as a picture, Maggie was—or at least she could have been, with her thick reddish hair (a little gift from me), her long legs (another gift), and her curvy form. Too bad she didn't have a lick of sense between the ears. Not that I didn't have sympathy for her plight. I knew what was troubling that gal. Oh yes, I knew. Not pretty, what had happened to her. But then, life isn't pretty, usually. Most of us get over it.

What really wasn't pretty, to my way of thinking, was that this little gal was last on earth to carry anything from Robin Rowe, and she seemed determined to *keep it that way. Depressing. Still, she was here. I was here. How hard could it be to bump Maggie onto the right path? A push here, a shove there, a hint or two or three.*

I was confident. I had all the cards in my hand, you see, and the deck was stacked.

Maggie Potter had never before heard a house call to her, but she heard this one. It stood in the warm April sunshine, two stories of gleaming stucco and red Spanish tile, and called out her name. Maggie stood in the middle of Hill Street and stared.

"Oh my! Isn't this just quaint?" Maggie's stepmother Virginia wasn't looking at the house. She was looking at the café across the street, aptly named the Haunted Hamburger. "Do you supposed it's really haunted?"

"I'll bet it is!" Catherine, like her mother, Virginia, was blond, blue-eyed, and plumpish. Unlike Virginia, her hair was not teased into a bouffant but fell in lustrous waves to her shoulders. Her eyes twinkled and her smile was as infectious as the cheerful sunshine. "I'll bet they have ghosts frying the hamburgers. Cheap labor, you know."

Virginia sniffed. "It's not so ridiculous. Jerome is a ghost town. Something should be haunted."

"Ghost towns don't have ghosts," Catherine told her. "It means the town is a ghost. You know, deserted. No longer alive. Get the connection?"

"I get the connection. And don't use that schoolteacherly voice on me. It's a cute name, all the same. I like the idea of ghosts flipping the hamburgers."

Only half tuned to their conversation, Maggie muttered, "There's no such thing as ghosts, Virginia."

"Don't be a spoilsport, Maggie. We're having fun." Virginia raised her sunglasses and peered at her stepdaughter. "What're you gazing at so intently, dear? You look a bit ghostly yourself."

"That house. That wonderful house."

"What house?" Catherine asked dubiously. "That house?"

"Yes."

"Well, I suppose it was wonderful at one time. Maybe."

"It looks as if no one's lived there in a while," Virginia noted.

The boarded-up windows and weedy yard hadn't escaped Maggie's eyes. They simply didn't matter. The house had something. It called with a siren's song, promising comfort, refuge, security. It promised home.

"Let's take a closer look." Maggie climbed the cracked and crumbling concrete steps that led from the street. The wrought-iron gate creaked when she opened it, and weeds batted at her ankles as she traversed the brick walkway to the front porch.

"Be careful, dear!" Virginia called. "It looks as if you could fall right through to one of those mine tunnels underneath the town."

A big front window had somehow escaped the damage of time. It afforded a view into a large, airy room with a huge fireplace and beautifully carved crown molding.

"Wonderful," Maggie sighed. She turned, and her face lit up at the sight that met her eyes. This house, like every other building in the old mining town of Jerome, Arizona, clung precariously to the side of Cleopatra Hill. The arrangement made for some exciting times, for buildings had been known to slide down the mountain, but it also ensured that every place in town had a sweeping view of the valley below, and beyond that, the Mogollon Rim country and the towering red buttes of the Sedona area.

An idea nibbled at her mind. A ridiculous idea. Ludicrous, farfetched, impractical.

But it was an appealing idea. Compelling, even. Why hadn't she thought of it before? It was just what she needed.

Virginia didn't think much of the idea when Maggie brought it up over a haunted hamburger, but Catherine's eyes lit up.

"What fun! And when school lets out next month, I'll have the whole summer to help you. Maybe we could buy the place together. I have some money put aside."

"That would be great. Look at the horde of tourists up here. And how many rooms are available to accommodate them? Twenty? Twenty-five?"

"You're both nuts!" Virginia chimed in. "There's a bunch of motels just down the road in Cottonwood. Who'd want to stay in an expensive bed-and-breakfast that's about to roll down the mountain when they could get a nice, safe motel room for thirty bucks?"

"The view!" Maggie enthused. "The ambiance! The history!"

"That old jail building we saw has slid a half mile from where it was built!"

"It hasn't slid a half mile," Catherine corrected her succinctly. "Only a couple of hundred feet."

"Always the schoolmistress. The point is, it's not where they put it."

"This house is fine," Maggie insisted.

"You don't know the house is fine."

"The house is fine. I know."

"That's silly. How could you know? Are you an engineer? Are you a contractor?"

Maggie shrugged, and Virginia gave her a suspicious look. "That's an odd smile on your face. Are you all right?"

"You're imagining things. And the house is fine."

"It's probably not for sale."

"It is."

"There was no For Sale sign."

"It's for sale."

"Something else you just know?"

"I . . . well, yes."

"I keep telling you, ever since you came home, that you should see a shrink. Someone who's been through what you've been through . . . well, you should see a shrink. It's no disgrace to need a little help. A shrink would help you more than a falling down house that's sliding down a mountain."

"Virginia . . ."

"Well, I think Maggie's idea is just wonderful!" Catherine interjected diplomatically. "Just think! Maggie and I running an inn in picturesque Jerome. Fresh air. Interesting people. It's ideal. Sedona's just down the road—big draw, there, with the scenery, the art stuff, and all the New Age gurus. And the Grand Canyon's just a couple of hours away. Tourists will be flocking to our front door. It's almost destiny, isn't it? We drive up here for a day's outing, and Maggie finds her life's mission. I think it's terrific!"

"Terrific, schmerific. It's insanity. That's what it is. Insanity."

Maggie tuned them both out. She was busy looking out the café window at The House. She smiled and somehow didn't think it odd that The House seemed to smile back.

One

June 2000

"I've never gotten such satisfaction from flushing a toilet." On her knees beside the porcelain throne, Maggie smiled as the water gurgled cheerfully down the pipe. At the same time, clean water flowed from a little spigot on the back of the toilet into a soupbowl-size sink in the porcelain lid—limited space used with maximum efficiency.

"Is it working now?" Catherine asked from the staircase, where she was sweeping away the last of the plaster dust.

Maggie raised her wrench in a gesture of victory. "It's working." She backed out of the closet-sized bathroom and regarded her handiwork with pride.

Catherine laughed. "That's not so much a half bath as an eighth of a bath."

"I think it's charming. How much room does a person need, anyway, as long as you can turn around and set your butt where it's supposed to be? Bless Eddie

Chalmers for finding the fixtures. Whoever would have thought of putting a sink right on the back of the toilet?"

"Someone else who's converting a coat closet into a bathroom?"

"And he was awfully nice to tell me over the phone how to get the thing working. It saved us the cost of a house call. Actually, everyone who's worked on the house has been really nice."

Catherine sat on a stair and regarded her half sister with wry amusement. "If you hadn't been running with the political hyenas so long, Mags, you'd realize that most people are nice. Not everyone thinks that loyalty, truth, and integrity are just words to throw into a sound bite."

"Don't start," Maggie warned. "I don't want to talk about it." Her eyes surveyed the lower floor with pride. Oak floors gleamed with fresh wax. Walls proudly displayed new wallpaper and paint, and new sparkling windows looked over the valley below. A huge gas cookstove dominated the kitchen, ready to cook breakfast for an influx of guests, and the rejuvenated garden boasted wrought-iron benches scattered about where guests could relax.

They were ready for their opening day tomorrow. More than just ready—they were poised on the mark and eager for the starting gun. Maggie was determined to make a success of this venture. It was about time she sprinted with an opportunity instead of stumbled.

Catherine sighed wearily. "Okay, Miz Handyman, since you got the can working and the house is swept and scrubbed and polished, why don't we kick back for an hour or so. I'll treat you to lunch."

"Your treat? Wow!"

"Take advantage while you can. I always get insanely generous the first few days of summer break, just because I'm so grateful to be free of school."

Maggie brushed the dust from her jeans and grinned. "The house has turned out to be really something, hasn't it?"

"It really has. Too bad you got stuck with most of the work."

"You were a big help on the weekends."

Catherine grimaced. "I would've been glad to trade my biology students at Red Mountain High for a pair of work gloves and a hammer."

"Ah, the freedom of unemployment." Maggie went into the living room and looked out the huge, east-facing window. The town of Jerome fell away below her, a mishmash of brick, stone, and frame buildings clinging to the hillside in seeming defiance of gravity. U.S. Route 89A snaked its way through town in a series of precarious hairpin turns that turned many tourist faces green, then ran a tamer course through the towns of Clarkdale and Cottonwood, far below Maggie's hillside perch. The Verde Valley stretched away east and south, dressed in its finery of new summer green. To the northeast, the spectacular red buttes of Sedona basked in the warm sun, and in the far distance towered the snow-capped San Francisco Peaks, one of Arizona's highest mountains.

"I could learn to love this place," Maggie said.

"Of course. I love it already. How many reservations do we have for tomorrow?"

"One. A pair of girls driving in from the Grand Canyon."

"Oh. Well, there'll be more. I have faith. We didn't mortgage our souls in vain."

Maggie sometimes wondered if she had a soul left to mortgage, but Catherine's cheerful smile pulled her away from that yawning pit before she could jump in. "I hear lunch calling. Let's go."

They walked down the hill toward the English Kitchen, which served good salads and sandwiches. Almost nothing in Jerome was far enough away to necessitate maneuvering the car through the narrow streets. Besides, Maggie enjoyed walking through the late spring sunshine. She'd been born in Phoenix, in the Valley of the Sun, and grew up in nearby Glendale, but the last few years living in the Midwest had made her almost forget the joy of Arizona's bright blue skies and golden sun.

This early June day was nearly perfect. Not too hot, but warm enough to make a person want to stretch out in the sunshine like a languid cat. Shop doors stood open, and the ice-cream parlor was doing a bonanza business. Store clerks waved to Maggie and Catherine as they walked by. Maggie's purchase of the old Robin's Nest, as the house had been called in its heyday, had been the town gossip almost before the ink was dry on the mortgage papers. The first day she had gone to the post office to collect her mail, the postmaster had greeted Maggie as "the lady who's refeathering Robin's Nest." A member of the Jerome Historical Society had been collecting her mail at the same time, and she'd bent Maggie's ear about the house's lurid past. Discovering her new home had originally been a house of ill repute didn't bother Maggie in the least. Such a wicked history was simply another angle of interest for the paying guests. Right then Maggie had decided to keep the original name—Robin's Nest—and research information about the original owner. She might as well play up the brothel angle, she had thought rather glumly, since the whole country believed she was a strumpet who should fit right in to such a place.

"Isn't this a beautiful day!" Catherine said with a happy sigh. "It's so much nicer up here than in Phoenix. I'll bet it's a hundred and ten degrees in the city today. Ah! There's some newspapers for sale. I'm going to buy one."

"Oh, groan!"

"Bug off. You don't have to read it if you don't want to. I'm not going to tie you to a chair and prop it in front of your eyes."

Maggie sighed and rolled her eyes as Catherine dropped coins in the slot and pulled out a copy of the *Arizona Republic.*

"I was almost right." Catherine glanced at the front page. "It's going to hit a hundred and eight. Ouch."

Maggie staunchly walked on.

"Don't be cranky," her sister advised. "You can read the comics while I catch up on the news."

"I'm not being cranky."

"Yes you are. You're going to have to deal with it, you know, Mags. You think you can get through the whole summer—with one major political convention in July and the other in August—and not read his name or see his picture or watch him flap his jaw on TV most every day of the week? You can't dodge it, no matter how hard you try."

"We don't have a TV. And I can avoid reading the newspapers."

"So you just stick your head in the sand like an ostrich."

"You sound like Virginia."

"Yeah. Well, Mother is occasionally right about something—once a year or so. You can't just pretend Jack Kilbourne doesn't exist and he didn't turn you into shark bait to save his own hide."

Maggie snorted. "Let's change the subject."

"Okay, okay." Catherine threw up her hands, then recovered her smile. "Let's talk about TV. . . . You know, you can get a great deal these days on one of those little satellite dishes, and you don't even have to buy it. Our guests are going to want a TV somewhere in the house, Mags."

"More likely my sister doesn't want to miss her soupy old romantic movies from the forties and fifties."

"They really knew how to make movies back then. I'd miss 'em," Cat admitted.

Maggie managed a smile. "How many times have you seen *Casablanca*?"

"I don't keep count. About thirty, maybe."

"And that thing with Cary Grant and—who was she?"

"Audrey Hepburn. *Charade*. That's one of my favorites. What do you think, Mags? We could put the TV way off in the sunroom, where you wouldn't ever see it, and it wouldn't bother the guests who want nineteenth century atmosphere instead of modern technology. The twenty-seven-inch in my apartment in Chandler is portable, sort of, and I could get it delivered up here by tomorrow, I'll bet. And I've already talked to the dish people. . . ."

They argued amiably the rest of the way down the block, until the appetizing smells drifting from the English Kitchen turned their minds to the more pleasant subject of lunch.

The English Kitchen was one of Jerome's larger restaurants, in that it had more than six tables. All but three tables were on the porch, but in Arizona, that was no disadvantage. Even in winter, the sun was often pleasant enough to eat outside. The place claimed bragging rights for being Arizona's oldest restaurant still in business. This day being Thursday, the restaurant wasn't crowded, and they had a choice of porch tables, each under its own shade umbrella. A college-aged girl in jeans and a halter top brought them water and took their order for sandwiches and iced tea.

"I think the house is ready, don't you?" Maggie asked when the server left. "Everything's cleaner than it will ever be again, probably. Everything's cozy and comfortable."

"Except the Red Room," Catherine reminded her.

"Except the Red Room. Funny how that room has been allowed to just sit and gather dust all these years. People have lived in the house off and on, and the other rooms had work done to them. You'd think that room would have been remodeled as well. It still looks like a den of sin."

"I think it's kind of spooky and mysterious." Catherine's voice dropped to a dramatic pitch. "Our latest Unsolved Mystery: the Room No One Can Change—opulent, steeped in sin, legacy of a decadent past."

"You *have* been watching too much television."

"We could advertise the place as a haunted house."

"That's not the kind of business we want. Good thing we don't need that room right away. But the minute I get time, I'm going to go up there with a few rolls of wallpaper, a bucket of paint, and a stiff scrub brush. It'll be good-bye to the Room No One Can Change."

Catherine shrugged. "Oh well. Too bad the workmen couldn't get to it."

"Just as well. I'd rather save the money and do it myself."

"Maybe the ghost scared the workmen off," Catherine speculated in a threatrical, shivery whisper. "They looked scared to me."

"Right."

The server delivered their sandwiches—a turkey

breast on rye for Maggie and a cheeseburger with fries for Catherine.

"Here comes another two pounds," Cat complained. "Why couldn't I live back in the days when a little extra flesh on a woman was considered sexy?"

"You've worked some off in the last week."

"Don't I wish. Oooooh. Speaking of sexy." Catherine lowered her voice. "There's an absolutely delicious man who just sat down, and he's looking your way. Oh my. Black, black hair, just slightly wavy. Very nice shoulders. Eyes that must be the envy of every woman he knows."

"I doubt very much he's looking my way. Why not your way?"

"Because you're the man trap. You always have been. Besides, it's obvious. He's definitely aimed at you. Not staring, mind you. Just a telling glance every minute or so. Holds it long enough to tip off his interest, but not long enough to be rude. Turn to your right just a skosh and check out the third table to the right."

"Not interested."

"Come on. Do it. He's a stud. Take a look."

"It wouldn't matter if he was Mel Gibson."

"He's better than Mel Gibson."

Maggie snorted dubiously.

"You'll never know unless you look."

On that challenge, Maggie looked. At the third table over sat the man of Catherine's description. Black hair, nice shoulders, maybe mid-thirties, dressed in a short-sleeved shirt, khaki-colored Dockers, and Nikes. Maggie guessed he'd top six feet when he stood. Muscular. Tanned. Probably worked out in a gym where he could admire his pecs in a mirror.

"He's not better than Mel, and he's not looking at me."

"Of course not when you're looking at him," Cat replied in an exasperated whisper. "He's not stupid."

"How do you know?"

"Does he look stupid?"

"He looks like a man," Maggie commented, as if that said it all. "Not interested."

"You're going to let that jerk Kilbourne sour you for life?"

"Jack Kilbourne is the end of a long line of . . ."

"Of jerks?"

"Let's just say he's at the end of a long line of unfortunate relationships. And I do mean the end. Eat your burger. I want to walk up to the post office bulletin board and leave an invite for one and all to tour the house starting tomorrow, and we still have to go to the grocery store down in Cottonwood."

"Slave driver."

"Just eat."

Colby Drake accepted a refill on his iced tea along with the flirtatious smile the waitress sent his way. He returned her smile with one of his own—friendly but neutral. He was accustomed to women's eager smiles. It was the killer blue eyes, his sister Sharon kept telling him, and his boyish smile. The poor girls didn't know he was a shark behind all that charm.

Colby denied both the charm and the shark. He was a nice guy, he kept telling his sister. True-blue, all-American, and wholesome as cherry pie. Almost. But his job sometimes made him look a bit bloodthirsty, metaphorically speaking. Whatever it took to get the job done, he did it, and whenever Colby Drake went after something, he got it.

Right then the something—or rather, the someone—

he was after was sitting on the porch of the English Kitchen, alternating bites of a sandwich and conversation with a bouncy blond. Maggie Potter was not quite what Colby had expected. He'd seen pictures, of course. For a few days in late winter her photo had been in almost every newspaper in the country, not to mention television newscasts and the grocery store scandal sheets. But most of those pictures had been shots taken of her trying to hide her face from the cameras. NBC news had used a file photo they'd obtained from the Ohio state personnel office, and that one made most driver's license photos seem flattering.

She was quite attractive, even in dusty jeans and a baggy T-shirt. The photos hadn't done her justice. But her looks didn't surprise him. He'd expected pretty. A woman didn't score in the game of sex-and-politics unless she had looks, and little Miss Maggie had scored big time for a while. What he hadn't expected was a smile that looked free of artifice, skin with a glow no cosmetic could create, and a laugh that had bells in it. She should have been harder, big-city sophisticated, with sharp edges and a jaded smile. That would fit better with what she probably was.

Not that he was in the least interested in Maggie Potter beyond a very narrow purpose. He liked women, generally speaking. He liked them as people, as friends, as bedmates. He even liked his big sister, who was his fishing buddy whenever they could make it to the Catskills to wet a few flies. But he had no use for the bimbos who hung around the halls of power, getting their kicks from bedding the scum who'd risen to the top of the political pond, basking in reflected glory, enjoying the rush of getting it on with men who influenced the fate of states and nations.

Maggie Potter was one of those. If she hadn't experi-

enced a turn of bad luck, she'd still be clinging to Jack
Kilbourne's coattails instead of looking wholesome and
unspoiled here in this Jerome café. She had landed one
of the big fish. As the polls now stood, Kilbourne was
front-runner for the Republican presidential nomination this summer, and there was a real possibility the
handsome, boy-next-door scumbag would be sitting in
the White House come January. Maggie Potter had
been on Kilbourne's staff in the Ohio governor's office,
then promoted to an "aide" in his campaign for the
nation's top spot. Three years she had worked for
the man, and for at least one of those years she'd taken
the handsome divorcé to her bed—until the press had
found out about their affair. His "family values" plat-
form already on shaky grounds because of his recent
divorce, Kilbourne had correctly concluded that he
couldn't survive a moral scandal, especially with the
press speculating that Maggie had been the driving
force behind his divorce. He'd thrown Maggie to the
wolves, and his spin doctors had made her out to be a
groupie and nymphomaniac who had taken advantage
of the governor's good nature and basic innocence. The
media, of course, had indulged in a feeding frenzy at
her expense.

But Colby hadn't tracked her to Jerome to hound
her about sexual hijinks with Governor Kilbourne. She
could turn the man inside out every night and upside
down during lunch hour, and Colby Drake wouldn't
spare her a inch of newspace in his column. No indeed.
He was after bigger prey. Governor Jack Kilbourne
himself. Colby was going to nail the man into a political coffin, and Maggie Potter was going to help. She
just didn't know it yet.

·   ·   ·

If there's anything that gets my back up, it's people who feel oh so sorry for themselves. Maggie thought she was an expert on unfortunate relationships? She should have tried my life for a while. A relationship that ends with the guy blasting you with a shotgun while you sit in the outhouse is a really bad relationship. One moment I was grumbling to myself about splinters on the seat, and the next I was looking down on the scene from above, ingloriously separated from my physical self.

Can you tell I'm still upset about that? Some things a gal just doesn't get over, even in a hundred years.

In my day, a gal didn't have time to whine about "bad relationships." Usually, she'd take any relationship she could get, because if a woman couldn't catch herself a husband, she was in trouble. She'd find herself teaching some other woman's children, or keeping house for some gal who did manage to catch a man, or maybe earning her keep by whoring. Whoring was where most of the opportunities were, as far as I was concerned. I did think about being a schoolmarm once, but somehow I just wasn't the schoolmarm kind.

Anyway, my point is this. Maggie Potter needed to sit up and smell the flowers, not complain about the fertilizer. "Poor me," she sighs. "Poor, poor, me. I can't read the newspaper because people are saying bad things about me. A man treated me like shit and I'm not going to look at a man ever again in my whole life."

What bull! Men treated me like shit all the time. Women, too. Virtuous ladies crossed the street to avoid passing me on the walkway. They had their prissy noses so high in the air that a good rainstorm would have drowned them. And the only gent who would greet me by the light of day was my banker, and only because I had enough money in his bank that the vault would purely collapse if I pulled it out. But you didn't catch me hanging my head and swearing off life. No sirree! I met life head-on and spit in its eye.

Now, understand, I didn't want Maggie spitting at anyone. What I wanted was Maggie married, popping out kids and teaching them to do better in life than my daughter and granddaughters did. And better than I did, too. Being a rich tramp was fun, but even I admit it's not something you want to write home about. Maggie was my last hope.

Hope—a wonderful state of mind, even for a ghost. And I was full of it. Good things were happening. The inn was about to open. Maggie's life was about to start turning cartwheels. And me? I had purpose again. I had energy, determination, and a mission. I had power, and I would use it.

Poor Maggie. She was about to be haunted.

D day had arrived. Zero hour. The inn's first potential customers wandered up the newly repaired sidewalk to the front door while Maggie and Catherine both peeked at them from behind the dining room curtains.

"They look like very nice people," Catherine said uncertainly. "The kids are cute."

The kids, as a matter of fact, looked like good prospects for tracking dirt on the rugs and smearing ice cream on the bedspreads. The two of them looked tired, bored, and hot. The boy was about ten. He sported a buzz cut and nerd glasses. The girl was younger—maybe six, with honey blond hair framing a pixie face with windblown curls. The parents were sunburned and tired-looking.

"Don't get nervous," Maggie advised her sister.

"I'm not nervous. Are you nervous?"

"Of course I'm not nervous. Why should I be nervous?"

"First customers and all. You've looked nervous all day long."

"I'm not nervous."

The doorbell chimed.

"Well," Maggie said with a sigh. "Here goes."

The family was Fred and Peggy Ferguson, with Fred junior and Shanna. The chamber of commerce had suggested they drop by, Fred senior told Maggie, as they were looking for an interesting place to stay. Maggie invited them in for a tour. Peggy exclaimed over the antique kitchen fixtures and cautiously admired Attila and Hannibal, the two lovebirds in their cage by the kitchen window; Fred junior spied Gorgeous George, Maggie's plush white cat, and gave chase, and little Shanna dropped her ice cream cone onto the living room floor.

"Oh, I'm so sorry!" Peggy declared at the spill. "How lucky that you have wood floors. They're so easy to clean, aren't they?"

She didn't make any mention of demonstrating her own cleaning technique on the raspberry mess.

"No extra charge for breakfast?" Fred asked suspiciously.

"Everything's included," Maggie assured him.

An indignant meow interrupted the conversation, followed by a giggle from Fred junior, who had cornered poor George in the dining room.

"Leave the kitty alone," the boy's mother advised.

"Mo-*ther*!" little Shanna complained. "He's such a brat!"

Maggie agreed, and wondered if she was really cut

out to be an innkeeper. "Would you like to see the upstairs?"

The Master Suite, with its bank of windows overlooking the valley, met with Peggy's enthusiastic approval, while the two children climbed into the claw-foot bathtub, dusty sneakers and all, pretending it was a boat. Ignoring them, Peggy cajoled her husband into staying.

"Do you have plenty of hot water?" he asked Maggie.

"Yes, sir. We have a very large hot water heater."

"And we get breakfast with the room?" he asked again.

"Breakfast is at eight-thirty. My sister is an excellent cook, and the meal she serves is truly a gourmet delight."

"I want an Egg McMuffin!" Fred junior declared.

"I want a hot dog!" Shanna added.

"Not for breakfast, Shanna. Get out of the bathtub, please. Do you want Miss Potter to think you're a hopeless hooligan?"

Peggy smiled apologetically at Maggie, and Maggie tried to smile back.

"We'll just bring our bags in, then," Fred senior said. He muttered on his way out. "Charm, schmarm. Pay three times the amount for a place with no air-conditioning and a cat leaving hair all over the place."

Catherine grabbed Maggie's arm as the Ferguson family unloaded their Toyota. "Yes!" She turned a thumbs-up.

"Yes," Maggie sighed.

"That's at least two rooms let tonight, counting the reservation from those girls. Oh, Maggie! We're going to make a fortune! I just know it!"

Maggie sighed. Success, she realized, was going to

require tolerance as well as hard work. As she cleaned up the spilt ice cream, George regarded her from the top of the dining room buffet, annoyed as only a cat can be annoyed. A sticky child-sized handprint decorated the French door that led from the dining room to the big side yard. Somewhere in the house, she thought she heard a throaty laugh—impossible, since only she and Catherine were there.

She'd dealt with only one set of customers, and already she was going insane.

Soon after the Ferguson family checked in, the reservation showed up. Heidi Bitner and Sheryl Best were two friends from North Dakota vacationing together in the Southwest.

They dumped their bags in Blue Room, as Maggie called the smaller of the front bedrooms, and headed out to explore the local watering holes. When the Fergusons left for an early dinner, Maggie and Catherine had the house to themselves once again.

Catherine regarded the deserted kitchen with dismay. "I spent hours fixing this snack mix and these cookies and rolls. I hope somebody besides us gets to enjoy them. Did you tell the Fergusons that they can make free with the fridge and the goodies in the kitchen?"

"I told them. Don't worry. They'll be back. So will the girls."

Catherine sighed happily. "I just feel so right doing this. I love fixing little things for people to eat. I love decorating the place. I don't even mind the cleaning."

"I'll reserve judgment until we've done it all summer, seven days a week."

"I don't think I'm going to mind, Maggie. I don't suppose we could make enough money that I wouldn't have to go back to teaching next fall."

"I'm supposed to be the one running away. Not you."

Catherine grimaced.

"Speaking of running away," Maggie said. "Have you seen Gorgeous George?"

"She was on top of the buffet a few minutes ago."

"I don't want her to be out once night falls. Too many coyotes in these hills."

"She's probably sulking somewhere. Don't worry. George can take care of herself. You spoil her, but beneath that pouty, silken exterior beats the heart of a bitch."

"Just like me." Maggie flashed her sister a grin.

"Except for the silken exterior." Catherine dodged a playful blow from her sister. "Go find your cat."

George was not in any of her usual haunts. Maggie checked all the nooks and crannies of the sunroom, where the cat loved to bask in the sun that poured through the floor-to-ceiling windows. She checked their basement apartment, a common site for an afternoon catnap. The linen closet sheltered no cat; the living room bookcase was empty of everything but books.

Outside, George wasn't lurking on the kitchen windowsill, licking her chops at Attila and Hannibal. She wasn't in the basement window wells looking for bugs, or slinking through the rose garden, or basking atop the retaining wall that held the hillside out of their yard. In short, she wasn't in any of the places she'd marked as her own since she moved into the house. Maggie was about to give up the search when she heard an enticing meow.

"George?"

"Meeehhr?"

"Where are you, you brainless furball?"

"Mauwwhr!"

Maggie looked up. George regarded her from a perch in the ash tree that shaded the side yard.

"Well, aren't we the superior one?"

"Meow!"

"I hope you can get down from there."

George's haughty expression matched her superior position. Maggie suspected the cat was very satisfied where she was.

"You'll be sorry when night falls and the coyotes start howling on the mountain."

The cat looked bored.

"Damn it! Get down here!"

George yawned.

"All right, you little snot. I'll fix your wagon!" Muttering about rechristening the cat George of the Jungle, Maggie stalked into the garage to fetch a ladder. The cat calmly sat up and started washing her face as Maggie propped the ladder against the tree. "Watch it, my fine girl, or you'll be an indoor cat from now on. No more bug stalking, mouse hunting, or birdwatching for you unless you behave."

Maggie uncertainly climbed the first few rungs. She was not all that fond of heights. Still, the damned cat was only ten feet above the ground. She climbed on.

"I'm going to hang a sign around your little furry neck: Free to Good Home. Or maybe Free to Any Home, Good or Bad. Surely one of the guests will take you."

"Maauwhr!"

"Same to you. C'mere, George."

As she balanced herself on the ladder, reaching toward the cat, George simply sprang to the next higher branch and gazed down from her new, higher resting spot. Her mouth stretched in a bored yawn that nearly popped the whiskers from her face.

"I am not climbing that tree to fetch you down, you devil-cat. The coyotes can have you. Now come down from there!"

"Do you often have conversations with cats?" asked a masculine voice from behind her.

Maggie jolted in surprise. The ladder tipped. And Maggie and the ladder both came tumbling backwards, piling onto the unfortunate soul who had startled her. They landed in a tangle of arms, legs, and ladder rungs, her fall cushioned somewhat by a sturdy masculine body, his cushioned only by the hard ground.

They lay still a moment, stunned. George offered a pithy comment from the tree.

Tangled as they were, Maggie couldn't see the face of the man she'd flattened, but she felt his chest vibrate in the beginnings of—of all things!—laughter.

"The cat says it all," he rumbled.

Maggie groaned. What a perfect ending to her first day of business.

Two

"Are you all right?"

The man's voice was breathless and strained—little surprise, since Maggie still lay atop him, her back to his chest. Poor guy. She was not, Maggie readily acknowledged, a petite wisp of a woman.

"I'm all right, I think. You?"

"Great. I think."

"I'll just get off you. I'm so sorry . . . oops!" Her elbow poked into what felt like a rib cage. "I'm stuck. This damned ladder. I can't get my arm unwedged."

"Hold still a minute. If I can get my leg out of this rung . . . ouch! Damn!"

Maggie chuckled—overwhelmed by a sense of the ridiculous. "We're stuck here forever, tangled in a ladder."

"Nope. I've got my arm free. From here it looks as if maybe your right leg . . ."

"Wait. Okay. It's coming . . . coming . . . yes!"

"Now try to turn. Slowly. Ow!"

"Sorry. Elbow again. What was that I hit?"

"You don't want to know."

"Here we go." She ended up still on top, but she faced down instead of up, and her arms were free, along with one of her legs. "Less like a pretzel."

As their eyes met, they both grew still, suddenly aware of the intimacy of their entangled position.

"Hi," he said, his smile entirely too charming for a man in such an undignified position. He had his leg between her knees and his face six inches from hers. Somehow a friendly, breezy hello didn't seem quite appropriate.

"What are you doing?" She demanded as he started to squirm beneath her.

"I think I can get my other arm free if . . . all right!"

Maggie jumped as his just-liberated hand brushed her breast. The passing touch was a shock through the thin cotton of her shirt.

He grimaced. "Sorry."

"Right."

"All groping is strictly unintentional."

"I'll try to remember that," she replied caustically.

"Maggie! What on earth?" Catherine's sneakers and ankles came into Maggie's range of view. She couldn't turn her head far enough to see the rest of her sister, but she could tell from the voice that Catherine waffled between embarrassment and concern.

"I fell."

"Goodness!"

"On top of this gentleman here."

"I can see that you did. Look at you!" Maggie felt her sister's hand on her foot, twisting to get it free of the ladder. Then the weight of the ladder no longer pressed her into her victim. "Let me help you up. Easy now!"

Maggie was careful not to put a knee or foot into any awkward parts of the man's anatomy as Catherine helped her up.

"Are either of you hurt?"

"I don't think so." Maggie drew a breath of relief. Whoever the guy was, he made a very hard mattress. "Are you okay?"

The man still lay flat, staring up at the two of them. "Never better. Just resting."

"Omigod! It's Mel." Catherine bounced with delight a couple of times.

"Actually, the name's Colby."

"Private joke," Catherine admitted with a smile. "Sorry." She offered him a hand up.

Maggie took his other hand to pull him upright. Now that Catherine recognized him, she did too. He was the "better than Mel Gibson" man from the English Kitchen yesterday. He wasn't better than Mel Gibson, Maggie decided. He didn't look the least like Mel Gibson.

But he was a hunk; there was no denying it. Black, black hair, just shaggy enough to be a temptation to a woman's fingers; sharp blue eyes framed in lashes that should have belonged to a woman. Brows that arched in a devilish curve, and a mobile mouth that looked capable of everything from wry humor to dark passion. Shoulders not too broad, not too narrow. They fit his lean build. Maggie knew from experience that there wasn't an inch of padding on that physique. He would make a better brick than a mattress.

"I'm sorry I startled you," he said to Maggie.

"I'm sure you are, considering what it got you. I'm sorry I smashed you flat."

"Not quite flat."

He gave them a grin that was a flash of pure

warmth. Wry, spontaneous, almost impish, it lit his whole face. Good thing she was immune to such things, Maggie reflected cynically, or she'd be as wide-eyed as Catherine.

"I look like someone named Mel?"

Catherine sighed, and Maggie gave her a quelling look. "No," she said. "It's a silly joke between sisters. You had to be there. You say your name is Colby . . . ?"

"Colby Drake, from the beautiful state of Virginia."

He held out his hand, and when Maggie took it he shook her hand as if she were a man, with firmness and purpose.

"We saw you in the English Kitchen yesterday," Catherine said.

"I know. You ladies caught my eye as well. I asked the waitress your name, hoping I'd luck out and you were part of the local color and not fellow tourists."

The admission caught Maggie by surprise. "You asked the waitress about us?"

"Yeah. Don't you love small towns where everyone knows everyone's name, income, family history, and probably what you ate for breakfast? She told me all about the inn you two are opening. Today's the opening day, right? I was hoping you had a room available for a week or so. I've been staying in a motel in Cottonwood, but it's a stucco egg carton—all these little cubicles with no personality."

"Of course we have a room," Catherine offered with an ecstatic grin.

Maggie eyed him suspiciously. "Why did you ask the waitress about us?"

"I'm nosy, and when a guy sees two beautiful women walking about without any men hovering nearby . . . Well, I was being a guy. It's sort of an incurable disease."

"Oh! We're not offended," Cat gushed. "By the way, I'm Catherine Potter. The lady who crashed down on top of you is my sister, Maggie."

Maggie braced herself for recognition to light his eye, for the pleasant smile to becoming a knowing smirk, but none of that happened. The name Maggie Potter seemed to ring no bells in his head. Maybe he read only the worthwhile parts of the newspapers, like the comics, and didn't bother with the trash. She relaxed a bit.

"Maggie can take you on the tour," Catherine offered. "And when you decide which room you want, we'll help you with your luggage. Right now I need to put out some more snacks. See you in a little while."

"Terrific. I was hoping for a complete tour. This looks like a work of art."

He wasn't looking at the house as he praised it; he was looking straight at Maggie—an annoying bit of obvious flirting. Did he think she couldn't see straight through him? Men! Still, she was in the hospitality business now. She should try to be hospitable.

"Come on, Don Juan," she said in a neutral voice. "I'll give you your tour."

"What about the cat? It's still in the tree."

"Oh damn! I almost forgot about George of the Jungle up there. Idiot cat!"

"Maybe I could get him down."

"George is a her."

"Oh. Well, then that explains her behavior."

"Really?"

"Obvious. She's a female—also an incurable disease."

Maggie acknowedged his score with a reluctant grin.

"It would serve George right if I just left her up there. She'll be sorry when the sun goes down. The air still gets cool this time of year."

"I'm too much of a gentleman to leave a lady in distress. Even a stubborn one."

"She's above the reach of the ladder. Even your reach."

"I was a pretty good tree climber at one time."

"You don't say? How many years ago?"

" 'Bout eighteen or so."

"Hm."

He arched a brow at her. "I was twelve."

"You think you still have the knack?"

"It's probably just like riding a bike. You know—once you learn, you never forget."

"If you come crashing down, I'm not going to break your fall by getting under you, like you did for me."

"Oh, that wasn't intentional. I'm not that much of a gentleman. Besides, I won't come crashing down. I wouldn't let myself look like a fool in front of a great-looking lady."

"That lady being me, or George?"

"Both of you."

"You are so full of bullshit."

He grinned. "Perceptive of you. But I bet my line will work on the cat."

"Only because she doesn't know men like I do," Maggie said half under her breath.

Gorgeous George watched with casual interest as Colby propped the ladder against the tree and climbed toward her perch. When he clambered onto one of the branches below her, though, she sat up and took notice.

"Mowwwhr!"

"I agree," he replied. "Maggie was very wrong to give a name like George to such a queenly cat."

George twitched her whiskers in irritation as he climbed closer.

"How do you keep that fur so white?" he inquired. "Is that some kind of female secret?"

"Meehr!"

"That's what I thought. You women like to be secretive, don't you? You think it keeps the men interested, hm?" He snapped a tender, leafy twig from the tree and dangled it temptingly just out of George's reach. "But I know you ladies. You're a sucker for the right bait. Like this, maybe?"

George batted at the twig, meowed an objection when she couldn't reach it, and jumped to the next lower branch.

"You want this? Pretty girl? Come on."

Lower and lower the cat pursued the twig, all thoughts of her glorious high perch driven from her mind. Colby worked down and down, until he was once more on the ladder and George was so fascinated that she scarcely noticed when he scooped her from the branch. Far from objecting to her seduction, the cat promptly forgot the twig and settled into Colby's arms with a feline rumble of contentment. This from a creature who was better known for sharp claws than sweet purrs.

"Little tramp," Maggie muttered, looking up with a wry smile. She had to give Colby Drake credit. It wasn't every man who would risk his neck to pluck a stubborn cat from a tree branch.

After taking a bow for his heroism, Colby wanted a complete tour of the establishment. He greeted Fred Ferguson, who was reading in the living room, with a friendly nod, smiled at the old daguerreotype of the original Red Robin in the hall, and perused the books that Maggie had painstakingly dusted only that morning.

"*Classification of North American Birds?*"

"My sister is a high school biology teacher in the real world."

"Chaucer?"

"From an English Lit class at the university."

"Nevil Shute? I didn't think anyone else besides me read Nevil Shute, and I haven't read him since I was eighteen."

Maggie shrugged. "I'm a romantic. Or at least, I was at one time."

He gave her a quick, probing glance, then turned back to the books. "It's amazing what you can learn about people from knowing what books they read. You must be very romantic. Danielle Steel, Iris Johansen, Maggie Osborne, Susan Elizabeth Phillips, Dorothy Garlock."

"Those are Catherine's. She devours romances."

"And you don't?"

She shrugged. "I've read some of them. They're good stories, if you take all that happily-ever-after with a grain of salt."

"You don't believe in happily-ever-afters?"

"I think they belong in fairy tales. I haven't seen many of them in the real world."

"Ah," he said in a neutral voice. "*Politics and the American Dream?*"

"That's mine."

"*The Building Blocks of Foreign Policy. Elections and Other American Games. The Role of the Press in American Politics.* Heavy stuff."

"I have a graduate degree in political science."

"You don't say. Oops! What's this? *The History of Opera?*"

"You told the truth when you said you're nosy."

"One of my few failings."

"Well, pry yourself away from my bookcase and come see the sunroom. You're welcome to watch TV in here whenever you like, as long as you keep the volume low after ten P.M."

He looked around at the banks of windows. "Nice view. A lot different from Virginia."

"The bedrooms are upstairs. I'm afraid the one with the best view is already taken for the weekend."

"Bummer."

Colby decided on the Yellow Room—the smallest bedroom in the back of the house with windows facing the hillside, not the valley. Once they got his luggage into the room, it looked even smaller.

"That looks like one fancy camera." His camera bag was as big as a small suitcase.

"Top-of-the-line Nikon."

Maggie's curiosity was piqued. "Are you a photographer?"

"Well . . . yeah. Among other things."

"And a laptop as well. Mine's a lot bigger. I wish I had a notebook size like that. You use that in photography?"

He smiled. "It's amazing what you can do with computers these days."

"Yes. Isn't it."

He sat on the bed, looking out of place against the ruffled bedspread and chintzy throw pillows.

"You're sure this room's all right?"

"Well, I suppose I could stay in that very interesting room down the hall with the scarlet decor. I take it you're trying to preserve the original ambiance."

Maggie laughed. "Not really. That room hasn't been redecorated yet. But the room across from it has a bigger bathroom than this one, and it's only five dollars more. The Wicker Room, we call it, because the chairs and headboard are wicker."

"This room's fine."

"Okay, well, don't forget you have the freedom of the house. We want you to feel like you live here. Come downstairs and I'll show you the kitchen."

George awaited them at the foot of the stairs. She arched herself against Colby's leg and purred loudly when he squatted to scratch her ears. The cat usually showed a queenly indifference toward anyone other than Maggie, and sometimes toward Maggie herself.

"It looks like you've won her heart," Maggie said. "That's a very unusual honor. She's a miser with affection."

"I affect all the ladies that way."

"Is that so?"

"You'll see. I grow on you."

"Like Virginia mildew?"

"Ouch. I can tell you're a tough case."

She smiled. "Tougher than you know. Come on. I'll show you what's available for your snacking pleasure. Catherine's goal is for guests to gain at least five pounds during their stay."

In the kitchen, Cat greeted them with a cheery hello and a subtle lift of a brow toward Maggie. "Did you give him the two-dollar tour?"

"That and more. What do you have down here for snacks?"

"Mmmm. Lots. I just put out some Gouda cheese and those great rye crackers. There's mixed nuts, beer nuts, banana bread, pretzels, lemon squares, and of course the bananas and apples over there."

Maggie opened the fridge. "In here there's white zinfandel, Chablis, Anchorsteam beer, Moosehead, lemonade, milk, pop, and cold water. Feel free to eat or drink anything you see."

Colby seemed more interested in the pair of lovebirds in their cage by the window than he was in food, however. Attila was putting on her usual show.

"That's Attila the Bird and Hannibal. Attila likes to flirt, especially with men."

"What a cute bird."

Maggie wondered if she should warn him. Attila was insufferably darling as she fluffed her feathers and preened for Colby's benefit. She was an expert at cocking her head, making appealing little bird noises, and sucking men right into her web.

Maggie decided to be magnanimous. "It's all a trick, Colby. She actually despises men. She's just trying to lure you close enough to rip your hand off."

"A tiny little bird like that?"

"Inside that tiny bird lurks the heart of a vulture. Believe me."

"It's true," Catherine confirmed.

Attila twittered innocently, cocked her dainty head, and gave Colby the bird version of a come-hither look.

"You can't be talking about this bird." He tapped the cage with a finger. Attila cheeped invitingly. "She likes me. I told you all the ladies—*yow!*"

Like lightning, Attila struck, and Colby drew back a finger missing a beak-sized chunk. Blood dripped onto the tile floor.

"Shit!" Maggie grabbed his hand and pressed a clean towel against the wound. "Don't you ever listen to warnings?"

"Yowch! Go easy with that towel. That little piranha is fast. And she seemed to like me so much."

"Oh my!" Catherine joined in. "Are you all right? Maggie, you have to put those birds down in our apartment."

Maggie glared at Colby. "If people would just leave Attila alone, she'd be fine."

He grimaced as she pressed harder with the towel. "Sorry. I thought you were exaggerating."

"Should we call the doctor?" Catherine asked.

"No." Maggie gingerly lifted the towel from his finger. "The bleeding's stopped. And it's not all that bad. After all"—she sent an arch look at Attila's victim—"she's such a very tiny bird."

Colby had the grace to look embarrassed.

"Cat, go into our bathroom and try to find the iodine. I think there's a first-aid kit down there. I'll clean it up with some antibacterial soap."

Colby didn't seem to mind her dictatorial nursing, and he didn't pull the usual macho pretense that a little bird bite didn't bother a big tough guy like him. Maggie had to give him credit for that. She squirted the soap into a basin, filled it with warm water, took out a clean cloth, and told him to sit at the table.

"Attila belonged to a guy once," she explained, pushing his hand into the basin. "He moved and abandoned her in his old apartment. She holds the whole male gender responsible."

He grimaced as the warm water hit his finger. "Don't you think you're anthropomorphizing a bit?"

"No, I don't. Birds are very intelligent, and they have very distinct personalities. This bird is a manhater. And she's very clever about it. Puts on the cute little bird act, flirts outrageously, then rips out a chunk once the guy falls into her snare."

"I've known a few women like that, actually."

Maggie snorted in disgust. "Life itself is sometimes like that."

He lifted an inquiring brow, but she didn't go on to tell him there were times when she sympathized with Attila's attitude toward the male gender.

Catherine came in waving a first-aid kit. "Here you go. Iodine, gauze pads, bandages, and a bunch of other junk. How're you doing?" she asked Colby.

"I think I need a large dose of that Moosehead to drown my humiliation."

Taking the hint, Catherine opened the fridge and took out a bottle of beer. "This'll make you feel better. How about some beer nuts?"

"Nope. Just beer. Best thing I know to take the sting from stupidity."

"Don't feel too bad," Maggie said. "You're not the first guy to ignore my warning about Attila."

"Well, she is such a cute little thing."

Maggie shook her head ruefully. "Sucks 'em in, every time."

Cat waved as she went out the door. "I'll be in the sunroom if you need me. *African Queen* is on TV tonight. Ta-ta!"

Left alone again, they suddenly seemed to have nothing to say. Only Attila's cheerful chirping broke the silence. The bird was in a good mood now that she'd gotten her pound of flesh. Gradually, Maggie became very aware of her hand where it rested on Colby's in the basin. Why was she touching him? she wondered. The man didn't need her help to keep his hand in place. The soapy water might sting a bit, but he was a big boy, after all. Knowing the wound had to be cleaned, he was perfectly capable of leaving his hand where it belonged.

If she took her hand away now, though, her retreat

would only call attention to their touching. That would start the wheels turning in his mind, and he would jump to the conclusion that she was using this excuse to get chummy.

Nothing could be further from the truth, of course. Charming men left her cold. Well, maybe not cold. Lukewarm. Lukewarm at best. It wouldn't do to give Colby Drake the wrong idea about her susceptibility to his smile and those glinting blue eyes. So it was best that she left her hand where it was.

Besides, touching Colby Drake felt nice. She was big enough to admit it. He was a hunk, and she was only human, after all. One didn't need to buy a fine painting to admire the artwork. That was all she was doing— admiring the artwork.

Colby swallowed a few sips from his beer, each swallow working the muscles of his neck. He had a nice neck and throat, Maggie decided. Muscular. Tanned. Topped by a strong, clean jaw and a well-sculpted chin. Jack had possessed a nice chin, but that was a necessity for a successful politician in today's television-oriented campaigning. Colby Drake had a better one.

Maggie realized she was staring, and he was returning her regard full measure. Abruptly she stiffened.

"How's the hand feel now?"

He smiled. Easy charm. Confident sexiness with just the right amount of vulnerability. Oh yes. He was a piece of work, all right. Dangerous.

"It hurts like hell." He glanced over his shoulder at Attila, who was still merrily chirping her victory song. "Hope you're satisfied, Birdzilla."

Maggie lifted the injured member from the basin. "I don't think you'll die. Maybe you'll have a little scar. It'll get you sympathy from all the ladies you charm."

He brightened. "That wouldn't be bad."

"Move over here where the light is better. I'll bandage it."

He moved to her side of the table, pulling the chair close. Very close, Maggie noted.

"This will sting," she warned, brandishing a bottle of iodine. "Try not to flinch, or I'll get it all over both of us."

"Real men don't flinch."

"They just yowl like a banshee when they're bitten by an itty-bitty bird."

"Ouch!"

"Sorry. One more drop."

"Sadist."

"Wimp."

She blew on his finger, then stopped abruptly when she realized how intimate an act that was. When she turned her face, her nose practically touched his. The beer on his breath mingled strangely with the odor of iodine. His skin smelled pleasantly of sunshine and soap.

For a panicked moment, Maggie thought he was going to kiss her. But that was just silly. They'd been acquainted all of two hours. He couldn't be that bold. And she certainly wasn't sending out come-hither vibrations.

Carefully, she pulled back. "Uh . . . does it still hurt?"

"Does what hurt?" Still focusing on her face, he seemed a bit distracted.

"Your finger."

"Oh. No. It's not as bad now."

"Then let's wrap it."

"Good idea."

She took a gauze pad and tape from the first-aid kit and carefully wrapped his wounded digit.

"I hope you're left-handed."

"Nope."

"Oh. Well, this is a good excuse to avoid writing postcards home."

"There's that."

"I guess I do owe you an apology. I should keep the birds down in our apartment, where Attila won't find a fresh supply of victims every day."

"I think you owe me more than an apology."

She looked up in surprise. His blue eyes glinted with mischief.

"I think you and Birdzilla owe me at least a dinner date. Though the bird can damn well stay home."

"Dinner?"

"And a personal tour of the local sights. It's the least you can do for a man maimed by your lethal pet."

Maggie searched for something to say. This was not a smart idea. The man was entirely too charming, and she was in no mood to be charmed. "Well . . . I can't leave, really. The inn is a round-the-clock sort of job."

"You don't have help?"

"Sure she has help," Catherine answered from the kitchen doorway. Maggie gave her sister an annoyed scowl. Catherine only grinned. "I'm the help. And it's about time Maggie did something other than work and fret about this place."

Colby's smile was triumphant. "Then you don't have an excuse, Maggie. You don't mind if I call you Maggie, do you?"

"But . . ."

"Maggie always pays her debts," Catherine said with a smirk. She went to the fridge and took out a

Coke. Behind Colby's back, she gave Maggie a thumbs-up and mouthed the words, "Go for it."

"Tomorrow, then," Colby said. "We can spend the whole afternoon seeing the sights."

"I can't possibly—"

"Okay. Three o'clock then. I'll be generous. What's there to see around here besides Indian ruins and art galleries?"

"You'll love Sedona," Catherine told him. "Maybe you and Maggie could take one of the jeep tours. There's some New Age tours that take you to the vortexes, you know, and you have to see Slide Rock, too."

Maggie sighed. Catherine rattled on, after neatly trapping her into a date with Colby Drake. Next time she was alone with her sister, she was going to throttle her.

Pay dirt! Hubba hubba! Just as I set out to snare Maggie a man, along comes this one. Classic tall, dark, and handsome. Has himself a fine education; you can tell by his smooth talk. A million-dollar smile, sparkly blue eyes, a complete set of teeth, broad shoulders, and he probably even takes a bath more than once a week.

He was Mr. Perfect. What live woman could resist? Hell! What dead woman could resist? A hundred years in the grave and I can still appreciate a firm set of buttocks when I see one. Not to mention a nice pair of muscular hairy legs. I truly do love this day and age when men parade around in short pants on a warm summer day. Those little dinky shorts the joggers wear would plumb give me a heart attack if I still had a heart.

Anyway, back to the point. Maggie had hooked herself a keeper, but she seemed determined to throw him

*back into the pond, or worse still, not pull him in at all.
If not for Catherine, she would have weaseled a way to
turn down his little proposition. Stupid girl. It was
hard to believe she had my blood in her veins.*

*I had high hopes that she'd come around, though.
Mr. Perfect wasn't discouraged, which I liked to see. A
real man, after all, shouldn't let a little feminine hesita-
tion put a chill on his cojones. The way he looked at
her when they were carrying his gear to the room, you
could boil an egg in the heat he was putting out. Of
course, he only did it when Mags wasn't looking. For
all of that, though, something in that look he gave
Maggie wasn't quite right. I guess I should have known
from the start that Colby Drake wasn't shooting
straight from the hip. It wasn't until much later that I
realized his intentions were a little more tangled than
what I thought. But then, I can't be expected to know
everything. Ghosts are just dead people. We're smart,
but not all-powerful.*

*Not that it would have made any difference if I had
known. Robin Rowe doesn't back down that easily, or
back off, either. Men are simple creatures, for the most
part. Easy to manipulate, if you know which buttons
to push—or perhaps I should say, which buttons to
unfasten. Besides, I've always liked a challenge, even
more if the challenge comes in the form of a man.*

*Things were definitely looking up in old Jerome.
Now that Maggie was here and this Colby fellow was
in the picture, things were going to start jumping
around the old place. Robin's Nest was coming to life,
and I planned to liven it up even more.*

*Time for the ghost to come out of the closet and
deliver a few kicks to the backsides of the living.*

Three

Colby leaned back in his chair and enjoyed the view out the living room window. The hour was early, but the sun was well up and the valley was beginning to lose the pinkish hues of morning. Sixty or so miles to the northeast, San Francisco Peaks was etched against the morning sky. Snowfields on the mountain heights sparkled in the crystal clear air. Closer to home, Sedona's red buttes acquired an even deeper color from the reddish morning sun.

Before this trip, he'd thought Arizona was nothing but desert, cactus, rattlesnakes, and scorpions. He'd been wrong. Surprise. There was a first time for everything.

Colby grinned, wishing he could truly claim such a sterling record for being right. Good newsmen learned that preconceived notions were made to be disproven. Bad newsmen clung to their version of the truth, bending the facts until they fit. Colby figured he, like most others, had some bad newsman mixed in with the good. He wondered what he would do if, by some amazing twist of reality, he came across evidence that Jack Kilbourne, governor of Ohio, current front-runner for the Republican presidential nomination, was an upstanding, true-blue candidate for American sainthood? Could he accept it? Or would he continue down the path of throwing stumbling blocks in the governor's political path? A cause once taken to heart was difficult to surrender. Not that Colby had anything personal against the man. Just because Kilbourne's slick talk, ready answers, and toothy smile irritated the hell out of him didn't mean the guy was dealing under the table. But Kilbourne was a crook. Colby knew he was right about that. The man's irritating personal qualities just made the pursuit that much more enjoyable.

Maggie Potter, though—he might have been wrong about her. She didn't strike him as the bimbo type. The woman was too down-home, too real. She climbed ladders to rescue cats, scraped her hair into an ugly ponytail, made excuses for deranged birds, and smelled of Pine Sol and open air rather than fifty-dollar perfume. Indeed, he'd been close enough to take a sniff of her heady, natural scent, thanks to her preoccupation with bandaging his bird-nicked finger. A bimbo would have either given him the classic "how dare you" stare or gone into automatic flirtation mode. Maggie had simply sputtered and blushed. She didn't make the grade as bimbo.

But with her past, she could hardly be Ms. Clean, either. Her shuttered, sometimes hostile eyes hinted at secrets that pricked his reporter's curiosity—secrets that perhaps had survived the media spotlight that pursued her. Nothing good, he suspected. Secrets seldom were.

Colby grimaced. Cynicism got old after a while. So

did believing the worst and being proven right. It would be nice to be wrong.

But he wasn't wrong about Kilbourne. And Maggie Potter, bimbo or not, had been intimate with the jackass at just the right time. She could still be of help, if Colby could persuade her. And he intended to do just that, by fair means or foul.

None of the other guests were stirring at this early hour, but sounds of activity came from the kitchen. One of the inn's hostesses was up and about, and Colby was willing to bet it wasn't Maggie. She didn't seem like a bright-eyed, early-morning sort of girl to him.

Once again he was proven right. Not five minutes passed before Catherine came into the living room, an old-fashioned bib-style apron covering T-shirt and jeans, a dab of flour streaking her plump cheek.

"Good morning, early bird. What brings you out with the sunrise?"

Colby winced theatrically. "Don't mention birds, please."

"Still smarting, are we?"

"That bird leaves a lasting impression."

"Well, she's safely hidden away in our basement apartment. Your finger's sacrifice wasn't in vain. She won't get the chance to lure any other innocent men into her trap. Seriously, though, how is the finger this morning?"

"My finger and I will both live, I think."

"Good. There's coffee and tea ready in the kitchen. And juice, too. Breakfast won't be ready for a while, but there's hot muffins."

He took her up on the offer, followed her into the kitchen, and inhaled the warm odors of fresh-baked bread and just-ground coffee beans. The brew in the coffeemaker was strong, the orange juice fresh-squeezed, and the muffins still warm. This was the ambiance of homeplace dreams. It was his guess that the Robin's Nest Inn was going to do very well indeed.

He peered into the oven, where four loaves of bread were just beginning to turn golden brown. "I don't believe you got up early enough to bake fresh bread this morning."

"Sure. Nothing to it."

He settled himself at the big stainless steel kitchen table and took a bite of muffin. "Um-mmm! I suppose this is homemade too?"

"Of course. Nothing but the best for our guests here at Robin's Nest."

"You're definitely wasted as a schoolteacher."

She smiled. "I think so."

"You think so what?" came a bleary inquiry. Maggie leaned against the kitchen door frame in sweatpants and a tunic-length tank top. Tousled auburn hair framed her face in a ruddy halo, and dainty freckles danced on her nose and cheeks. The freckles were the only things about her that danced, however. Her head listed sleepily toward one shoulder, and her eyelids drooped over groggy eyes.

"That I'm wasted as a schoolteacher."

"Huh?"

"Colby thinks I'm wasted as a schoolteacher. I've been using him as a guinea pig for my domestic skills."

Maggie jolted visibly when she noticed Colby sitting at the table. Her freckles instantly swarmed into a blush. "Oh geez! I thought no one else would be up at this hour, or I wouldn't have come up like this."

"You look fine," Colby assured her.

As far as he was concerned, she looked better than

fine. She looked great. There was nothing that showed a woman's true colors better than early-morning au naturel. This one apparently woke up sleep-warm and rumpled, with flushed cheeks and sooty, slumberous eyes. The effect was engaging. It was amazing, in fact, how any woman could look so completely sexy first thing in the morning, before she'd done so much as run a brush through her hair. No wonder Mr. High-and-Mighty had been willing to risk a political career to climb into Maggie Potter's bed.

As soon as the image entered Colby's mind, his enjoyment of the morning curdled like sour milk.

"I don't look fine." Maggie flopped into a chair at the table as Catherine poured her some coffee. She cupped the steaming mug in her hands and sighed. "I didn't sleep very well last night. Weird dreams." Her eyes pinned Colby accusingly, as if he had been responsible for her uneasy dreams.

"I slept great," he commented.

Maggie responded with a resentful grunt.

"You could go back to bed," Catherine told Maggie. "I've got everything under control for breakfast."

Maggie groaned. "You shouldn't do all the work. I'm sorry I slept so late."

"It's only seven-thirty."

"Yeah. And look at you both. You look so bright and perky. It's disgusting." She sighed and pushed herself up from the chair. "I need a shower and eight more cups of coffee. Shower first."

Catherine shook her head as Maggie dragged herself out of the room. "Poor Mags. She hasn't slept well since she moved in here. She's usually such a ball of fire."

A ball of fire indeed. Colby reminded himself what

happened when a man was careless around a ball of fire.

The man got burned.

Breakfast was served at eight-thirty sharp. A long, hot shower had made Maggie feel like, if not a new person, at least a person who might get through the day without collapsing onto the nearest bed. She sat at the head of the big oak dining room table while Robin's Nest's guests stuffed themselves with Catherine's excellent fare and exclaimed over the warm bread, delicious omelets, marinated beef, and unique granola. Right then she knew that the inn was going to be a success. The combination of great food, good service, and turn-of-the-century charm was unbeatable. Together, she and Catherine were going to make it. For once she wasn't going to sabotage herself.

As stomachs filled, the guests' conversation turned to happy get-acquainted chatter. The only guest who didn't participate in the friendly gab was Colby Drake. He sat on Maggie's left, and though he contributed a comment or two to the table conversation, Maggie got the feeling his real focus was on her. He wasn't blatant about it—at least not so much as to be rude. But even when his eyes were turned away, she could almost feel his mind focused in her direction.

She didn't need this. Not at all. What she needed, in fact, was a vacation somewhere where there were no men, especially no charming, attentive, overconfident, on-the-make men.

Colby's voice interrupted Maggie's silent complaints. "Do you cook like this too?"

"What?"

"Are you as good a cook as your sister?"

"Hardly! I do well to boil eggs. Cat and I have a deal, for this summer at least. I do most of the cleaning, and she does most of the cooking. I don't know what we'll do when she has to go back to teaching school next fall."

His eyes followed Catherine as she went to the kitchen to fetch more eggs and beef. Her sister spent more time dashing to the kitchen than she did eating, but her eyes sparkled with every request for seconds, and a genuine smile never left her face.

"Your sister seems to be in her element here."

"That's the truth," Maggie agreed.

Neither of them was really thinking about Catherine right then, however. Maggie knew it, and Colby knew it as well. It was there in his eyes. She was in his eyes.

She didn't need a man, Maggie reminded herself. Not even a brief flirtation. Not right now. She was on vacation from men—maybe a permanent leave of absence. Some people were allergic to cats, or dogs, or nuts, even though they liked them. Maggie Potter was allergic to men. Every time she indulged, she ended up with hives on her heart.

Equally deep in contemplation, Colby scarcely tasted the excellent breakfast for having all his senses riveted on Maggie. He'd never known a woman to send more mixed signals than she did. Since she'd come crashing down on top of him the day before, she had alternately bristled and smiled, rebuffed and flirted. Okay, maybe flirted was too strong a word. But sometimes she was a hell of a lot friendlier than other times. A smile that thawed one moment could chill the next. The gay sparkle in her eye could freeze instantly to crystals of ice. She was skittish as a wild rabbit and twice as cautious, yet there was an occasional flash of warmth, a rare relaxation of the barriers that let him glimpse the woman behind all that caution. If she could be herself, he might like her. Not that he really wanted to like her. That complication he didn't need.

But if Maggie Potter liked him, what an advantage that would be. She was beginning to do just that. Her eyes returned to him time after time. If he leaned her way, she leaned his—just the slightest bit. So slight that she probably didn't notice. But Colby noticed. He made a living by being observant, from weaseling the truth from those who didn't always want to yield the truth. The truth was that Maggie Potter was attracted to him. And if he had the guts to admit it, he was attracted to her as well.

"Pass the pepper, please."

Colby jerked himself out of his woolgathering. Heidi Bitner was smiling at him, her eyes sending an unmistakable message. The pepper wasn't all she wanted. She was attractive—sleek, confident, probably more than ready to have a little casual fun. He wasn't interested, Colby told himself, because he was absorbed in his work, in the problem at hand, not because all of his hormones were focused on Maggie Potter.

"Do you want the salt too?"

"Just the pepper. I like things spicy."

I'll just bet you do, he thought. Her friend Sheryl jabbed her discreetly in the ribs and rolled her eyes. Colby tried to feel some regret that he hadn't met Heidi some other time, when he could have taken her up on the offer. On the other hand, if he had met Maggie Potter under other circumstances . . . He was tempted to speculate on the possibilities, and had to jerk himself back to reality when Maggie spoke.

"More bread, Colby?" Maggie asked.

He looked up and caught her gaze upon him. How

could a predatory bimbo have such clear, guileless eyes? "Uh . . . I've had enough, thanks."

"You still look hungry."

Hungry, yes, but not for bread.

"We've got to be off," Sheryl said. "We decided to take the drive to Payson today. I hear that road's really pretty."

"I hope you enjoy the rest of your vacation," Maggie said with a smile.

This was Maggie Potter, Colby reminded himself. The Maggie who bedded with the movers and shakers, or at least with one of them.

"We'd like to extend our stay over tonight," Peggy Ferguson said. "Do you have room?"

"Of course we do," Maggie told her. "We'd be happy to have you for as long as you want."

"I want to see the Grand Canyon!" Fred junior demanded. "I want to ride a mule!"

"It'll be much better when it's not so crowded," Maggie cajoled the boy with a smile. "On Saturday and Sunday there are so many people there you wouldn't have much fun."

"Yes I would!" the boy insisted.

This was the Maggie who'd slapped a reporter who'd asked her if Kilbourne was good in bed. This was the Maggie who Kilbourne's staff had accused of pursuing the poor innocent politician until he'd succumbed to her seduction. This was the Maggie who'd been an active player in a rough world, a cutthroat game, and had fled with her tail tucked when she'd lost.

She couldn't be as ingenuous as she seemed, nor as straight-arrow. And Colby Drake had best remember why he was here and what he was after. No reporter worth his salt should be distracted by a winning smile and a pair of clear hazel eyes.

"You look sour as a lemon," Catherine commented as she cleared Colby's plate. "Didn't you like the omelet?"

"The omelet was great. Everything else, too." He got up and tossed his wadded-up napkin onto the table. "Don't forget our date," he told Maggie. "Three sharp."

Catherine raised her brows as he marched from the room. "Well, something must have gone down wrong."

"Two o'clock. The cleaning's done. The snacks for tonight are made. And last night we took in three hundred and forty dollars."

Sitting cross-legged on the moth-eaten rug in the Red Room, Maggie laughed at her sister's ecstatic expression. "Mercenary."

"Not mercenary. Businesslike."

"Okay then, Miss Businesswoman. Figure the expenses for last night as well as the take. Prorate the mortgage, taxes, utilities, grocery bill, and remodeling costs, deduct them from last night's room rentals, and then see how much profit we made."

Catherine waved a hand in airy dismissal. "I'll do that at the end of the month. Let me enjoy the dream while I still can. Besides, I think we're doing very well."

"What do you think of this wallpaper sample?" Maggie held up a cheerful floral design with a light beige background.

"Boring."

"What if we combine it with this color paint?"

"Boring."

"Well, what do you want? This is a bedroom. People

are supposed to sleep here, not oooh and aaah over the wall coverings."

"I think we should leave some of the original ambiance."

"It looks like a bordello!"

"That's what it was. It's history!" Catherine swept the air with her hand, as if painting an advertisement. "Come experience the wicked Old West! Sleep where Jerome's hottest madam slept!"

"Oh, please!"

"I think it would be a hoot!"

"You think everything's a hoot. Help me take down those curtains. They're disgusting."

Pulling the old curtains from the rod put enough dust in the air to make them both sneeze. Holding her breath, Maggie wadded them up and stuffed them into a trash bag.

"This room has a really nice view," Catherine said. "Do you think it was really Robin Rowe's private digs?"

"Who knows?"

"Oooh! Look. There's Colby Drake walking down Main Street. What did you say to him this morning that sent him out of the house in such a bad mood?"

"I didn't say much to him at all."

"Maybe that was the problem."

"I was perfectly courteous. That wasn't the problem. Besides, what makes you think there was a problem? Maybe he's just naturally moody."

"He doesn't strike me as moody. He seems like a really cool guy. You could do worse."

"Oh, for heaven's sake. I've known the man for all of twenty-four hours. Less, actually."

"I knew from the minute I saw him that he was a catch."

"I'm not fishing."

"You know what they say—when you get dumped off a horse, you have to climb right back on."

"Cat?"

"Yeah?"

"Get your metaphors straight. I'm not fishing, and I'm not riding a horse. We're redoing a room here, not my love life."

"You don't have a love life."

"I like it that way. Come over here and look at these swatches of drapery fabric. If we go with that wallpaper—"

"The boring stuff?"

"Yes. The boring stuff. And this paint . . . then how about this material for curtains? And don't say it's boring."

Catherine sighed. "I'm sure an interior decorator would love it."

"Okay."

"If the interior decorator is over sixty. And I don't see how you can not think Colby Drake is hot."

"Okay, he's hot. He's charming, sexy. But he's a man. I'm allergic. Besides, he's a little too charming. I don't trust him."

"You don't trust anybody these days."

"I'm a slow learner, but when the lesson gets through, it sticks. Besides, I do trust someone. I trust you."

"That doesn't count. I'm family. I think you should give Colby a chance."

Maggie merely snorted.

"Mags, you have no romance in your soul!"

"And you have too much. I think I will go with this color scheme. Let's start stripping the wallpaper and get rid of some of this awful furniture. I'll be glad to get this room cleaned up so we can put a guest in here. I can't believe it hasn't been remodeled before now."

"The realtor that showed us the house seemed quite proud of that."

"Most realtors would call a plugged-up septic field free fertilizer if they thought it would sell a house. That's a realtor's job."

"Speaking of plugged up—I think the heating vent in here is blocked. Have you noticed how cold it is sometimes?"

"Cat, it's eighty degrees outside."

"Well, it probably cools down at night, and the heat doesn't get up here . . ."

"We turned the furnace off two weeks ago."

"Well, then we need one of the space heaters. I'm freezing."

"Then go get a heater. And bring up the heat gun while you're at it. We may need it to get this wallpaper off."

While Catherine was out of the room, Maggie puttered. She took the pictures from the wall, shaking her head at the dust and grime that clouded the glass of the old prints. Thinking they might be worth something as antiques, she set them carefully aside.

The rug definitely had to go, Maggie decided. Even if it weren't moth-eaten and stained, who knew what had once taken place on that very rug if it was the original decor? She'd heard ladies of the evening could get pretty creative.

Not that she believed that the room's decor was really original. After all, Roberta Rowe, alias Red Robin, had died a hundred years earlier, and the house had gone through several transformations since then. Still, the room certainly looked like the den of a notorious whore.

Next she moved the lamp from its place by the bed table to an out-of-the-way spot by the door, where it could wait to be dumped in the trash. The lamp was a cheap electric one, but the supports on the shade didn't match the metal on the lamp. The shade itself might be older than the lamp, Maggie mused. Crimson with gold tassels, it certainly looked like a fancy lady's stereotypic idea of style.

"Trash, trash, trash," she muttered. She should feel good about finally getting this room in shape, but somehow her mood got darker the longer she worked. Even the room seemed to get darker and colder, as if someone had drawn a shade on the window to block the sun. But the window no longer had a shade or curtains, and outside, the sun shone as brightly as ever.

She sighed and opened her book of sample paint chips and fabric swatches. The room would need a miracle to make it seem bright.

"Honey," said a throaty voice behind her, *"even a common streetwalker has better taste than that."*

For a moment Maggie froze. Goosebumps prickled her skin. Slowly she turned and felt the blood leave her face.

"And a big friendly howdy to you, Maggie Potter. Welcome to my home."

Every woman loves to make a grand entrance, and I'm no exception. Back when I was Jerome's classiest madam, I always timed my nightly entrances down the staircase to reap the greatest attention. What a scene that was. Me with my red hair and hourglass shape, oozing sex appeal in the most scalding red gown you can imagine. The bodice didn't leave much to the imagination, let me tell you. A rose in my elaborately coiffed hair—it was my trademark. Gold and diamonds around my wrist and neck, diamond earbobs dangling from my ears. All eyes would turn my way, and my girls knew better than to try to divert attention away from Red Robin. I was the classiest tart in town—and everybody knew it. The gentlemen who came to Robin's Nest expected the best, and that's what they got.

After being dead for a century, I was afraid I'd lost the knack for impressive entrances, but it ain't so, sweetie. My debut as a ghost was a doozy. You should've seen Maggie's face. She looked positively haunted. Get it?

Okay, poor joke. Even when I was alive, my sense of humor didn't go over that well, and death doesn't give you much help in that direction. But my success did lift my spirits. No pun intended. Maggie turned white as a sheet, and her eyes looked like big round wells of astonishment. Of course, I didn't let her stay that way but a few moments. I'd grown fond of the little gal, and I didn't want her to croak from heart failure just as I was ready to introduce myself.

"Don't shit your bloomers," I advised her. "Haven't you ever seen a ghost before?"

Maggie's mouth opened and closed a time or two, so that she looked a lot like a fish. Very unattractive.

"Don't recognize me?" I asked. "What? Don't tell me I've been completely forgotten. After all, I built this place."

This was my first try at materialization, so I probably didn't look truly solid. But I was pretty sure I was substantial enough for Maggie to recognize. After all, my daguerreotype hung in the hall by the stairs. Really experienced ghosts can look as solid as living flesh, but that takes a lot of skill and energy. I would get better with practice. Still, Maggie seemed to be impressed by this first effort. Her eyes followed my every move with something bordering on horror.

"Don't look like that, honey. We're going to be friends. I'm here to help you out of the mess you've made of your life. But you've got to show some respect. Some things a lady just doesn't want touched, and this room is one of them."

Her mouth moved again. She looked as if she might have trouble breathing. Chicken. That's what she was. Since she wasn't willing to carry on a civilized conversation, I drifted over to the sample book she'd laid on my bed. By exerting just a bit of energy, I found I could flip the pages without even moving a ghostly hand.

"Dull," I concluded about the wallpaper. "Ugly. Sweetie, you've got no taste at all. Not that this room couldn't use a little sprucing up. But I want my tasseled lamp back, and the new curtains have to be scarlet velour. Red's my color, you know. Scarlet, vermillion, rouge, crimson—all of those. It's because of my hair, honey. Everyone says we redheads can't wear red. But in all of my life, whenever I heard the word 'can't,' I made it a point to do whatever I supposedly couldn't do."

"You . . . you . . ." Her jaw was flapping again, but nothing much came out. For a woman who'd been in politics, she sure wasn't much for thinking on her feet.

"And another thing, while we're at it, Mags. Do you have to let that damned cat wander all over the house? Just yesterday she brought in a mouse. A dead one. That sort of thing could give this house a bad rep. Back in my day we knew better than to let animals run about the place. Except our clients, of course." I smiled as memories came flooding back. "You might say that a

lot of our gentlemen were animals, in their own way. Like Big Tom McCleary, who never could hit the spittoon, and Gilbert Rawlins, who let loose a wolf howl every time he got his money's worth with one of the ladies. Gilbert didn't get his money's worth all that often, as he had a lot of trouble with his willy.

"But at least our gentlemen animals used the necessary out back. They didn't pee into a sandbox in the boiler room. And they didn't drag in dead rodents from the outside."

I flipped through the book, humming, having a good time on this maiden voyage into haunting, and decided to give the little gal a bit of decorating guidance. "All these are so plain. Very drab. Where's the velour patterns? The silks? The big florals? And these drapery materials? Eccch! These will never do. Maggie, Maggie, Maggie! Elaborate means wealth. Lavish means success. Ornate shows you've got class, and high-toned taste. Simple just means you can't afford anything else."

I really didn't mind if Maggie wanted to restore my room, but restore was the word. Not redecorate. Obviously the girl didn't have the taste to be trusted with that task. This room was very special to me, after all. I had lived here, both alive and dead, a long time. Besides that, it held a lot of my memories.

"We're going to have velvet draperies," I decided. "Just like the old ones. You can afford it, can't you? And a red satin counterpane." I closed the sample book with a snap and dusted off my illusory gown with a brush of my hands.

Mags backed slowly toward the door, shaking her head and muttering something meaningless. She didn't look pleased.

"Now don't you get stubborn about this, sweetie.

You don't want to get my back up. I had a spitfire temper when I was alive, and gathering cobwebs in my grave hasn't helped it any."

It was very rude of Mags to try to leave, I thought, and as soon as the notion crossed my mind, I shifted places, placing myself between her and the door, blocking her escape. She let loose a surprised little shriek and turned, only to see me close enough to reach out and touch. I had to laugh at the expression on her face. Yes, I know. It was rude to laugh. But I just had to.

And that was that. Maggie's eyes rolled up in her head and she folded up like a drunk miner. Flat on the floor, she was. Tsk. It was such a shame. Modern girls are so fragile.

Four

Catherine popped through the door to the Red Room, an electric heater beneath her arm and a heat gun in her hand. "Do you know that the only working space heater in this whole house is the one in our apartment? Haven't used those others much, have you? We'd better—Omigod! Maggie!"

When she spied Maggie lying flat out on the floor, she dropped the appliances and hurried to her side. Kneeling beside her unconscious sister, she grabbed a cold hand and tried to chafe it back to life, as she'd seen done in so many movies.

"Oh, Maggie, wake up! Wake up, wake up, wake up! Oh, what'll I do now. Maggie?'

Maggie didn't stir, so Catherine ran across the hall to the bathroom. A moment later, she returned to press a cold washcloth to the patient's cheeks and brow. Finally, Maggie stirred and groaned.

"Mags, are you okay? What happened?"

For a moment Maggie looked blank. Then her expression turned to one of incredulity. Her eyes darted around the room as if she looked for a monster to pop out from beneath the bed or behind the dresser.

"What?" Catherine demanded. "What's wrong?"

"You didn't see her?"

"See who?"

Slowly, Maggie got to her feet. Her hands shook; her face was parchment white.

Afraid her sister would faint again, Catherine pulled her toward the bed. "Sit!" she ordered in her sternest schoolteacher voice. "You're pale as a ghost. Tell me what happened."

"Pale as a ghost . . ." Maggie laughed, hitting a note that bordered on hysteria. "Ghosts aren't pale. They have sultry eyes and wear red dresses—and diamonds and gold, and roses in their hair."

"What?" Catherine's heart sank. Her mother had been right. Maggie should have seen that shrink. "Mags, what are you talking about?"

"I . . . I saw a ghost, Cat. Right here in this room."

For a moment Catherine could think of nothing to say. Her sister was having a breakdown before her eyes, and she didn't know what to do. She was a biology teacher, not a psychologist. "Mags . . . you've been under a strain. . . ."

"I saw a ghost!"

"You didn't eat lunch, did you. All day you've been going strong at the cleaning. You're just tired. I read an article in *Psychology Today* about people hallucinating when they get too tired or go without sleep too long."

"I am not hallucinating! I saw a ghost!"

"Or maybe you have a virus."

Catherine felt Maggie's forehead, only to have her hand slapped away.

"She was wearing a red silk gown, diamond earrings, and a bracelet that must have cost a fortune. And she said, 'Welcome to my home.' "

"Welcome to my home?" Catherine began to feel a quiver of doubt. "What else did she say?"

"A bunch of malarkey about my reprehensible taste in decorating. She wants the room done in crimson velvet and silk."

Catherine's heart started to race. Her eyes scanned the room with an unease that matched Maggie's. "You know, Mags. When I talked about the place being haunted, I was only teasing. I didn't mean it."

Maggie was silent.

"It was a joke."

"I'm not joking. I don't think the ghost was either."

"Dressed in a fancy gown and diamonds. Red hair? A rose?"

"Yes."

"What color eyes?"

"I don't know. She was kind of fuzzy, and kept fading in and out. Sometimes I could see right through her, and other times she seemed as real as you are."

"Do you suppose it could be . . . Roberta Rowe?"

"Jerome's queen of the whores?"

"Don't call her that," Catherine whispered. She glanced over her shoulder to make sure no one was listening.

"That's what she was. Come to think of it, the ghost did mention something about her gentleman clients being animals. That would fit. She certainly didn't seem shy about admitting what she was."

"Oh, Mags! We're haunted!"

They shared a moment of agonized silence, then Maggie groaned.

"Maybe this is just a bad dream."

Catherine let her mind chew on this new development for a moment. It was disturbing, yes, but . . . it might be exciting, also—to actually see a real live ghost. Of course, live wasn't the proper word. She wondered exactly what the proper word was to apply to a dead lady of the evening who paraded about in diamonds. Excitement began to crowd out distress.

"Did you look at the picture of the Red Robin in the hallway? The one I hung yesterday?"

"No. Why?"

"I thought you might have seen in, absorbed it, and then maybe you got light-headed from not eating and imagined that you saw her."

"The only thing I've absorbed lately is too much dust from this godforsaken room. I didn't imagine anything, and I certainly haven't had time to look at that picture."

"Then let's go look at it now. Maybe you can tell if it's the same person."

Cautiously, looking about as if a spook might pop from every shadow, they went downstairs. Catherine plucked the framed daguerreotype from the hallway wall before Maggie could look at it. "Describe the woman you saw," she instructed Maggie.

"I told you. She wore a red silk dress—"

"This photograph is black and white."

"Oh. Well, her hair was piled on her head in some sort of fancy arrangement of curls. And she had a rose twined in the curls."

"Go on."

Maggie closed her eyes. "She wore bracelets and dangly earrings."

"Uh-huh."

"Her nose was rather long. And she had a spot—a mole—high on her cheek, just below her right eye.'

Catherine's heart pounded. "Are you sure you didn't take a look at this picture?"

"I haven't had time to look at any picture, damn it!"

Cat turned the picture so Maggie could see it. Maggie's face grew even paler, if possible. "The earrings are different," she said, her voice strained. "The dress isn't the same one."

"The mole is the same, isn't it?"

"The mole, the face, the hair. Oh, God!"

Catherine looked up the stairs, her eyes drawn irresistibly. She couldn't decide if this was exciting or horrible. Maybe somewhere in between. "Oh, Mags! We're—"

The back door shut with a bang, sending them both jumping nearly to the ceiling. But nothing more frightening than Colby Drake came around the corner into the hallway. A swift exchange of glances warned Catherine to keep the ghost of Robin's Nest their own private secret.

"You ladies look as though I just grew horns," he told them. "Something wrong?"

"Not a thing!" Catherine insisted.

"Of course not!" Maggie said at the very same time.

He looked from Maggie to Catherine, then back to Maggie. "What's up, you two? Maybe I can help."

"Why would you think something's up?" Maggie asked.

Catherine marveled that her sister had gotten along in politics if that was her best innocent tone.

"You look jumpy as two cats on a hot stove."

"Oh no. No," Maggie protested. "We're just standing here . . . standing here . . . dusting this picture."

Colby had a very penetrating gaze when he leveled those cool blue eyes at a person, Catherine thought, and the man looked positively predatory when his eyes fastened onto Maggie.

"You're sure there's nothing wrong?"

Maggie took a deep breath. "Nothing's wrong."

"You're acting strange."

"I just . . . I just get jumpy when I'm tired. I've been working too hard. Cat tried to warn me."

"I tried to warn her."

He still looked suspicious.

Maggie fumbled at hanging the picture back in its place. She dropped it, but before it hit the floor, it miraculously seemed to slow for just a spilt second. It didn't break.

Both Catherine and Maggie stared as if the picture might bite them. Colby didn't seem to notice anything unusual. With the two sisters standing frozen, he picked it up and hung it back on the wall.

"She was a looker, wasn't she?"

A warm draft blew down the stairs, tinkled in the decorative wind chimes hanging by the front door, swirled cheerfully around the three of them for an instant, then was gone. Catherine shivered, and Maggie jumped back with a groan.

"Whoa!" Colby chuckled. "You *are* nervous. Good thing you're going to relax the rest of the afternoon."

"What?" Maggie looked blank.

Colby checked his watch. "Three o'clock. Remember? You owe me a date." He grinned. "I'm collecting."

Maggie looked at Catherine, then Colby, then back to Catherine. "I . . . I couldn't possibly," she finally stuttered. "Not today. I'm sorry, Colby."

As Colby's brows knitted in annoyance, Catherine jumped in. She wasn't about to let Maggie trash this opportunity. "Of course you can, Mags. You promised."

"I can't leave you alone here," Maggie said with a quelling look.

Colby raised a questioning brow, and Catherine hastened to repair the damage.

"Maggie, don't worry. The Fergusons will be back tonight, and in an hour we open for check-in. I'll probably be really busy with tours and . . ."

Catherine saw Maggie's eyes close painfully at the reminder of tours—of the upstairs, of the Red Room. Catherine veered away from the thought. She hoped they had a full house tonight. She absolutely did not want to be alone with whatever it was upstairs. But she continued staunchly. "You just go and have a good time, Mags. After all, you did promise Colby."

"I couldn't," Maggie declared.

"You can. Absolutely. Go change clothes. Your jeans are covered with dust, and so is your shirt."

Maggie glanced down at her clothes and shook her head, but she obediently moved toward the basement stairs. In only a few strides she stopped. "There's garlic in the kitchen. Isn't that supposed to keep away . . ."

"Vampires?" Colby inquired archly.

"Of course not! Garlic is for—"

"Bugs!" Catherine interjected. "Insects, you know. Roaches. Fleas. Yes! Fleas! George has fleas!"

"Well," Colby drawled. "It's nice that you're so happy about it."

"We're not happy," Maggie denied frantically. "It's just that . . . we should give the garlic a try, Cat. I've heard it's good for repelling all sorts of pests. Just spread it around where you don't want them to be."

"It won't work on me," Colby said with a grin. "I love garlic."

"Did I say you were a pest?" Maggie asked.

"It wouldn't be the first time someone's said so."

She rolled her eyes. "I'm obviously too tired to carry on a sensible conversation."

"Go get dressed," Catherine advised. "You're going out."

"All right. You win."

As Maggie headed toward the basement stairs, Catherine gave Colby an apologetic shrug. "We've both been working too hard. I need some wine."

With that, she fled to the kitchen, leaving him standing in the hallway to wonder if mental instability ran in the Potter family.

Once away from the house and on the road to Sedona in Colby's rented Ford Taurus, Maggie was tempted to think the whole Red Room incident had been stress preying on her mind rather than an actual ghost parading about Robin's Nest. The outside world seemed so normal—the same world she greeted day in and day out. The sky was still blue, the ground firm beneath her feet, the mountains still solid and unmoving as they always had been. She'd gotten a little too engrossed in Jerome's history, in the house's history, and her imagination had taken flight. That was all. Nothing a nice relaxed afternoon and a good night's sleep couldn't fix. She shouldn't have involved poor Catherine. Of the two of them, Cat had always been the giddy one, eager to embrace flights of fancy. In spite of her brave words, she would probably tremble within a circle of garlic cloves until Maggie came home.

Ghosts, Maggie told herself, belonged in fairy tales and campfire stories. When people died, they went somewhere else. Exactly where wasn't clear in her mind. But she knew they didn't stick around to protect the decor of their onetime bedrooms and scare the wits out of the owners of their onetime houses.

"Are you sure you feel all right?" Colby asked. "You're very quiet this afternoon."

"I'm just tired. You're right. I need to get away from the house for a while."

"Happy to be of service."

She gave him a smile. "You must think we're totally insane."

"Not totally."

"But a bit?"

He thought for a few seconds, then grinned engagingly. "Maybe just a touch. What was all that back there?"

"Overstretched nerves. We tend to babble. It runs in the family."

"You must have really interesting family reunions."

"Fortunately, it's a small family. And I'm feeling much better, thank you. It seems as if I've been cooped up in that house since the beginning of time."

"Have you? Are you a Jerome native?"

"Oh, no. Actually, I am an Arizona native, but I've been living in the Midwest for a while—deadly dull compared to what we're driving through." A sweep of her hand indicated the countryside around them, where dusty sage and juniper softened the bleached white of stark limestone buttes. Ahead the country rose toward the Mogollon Rim, and at the base of the Rim, Sedona nestled among fanciful castles, fortresses, towers, and spires of red sandstone. "Is this your first trip to Arizona?"

"I've been in Phoenix a couple of times. Never up here."

"What do you think?"

"It's spectacular."

It was, Maggie agreed. The scenery inside the car was rather spectacular also. Colby Drake might not be better than Mel Gibson, but he was nothing to sneeze at. Being tall herself, Maggie appreciated tall men. Colby was tall enough that his head brushed the top of the Taurus, and Catherine had been right about his shoulders. They fit the rest of him perfectly. Not too broad, but certainly not wimpish. He was lean and fit, with a tan that made his blue eyes downright startling and a smile that would make most women drool.

Not Maggie, though. She'd fallen for too many smiles like Colby Drake's.

"It is spectacular, all right," she agreed. "But wait until we get to Sedona. It looks pretty from here, but once you're right there among the red rocks, it's totally unbelievable."

"Since you love this country so much, how'd you end up in the Midwest, of all places?"

Maggie hesitated. She wanted to think about her years in Ohio even less than she wanted to contemplate the ghost in the Red Room. "Youthful yen for adventure," she said finally. "Isn't there a time in everybody's life when home is the dullest place imaginable, and anyplace else has to be cooler and more interesting?"

"The grass-is-always-greener syndrome."

"Something like that. Leave home, make waves, save the world."

"Did you save the world?"

She laughed humorlessly. "Hardly. Watch it, the road gets really curvy through here. We're almost to town. Do you believe how beautiful this is?"

Maggie didn't want to sound like an overwound tour guide, but any subject of conversation was better than the direction they were heading. She did not want to talk about Ohio, about her past, or even about her uncertain future. She had been dragged into this "date," but that didn't mean she had to get personal. Besides, she wanted to forget herself for once. Forget politics, betrayal, business concerns, and . . . ghosts.

Denial could become a total lifestyle if she wasn't careful.

As they rounded a curve, sage and juniper gave way to a motley collection of buildings that crowded the margins of the road. The structures had only one thing in common, and that was a look of tawdry impermanence. Built of brick, stone, stucco, or fake adobe, they were bright with signs announcing services ranging from palm reading to dry cleaning.

"This is the fabled Sedona?" Colby was clearly disappointed.

"I said the setting was beautiful. Not the town. It gets much better up the road, but everything near the highway is pretty much a tourist trap. The art galleries and restaurants are great, though, and if you like golf, the links are wonderful. Or so I'm told. Back in the hills are some homes that even Bill Gates couldn't afford."

Colby laughed. "Is there such a thing?"

"If there is, it's probably here. That's the unique thing about this town. From one shop to the next, from one street to the next, you can go from sublime to just plain silly."

"Chimera Crystals, Earth Mother Bookstore, Madigan Art Gallery, Bashas' Grocery." He chuckled at the diversity of signs. "Vortex Tours. Good grief! What's a vortex, and why would I want to tour it?"

"A vortex is supposedly some big whirlpool of psychic energy, and all the New Agers in town will tell you there's a couple of humdingers around here. Sedona is reputed to be a very magic place. Oops! Talk about magic! There's a parking spot. What luck!"

Colby obligingly turned into the empty spot, and once they were walking along the street, taking in the galleries and shops, the conversation turned to southwestern art, tourist traps, and the likelihood that the "Native American" curios had come from a factory in Taiwan. Almost against her will, Maggie found herself having a good time. Colby Drake was a difficult man to dislike.

Not that it mattered. This afternoon was simply a very short detour on her road of completely not needing a man. A very temporary detour.

Colby Drake prided himself on his instinct about people. It seldom took long for him to figure someone out. Perceptiveness was one of the things that made him a good reporter. Or so he believed.

In Maggie's case, Colby's instinct was fighting a battle with comfortably preconceived ideas. The more time he spent with Maggie Potter, the more his instinct insisted she was not the ambitious, amoral sharpie the TV-watching, tabloid-reading public believed her to be—just an honest woman who wasn't too smart about her affairs of the heart. His job might be easier if Maggie were on the make for power, money, or celebrity. She would be a heck of a lot easier to manipulate.

He didn't like being the kind of man who would think such a thing, but he was that kind of man. To do his job, he had to be. And his job, Colby reminded himself sternly, was worth doing.

As the afternoon progressed, he discovered that Maggie Potter was a number of things he hadn't expected her to be. As they wandered Sedona's main street—a commercial nirvana—the awkwardness between them gradually eased. In the galleries, he discovered that she liked most of the same art that he did. She laughed at his jokes—genuine laughter, not polite "date" laughter. She shared his disgust that civilization ruined every beautiful spot on the planet with curio shops and ice-cream parlors; and she shared his opinion that Joe Montana was one of football's all-time greats.

How could a man not be taken with a woman like Maggie Potter? When Colby had first seen her in Jerome, he'd thought her attractive. When she'd landed on top of him at the inn, he'd noticed she was sexy. More and more he was tempted to like her. Like her a lot. That made his job harder, but he wasn't going to let it trip him up.

During dinner at Poco Diablo, Colby got down to work. Fun time was over, and the trick was to not let the lady know it. Subtly, skillfully, he probed Maggie for information—and she nimbly dodged every attempt to get her to talk about life before Arizona. The lady was clever. She wanted to know about him as well. Colby had every intention of telling her the truth, but not yet. He didn't want to lie, but he was very skilled at half-truths and evasions.

Yes, he told her, photography was a difficult way to make a living. It would be, he thought, if that was his profession instead of his hobby. Maggie was the one who jumped to the conclusion that he was a photographer—maybe with just a little push from him.

And yes, he was on a working vacation. More work than vacation, he added silently, and his work was as a newspaper columnist, not a photo bug. He was here stalking Maggie Potter, not photogenic scenery, and soon, after she was thoroughly convinced what a nice, trustworthy, utterly likable guy he was, he would tell her that. Gently, of course. Tactfully. In a way that would make her want to cooperate with him, not boot his sorry butt out of her house.

Their drive back to Jerome was amiable. Maggie seemed much more relaxed than she'd been in the afternoon. Of course, the night was a soothing one. The breeze was warm, full of the scent of sage, juniper, and pine. The full moon rode high in a black velvet sky, and the lights of Jerome twinkled high up the side of Cleopatra Hill. Who could not be relaxed on a night like this? Colby wished he could break out a can opener and peel the top off his rental car. The night was made for a convertible.

When they arrived back at Robin's Nest, however, Maggie tightened up like an overwound spring. He could see the change in her eyes, her posture, the set of her shoulders, the line of her mouth. And a very nice mouth it was, too. He couldn't help but notice. A man couldn't spend the whole afternoon and evening in company with a great-looking woman and not notice some of those little details.

When they parked the car and approached the front door, he sought to stretch the evening a bit. "I like this front porch," he said lamely. "If my job allowed me any time to spend at home, I would have a porch just like this one."

She seemed eager for an excuse not to go inside. "We can sit awhile, if you like. That's why we put the swing out here."

The old-fashioned porch swing was perhaps more appropriate to small-town Midwest than ghost-town Southwest, but it was comfortable all the same, and a great place to sit with a pretty girl.

"Tonight was a nice time," she said after a few moments of comfortable silence. "Thank you for bullying me into going."

He should dispute the comment about bullying, but it wasn't far from the truth. "Thank you for allowing yourself to be bullied."

She gave him a moonlit smile, and his heart flip-flopped like a green boy's. He wondered what he was doing. Certainly his aim wasn't seduction. He would stoop fairly low for a story nailing Jack Kilbourne, but not that low.

Yet here he was, and here she was, and there was no denying that Maggie Potter needed to be kissed, wanted to be kissed, absolutely had to be kissed. He knew it in his very heart.

So he kissed her, pressed his mouth gently to hers, then less gently, then reached out to gather the rest of her as close as possible. Their bodies fit together as if made for each other, her hips tucked against his thighs, her breasts cozy with his chest. Their mouths flowed together without any awkwardness. She fit perfectly in his arms, and he fit perfectly in hers. For a moment it seemed as if much more than their bodies drew together, more than their lips joined forces.

And in that moment Colby knew he was in very deep trouble.

Five

Maggie lay in her bed staring into the dark. She couldn't sleep, and that wasn't surprising, considering the circumstances. In the space of one day, she had acquired not only a ghost, real or imagined, to complicate her life, but a man who could turn her inside out with one kiss. Not that she had let Colby know how his kiss had affected her. She'd forced herself to be cool, casual, properly nonchalant, but beneath that facade she'd been buzzing with reaction. One would think a twenty-six-year-old woman wouldn't start bouncing around on cloud nine from a simple kiss, but then, Maggie had never been very smart when it came to men.

The last thing she needed, Maggie sternly reminded herself, was a man. She was a fool if she let good looks and charm melt her defenses. How many times did she have to be burned before she stayed away from the fire?

"Damn!" she muttered aloud. She was too restless to stay in bed, but she didn't want to go upstairs to the living room or kitchen. She might run into Colby—if he was having similar late-night unrest. Or worse, she might run into something else, something she would rather avoid thinking about. Thinking about her unease with Colby Drake was much less disturbing than thinking about a hallucination in a red silk gown.

She got up, went into the bathroom, and filled a glass with water. Back at her bed, she set the glass on the bedside table, sat forlornly on the mattress, then got up again. Pulling on a robe, she went to the stairs, hesitated, and walked back to the bed.

"Maggie?" came a sleepy voice from Catherine's section of the apartment. "Is that you?"

"It's me. Sorry I woke you."

After a few moments of rustling behind the curtain, Catherine emerged, her hair in chaos and her eyes at half-mast. "Did you have a good time?"

"Yes, I did. I'm sorry I came in so late. I didn't want to wake you, but I just can't sleep."

Catherine's eyes popped open in sudden alarm. "You didn't see . . . anything, did you?"

Maggie knew very well what "anything" was. "No. Did you?"

"Uh . . . well . . . maybe, but I'd had a bit of wine."

"You saw her!"

"I think it was just the power of suggestion, Mags. Really. You know what wine does to me."

Maggie looked at her wide-eyed for a moment, then groaned. "Yeah. Wine. And as for me, my wits are just shredded. Maybe I should have taken Virginia's advice and seen that shrink. It's just silly to think it was a real ghost. A nervous breakdown would be much easier to accept. And I certainly deserve one."

"I can't argue with that." Catherine sighed wearily.

"I'm going back to bed. Oh, by the way, a couple from Tucson dropped by after you left and decided to take the Wicker Room. They'll probably be here for three nights."

"Great." The Wicker Room was right across from the Red Room. Maggie hoped their new guests didn't see any visual effects from the past during their stay.

"We're going to make a great success of this venture, Mags."

"I know we are. We won't let it be any other way."

"And I'm glad you had a good time with Colby. You don't need to get up and help me with breakfast. You're more bother than help in the kitchen, you know."

"Thanks," Maggie replied wryly.

"Sleep in, Mags. You need it. Good night."

"Good night."

Maggie huddled in her bed, listening to Attila and Hannibal making bird noises, wishing sleep would come to drive ghosts and Colby Drake from her mind. Colby Drake. Kissing Colby Drake. The memory made her feel guilty. Guilty and idiotic. The man was much too charming, too handsome, too likable. One couldn't trust a man with all those qualities; he was either a politician or a jerk.

So why did his smile make her want to smile in return? And why did something as simple as a kiss turn her upside down and inside out? One would think by now she would have learned. Men. Ghosts. Insanity. Men. Didn't life have anything to offer but problems?

Still, she couldn't keep a smile from her face as she fell asleep.

•   •   •

Morning came much too early for Colby. He woke at seven, a full hour later than his usual rising time, and even then he didn't get up. The bed was very comfortable. Outside the open window, birds trilled a greeting to the new day. A pleasantly cool breeze belled the curtains and scented the room with pine and juniper.

It was such a goddamned perfect country morning that it ought to be bottled, Colby thought. He could make a fortune selling it to the asphalt-pounding, auto-exhaust-sniffing denizens of Washington, D.C. And not just Washington. There were markets all over the world that could use bit of Jerome's morning. New York, LA, Chicago, London, Tokoyo, Moscow, to name just a few. He would make a fortune, then retire to someplace where the stupid birds didn't get up at five in the morning and the air had some solid substance to it. Forget all this pine-scented, smog-free purity.

Not that he really minded the noisy birds, and he rather liked the novelty of sucking in a lungful of air without the usual load of pollutants. But in his line of work, a good dose of cynicism started the day rolling in the proper mood. It wouldn't do to let his wits be dulled by the country air—or his mind to be clouded by the appeal of a certain infamous but very attractive woman.

With that in mind, Colby dragged himself out of bed. He'd actually slept the night through without waking, an unusual feat for him. Usually his mind churned so actively with plans, problems, and possibilities that he couldn't sleep more than three hours at a stretch. This place was much too peaceful. Or maybe Maggie Potter had a soothing effect on him. He would just have to ignore it.

After inhaling Catherine's delicious breakfast—at which Maggie was notably absent—Colby took his camera for a stroll through town. He did love photography, even though he didn't make his living at it. He liked capturing different aspects of the same object or scene, using angles to vary character and presentation. On the whole, photography was a lot like writing. But there was more money in capturing the character of a presidential candidate than the beauty of red buttes basking in the sunshine.

Except, of course, that the red buttes would be there long after Jack Kilbourne and Colby Drake were both dust.

He paused to shoot a couple of frames of the awesome landscape, then wandered into the post office. When Colby walked in, the place was empty. Traffic in the post office was light today, as it was Sunday, and only the lobby was open. He glanced at the cluttered bulletin board of community notices—puppies for sale, a seminar on finding your spirit guide, a community theater production of *As You Like It*. Small-town homeyness wed to New Age weird. Quite a comedown for Maggie after running with the big dogs.

He dropped his mail in the slot—a letter to his sister and postcards for her kids—and was getting ready to leave when Maggie herself came through the door. She walked straight to her mailbox, apparently not seeing him as she passed from bright sunshine into the dim light of the lobby. Shadows beneath her eyes were a clue that she hadn't slept nearly as well as he had. He wondered if thoughts of Jack Kilbourne kept her awake at night, and experienced an unexpected flash of jealousy.

"Hi there."

She jumped at the sound of his voice. "Oh! Colby. Hi."

The instant their eyes met, Colby recalled exactly

how their kiss had felt. His body responded with a rush
of heat, and for a moment, he felt like an out-of-
control adolescent. If the sudden color in her face was
any indication, Maggie was experiencing the same difficulty. Her eyes didn't hold his for long before they
slid away to the bulletin board, the stamp posters decorating the walls, the cracks in the floor.

"You missed breakfast," Colby said.

"I slept in. As Cat says, I'm more hindrance than
help at cooking, and I figured the guests could do without my playing lady of the manor at the table."

Colby wanted to say he had missed her. But telling a
woman something like that gave her a distinct advantage.

"I'm lucky that Cat doesn't mind taking on the
breakfast duties by herself."

"She does a great job."

"Yes. She's a good cook, and good with people
too."

They were neither of them talking about the thing
that was foremost in their minds. He could see last
night's embrace in her eyes, just as he could feel it in his
own mind. It was crazy, Colby thought, for two adults
to let a single, casual, offhand little kiss throw them
into a tizzy of awkwardness. What were they, thirteen-
year-olds?

"Do you know how long you'll be staying?" Maggie
asked.

"Uh . . . I'll be around a few days longer, at least.
Is that a problem?"

"No problem," she hastened to assure him.

Did he detect just a bit of pleasure in her voice? If
so, he was succeeding at the first step of his strategy.
Why did he feel as if he was teetering on the edge of
losing control of the situation?

"Well," she concluded, "I'll see you tonight, if not before. And . . . thanks again for dinner last night."

As she walked out, he admired the gentle sway of her hips and wished he were a straightforward guy putting the moves on an ordinary girl. But life wasn't that simple. He wasn't a straightforward guy. At times, he was as underhanded as they come; it was part of the job. And Maggie Potter was far from an ordinary girl.

And Colby Drake had better start working at being underhanded, or he was going to lose this story.

Up the street a ways, a shaded bench looking out over the valley below afforded a measure of privacy. Colby took a cell phone from his camera case and punched in *America Today*'s general number. When the receptionist answered, he said, "This is Colby Drake. Let me talk to Rich Michaels."

His editor came on the line immediately. "Yo, Colb. It's about time. Where are you?"

"Where I need to be, Rich. I'm on a cell phone—not the most private piece of equipment—and I don't want every rival in the business flocking to . . . let's say, Tioga, North Dakota."

"Oh. Gotcha. You get what you need?"

"I'm in the process, on target. No problems. I'm just lying low for a few days to map out the best way to get our subject to talk."

"Listen, man. We don't have all summer, you know?"

"I know, I know. But if I just spring out of the woodwork and announce to this woman that I'm a political columnist for our esteemed newspaper, she'll lock all her doors and windows and then set her attack bird on me."

"Attack bird?"

"Yeah. You'd have to see it to believe it."

"I'm not sure I want to."

"Don't worry, Rich. I'm making progress here. Our girl isn't quite what I expected. This is going to take some subtlety."

Michaels snorted. "You? Subtle?"

"Hey! I can be subtle when it's called for. This is too important for me to get in a hurry and blow it. I can get the goods, given just a little bit of time."

"How long, Colb?"

"How the hell do I know? This is a woman we're dealing with, not an airline schedule."

"Well, you'd better get what you need, buddy. Have you seen the latest polls?"

"No. I'm out in boonieland, remember?"

"What? You don't get TV in . . . North Dakota?"

"I've been busy."

"Well, let me tell you, it's not only his own party that's cozying up to Jack Kilbourne. He's going to win not only the nomination, but the election hands down."

"No he won't. Too many questions have been raised about all this wheeling and dealing in Ohio. And he's divorced. That always alienates fundamentalists and little old ladies. And then there's Maggiegate."

"Don't fool yourself. You've been out there in boonieland too long. Kilbourne's come out of the Maggie Potter thing and the divorce looking like a good-hearted down-home boy taken advantage of by a scheming slut. He's got a couple of good spin doctors working every angle. And the allegations about the wheeling and dealing in Ohio aren't going to stick unless someone comes up with something concrete. The guy's Teflon."

"Give me a little time," Colby said. "I'll get enough concrete to make a major dent in Kilbourne's head."

"You'd better. Speculations don't sell papers anymore, and they don't win or lose elections, either."

"Trust me, Rich."

Michaels made a rude noise. "Where have I heard that before?"

Colby punched the End button and grimaced. He definitely had to get back to work.

Maggie walked out of the post office in a better mood than when she'd walked in. Her footsteps were light, and a smile played at her mouth. The morning seemed sunnier, the sky bluer, and the distant red-rock country more vivid—because of Colby Drake? He truly was a hard man to dislike. She tried to remember why it was important to dislike him. The reasons were becoming foggy. Cynicism and disillusionment weren't packing the same punch they had a week ago.

She walked by the open door of a stained glass shop and waved at the proprietor.

"Hi, Maggie!" The woman behind the cash register waved her in. "How's it going?"

"Great. How 'bout you?"

"Business is pretty good, considering it's June. I wish tourists would get it through their heads that not all of Arizona is blazing hot during the summer months. So how's your grand opening weekend?"

"We're doing okay. Can't complain."

"Well, if anyone asks for a nice place to stay, I'll send them your way."

"Thanks, Midge. You still holding that sun-catcher I want?"

"Got it in the back."

"Great. Gotta go. I'm going to treat myself to one of

those pots down at the Clay Company. Talk to you later."

She stopped to chat at two more shops. In others, clerks waved to her through a window or open door, a couple congratulating her on a good first weekend of business. Everyone in Jerome seemed to know her, but only because she'd bought an old landmark and restored it. Only one or two had connected her with the notorious Maggie Potter of dubious Maggiegate fame, and those, to her face at least, had been more indignant for her than about her. Jerome was certainly a unique town with unique people.

"You're not a-kiddin', honey. You should've seen it a hundred years ago."

The voice was crystal-clear in Maggie's ears, but when she whirled about, looking for who had spoken, no one was there.

"Watch where you're walking, sweetie. Jerome isn't the kind of place you want to be stumbling around backward. You'll find yourself stepping off into thin air, and that would hurt a mite."

"Who . . . ?"

"Who do you think? Now don't get all swoony on me, gal. It's not like we haven't been introduced."

She was going mad, Maggie decided. And just when she'd been feeling so good.

"You're not bonkers, you ninny. I told you we were going to be friends, so don't look so put out. I'm here to help you. I can give you advice, you know. One woman to another."

Maggie tried to ignore the voice. People were beginning to look her way. Turning circles in the middle of an empty sidewalk, staring about her as if there were someone to see, she probably looked like a lunatic waiting for the padded wagon.

"And you do need advice, Maggie girl."

This was her imagination reacting to stress. Delayed stress syndrome, that's what it was. If she ignored it, it would go away.

"Now, Maggie, I'm not going away until we have a little talk."

"Get out of my head!"

Three small children stopped to stare at her before their mother hastily pulled them away and herded them up the street, glancing over her shoulder to make sure the crazy lady wasn't following.

"Damn!" Maggie muttered. She moved to the edge of the sidewalk, looking out over the valley so that people on the street could see only her back. At that spot, no building fronted the sidewalk. The ground fell away abruptly, tumbling down to the next street, and a sturdy rail bordered the walk to keep the tourists from tumbling after. Maggie grasped the steel pipe of the rail as if it were the sanity she was trying to hold on to. Her knees felt wobbly, and her heart was beating double-time. She wasn't seeing anything, but she was hearing entirely too much.

"You want to see me, Mags? I aim to please!"

The apparition popped out of thin air, fancy red dress, diamonds, and all. It was the exact same vision she'd had before.

"Don't worry, honey. Only you can see me this time. I haven't had much practice, but I'm getting damned good at this, if I do say so myself." She spread her arms in an invitation to inspection. *"Not bad, eh? Betcha can't even see through me."*

Maggie forgot to breathe. Spots swam in her vision. She closed her eyes, took a deep breath, and hoped when she looked again the apparition would be gone. It wasn't.

"You know, Mags, you're one very lucky girl. There aren't very many men like that Colby Drake running around loose for a spinster to scoop up. And he's sweet on you. A blind man could see that, or a dead woman. Heh, heh. A little spook humor there."

Maggie groaned softly.

"All right, it wasn't that funny. What do you want from me? Chain-rattling and wailing? I'm not into that sort of thing. I have more class. What I came to tell you, Mags, is that you're going about getting your man all wrong. It's no wonder you're a spinster at—what are you? Twenty-six? Face it, sweetie, you're way over the hill. You'd better start paying attention to business. Playing hard to get isn't a good idea at your age."

Maggie stared out over the valley to the cliffs beyond, refusing to look directly at the outlandish creature who leaned indolently against the railing beside her. Nevertheless, she was painfully aware of every detail of her nightmare—the jewelry, the elaborately curled red hair with its rose, the lavish gown, the tiny mole beneath her eye, and the dimple beside her mouth. The thing looked so solid, so real. Why hadn't she listened to Virginia and talked to that shrink?

An elderly lady in shorts, T-shirt, and Nikes strolled up to Maggie with a polite smile. The woman looked right through the apparition without seeing it. Worse, she walked right through it without so much as flinching.

"Excuse me, dear. Do you have the time?"

Trying to breathe at a normal pace, Maggie glanced at her watch—just as if she weren't standing at the rail with a ghost, and this nice lady weren't standing inside the ghost. "Ten o'clock."

"Thank you. It's certainly a lovely day, isn't it? I

declare, these Arizona people are absolutely spoiled for good weather."

Maggie could manage only a twitch of her lips, and the result felt more like a grimace than a smile.

"Well, have a nice day," the woman said. She walked away with a pace that did the Nikes justice, apparently suffering no ill effects from her close encounter with the spirit world.

"*See?*" the ghost said. "*They can't see me unless I want them to. Feel better now?*"

"I'd feel better if you went the hell away."

"*Tch! Is that any way to talk to a hundred-and-thirty-eight-year-old lady? I was only thirty-eight when I was shot, you know. What do you think? Do I look thirty-eight? I always thought I looked younger.*"

Maggie gave the ghost a murderous look.

"*Yes, well, back to your problem. You're not getting any younger, either, so you'd better appreciate an opportunity when it walks up and kisses you. Oh yes! I saw. You can't tell me that Colby Drake leaves you cold. Lordy! He wouldn't leave a block of ice cold. Those blue eyes of his could make a girl melt her bloomers, and that wavy black hair, those nice, solid muscles . . . um! Not to mention that he fills out his jeans just the way a real man should.*"

Maggie nearly choked.

"*Don't give me that wide-eyed innocent look, girl! I've seen your eyes drop below the belt a time or two. There's no shame in it. Curiosity's just natural. He looks like a good kisser, too, but you'd know that better than me. That's important in a man, you know. In my line of work, most gals don't care for kissing. The other stuff you can serve up without getting real personal, but kissing is for lovers. Most fellas are sloppy at it, anyhow, slobbering and smacking like pigs. But*" *your Colby looks like a real gentleman with his mouth, and probably his other parts, too."*

That was too much for Maggie. She pushed violently away from the rail and proceeded down the street in purposeful strides, her purpose to escape whatever it was that was hounding her—imagination gone awry or a real live ghost. The apparition followed, matching her stride for stride.

"Go away!" she whispered vehemently. "Please!"

"Hell, no! I'm having too much fun. Do you know how long it's been since I've had fun?"

"Who are you?"

"You know that, honey. Roberta Rowe, the Red Robin herself, in the ghostly flesh. You can call me Robbie, since we're friends. Oh my! Look at the dress in that window. It's leather, do you believe? In my day, leather was for harnesses and saddles, and maybe chaps, if a man had to work in the brush. But ladies' dresses? And would you look at the slit up the side? I wouldn't have let any of my girls wear that. The ladies of Robin's Nest had class."

"I don't believe this."

"Not that the way you dress is anything to be proud of. Really, Mags, how do you expect to hook a man dressing the bait in denims and a T-shirt? You look like a twelve-year-old boy. And we both know you've got something to show off if you wanted to."

Desperately, Maggie ducked into the Jerome Artists' Co-op gallery. Bracing one hand against the wall, she closed her eyes and prayed. When she looked up, Robbie was gone.

"Hi! Can I help you?" From behind a glass display case, a young woman with waist-length curly brown hair regarded Maggie with sympathy. "Sun get too much for you? Arizona can do that to the unwary.

Even when it doesn't seem hot, the dry air can suck the energy right out of you."

Maggie sighed. "I'm fine. Thanks, though."

"You're Maggie Potter, aren't you? The one who opened the bed-and-breakfast up the hill?"

"That's me."

"Well, if you need some pottery or sculpture to help decorate the place, we've got some really dynamite stuff from a guy who lives over in Prescott. He uses gourds, and what he creates is absolutely beautiful."

"Thanks. I'll take a look."

Maggie was so relieved to escape her ghostly shadow that she would have looked at a blank wall to avoid going outside. But the artistic gourds were actually very nice, and the price was reasonable. She bought one. By now, she had forgotten what she'd originally come into town to buy.

"Good choice!" the girl congratulated her. "It's nice to have people around who'll support the local artists."

Maggie was all for supporting the local artists; she just didn't want to get stuck with the local ghost. Clutching her package, she nervously ventured outside.

"What'd you buy?"

"Geez!" She jumped practically out of her Reeboks.

"Art doesn't really grab me, you know? So I went up the street to look at jewelry. I've always been partial to diamonds. They had a few, but mostly they sold this handcrafted artsy stuff. It's all right, I guess, but if a girl wants to show what she's worth, diamonds are the ticket."

"Go away!" Maggie pleaded under her breath.

"Don't be rude, honey. You oughta be honored. In a hundred years, you're the only person I've talked to. Oh, it is good to be out again! Do you know there's a

candy store around the corner? I would die for chocolate. What I would give to be able to taste again."

"You're a figment of my imagination."

The apparition swung in front of Maggie and blocked her way, hands braced on silk-swathed hips. *"Don't get pert on me, Maggie girl. I'm not a figment of anything. I'm me. Or at least what's left of me. And you'd better watch yourself with your insults, missy! Figment, indeed! I might be your last, best hope of leading a normal life. Heaven knows you haven't done such a hot job managing it on your own. You just remember that next time we visit."*

With an annoyed huff, the "figment" disappeared, leaving Maggie standing on the sunbaked sidewalk, feeling as if she had just awakened from a dream. Last, best hope for a normal life indeed! Just what about this morning could be described as normal?

Six

The bookstore smelled like every other new-and-used bookstore Catherine had ever walked into. The mall stores that sold only pristine new volumes didn't have this wonderful smell. It came from old paper, cardboard hardcovers, and worn pages that had already known the loving touch of human fingers.

Catherine inhaled happily. She supposed it was the schoolteacher in her, but she did love books.

"May I help you?"

A man came from among the stacks. He smiled at her, and instantly Catherine melted. *Harrison Ford with glasses,* she thought. Better than Mel Gibson, Cary Grant, Humphrey Bogart, and Cliff Robertson all rolled into one.

"Are you looking for something specific?" he asked.

She'd been looking for someone specific all her life, and now she'd found him. Most people pooh-poohed love at first sight. But Catherine believed.

He tilted his head in inquiry, and she struggled to remember why she'd come into the store. Oh yes. Their little problem. How could she forget? Poor Maggie had been close to frantic the afternoon before when she'd recounted her adventure with ghostly harassment on the streets of Jerome. It had taken two glasses of wine to calm her.

The clerk gave her an inquisitive smile—slightly wry, gently patient, and entirely heartstopping. Shyly she returned his smile. "I . . . was at the library in Jerome, and they said of all the bookstores in the area, Matthews' in Cottonwood was most likely to have books on . . . uh . . . ghosts."

"Ghosts, eh?"

She waited for a condescending chuckle or a tolerant smile, but neither came. Instead, a spark of interest fired his eyes—and very nice brown eyes they were, Catherine noted. "So happens the library sent you to the right place. I have a whole section of ghost books."

"Really?"

"It's in the back, between history and gardening. I'll show you."

She had indeed come to the right place. He had everything from ghost story anthologies through theoretical studies of hauntings to back issues of the *Journal of the American Society for Psychical Research*.

"You really do have a whole section. Goodness! I don't know where to start."

"What exactly were you looking for?"

"Just general. How ghosts come to be, what one can expect of a ghost, how to get rid of them . . . stuff like that."

He took down a book by Hans Holzer. "This fellow can be very interesting. Entertaining, too. He's a ghost hunter of some repute."

"Ah."

"And this fellow over here tried to debunk haunt-ings and ended up writing a book on why they're real."

"Oh?"

They went through the shelves, and with the man's help, Catherine selected four books that were sure to tell her more about ghosts than she ever wanted to know. As they headed toward the cash register, she slid him a sideways glance.

"You seem very conversant with this subject, Mr.—"

"Matthews. Tom Matthews."

"Oh! You're the owner?"

"Owner, chief clerk, cashier, and janitor. And my own most loyal customer as well."

She laughed. "That's wonderful. I've always thought it would be fun to own a bookstore."

"Fun isn't always the word to describe it, but I do enjoy it. Mostly I enjoy the books."

"And you seem to know a lot about ghost books."

"Ghosts are a hobby of mine. I've been fascinated by the subject ever since I was a kid and thought I saw my grandfather's spirit."

"You actually saw a ghost?"

"No. It turned out to be a good dose of pizza mixed with a kid's overactive imagination, but it started my interest just the same."

He slipped behind the counter, and she set the books in front of him. He had an old-fashioned cash regis-ter—the kind that had become obsolete when com-puters took over the business end of business. Though his work space included a PC, Tom Matthews obvi-ously appreciated things from the past.

Better and better, Catherine thought.

"So you know a lot about ghosts?"

"I've read a lot, is all. And you? What's your take on ghosts?"

"I don't have a take. I'm just trying to learn a bit. Are there many hauntings around here that you've read about or heard of?"

"The usual stuff. All the New Age wizards in Sedona tend to see spirits, aliens, and vortexes wherever they look. They're more into that than ghosts. But this area has a fairly violent history. Many of the well-documented ghosts around the world seem to be the result of violent deaths, so I'd be surprised if there weren't a few haunts around here."

"Violent history? I didn't know that. Tell me more."

He gave her a keen look. "I don't usually pick up pretty women in my own bookstore, but . . ."

Catherine's heart flipflopped. He'd called her pretty. Of course he was just being polite, but it gave her a lift just the same.

". . . but maybe you'd like to catch lunch? It is noon, and I like to talk about my favorite subject."

"Oh yes!" The enthusiasm gushed out before she could dam it up. Immediately she tried to look nonchalant, as if she accepted lunch dates with endearingly bookish hunks every day of the week.

Catherine scarcely noted what she ate at Diego's Mexican Restaurant where they drove in Tom's 1988 Ford Bronco. She was accustomed to being smitten at first sight; she'd been doing it since she was fourteen. But getting attention from the object of her interest was a new experience.

Not that she'd never been out with a man before. Of course she had. But the men she went out with were not the men who made her heart do somersaults—until now. Of course, this impromptu lunch wasn't really a date, and Catherine didn't have Tom Matthews's undivided attention. His interest focused on the subject of their discussion, not the color of her eyes, the fetching tilt of her nose, or the loving heart that lay beneath her rather well-padded exterior. But Catherine allowed herself to hope just the same. One could not be a true romantic without hope.

Tom Matthews was a wealth of information about ghosts—ghost theories, ghost pranks, ghost habits, ghost dislikes. He told sad ghost tales and funny ones. Tales that ranged from the heartstring-puller to the unbelievably scary. He'd read about ghosts, attended lectures, and even taken a class in the supernatural via the Internet.

Catherine didn't have any ghost tales to tell except the one she'd experienced herself, and both she and Maggie believed the fewer people that knew about Robbie, the better. After an hour and a half munching tostadas and listening to Tom, however, she caved in.

"I think it's great what you and your sister are doing," Tom said when Catherine told him about the inn. "Hard work, I guess, but in that location, I'd guess that you could make a success of it."

"That's what Maggie thought when she convinced me we should buy the place. We've only been open a few days, but we already have quite a bit of business."

"I'll have to come up sometime. I love the old buildings in Jerome. They have so much character."

"Well . . . yes." Catherine wondered whether Tom Matthews would believe in a ghost that was not some fascinating specter documented in the pages of a book, but a loud and brassy strumpet from the last century. "Robin's Nest has a lot of character. One character in particular. We've got a real ghost, Tom. The lady who built the place and ran a brothel there is still in residence."

He gave her an intense look. "You're kidding!"

"Believe me, I wouldn't kid about such a thing. It's scarier than having cockroaches."

She got no skepticism from Tom Matthews. He wanted to hear all about Red Robin Rowe—her history, how she looked, how she sounded, what she wanted.

"I don't know what she wants," Catherine admitted. "Except she seems strangely interested in my sister's love life. Poor Maggie."

He wanted to hear every detail that Maggie had told her about the ghost's appearances. Catherine was amazed he didn't think both she and her sister were a brick short of a full load.

"Maggie can't decide whether she's walked into an episode of *The X-Files* or into a mental ward. She was hoping to get some peace and normalcy for a change, and now she has a troublemaking ghost on her hands. If you tell anyone about this, she'll kill you right after she kills me for telling you about it. Maggie doesn't want to scare off the guests, and she doesn't want any more notoriety than she already has."

Catherine wasn't afraid to allude to Maggie's state of mind. While they'd still been on the chips and salsa appetizer, Tom had recognized the name Maggie Potter and agreed wholeheartedly with Catherine that her sister had gotten a raw deal.

"From what you've said so far, this ghost sounds more interesting than troublesome."

Catherine grinned. "It seems that way to me, but then I'm not the one who Red Robin's following about like a Jewish yenta."

At the end of two hours, Tom announced that he had to get back to his store before his customers decided he'd closed for good. Catherine couldn't resist inviting him to the inn that evening for a look-see at Robin, and he jumped at the opportunity. Maggie would not be pleased, but what harm could be done, Catherine thought, by letting a knowledgeable ghost aficionado in on their secret? Besides, Tom Matthews was so fascinated by ghosts, he might hang around the inn a lot. And if he was at the inn a lot, he might eventually discover that there was something at Robin's Nest more desirable than a long-dead tart. Namely, Catherine Marjorie Potter—very much alive and quite willing to be a tart for the right man.

Maggie felt like kicking something—preferably the hot water heater. They'd been open for business four lousy days and the thing was already on the fritz. The gurgling she'd heard the night before hadn't been Robbie having trouble with ghostly stomach gas; it had been the hot water heater complaining of a similar problem. Maggie didn't know exactly what was going on. She wasn't conversant with appliances. What she did know was that the water heater was gurgling, the pipes were belching when the hot water taps were turned on, and the water wasn't as hot as it should have been.

The joys of being an innkeeper! Maybe if she stood staring at the thing for a few hours, it would heal itself.

"Hi there! Here you are."

Maggie turned to find Colby halfway down the basement stairs. Attila greeted him with a seductive chirp.

"Not this time, you hussy," Colby told the bird. "I can't be duped twice."

"I thought you were going to the Grand Canyon today."

"When I couldn't persuade you to go with me, I

decided to stay here. I thought I might be able to steal you away for just a few hours to show me Oak Creek Canyon. It's a lot closer."

She puffed out a breath of exasperation. "What am I going to do with you, Colby?"

"I could suggest some interesting things," he said with a waggle of his brows. "And we wouldn't even have to leave the house to do them."

"Typical man."

"You have something against men?"

"The exasperation of a superior life form for an inferior one."

She delivered the cut with a smile on her face, and he laughed. "You ought to smile more, Maggie. Come play with me, and I'll make you smile."

"You're impossible, Mr. Drake."

"Well, I did offer a nice, chaste tour of Oak Creek, but you didn't seem too pleased with that."

"I won't be too pleased with anything until I get this hot water heater fixed. And I'd guess that you and the other guests won't be too pleased if it craters and you end up taking a cold shower tonight."

"Take me up on my offer and I won't need a cold shower tonight."

Maggie gave him a face.

"You left yourself wide open for that one." He grinned engagingly and came the rest of the way down the stairs, just as if she had invited him into her private sanctuary—the sanctuary she shared with Catherine, George, the lovebirds, the hot water heater, the furnace, and the washing machine. "Nice digs," he lied politely. "What's wrong with the water heater?"

"How should I know? Do I look like the Maytag man?"

"This is a Sears model."

Maggie made a rude sound.

"Cranky, cranky."

"I'm sorry." She sighed. "Just because the water heater is making ill-mannered noises is no reason for me to take it out on you. I don't suppose you know anything about hot water heaters—something more than reading the brand name, that is."

"A real man knows a little about everything," he told her with a twinkle in his eye. "Let me take a look."

Maggie sat on the bottom step of the stairs to watch him poke, prod, and frown at the appliance. She doubted he knew anything more about water heaters than she did. He was a photographer, after all, not a repairman. But his banter and unquenchable good cheer lightened her mood. She smiled and realized that for the first time all day, smiling was not an effort.

Colby Drake did that to her—made her smile, inspired her to laugh, tempted her to dream. She didn't need a man and didn't want a man, but his teasing and trying to lure her into spending time with him felt good. Kissing him felt even better. Parts of her she had thought dead suddenly came to life.

His flirtation was all a game, of course. In a few days, a couple of weeks at the most, he would be gone. All Colby Drake wanted from her was a little vacation entertainment.

But what if she was wrong? What if he wanted more? Suppose his interest was more sincere than a few days of shallow flirtation? How would she feel then? Maggie wondered. How would she react if he announced he was staying the summer? Suppose he said she was special, that they should hook up, discover each other, explore what they had together? She would resist, of course, and let him know that she'd been there, done that, got the T-shirt, and was done with such games.

Oh, to still have the luxury of romantic illusions, as Catherine did, as Maggie once had. Colby's cheerful persistence tempted her to lower a few barriers and let some warmth thaw her heart.

Shit! What was she thinking? Feeling a sudden twinge of panic, Maggie had the urge to run. "I'm going upstairs to start cleaning," she told Colby. "Do you mind?"

"I'll just take a few more minutes to look at this thing. Do you have a screwdriver?"

"Top drawer of the desk. Fix it, and I'll give you two days' free room. If you're staying that long."

"With an offer like that, how can I not stay?"

Idiot, Maggie scolded herself as she climbed the stairs. Now he thought she wanted him to stay. She didn't. He could leave tomorrow, and she would be delighted. Wouldn't she?

Colby watched Maggie ascend the stairs, admiring the rear view. Then turned to look at the desk. A wry smile lifted one corner of his mouth. He would have expected someone who'd been through the mill, as Maggie had, to be less trusting. This was so easy he should feel guilty. He did feel guilty. Betraying someone's trust was rotten, and he was slime. But then, he was a reporter. Sometimes being slime was part of the job description.

The desk was unlocked—not only the middle drawer, where Maggie had directed him to find the screwdriver, but all the other drawers as well. He didn't know exactly what he sought—something with Jackass Kilbourne blazoned on it in big red letters would be nice. Nice, but unlikely. He found the screwdriver, an interlocked mess of paper clips, state and federal tax files, mortgage papers on the house, title to a 1998 Saturn, and receipts for everything from window coverings to the Saturn's last oil change. He blessed Maggie for being a very organized person. Every file and envelope was labeled and dated, which made invading her privacy so much easier.

After only five minutes of search, Colby found something that set his heart to racing almost as much as Maggie herself could. A series of files, neatly organized by date and labeled simply "office logs—personal." A quick perusal of the first folder confirmed Colby's hopeful guess. All the time she'd worked in Kilbourne's office, Maggie had kept a personal log of who, what, when, where, and why. Names, dates, and purpose of visit was all there. Why a smooth operator like Kilbourne had let her get out of the office with such a thing was beyond guessing, unless the guv didn't know the logs existed. They were handwritten, with the dry account of office ins and outs interspersed with personal observations. No doubt a more official log had been typewritten and stuck strictly to business. And no doubt that official copy had been doctored if it included a record that would implicate Kilbourne in anything slimy. That was a certainty if Kilbourne knew what was good for him.

In Colby's experience, politicians who advanced high in their party's political structure did know what was good for them. They didn't survive, otherwise. Wouldn't it be interesting to compare these personal logs with the corresponding official logs, especially during the time of the alleged gubernatorial meddling in the bid process for the new Toledo airport? Very interesting indeed! The trick would be convincing Maggie to let him use them.

Maggie's call floated down the stairs. "Colby? Have you eaten lunch? Do you want a sandwich or something?"

"Sure. Thanks." He hastened to replace every file just the way he'd found it. "I'll be right up." He gave the ailing hot water heater a friendly slap as he left. "Thanks, pal."

"Ham, turkey, or salami?" Maggie asked when he got to the kitchen. "Cat's still out, so you have to put up with my cooking."

"Salami. I thought you never unchained Catherine from the kitchen stove."

"Every once in a while I let her out," Maggie said with an impish grin. "Even slaves need an hour or so off now and then. Mustard or mayonnaise?"

"Both, please."

The guilt was setting in but good, now. Nothing made a scoundrel feel lower than being treated nicely by his victim. As he sat at the table and Maggie put a glass of iced tea in front of him, Colby had to remind himself that he wasn't really doing Maggie any harm. He was after Kilbourne, not her. In fact, when all was said and done, Maggie might consider that he was doing her a favor by going for Kilbourne's throat. Most women were big on revenge.

"Did you fix my water heater?" she asked.

"Can't. You have a pinhole leak that's letting in air. It's dripping a bit around the back. And probably your thermostat's shot."

"Well, hell!" She plopped a sandwich in front of him with unnecessary force. "How many billion dollars does a new water heater cost?"

"I might be able to replace the thermostat for you,

and even with the leak, the tank should last a little while yet. It's not something you need to rush down to the appliance store about."

"I can't ask you to go to all that trouble."

"Sure you can."

"I would pay you."

"You don't need to."

She sat across from him with a sandwich considerably smaller than the one she'd built for him. "How does a photographer come to know about thermostats in hot water heaters?"

He smiled and shrugged. "Jack-of-all-trades. I'm a handy fellow to have around."

Her hazel eyes were clearer, her gaze friendlier than in days past. With a sharp jab of conscience, Colby realized she was beginning to trust him. He wished suddenly that he really were what he pretended to be— an amiable guy on vacation putting the moves on a pretty local woman.

He should tell her who and what he was, Colby thought. Maybe she would jump in with both feet, eager to help him hog-tie Jack Kilbourne. And maybe the moon was made of green cheese, too.

"Have you been sleeping all right in your room at night?" Maggie asked. To Colby's ear, which was practiced in detecting subtleties of beating around the bush, her tone sounded just a bit too casual.

"I've been sleeping great. This fresh air makes me snooze like a baby."

"No disturbances or strange noises keep you awake?"

"What kind of noises?"

She shrugged. "I don't know. Noises."

The questions were a bit odd, Colby thought. "I slept like a baby." The only disturbance in his night had been his vividly graphic dreams starring himself and sexy Maggie Potter, and those had been in the realm of entertainment, not disturbance. He wished he could dream up a confession smooth enough to admit who he really was and still remain in Maggie's good graces.

He was contemplating the possibilities when Catherine breezed in the back door and called out a cheerful hello. She sailed past the kitchen door and went down the stairs to the basement apartment, talking all the while.

"You can't imagine my luck! I found out all sorts of things about our unwanted guest—not her in person, but the species, at least. I've got books galore." The words were accompanied by the sound of books being thumped down upon the desk. "There'll be something in one of these to let us know how to deal with the lady. And you'll never guess who I met!" Catherine trotted up the stairs and burst into the kitchen, pink-faced with excitement. "The most wonderful, glorious, handsomest, smartest man! He knows all about— oops!" She belatedly noticed Colby sitting at the table. "I'm sorry. I thought Maggie was alone."

"She was kind enough to let me mooch a sandwich. You having trouble with one of the guests?" He couldn't think of anyone at the inn that could qualify as a "problem guest," except him, and whatever anyone said about Colby Drake, he was no lady.

"Trouble with a guest?" Catherine was all wide-eyed innocence. She looked to Maggie for help. "No. Of course not. This is just . . . you know . . . a theoretical problem guest. We like to practice problems ahead of time. Sort of like a war game in the army. Not that it's really a war." She glanced quickly about the kitchen as if she expected someone to be lurking in a

corner, eavesdropping. "It's more a game than a war.
We wouldn't dream of . . . of being nasty to anyone,"
she trailed off apologetically.

Catherine was no better a liar than Maggie. Colby
let the matter lie. Whatever little secret was making the
sisters so jumpy, he had secrets of his own that were
going to cause problems. He was glad Catherine had
interrupted before he could confess. He needed more
time to prepare, Colby decided, more time to think of a
diplomatic way to smooth over the truth and get Maggie on his side.

"Well, Catherine, your sister has refused to desert
her post here and join me for a drive up Oak Creek
Canyon, so I guess I'll just take myself off as a solitary
traveler. Thanks for lunch," he said to Maggie. "I'll see
if I can pick up a thermostat for your water heater in
Cottonwood."

"Thanks, Colby. That's very nice of you."

"I'll install it for you if you'll have dinner with me
tonight. Ah-ah!" He forestalled her answer with a finger pointed at her nose. "Think of your duty. Think of
your houseful of paying guests taking cold baths tonight."

"I was going to say yes," Maggie told him with an
amused smile.

Colby wondered how amused she would be when
she got the truth served up as dessert tonight. He'd
make sure she didn't have any food left to throw before
he told her.

Maggie hadn't done so much housecleaning since she
was thirteen, when Virginia had grounded her for a
week and slapped her with spring-cleaning chores as a
punishment for smoking with her friends in the garage.

This time the punishment was for starting up an inn. Her inspired vision of being hostess at a bed-and-breakfast had lacked some of the nitty-gritty details—such as the requirement that every nook and cranny of the house be swept, washed, waxed, shined, and disinfected day after day after day.

Nor did the vision include the unique problems of having a ghost on the premises. She had just finished cleaning the Master Suite. The guest—a Mrs. Stromberg—had left her a polite note. While her singing voice was lovely, the note conceded, would Maggie kindly restrain herself from singing in the small hours of the morning? Mr. Stromberg had a bad heart, and he needed his rest.

The note was very polite, and the Strombergs were staying two more nights in spite of the singing. Maggie hadn't been the one singing, of course. Neither had Catherine. They'd been innocently asleep in their basement apartment. Apparently Robbie fancied herself a musical performer. Maggie could just imagine what kinds of songs she warbled.

Just as soon as she finished cleaning this last room—Colby's room—she intended to dig into the books Catherine had brought home and find out how to deal with the late Madam Robin Rowe, who was no doubt chortling about her mischief-making at this very moment.

She ran a duster over the dresser, carefully avoiding Colby's personal items. The room was unnaturally cold, considering the way the sun was beating down upon the house, so Robbie was lurking somewhere close.

"I know you're in here, you pain-in-the-ass ghost. No use hiding. You might as well show yourself. I have a few things to say to you."

"You should show more respect to your elders, Mags. You don't have to bellow like a bullwhacker. It's very unattractive in a lady." Robbie was suddenly sitting in the rocking chair, one arm artfully draped over the back.

"So is eavesdropping on conversations. I know you were listening to me and Colby earlier. And that was you who added mayo to my sandwich when I was making lunch."

"You need some meat on your bones, girl. A man likes a little padding in a woman."

Maggie wasn't about to be bested by a nosy holdover from nineteenth-century debauchery. "You can mind your own business, Robbie. And I am not your business. Understand?"

"You can be a very unfriendly person, Maggie Potter."

"Yes, I can." Fists braced on her hips, Maggie stood firm. "This isn't your house anymore. It's mine. And I'm not going to be driven away."

"I'm certainly not trying to drive anyone away, sweetie. Do you know that duster in your hand looks just like a fuzzy tail when you stand like that?"

Maggie shifted to cross her arms over her chest, then caught Robbie's smile. "Think you're very funny, don't you?"

Robbie shrugged shoulders left bare by her low-cut gown. *"A ghost has to grab at every chance to laugh. Once you're dead, life isn't all that entertaining."*

"Well, I have not been entertained the last few days. I want you to leave me alone."

Robbie pulled a fan out of nowhere and fanned herself nonchalantly.

"And quit haunting my guests. Don't roll your eyes,

you troublemaker. I heard about the singing last night."

"I like to sing. I've been told that I could have been on the stage."

"This isn't a stage. It's a place of business. My business. And I don't want you ruining it."

Ghostly lips pursed in a little moue. *"I wouldn't think of ruining your business, dear. I was a business-woman myself."* Her expression warmed to a ghostly grin. "I certainly wouldn't mind doing a bit of business with that Colby Drake."

Maggie slapped the duster down on Colby's bed. "Leave him alone!"

"Tch, tch. Such a temper, Mags. Also very unattractive in a lady. I'll leave the poor man be if you'll just keep him busy. You wouldn't be disappointed in him, honey. He's got the look of a man who could make a long winter night a lot of fun."

"You are disgusting!"

"Now, now. Don't be such a starched prude. You're no cringing little virgin, after all."

"How do you know what I am?"

Robbie smiled benevolently. *"I know a lot about you, Maggie Potter. I know you've been very stupid about men all your life. I know it's gotten you into a passel of trouble. And I know you need my help in the worst sort of way."*

"Well! You know just about everything, don't you, then? But you're not nearly as smart as you think you are, Madam Icebox Breath." Maggie marched to the window and opened it, trying to let some warm outside air into the ghostly cold room. "You're not nearly as smart as you think you are, because—"

A gust of warm breeze belled the curtains and blew an issue of the *Arizona Republic* from the narrow win-

dow seat. The newspaper landed on an upright briefcase, which fell to its side, spilling some of the contents
onto the floor.

"*See what you did now!*" Robbie chided. "*A fit of
temper never helps matters.*"

"I didn't do anything." Maggie reached for the mess
on the floor—two folded newspapers and a small tape
recorder. "The wind did this. Uk. *America Today.* I
can't believe Colby reads this trash." Maggie took a
closer look at the paper in her hand. It was folded to a
page that displayed a small picture of Colby's face,
smiling that smile she knew so well. No wonder he had
a copy of the paper if there was something printed in it
about him.

Robbie drifted over and peered over Maggie's shoulder. "*That's our Colby.*"

"Not our Colby. My Colby. Damn it, not my Colby,
either! Would you leave?"

"*No. Oh my! What's this?*"

"It says . . ." Maggie's heart dropped right
through the floor. "Shit! It isn't about Colby Drake; it's
written by Colby Drake. Colby isn't a photographer.
He's a lying, slimy, bottom-feeding, bloodsucking
sneak of a reporter!"

Seven

Colby was whistling as he walked up to the front door of Robin's Nest. He'd accomplished a lot that afternoon: gotten a haircut, bought some comfortable new shoes, and spent a good long time calming Rich Michaels over the phone. Editors could be such worrywarts.

This evening he was taking Maggie Potter to dinner, and from then on, things were going to move a lot faster on this story. He had convinced himself that Maggie would be reasonable. She was an adult, after all. She'd been out in the big, bad world and knew how it worked. Yes, he'd fibbed. Yes, he'd weaseled his way into her life under false pretenses. But that was the way the game was played. During her years in politics, she'd played it herself a time or two, he'd wager. None of it was personal.

Not that he wouldn't welcome the opportunity to get very personal with Maggie Potter. He'd come to Jerome expecting to find a high-class bimbo. What he'd found was a smart, sassy woman who was not only easy on the eyes, she was easy on the heart. She made him smile, made him ache, made him want to gather her in his arms and not let her go.

Beneath that cool, cautious crust, Maggie had feelings for him. He knew she did. Colby Drake was a good reporter because he had instinct, and instinct told him that Maggie Potter thought about him as much as he thought about her.

The first thing he saw when he stepped through the front door were two duffels in the hallway that looked remarkably like his own very old but serviceable set of luggage. But these couldn't be his, though, because they were sitting in the middle of the hallway, and odd corners of clothing stuck here and there from pockets. Whoever had packed them had done a very sloppy job.

The second thing Colby saw was his copy of *America Today* propped on the floor against one of the duffel bags. It had been in his briefcase—the briefcase that sat to one side of the suitcases, the briefcase with papers jammed in every which way. His mouth suddenly went dry.

The third thing Colby saw was Maggie Potter coming around the corner from the kitchen. Her eyes spit lightning and her lips were shut tighter than *America Today*'s budget.

"There you are, Colby Drake, you lying, maggoty, rotten piece of pig liver. You are out of here. Out! O-U-T out! I'll send you a bill. Or should I send it to *America Today*? Do you have an expense account to invade people's privacy and slither your way into their personal lives?"

Colby flinched. "I was going to tell you—"

"Sure you were, you lying dog turd. You sneaked into my inn under false pretenses."

"Yes, well—"

"You tried to charm your way through my defenses."

"But—"

A young couple were coming through the yard to the front porch. It was past four o'clock, when the house opened for tours and check-in. Maggie grabbed the front of Colby's shirt and hauled him through the hall, out the back door, and into the back garden.

"You have guests," he said hopefully.

"Cat will see to them. I'll see to you." She pushed him against the back wall of the house. "Just how far were you prepared to go with this, Mr. Drake? Were you going to seduce me? Get me to air my dirty laundry as pillow talk?"

"No. Well—"

"What do you suppose you could write about me that hasn't already been written by your colleagues in sleaze? Maggie Potter is a slut, a political power groupie, an opportunist, a Delilah who took advantage of an upstanding, naive, political Samson? Sorry, that's already been said."

Her voice was pitched low in deference to the guests, but the words hit his ears with a bitterness that stung.

"Or how about writing that I'm a piece of predatory trash that typifies the fringes of political might, just as camp followers hung about the margins of military might? Oops! Sorry. That's been said too. What cliché or image can you use about me that isn't already old hat?"

"Maggie, listen to me. It's not that way at all. I was going to tell you."

"When? After you got the Pulitzer for tabloid sleaze?"

"I was leading up to it at lunch today, but then

Catherine came in and—well, I wanted some privacy. So I was going to tell you at dinner."

"Likely story."

"It's true. And I never actually lied to you. You just assumed I was a photographer because of all the equipment."

"A lie is a lie, scumbag. Go. Get away from me."

She turned her back on him and marched along the flagstone walk to the big side yard. He followed with determined stride.

"And I wasn't trying to climb into your bed. Okay, okay, the thought occurred to me, but not just so you would talk to me."

"You're trespassing, Romeo. Go before I call the police."

He caught up to her and grabbed her arm, forcing her to face him. "Maggie, look at me! This is ridiculous! I'm not after a story on you."

She scowled at the hand imprisoning her upper arm. His fingers almost burned from the heat of her eyes. Carefully, he released her.

"Maggie, I would never write sleaze about you."

"Right. That's why you slithered in here under a cover of lies."

"I'm writing sleaze about Jack Kilbourne. I mean, damn it, that I'm doing a series of political columns on Kilbourne. I don't write sleaze! Even though our friend Jack is worthy of sleaze if anyone is."

She poked his chest with a stiffened finger. "Go away, toad."

He backed up a few steps. "My interest in you wasn't a lie, Maggie. I came here expecting to find Kilbourne's bimbo, and found you instead. We could have something together. Something with potential. Don't deny it."

"In your dreams, buster!" She poked his chest again, harder.

He backed faster. That finger of hers was a lethal weapon. "Don't you want everyone to know what a lowlife Kilbourne really is?"

"Get out, worm."

He backed through the rear door of the house and along the hallway, where retreat was blocked by the pile of his luggage. "This can't end here, Maggie."

"Watch it." She holstered her finger and smiled maliciously. "Your luggage, sir."

The glint in her eye reminded him that discretion was the better part of valor. He picked up his duffels. She slid his briefcase under his arm, then took the offending copy of his employer's newspaper, folded it over once, and slapped it against his chest as if he were a fly that needed swatting. Her voice was flat and controlled, but her eyes spat enough venom to kill an elephant.

"Mr. Drake, it has been neither an honor nor a pleasure. Now, take your cheap smile and your fake charm, and get out of my house—or I will kick you down the porch steps and let Attila loose to chase you into the street, where hopefully you will get run over by a very big truck."

When the front door closed behind him with a carefully restrained thunk, Colby shook his head. Fake charm? Cheap smile? Setting his luggage on the porch, he looked back through the big living room window. The curtains whipped shut, leaving him to face his own sorry reflection.

"Nice going, Colb," he congratulated himself. "A real smooth operator, that's what you are."

•   •   •

She'd gone and done it now, the nitwit. Served up a man on a silver platter, and what does Maggie do? She chucks both man and platter out the door. That girl does have a temper on her, and she doesn't know any better than to let it run away with her. If she'd been raised up by my pa, she would've spent more time in the woodshed than she did in the kitchen.

My pa didn't put up with mouthy sass from us kids. My brother grew up too big for Pa to whup. Past the age of fourteen, Seth would likely whup Pa rather than it being the other way around. But us girls had to keep learning our manners the hard way, at the end of Pa's belt. It taught me to hold on to my mouth, but it was clear as day that no one had taught Maggie that lesson.

I caught up with her in the basement. She was mighty put out. I could tell from the way she stomped around, kicking the desk, pounding the bed with her fist. Like I said, Maggie has a temper on her. But I was put out myself. I'd figured I was well on my way to getting Maggie hitched, and now she had put a Grand Canyon–sized dent in my plans. My job would be a hell of a lot harder all because of her persnickitiness. So maybe I wasn't as tactful as I could have been when I called her on the carpet.

"You've really done it now," I told her. "Do you think men like Colby Drake grow on bushes? You think they're just lying around waiting to be snapped up by some spinster gal, so many that you can afford to kick around a fourteen-carat hunk like he was a mongrel dog?"

She whirled around, mad as a bee-stung bull. "You! You must have known what he really was, with all your spying on people and digging around in their secrets. You knew, and you didn't tell me! You're as low as he is!"

"You really should watch your temper, Mags. Men don't like a gal with a temper. I remember Eliza Dare learning that lesson the hard way. She found out that her man Amos was cruising the Tenderloin District after hours instead of cleaning his store like he told her. Gave him such a tongue-lashing that folks could hear clear down at the other end of town. Now Amos, he was fit to be tied. Didn't take to being dressed down in front of the whole town. He packed Eliza off to Prescott to live with her widowed sister. Claimed his prowling around the fancy ladies was all Eliza's fault, since she was the one who nagged him into taking work at the mines here."

Maggie gave me a blank look. I could see she didn't get what I was driving at. It's probably a good thing that I decided to become a whore instead of a teacher.

"What I'm saying, Mags, is that a temper doesn't look good on a woman. What's more, you can't call a man names and boot him out the door then expect him to still pay court to you."

She laughed, and it wasn't a pleasant sound. "Colby Drake can pay court to the devil for all I care."

"Now, honey. You don't mean that. If you didn't care something for the man you wouldn't be standing here spouting off so much steam."

"I hope he falls off the side of the mountain. He lied, he sneaked, he played me as well as Fodor plays a violin. And to think I was beginning to trust him, to think he was a decent guy. What a pathetic fool I was. He turned on all that charm, treated me as if he liked me, and all the while he was out to dig up dirt."

Her tone was so black that I actually bucked up a bit. What I'd said was true. If she wasn't sweet on the guy, she wouldn't be in such a snit.

"Now, honey, he might've been digging up dirt, but he wasn't digging in your garden."

She sat down on the bed and huffed out a pathetic wheeze of a sigh. "What's that supposed to mean?"

"He told you he was gunning for your old boss, not for you."

"Slime is slime. Colby Drake is a bloodsucking reporter."

"The man's got to earn a living somehow, girl. Photographer. Huh! No real man earns his way taking pictures. You oughta be grateful, if you ask me. The man's out to get the no-good who caused you all that grief. You should be cheering him on, giving him a helping hand. Now, if a stalwart fella came up to me and offered to take down Jackass Jake Schmidt, the snake that shot me dead, I'd offer to load his gun and polish his gunbelt, and anything else the fella wanted."

"What happened was not Jack Kilbourne's fault. He did what he had to do. It hurt him as much as me."

I answered with a very rude sound, and I have an impressive stockpile of rude sounds. "It hurt him as much as me!" I mimicked. Silly girl. She obviously didn't understand men at all. "Wake up, honey. The man's a louse. To my way of thinking, Colby Drake's a hero riding in to save the day—just like in those movies your sister watches. You should be getting on your knees and kissing his feet, or any other part of his anatomy that he wants kissed."

I guess I went a bit too far that time, because Maggie grabbed a paperweight from the desk and threw it at me. When the little leather beanbag whacked harmlessly against the wall and splotted to the floor, she let loose with a cuss word that impressed even me.

"You watch your unladylike language, Maggie. No man wants a woman with a trashy mouth."

"Butt out, Robbie. Just butt out."

I took that as my cue to leave. Maggie had left us in a pickle, and I had a lot of plotting to do.

That evening was very quiet at the inn. Three rooms were rented, but the guests were out enjoying dinner or shopping in town. Sitting alone in the living room, Maggie enjoyed the peace and quiet. She was in no mood to deal with either people or ghosts. Catherine was in the sunroom watching a Tyrone Power movie, and Robbie had been very quiet since Maggie had told her off that afternoon. Only Gorgeous George kept Maggie company, and that was fine with Maggie. George could be a menace at times, but at moments like this, when the cat curled warmly in her lap and purred every time Maggie's hand brushed her fur, George seemed a friend without equal. She didn't scold, didn't advise, and expected nothing more than a bowl of cat food every day and a soft lap to sit in.

George butted her hand for more attention, and Maggie chuckled. What George really demanded was a full-time human slave to do her bidding. In that way she was like most other cats. All the same, Maggie often preferred George to almost anyone else she knew. The cat had never sacrificed her to political expediency, lied about her, lied to her, betrayed her, or advised her to go to a shrink. She thought about her friends in Ohio who had given her the cold shoulder once Maggiegate had hit the papers. She thought about Jack Kilbourne's stumbling, red-faced apology for his decision to throw her to the wolves. She thought about the reporters from television and newsprint—the blood lust in their eyes, the feeding frenzy mentality that sent them swarming to dig out her every sin, from a failing grade in junior high PE to the university party her freshman year where everyone had been smoking pot. The more she thought about it, the gladder she was to have a cat.

Her peace and quiet was interrupted by the front doorbell. She looked at her watch. Seven-forty-five. Theoretically, they were open for tours and check-in until eight.

The man at the front door didn't look like a tourist. He was tall, nice-looking, spectacled, and had a lop-sided smile that reminded her of a stuffed bear she'd once had. Under one arm he carried a load of books.

"Uh . . . hi. Are you Maggie?"

"Yes," she said warily. Surely this couldn't be yet another reporter come to hound her.

"I'm Tom Matthews. I have a bookstore in Cottonwood. Your sister Catherine invited me up to—"

"Tom!" Catherine flew in from the sunroom. "Maggie, this is Tom Matthews. I told you about him, remember?"

Maggie remembered vaguely that her sister had gushed something about meeting a man earlier in the day. Maggie had been preoccupied with feeding lunch to Colby, then later she had been equally preoccupied with throwing Colby out of the house.

"Ah. Sure. So this is Tom Matthews."

"I'm really grateful for your inviting me up to take a look around."

"Any time," Maggie said, slightly perplexed.

"You remember I told you that Tom's a real ghost expert."

"I'm a long way from being an expert, I'm afraid."

"Well, you're closer to being an expert than either me or Maggie. Why don't you poke around a bit, Tom.

The place Robbie seems to like the best is the Red Room upstairs, but she pops up all over the place."

Excitement gleaming in his eyes, Tom didn't hesitate to take Catherine up on her invitation. He laid his load of books on the nearest table and set off up the stairs with the mien of an explorer pursuing hidden treasure. Catherine started to follow him, but Maggie pulled her into the kitchen.

"You told him about Robbie?"

"I told you that I told him."

"I wasn't listening."

"Well, that's not my fault."

"We agreed," Maggie scolded. "Robbie was to be our secret!"

"Tom's an expert. He knows all about ghosts. He can help us."

"Yeah, right."

"Maggie . . ." Catherine's puppy-dog eyes pleaded with her sister.

"Oh, Cat . . ."

"Isn't he wonderful? He looks like Harrison Ford with glasses, doesn't he? And he has the nicest smile, and he's very intelligent. Loves books. Has his master's degree in English literature."

"You found out a lot in one meeting."

"Maggie! Don't sound so cynical. I'm sorry that Colby Drake disappointed you, but that has nothing to do with Tom."

"And just how are we going to deal with it when this guy trumpets far and wide that Robin's Nest has a genuine, in the not-so-living flesh, ghost?"

"I told him he couldn't tell a single soul."

"Then I hope he keeps a secret better than you do."

"Give me some credit, Mags. I've got as much invested in this place as you do."

Maggie flopped wearily down at the dining room table. "Okay. I'm sorry. It's just that one of us stepping in a romantic pile of manure is enough for one summer."

"Don't worry. Tom Matthews is special."

Regarding her sister with affection, Maggie shook her head. "Cat, you think everyone is special."

"No! Really, Mags! There's a spark between us that I felt the first time I saw him. It feels so wonderful! All my life I've fallen in love with movie idols, but that isn't real. This is real. Finally I feel it. I just need him to feel it too."

"You don't think he does?"

"He's so fascinated with ghosts, I don't think he'd know what to do with a live woman."

Maggie scoffed. "Wanna bet?"

"Don't be that way! I'm just hoping that if he finds Robbie interesting, he'll hang around enough to see that I'm even more interesting. It could happen."

"If he doesn't think that you, Catherine Potter, are more interesting than a dead whore, then he's not worth mooning over."

"Well, I think he's worth mooning over."

Catherine's smile went deep. Her sister was really gone, Maggie reflected.

"Okay. If that's what you want, let's hope that Robbie puts on a show—as long as she does it before our guests get back."

Maggie let Catherine tag after the object of her affection while she enjoyed a few minutes of solitude to read the novel she had started. Before long, however, Tom and Catherine came down the stairway. They paused to examine the photograph of Roberta Rowe that hung in the hallway, then joined Maggie in the living room.

"Can I get you some wine, Tom?" Catherine offered. "Or a beer?"

"A beer would be great."

"Coming up."

Tom sat on the sofa across from Maggie. He lacked the usual self-consciousness of a new acquaintance visiting for the first time. Instead, he seemed totally absorbed in looking at every corner of the room.

"See anything interesting upstairs?" Maggie asked.

Catherine walked in with their drinks. "We didn't see a thing. Not even in the Red Room." She sounded embarrassed.

Maggie pondered the irony of actually wanting Robbie to appear. Of course the tawdry tramp wouldn't manifest the one time she was truly invited. "Usually she's there every time I turn around. Do ghosts take time off?"

Tom smiled. "Not that I know of."

His smile had an appealing nerdish quality, Maggie noted. She wasn't surprised that Catherine liked him.

"Tom probably thinks I made the whole thing up," Catherine said sheepishly.

"Don't I wish!" Maggie commented with a quiet laugh. "If you're here enough, Tom, you're bound to see her. Knowing Robbie, I wouldn't be surprised if she's floating around spying on us right now. I've heard of scary ghosts, malevolent ghosts, mysterious ghosts, but I never thought to meet a busybody, know-it-all, buttinsky ghost like this one. She's into everything, and she specializes in meddling in my personal life."

"Fascinating," Tom said.

"She really does exist," Catherine assured him.

"I don't doubt it for a minute. I can almost feel her in the house."

"Have you been acquainted with many ghosts?"

Maggie was somewhat skeptical of just how expert Catherine's ghost authority was.

"Actually"—he smiled wryly—"not a one. Running into Catherine was a piece of incredible good luck. I've been waiting for this chance for a long time."

So had Catherine, Maggie acknowledged, but in an entirely different way than Tom Matthews meant.

Robbie continued to frustrate Tom and Catherine by her silent act. The Strombergs came in, said hello, then disappeared into their room for the night. Somewhat later, the Cranes—the young couple who had almost gotten an eyeful and earful of Colby's reluctant exit— returned from their night on the town. Their car pulled up to the garage, and their laughter floated into the house through the open living room windows, but they came through the back door and went straight to the Yellow Room—Colby's old room—without stopping to chat.

With the house quiet, Maggie decided to retire early and let Catherine take care of her new friend. Her sister was trying her best to be entertaining, and Tom was a model of courtesy, but his attention was focused on the house rather than Catherine. If her sister truly wanted this fellow's attention, Maggie decided, she was going to die and stick around in ghost mode. Some men didn't know a treasure when it sat down right beside them.

"I'm going to say good night," she told them. "I hope we'll see you up here again, Tom."

"Thank you for letting me intrude."

"You're not an intrusion," Maggie assured him.

Once in her bed, Maggie let down her guard to allow the events of the day wash over her. The night was very still. Even the hot water heater—which hadn't been fixed—was silent. Attila and Hannibal slept in their cage, and George snored delicate cat snores, curled at Maggie's feet. She was unconsciously listening for Colby's footsteps in the hallway, Maggie realized, and mentally kicked herself. How hopeless a case was she? After knowing the man just a few days, she could distinguish his step from any other. Foolish, foolish girl! Fresh from the romance disaster of the century, she let herself be taken in by an underhanded, dirt-digging bottom-feeder just because he had a winning smile and kissed like a twentieth-century Don Juan. She recalled the funny little twist to his smile, the way his slightly-too-long black hair curled around his collar in back. And his eyes! Did any man ever have a bluer pair of eyes? When he smiled, which was often, the smile lit up those eyes as if someone had switched on a light bulb inside his head. That man's smile could coax a woman from a blue funk and set her on the road to heaven.

She caught herself just in time. Colby Drake was a fake, a shallow charmer who used his looks and wiles to deceive. He probably practiced that winning smile in front of his mirror a dozen times a day, just to be sure he really had it down pat. No doubt he arranged his hair to be just mussed enough to tempt a woman's fingers, and she could imagine that he had his smooth pickup lines neatly filed somewhere in his office in Virginia. At least she'd given him a new opening gambit to add to the files: allow your intended victim to fall out of a tree on top of you, smashing you flat, and then rescue her stupid, stubborn, but much-beloved cat from said tree.

Tears stung her eyes, but she didn't want to cry. She'd cried buckets over Maggiegate, and tears hadn't changed the situation one iota. Besides, what right had she to feel sorry for herself about Colby Drake? She hadn't started to trust him, had she? She hadn't really let him get past her emotional defenses.

Yes, she had. And she'd gotten exactly what she deserved.

Of course, if a certain spook hadn't popped up around every corner, gushing over Colby's blue eyes, applauding his physique, harping on how every sane woman needed a man, Maggie might have shown more sense. Robbie Rowe definitely had to take some of the blame for Maggie's misery, and Maggie swore she'd make the interfering Jezebel sorry she'd meddled in Maggie Potter's life.

"You're not going to show up when I'm in the mood to give you a good tongue-lashing, are you?" Maggie asked the empty air.

No answer.

"You can nag all you want, Robbie. Colby Drake is history. Fini. Water over the bridge. Go matchmake for someone else. Like Catherine. Tom would be ecstatic to make your acquaintance. You could have your own one-man fan club. And Cat could use your help."

Silence. Even the mouse in the wall was asleep. Maggie punched her pillow and yanked the covers up over her shoulders, wishing she could wrap herself up in a cocoon, like a sorry caterpillar, to eventually emerge a new creature, clean and beautiful. She would rather emerge from her cocoon smart than beautiful, Maggie decided. No man would ever fool her again.

She turned her face into her pillow and finally let the tears come.

Catherine felt as if she had egg all over her face. Of course this would happen. It was fated to happen. As soon as she lured Tom Matthews here to meet their spectral roommate, Robbie took herself elsewhere. What use was being haunted if Catherine couldn't impress the local ghost buff, who just happened to be the hunk of her dreams?

"Robbie appears to take a very personal interest in my sister," she explained.

"That's unusual," Tom said. "In many ghost sightings, the ghost doesn't even seem aware of other people."

"Oh, Robbie's aware. If she didn't pop in and out like some kind of Hollywood special effect, you'd think she was a real person. She has a little different perspective on things, though. You can tell from her take on the world that she's not exactly part of the twenty-first century. Of course, when I look at some of my students at Red Mountain High, I don't feel like part of the twenty-first century, either. I did tell you I'm a high school biology teacher, didn't I?"

"Yes, you did. I think it's wonderful that anyone has the courage to teach school these days. Tell me, have you yourself seen the apparition?"

Catherine's face grew warm. She gave him an uncertain smile. "Maybe. At night. Outside on the porch. But . . . I'd had a glass of wine, and . . . well . . ."

"Did she look exactly as she did in that photograph in the hallway?"

"Not exactly. The dress was a different one. The hairstyle was the same. The features were the same."

"Did she say anything?"

Catherine felt a blush coming on. "She told me I should teach my sister a thing or two about how to maintain a . . . a man-catching figure."

Tom's eyes instantly went to Catherine's unfashionably ample curves, and now it was his turn to color up.

His eyes darted away, and he cleared his throat awkwardly. For a moment Catherine thought he'd choke.

She laughed suddenly—an open, relieving laugh that swept the tension from the room. Her plot was hopeless. Every time she tried to shift the subject away from ghosts and toward more a more personal conversation, Tom took them right back to Robbie. The one time he did notice something personal about her—and it had to be her figure, thanks to the unfortunate direction of the conversation—he just about choked on his embarrassment. She had to either laugh or cry, and laughing seemed more worthwhile. "Don't worry about it, Tom. You don't have to say anything. If this figure is the nineteenth-century version of supermodel svelte, that's one part of the Old West I really would have enjoyed."

He got even redder. "You look just fine to me."

"Thank you, Mr. Matthews. You are a true gentleman. But as you can see, I not only enjoy cooking, I enjoy eating what I cook."

"I . . . I brought some more books I thought you might like to look through. There's even some good tips in here about how to get a ghost to leave you alone." His lips twitched in a brief smile. "Not that it seems a problem tonight."

"I'm sorry. After last night, I was sure she'd be haunting us every single moment."

"Maybe I should just keep coming around. The ghost would never show, and I'm sure your sister would be delighted."

"That would work." Hope flickered to life again. Catherine grinned hugely. "Maggie would probably pay you to hang out here if that would guarantee that Robbie would keep quiet."

"I'll see what I can do." A touch of humor quirked his smile. "Thank you for inviting me, Catherine. Let me know what the next chapter of Robbie's saga is, will you?"

"Maybe you'll get lucky and witness it yourself."

He bid her an entirely too-gentlemanly good night, but Catherine gave herself a thumbs-up when the door closed behind him. Robbie hadn't shown up to impress him, it was true. Tom hadn't looked at Catherine and realized that this particular living, breathing woman was more interesting than any ghost. But there was hope. He had felt his way around the subject of coming back. Very good! Extremely good! And he had lent her a stack of books that she would need to return—a perfect excuse to see him again, even if he didn't come back.

Romances seldom just happened, Catherine reminded herself. Did Katharine Hepburn not have her troubles with Humphrey Bogart in *The African Queen*? And what about Anne Heche and Harrison Ford in *Six Days, Seven Nights*? She would not give up, Catherine vowed. Tom Matthews might not know it right then, but he had met his soulmate.

She hummed a little tune and danced her way down the hall toward the basement stairs, waving to Robin Rowe's photograph as she waltzed by. "You should come out and meet him, Robbie. You'd like him." She hugged herself and smiled dreamily. "I certainly do."

Eight

Colby Drake wouldn't have been a good reporter if he didn't truly enjoy being a pain in the backside—which is why he showed up at Robin's Nest for breakfast the morning after he'd been tossed out like a piece of over-ripe liverwurst. When he walked through the front door and sauntered casually into the dining room, the inn's guests were already seated around the big oak table. Mr. and Mrs. Stromberg he already knew. The other two guests were obviously a couple. They sat close enough together to be welded at hip and knee.

"Hi!" Colby greeted them all cheerfully. "Beautiful morning, isn't it?"

The Strombergs greeted him with friendly hellos. "You almost missed breakfast," Mrs. Stromberg chided him in a motherly tone.

"Wouldn't want to do that," Colby said with a wide smile. "Not when Catherine's cooking." He beamed innocently at the new guests. "Colby Drake's the name. Don't believe we've met."

"We're the Cranes," the man answered. "Stephen and Harriett."

The young woman beside him smiled self-consciously. "We're on our honeymoon," she told him in a near-whisper, as if it were a secret.

"Your honeymoon!" He pulled out a vacant chair and sat down. "That's great!"

Catherine came through the door from the kitchen carrying a pitcher of juice and a plate of steaming omelets. "Colby!"

"Morning," he said casually.

"What are . . . what are . . . ?"

"Thought I was going to miss breakfast, did you?"

For a moment she was dumbfounded.

"Don't drop the food," Colby advised. "You haven't lived until you've tasted Catherine Potter's cooking," he said to Stephen Crane.

Nervously, Catherine glanced over her shoulder at the kitchen door, then back at Colby. "You've got nerves of steel, Colby Drake."

"She's kidding," Colby assured the Cranes. "It doesn't take nerves of steel to eat Catherine's cooking. Just ask them." He pointed a fork toward the Strombergs.

"You're flirting with reportercide," Catherine told him with narrowed eyes. "But I guess you deserve a decent last meal."

"You're a saint. And speaking of angels, where's your angelic sister this morning? Still lolling in bed?"

"I'm right here, Mr. Drake."

Maggie stood in the kitchen doorway, a crock of jam in one hand, a plate of sausage patties in the other. Colby wondered if he was going to get one of these breakfast delights in the face. The look in her eyes made the possibility quite likely.

"Look who made it for breakfast!" Catherine said too cheerily.

Maggie's lips pressed together in a stern line. Colby could almost hear the words she wanted to fling his way, but she didn't dare with her guests gathered around the table. At least that was what Colby had hoped when he'd walked in. Violence, both physical and verbal, would be bad for business. One didn't get a reputation for hospitality by bloodying a guest at breakfast.

"Maggie," Catherine prompted nervously, "we're ready to eat."

Stiffly, Maggie set her burdens on the table and took the seat at the head. Catherine took the seat at the foot. "Dig in," Catherine invited.

Colby did so with gusto. Danger always whetted his appetite. "So you two are on your honeymoon, eh? When was the wedding?"

"Two days ago," Stephen answered. He took his bride's hand, and they gazed at each other as if nothing else in the world mattered.

"Ah, love!" Colby rhapsodized. "Isn't it great? Love makes the rest of life bearable, makes the stars brighter, the night softer, the sun more golden, the grass greener—"

"*The Grass Is Always Greener over the Septic Tank*," Maggie interrupted, narrow-eyed. "Ever read that book? It's by Erma Bombeck."

Colby returned her glare with an innocent smile. "That's one of the most amazing things about love. It can grow right out of slime and shit."

"Colby!" Catherine scolded. "We're eating breakfast."

"And an excellent breakfast it is!" He continued relentlessly. "Can you imagine that some people actually fear the prospect of a romantic relationship? So much so that it can walk right up and slap them in the face, and they refuse to even see that it's there." He waved a forkful of omelet in the Cranes' direction. "Obviously, these two have the courage it takes to stand up and acknowledge Cupid. They're willing to accept each other the way they are, with all their faults and foibles, recognizing that trust and forgiveness are the lifeblood of any relationship."

"Stephen would never do anything that would require forgiveness," Harriett claimed. "Not that I wouldn't forgive him if he did."

Maggie attacked a piece of sausage with her knife. "Forgiveness is highly overrated, if you ask me. If men want respect, affection, and *love*"—she gave the last a syrupy flavor—"then they should earn them by being decent, honorable, and honest. Don't you agree, Harriett?"

Harriett looked confused, her eyes traveling from Colby to Maggie and back again. "Well, I suppose so. But of course, I never would have married Stephen if he weren't all those things."

"That's because you're smart," Maggie complimented her. "Not to mention lucky. Men with those qualities are as rare as . . . as rare as newspaper correspondents with ethics."

While Maggie smirked triumphantly at Colby, Harriett looked a question at her groom, as if to ask if he understood the odd conversation.

Mr. Stromberg seconded Maggie's point. "Ethical reporters! Hah! That's an oxymoron if I've ever heard one. I tell you, it's never worse than in an election year. I get so tired of the second-guessing and rumor-mongering that by election day I almost wish we lived in a dictatorship."

"Oh, Carl! What a thing to say," his wife scoffed.

"It's true," he insisted. "And the TV types are even worse."

"They're all worms feeding on sh . . . dirt," Maggie amended at a stern look from Catherine. She shot Colby a venomous smile. "I suppose we shouldn't be knocking the media, though, since Colby here is one of the—"

"More sausage, anyone?" Catherine broke in. "There's more eggs on the stove, too."

Polite murmurs of refusal were followed by effusive praise for the the meal.

"We're going on a jeep tour of the red rock country today," Stephen told everyone.

"And we're going to Phoenix to catch a plane back to New Jersey," Mrs. Stromberg lamented.

The guests became engrossed in comparing vacations, both past and present, and then competing for the honor of having to return to the most miserable place to resume their normal lives. Maggie started clearing the table, taking the plate still piled with eggs and sausage from in front of Colby without so much as glancing at him.

"Hey!" he objected as she whisked the food to the kitchen, and was rewarded only with a toxic look over the shoulder. With a rueful smile he conceded her victory.

The other guests scattered to start their day, leaving Colby alone with Catherine. She pushed back her chair and in a quiet voice said, "She has ample reason to be angry, Colby."

"Granted."

"She's not the lowlife you media types made her out to be."

"Don't include me in that number, Catherine. Maggie's name never appeared in my column. I'm not here after stories of bedtime antics. I'm after Kilbourne."

"But you did lie to her."

"I didn't . . ." He paused at Catherine's skeptically raised brow. "Maybe a lie of omission."

"And you plotted and schemed."

"It's part of my job description."

She gave him a disgusted look. "Maybe you'd better get another job, then. Don't you have something to say to Maggie—like an apology—while you two can be alone in the kitchen?"

"I'd rather talk to her in a room that didn't have so many knives available. She'd rather slit my throat than listen to me."

"Maybe. Maybe not. Try getting down on your knees and saying you're sorry."

He grimaced. "Abject humility?"

"They say it's good for the soul."

He pushed back his chair, feeling like a man headed for the guillotine. Catherine speared him with uncharacteristically serious eyes. "Colby?"

"What?"

"Was all that spouting off about love just empty chatter?"

Colby made a face. He was a fast draw with words. That was part of his job. But some words were much more than the sounds required to produce them, the ink required to print them. There were words that could destroy a spirit or heal a soul. And words that could take over your life. *Love* was one of those. Should a word as powerful as *love* be invoked after an acquaintance of mere days? "I can run off at the mouth," he admitted. "But I don't generally take the word *love* in vain. A man can get in trouble that way."

"You don't strike me as a man who avoids trouble."

He grinned. "Okay. Let's just say I think that Maggie's a special lady."

"She is. Just remember that when you're dealing with her. Please?"

Maggie scraped food from the dishes and stacked them with an unnecessary amount of clattering. Her insides roiled, her mind seethed, and her jaw ached from being clamped down so tightly. George, in the perverse way of cats, walked figure eights around and between her legs, purring for attention. Normally, Maggie would have picked her up and given her a cuddle. This morning the cat's insistence just made her all the madder.

She was surrounded by creatures who thought of her as something to be used, pushed around, and manipulated. George, Jack Kilbourne, Colby, Robbie, even Catherine joined in the game now and then. Sometimes it was enough to make a girl want to lock herself in a room and start throwing things.

"Hi there."

Maggie whirled around at Colby's tentative greeting, dropping the glass in her hand. It shattered on the hard tile floor.

"You have a nerve, Colby Drake! If you knew what was good for you, you'd be miles away and out of my reach."

"You're going to cut yourself. Let me clean up that glass."

"Just leave."

"Now, now. You'll never be a good innkeeper with that kind of inhospitable attitude."

Maggie almost enjoyed the slow boil of her temper as he searched out a broom and set himself to the task of sweeping the broken glass from the floor. Colby

Drake, damn him, made her feel alive. He made her feel, period. Feel giddiness, feel laughter, feel desire, feel fury. Her senses burdened with the misery of Maggiegate, she'd become numb to life—until Colby Drake came along.

She wondered if feeling frustration and outrage was better than not feeling at all.

"What did you think you would get by coming back, Colby? Other than talking my softhearted sister out of breakfast."

He dumped the glass shards into the garbage pail. "I thought you might be calmer this morning. Maybe you'd be ready to listen to my side."

"You don't have a side. You're slime."

"I'm slime," he agreed readily.

His boyish grin threatened to cool her anger. Maggie reminded herself that slippery charm was the man's stock in trade.

"I'm slime, dog snot, worm turds, whatever. But I'm good reporter, Maggie. And like it or not, the press is a very necessary ingredient of a free society."

She made a rude sound and turned back to the sink. Flipping the hot water spigot, she listened for his footsteps leaving. They didn't.

"You wash, I'll dry," he offered.

"Just go."

"You're using too much soap, you know. You'll never be able to get the dishes rinsed."

"Are you suicidal?"

The man was unbelieveable, Maggie decided. Insane. Certifiable. She ignored him.

George didn't ignore him. Since she couldn't get attention from Maggie, the cat brushed pleadingly against Colby's legs. Maggie had thought George had better taste. But then, the little furball liked dead mice, too.

"Hi, Gorgeous." Colby picked her up and gave her a squeeze. George purred loudly.

Colby was good at getting around females, Maggie noted. But he could just forget getting around her!

"Your mom's mad at me," he confided to the cat. "She doesn't realize I'm here to help her. I'm on her side, you know."

Maggie made yet another rude sound. If Colby insisted on hanging around, she was going to go completely through her repertoire of rude sounds.

He set George down and grabbed a dish towel.

"Don't get cat hair on the dishes," she said.

"What! You think I know nothing about drying dishes?"

She froze him out with silence.

"I'm telling the truth, now, you know. I'm here to help you. Don't you want to see Jack Kilbourne hung out to dry after what he did to you?"

"Jack Kilbourne didn't do anything to me. The media did."

It was Colby's turn to make a rude noise. He was much better at it than Maggie was.

"It's true." She swished a dirty glass with enough force to cause a tidal wave in the dishpan.

"The louse fed you to the sharks, Maggie."

"And you're one of the sharks."

"Okay. I'm a shark. But I'm a shark who's after the real bait, not the diversions. I'm not interested in sleaze or bedtime stories. I want to shine a light into places Jack Kilbourne wants to keep dark. Places the public should know about when they concern a man who's running for president."

"I can't help you with that."

"I think you can."

"Well, Mr. Know-it-all, you're wrong."

"What about those daily logs you have from his office? They're the originals you made for yourself, right? If we could—"

"Logs? You searched my files?"

"Well . . ."

"Oh! You are lower than I thought!"

"Maggie! I'm doing a legitimate, important piece of research."

"By breaking and entering?"

"I didn't break and enter anything! You left me down there and invited me into your desk. There's nothing illegal about looking around."

"In my drawers?"

His instinctive, very male interpretation of that statement was immediately obvious in his face. Maggie felt her own face flush. "You are despicable."

"I'm not! I'm a nice man, Maggie. Trust me."

"Oh, sure! Like I've never heard that line before!"

"I'm just looking for the truth about Jack Kilbourne and the deals he made in Ohio."

"*America Today* shuns sensationalism for the truth. That would be a first."

"*America Today* might be sensationalist. But my column is for real. I don't write trash."

"Uh-huh." She slapped the wet dishrag onto the counter and began to scrub. "You're Mr. High Road, all right. I don't think so! You'll do anything for a story, won't you? Lie about who you are. Sneak around private, personal files. Romance some gullible, down-and-out female so she'll spill her guts for you to write about."

He took the dishrag from her before she scrubbed a hole in the countertop. "You don't look so down and

out to me. In fact, you look pretty good. You want
stark honesty from me? Okay, I'll be honest, Maggie."

"Don't strain yourself."

He turned her around to face him. She didn't want
to. Those blue eyes were too dangerous, that smile too
beguiling. His voice was gentle, but relentless. Pinned
by his eyes like some poor insect skewered to a board,
she couldn't look away.

"I confess. I came here expecting to find some good-
time girl with big hair and stiletto heels. But look what
I found." He touched a tendril of auburn hair that had
escaped her ponytail. She flinched, and he shook his
head gently. "At first, I figured I could sweet-talk you
into cooperating. But I ended up sweet-talking myself
into . . . into really caring about you, Maggie. You're
not at all what I expected, and I'm so glad. You took
my heart completely by surprise. I know you think I'm
handing you a line, but I'm not. You've become as important to me as the story."

"Bull."

"And if you weren't so scared of me, you'd see the
only fair thing is to accept my apology and grant me a
second chance."

Maggie felt trapped. She was backed against the
counter, and his body blocked her escape. He was too
close, heating the air around her, breathing the air she
breathed. She didn't know where to put her hands
without touching him. She wanted to touch him. That
was the hell of it. Goddamn her foolish heart. She
wanted to touch him.

"I'm not afraid of you," she lied. "That's ridiculous."

"You're scared that you might actually fall for me.
You're scared if you try to see things from my point of
view, you might discover that I'm not such a bad guy

after all. You're scared if you touch me, you might feel a healthy desire. You might be tempted to take a chance with me. It's easier to hate me, isn't it, coward?"

She wanted to shove him away from her, but that would require touching him, and she didn't dare touch him. She would be lost if she touched him. "You've got it all wrong, smart guy."

"Prove it. Kiss me."

"What?"

"Kiss me." His grin was pure challenge. "Kiss me without your heart speeding up and that pretty blush coming to your cheeks. Prove you don't feel a thing for me. That you feel only revulsion and contempt."

"I'd rather kiss the hairball George threw up this morning."

"Kiss him, honey."

Maggie could have screamed. The last thing she needed was Robbie cheerleading for Colby inside her head.

"Kiss him a good one. Let yourself go."

Robbie and Colby both were too much for Maggie to deal with at one time. Before she could gather her thoughts to object, Colby's mouth came down on hers. His arms drew her away from the counter and gathered her close, pressing her to him in places that proved his desire was most certainly real. Her desire was just as real. He coaxed her mouth open, inviting her tongue to play. The heat of him melted her every objection, and when one of his hands slipped upward from her waist and began to explore her breast, her knees turned to jelly and every nerve shivered with pleasure—until her eyes slitted open and she saw Robbie, plain as day in the virtual flesh, give her a knowing, wicked smile and a big thumbs-up.

"Ooooo la-la!" the ghost mouthed silently.

"Aaaagh!" Maggie heaved Colby away from her. Furious at him, at herself, at Robbie, and the world in general, she smacked him across the face—something she had not done in her entire life.

Colby looked at her as if she'd gone insane. "What was that for!"

"What do you think, Romeo?"

"Hey! You weren't exactly objecting."

"Hah!"

Behind him, Robbie snickered silently and did a little victory dance.

"Get out of here!" Maggie cried.

"That's very rude. Especially after I dried all those dishes."

"Not you. Her!" Somehow, keeping Robbie a secret didn't seem important any longer. Her life was going to hell anyway. She pointed to the kitchen table, where the ghost now sat, smiling beatifically, legs seductively crossed.

Colby raised one doubting brow, and Maggie gave him a wicked smile. "Behind you, hot shot."

The minute he turned, Robbie waved playfully and blinked out.

"Am I supposed to see something?" Colby inquired with exaggerated courtesy.

"She disappeared when you turned."

"Who disappeared?"

"The ghost."

"How very convenient. Come on, Mags. You can think up a better story than that."

"She's real," Maggie insisted. "The ghost is Red Robin Rowe, and she built this house as a brothel." She grinned wickedly. "I'd run if I were you, Colby, because Madam Rowe likes you a lot."

He chuckled and settled into a kitchen chair very near to where Robbie had been sitting. "If you want to distract me from those logs of yours, you'll have to think up a better diversion than a haunted house story."

Behind Colby, Robbie popped in again and did a little dance on the table. *"I could be featured in the newspapers!"* she said gleefully in Maggie's head.

"I'm not interested in some worn-out ghost story," Colby scoffed.

Behind him, Robbie's face fell.

"As I said before, I don't write trash."

"You are trash, Colby Drake."

He sighed and got up. Behind him, Robbie took the measure of his shoulder breadth and nodded her head approvingly. Maggie ignored her.

"Be rational, Maggie. Don't make me get tough on this. Nothing I've said to you today is a lie. I like you. I more than like you. But I'm going to get this story."

"Mr. Drake, you don't know what tough is until you've come up against me. So don't try your scare tactics."

"I usually get what I'm after, Mags."

"Not this time. The front door is that way." She pointed a finger with grim finality. "Use it. And don't bother coming back."

Finally, when he was gone, Maggie allowed herself to slump into a kitchen chair. How could she still be attracted to the jerk even though she knew what he was? Was she the ultimate chump? Dangle an attractive man in front of her and her brains automatically shifted into neutral.

He was a liar. A snake. A weasel. He was a reporter, which was worse than any of those. Yet when he kissed her, she felt as though she could melt. When he smiled, her heart skipped a beat.

Maggie groaned. "Damn!"

"Yeah. That goes for me, too."

When Robbie blinked into sight, a sultry specter sitting on the kitchen counter, her silk skirts rucked up to reveal shapely calves and ankles clad in fishnet stockings. The rose in her red hair looked as fresh as ever. Like Robbie, it defied wilting.

"You're thinking you're a moron? Well, I agree. I've never seen any spinster so choosy."

"Butt out, Robbie. Maybe back in your day every woman was expected to catch herself a husband, but the rules have changed."

"Sheesh! I know the rules have changed. I've been dead for a hundred years, not asleep. But I'll tell you one thing that hasn't changed, sugar. When I'm not happy, I'm not an easy gal to live with; and without Colby to entertain me, I'm not a very happy ghost. I don't think you want an unhappy ghost around the place."

Robbie winked out of sight. Maggie glared and called after her, wherever she was. "How about not having a ghost around at all?"

Colby pulled off the highway at the Taco Bell in Cottonwood. He wanted to get well out of Maggie's range before he stopped. She was in one heck of a snit, and he wouldn't have put it past her to come after him with a skillet if he'd stayed within reach. He had to give the lady credit, though. Even after the beating she'd taken these past months, Maggie still came out of her corner fighting. And she wasn't going to be charmed out of her rancor, either. He deserved it, Colby supposed, looking at the situation from her point of view. Maybe too many years chasing unpleasant truths had inured him to his own sometimes questionable methods.

But what was he supposed to do? If he had been truthful about who he was, she wouldn't have given him the time of day, much less a room at her inn and some of the best food he'd had in years. He would never have gotten close enough to get a look at those logs.

More important, he wouldn't have gotten close enough to know her, much less steal a couple of kisses. Those kisses had been real eye-openers. Kissing could be an ordinary sort of thing. On the other hand, with the right person, the right connection, kissing could knock a man right out of his socks. Kissing Maggie Potter was definitely in the second category.

Even if there weren't a story at sake, Colby couldn't have given up on Maggie. A connection like theirs didn't happen every day. She would realize that sooner or later. He would make her realize it. Sooner. Not later. Even if it meant sinking lower than he'd already gone.

Colby dug the cell phone from his camera case and dialed. When the operator at *America Today* picked up, he asked for George Masters.

"Hey, buddy!" George greeted him. "How's the Wild West?"

"Wilder than you know," Colby assured him. "I need a favor."

"I think you're the one who owes me a favor. Weren't you the one who promised me a steak dinner when I put you on to that story about the president's dog?"

"Yeah, well, as it turned out, that story was worth a

box of dog cookies, not a steak. Listen, I need you to dig up information for me."

"Does this one rate a steak?"

"It rates lobster thermidor, pal. This is what I want . . ."

At the end of several minutes, Colby punched the End button, then sighed. He reminded himself that stockpiling ammunition didn't mean he was going to pull the trigger. With a wry smile on his face, he looked west, toward Cleopatra Hill and the little town of Jerome perched halfway up its slope.

"In the words of the great Schwarzenegger: I'll be back. Don't think you've gotten rid of me, Miss Maggie."

Nine

The English Kitchen was loud with the clatter of dishes and the voices of vacationers. The day was a bright, warm Sunday—an ideal day for both tourists and local folk to be out and about, enjoying the wonderful weather and a day of rest.

Sunday was hardly a day of rest for Maggie and Catherine, but they were taking a few hours off. Directly after the last Saturday night guest had checked out and the breakfast dishes were washed, they'd set out for a meal cooked by someone else, on dishes they wouldn't have to wash. Later they would clean rooms and prepare for the check-in hour of four o'clock.

"Somehow I didn't picture running an inn as being so much work." Maggie poured a dollop of ranch dressing on her Verde Valley Greens. "I think what I pictured was me lounging gracefully on the porch swing, chatting up Mr. and Mrs. American Tourist with their two well-groomed, perfectly behaved kids, accepting compliments on the beautiful house and wondering how to spend the money that simply keeps rolling in.''

Catherine snickered.

"Well," Maggie amended, "maybe I wasn't that ignorant, but I certainly didn't imagine feeling like a used dishrag hung out to dry day after day. And you work harder than I do. I didn't do you any favors by getting you into this, did I?"

"I'm having a wonderful time. I don't think I've ever been so happy."

Catherine's smile was infectious. And the salad plate was cooling and tasty. Maggie's mood began to lift. "It does look as if we might make a success of this. We've only been in business a little over two weeks, and the last two nights we've been full. Of course, if we can't think of something to do with you-know-who, we'll have to look for customers from Lower Slobbovia, because they're the only ones who won't have been warned away by our reputation."

"She hasn't been that bad. Truthfully, Mags, I think Robbie's sort of fun. How many people in this world get to keep company with a real live ghost?"

"Hush, Cat! You want everyone in the restaurant to know?" At Catherine's unconcerned shrug, Maggie drove home a warning. "All we need is for word to get out. Eventually we'd have Geraldo or someone like him up here with a camera crew. The only customers we'd get after that would be thrill-seekers and nut cases."

"It wouldn't be that bad."

Maggie was unconvinced. She'd told Colby Drake about Robbie in a moment of rash anger, and now she was glad he hadn't believed her. She hoped he'd been telling the truth about that, at least. The last few days, she and Catherine had needed to be fast talkers to explain some of the things that were happening at the inn. Catherine wasn't as worried as she was, but Maggie couldn't picture life ever settling down to normal if the whole world knew that Robin's Nest still had its Robin.

Just last night they'd all been treated to a medley of raucous songs that would have made a sailor blush. The night before that, Maggie had awakened at 3:00 A.M. to the sound of clattering. Trundling upstairs to the main floor in T-shirt, sweatpants, and slippers, she'd discovered the kitchen in a mess and an invisible cook whipping up a cake batter that used almost all the eggs and butter in the house. The instant Maggie had walked through the kitchen door, the cook had popped into view from thin air. A busy, smiling Robbie had lectured her on the need to round out her womanly figure and the dangers of the boring diet she ate.

" *There's nothing wrong with a good, healthy dose of bacon fat,*" Robbie had declared. "*And a heap of fried eggs and pancakes. Fat's good for you. Puts shine in your hair and a twinkle in your eye.*"

Robbie had disappeared in a huff after a scalding rebuff from Maggie, and Maggie had spent the rest of the night cleaning up the mess. An early-morning visit to the grocery store in Cottonwood had been necessary to get enough food in the house for breakfast.

"I think Robbie misses Colby," Catherine speculated. "She didn't cause nearly as much trouble while he was staying with us."

Colby. The instant acceleration of her heart made Maggie grimace. The reaction was from anger, she told herself. Anger and nothing else. "Well, *I* don't miss him! He can fall into the Grand Canyon for all I care."

Catherine gave her a canny look. "Well, Robbie certainly seemed to like him a lot. And I think she's frustrated that no one else has shown up to fall in with her matchmaking schemes."

Maggie chuckled. "There were Mick Ames and Terry Hardin."

"Poor Robbie. She did everything but put a love potion in Mick's orange juice. Then she started in on Terry."

"Until I explained to her that gay didn't mean the fellows were exceedingly cheerful. Poor Robbie, nothing! Poor Mick and Terry! I'm glad they weren't treated to Robbie's comments on the subject of their sexual orientation."

Catherine did a fair job of mimicking Robbie's voice. "Those fellas just don't know a good thing from a kick in the ass. If I was still alive and kicking, I'd show 'em that a real woman's worth their attention."

Maggie laughed softly, then glanced uneasily over her shoulder—a habit that had become instinctive over the last few days. One never knew when Robbie would be lurking about, ready to take offense at some comment or inject herself into the conversation.

"We really do need to find a way to persuade Robbie to move on," Maggie said with a sigh. "I feel as if I have a malicious fairy godmother hanging over my shoulder."

"Oh, Mags! Robbie's not malicious."

Maggie spitefully stabbed a tomato in her salad. "You weren't up half Thursday night cleaning the kitchen and feeding yellow cake to the sparrows and squirrels."

"That's true."

"Nor were you the one who got pushed down the porch steps into poor Terry Hardin's arms. I'm sure the poor man thought I was coming on to him."

"He did look a bit wary of you when they checked out."

"How much does it cost to hire an exorcist?" Maggie wondered aloud.

"I think exorcists are for demons."

"Well?"

Catherine chuckled. "Those books Tom brought had a few suggestions about expelling ghosts."

"Such as?"

"We could find Robin Rowe's grave and rebury her remains."

"Uk. I don't think so."

"We could change the environment so she feels uncomfortable."

"Like tear down the house. That would do us a lot of good."

"There's always a séance."

"We don't need a séance to talk to Robbie. She's there every time we turn around."

"But maybe someone who knows his way around ghosts might actually have some power over her. You never know."

"Too dramatic. I can't see sitting around a table with candles flickering and incense stinking up the place. Robbie would die laughing at us, if she weren't already dead." Maggie gave her sister a knowing look. "But maybe we should consult someone who does know a lot about ghosts. Why don't you talk to your friend Tom and see if he has any suggestions?"

Catherine immediately brightened—as if she hadn't been leading up to the idea all through the conversation. "Tom Matthews? What a good idea!"

"Yes, isn't it?" Maggie indulged her sister with a droll smile, and Catherine's cheeks grew red.

"Don't make fun, Maggie. Tom's a very nice guy. And he's a hunk."

"Very hunky," Maggie agreed.

"Do you think I'm acting like a teenager?"

"It does a girl good to act like a teenager every once in a while." Maggie recalled her wild swings of emotion during the time she'd thought that Colby Drake was an honest-to-God real person instead of a reporter. It had been fun. Foolish, but fun. Now that she thought about it, those gyrating emotions hadn't calmed much since she'd banished him. Now, however, her feelings bounced between rage and regret, not caution and infatuation.

She'd been sitting right at this table when she'd first seen him, Maggie remembered. He'd been sitting alone, three tables over, looking casually handsome in shirt-sleeves and khakis. Catherine had thought he'd been eyeing Maggie, and it turned out she was right. He'd been more than eyeing her. He'd been stalking her—a silver-tongued, affable snake with his boyish smile and wickedly delicious kisses. A rotten reporter. Rotten, rotten, rotten.

Why did she miss him?

"Do you really think so?" Catherine asked.

"Think what?" Maggie jerked her thoughts back to the present. Colby still had the power to draw her away from reality. Damn him.

"That it's good to act like a teenager every once in a while."

"Well, I wouldn't pierce your navel and start wearing blue nail polish, but where romance is concerned, yes."

"Do you like him?"

"Like Colby?"

"No, idiot! Like Tom."

"He seems nice enough."

"He can't see me for the ghosts on his brain. I think he's shy."

"Shy is good," Maggie said. "It's the smooth charmers"—*like a certain reporter,* she thought silently—"who do you in. If he has a brain in his head, he'll notice you eventually. If he doesn't recognize what a treasure you are, you don't want him, because he's a numbskull."

Catherine gave her a grateful smile. "Sometimes you make me really glad I have a sister."

The bell tinkled on the bookstore door as Catherine walked through. She smiled and inhaled. From now on, the old-ink odor of books, whether in a library or bookstore, would remind her of Tom Matthews.

His head poked out from behind one of the stacks. When he saw her he pushed his glasses up the bridge of his nose as if to make sure it was really her.

"Hi," she said with a smile.

"Hi . . . uh . . . Catherine. Hi."

"I brought your books back."

The rest of him emerged from behind the shelves. His T-shirt proclaimed, *Outside of a dog, a book is man's best friend. Inside a dog, it's too dark to read,* and attributed the quote to Groucho Marx.

"Clever," she said.

"What?" He looked down to where her eyes rested. "Oh, yeah. You'd be surprised at the number of people who don't get it."

"No, I wouldn't. I teach school, remember?"

"That's right." He chuckled. "Brave woman."

"Thank you for letting us borrow your books."

"You're welcome." He relieved her of the heavy pile,

and in taking the books from her arms, they became briefly entangled. Embarrassment made them both stammer.

"Sorry," they said at the same time.

Catherine smiled, and he returned the smile with a self-conscious twitch of his lips. "Uh . . . has your friend been around?"

"Up to all sorts of mischief. You should come up. Maybe she'd go away."

He laughed and set the books on a table. "She probably would. Are you sure you wouldn't like to keep these a while longer? You didn't need to bring them back so soon."

"I've read every line. Speed reader."

"Really? So am I."

Catherine ticked off another reason why they were perfect for each other, if she could just get him to realize it. "Speaking of coming up the hill again, I'd like to . . ." How was she going to phrase this invitation, Catherine wondered, so that he didn't think she was an old maid on the prowl?

"Oops! It's almost three. I almost forgot that I'm supposed to go over to Tuzigoot with Martha."

Catherine's heart plummeted. He had a girlfriend, a lover, maybe even a wife. Of course he did. Just because he didn't wear a wedding band didn't mean he was available. A man like Tom Matthews had to be taken. She should have known.

"Oh," she said meekly.

"Why don't you come? Do you have time?"

She strained to smile. "I wouldn't want to crowd you."

"Crowd me?" He chuckled. "You could protect me, seeing as you have experience with kids. My sister works at a summer day camp, and she always snookers

me into going along when she takes the kids up to
Tuzigoot. I've done some reading on the place, and the
kids like my stories, she claims. There's a whole van
full of twelve- and thirteen-year-olds. A sight more
frightening to a bachelor is hard to imagine."

"A sight more frightening to anyone is hard to imagine," Catherine agreed with a laugh, suddenly cheerful.
"Martha is your sister?"

"My older sister." He gave her an irreverent grin
that revealed a side to him she hadn't imagined. She
liked it. "I keep reminding her she's my *older* sister,
and she hates it. It's revenge for duping me into this
trip three times every summer."

He was perfect, Catherine reflected. Absolutely perfect. Cupid had made Tom Matthews just for her.

Tuzigoot National Monument was the remains of an
ancient pueblo perched on a limestone mound high
above the Verde Valley floor. The ranger who con-
ducted their tour told them the Sinagua people built the
village sometime after 1125 and abandoned it in the
early 1400s. During the ensuing centuries rooms collapsed, walls crumbled, and the plaza eroded, suc-
cumbing finally to a crop of weeds. But considering the
time that had passed, Catherine thought the pueblo
had come through quite well. Whether it would survive
an onslaught of Martha Dodge's summer camp kids
was another question entirely.

Driving from Cottonwood to the monument, the
van nearly rocked with preteen exuberance. The kinetic
energy of adolescents released from school then recap-
tured by summer camp was a frightening thing to be-
hold. Martha, driving the camp van, was phlegmatic.
Tom looked like Indiana Jones trapped in a cave full of

snakes. And Catherine spent the whole ride smiling—at the kids, at the sunny afternoon just made for goofing off, and mostly, at Tom.

Upon arriving at their destination, the little campers filled the Tuzigoot museum to bursting. The place was roomy enough, but a handful of twelve- and thirteen-year-olds could make a football stadium seem crowded. They skimmed past the displays, the boys searching for illustrations of women à la *National Geographic* and occasionally granting a "Cool!" to some account of war or illustration of a grisly hunting scene. The girls stayed together in a little knot of giggles, giving the boys more attention than they gave the displays.

Once on the ruin itself, the campers managed to restrain themselves, under the encouragement of Martha's stern eye. The ranger seemed to be a kid person, used to dealing with the excess of energy, and tailored his presentation to catch adolescent interest. Soon the little savages were sufficiently diverted for Martha to fall into step with Catherine. Tom brought up the rear, some fifteen feet behind them. The girls surrounded him. Next to the boys in their group, Martha's brother was the one who fixed their interest. Catherine didn't blame them one bit.

"So you're the one who has that new B and B up in Jerome," Martha said. "Tom mentioned you."

"It's my sister and I, actually. We run it together."

"I've always thought it would be cool to own a bed-and-breakfast."

"It's a lot of work."

"Isn't everything? I have a husband, three kids, and a job as a school counselor. Tell me about work!"

"Oh? You're a school counselor? I teach high school in Chandler in real life. I'm actually just helping my sister out for the summer at the inn. Then I'm afraid I'll have to be a silent partner."

"Tom told me you were a teacher."

They chatted about their schools while listening with half an ear to the ranger's lecture. Catherine liked Tom's sister. She was a no-nonsense person who didn't mince words or soft-pedal her opinions. Catherine recognized critical assessment in the woman's eye, no doubt because Tom had mentioned her. And perhaps, just perhaps, Tom did not mention many women. Catherine's heart soared. He had talked about her to his sister. Surely that was something.

They climbed past the outlying rooms defined by crumbled walls of limestone block and ascended toward the main pueblo. Two stories high, it was an impressive piece of architecture for a people who had possessed only hand tools and their own cleverness. Catherine had been here before, several times, and the ruin always made her wonder how it might have been to live here when the pueblo was alive with families going about their daily lives, bringing in their crops, hunting, weaving cloth, and making pottery. The place would have been loud with the voices of women chatting, men calling out to companions, children shrieking and playing in the plaza. Would life have been more simple then? Or did the vantage point of time and distance only make it seem more simple?

In the steeper parts of the ruins, Martha went to the front with the ranger, urging each of her charges to be careful on the steep path. Catherine eased to the back to walk with Tom—just another female in his little entourage.

Some of the rooms in this part of the pueblo had been restored, and one had been decked out with pottery, stone tools, and a hide stretched for tanning to give it the lived-in look. The boys, Martha, and the ranger were trooping out as Tom and his group entered.

"It's dark in here!" a pint-sized blonde beauty complained. "How did they see?"

"They had fires, stupid," a frizzy-haired redhead said.

The room was dim and cool after the blazing June sunlight. The only light came from above, where an opening served as both entrance and smokehole for the family who had lived here. A crude ladder provided a way up.

"Stay away from the ladder!" Tom put a large hand on top of a ponytailed head and gently guided its owner in a U-turn. "That's for looks, not for climbing."

"Well, then, they shouldn't put it in here," the redhead said indignantly.

"Yeah," the other girls echoed.

He quickly diverted the incipient rebellion. "Did you know that children who died here were often buried beneath the floor of a room like this?"

"Eeeewww! Gross!" the girls exclaimed in unison. Catherine felt like joining them.

"It wasn't gross," Tom insisted. "Their parents believed that the dead child's spirit would linger and still be part of the family's life."

"It's still gross!" The redhead made an exaggerated face.

"Did kids die often?" the little blonde asked.

"Yes, they did. These people didn't have vaccinations and doctors and antibiotics as we do."

"Yeah, and like, they didn't have to go to school either!" the redhead reminded her friends.

With a giggle or two, the girls left to catch up with the boys, leaving Tom and Catherine alone.

"Is that really true, what you told them?" Catherine asked.

"It is. The Sinagua had a Stone Age technology, but they were a spiritually sophisticated people."

A little shiver went up Catherine's spine. Suddenly the people who had built Tuzigoot seemed not so far away. She could almost hear their voices, their footsteps on the gravel paths. "They seem so real," she commented.

He seemed to know exactly what she meant. "These rooms don't feel empty, do they?"

"No. Do you . . . do you think their ghosts are still here—the people who lived here?"

"I wouldn't be surprised if there was a ghost or two here. Though they've managed to evade me as efficiently as your Robbie. I'm beginning to think I am to ghosts what garlic is to vampires."

She laughed, and they stepped out into the sun. Temporarily blinded, she grabbed on to his arm, then pulled her hand away, suddenly mindful of the intimacy of the gesture. Her heart skipped when he took her elbow.

"Watch your step here, Catherine. The path's rough."

"Thank you." Her skin blazed where he touched her, and warmth that had nothing to do with the sun suffused every part of her. She told herself she was acting more like a hormonal idiot than the gaggle of girls who bounced along the trail ahead of them. At the least the girls had an excuse: adolescence. What, Catherine wondered, was her excuse?

"Speaking of ghosts . . ." She tried to focus on her

original reason for seeking him out. "I was going to ask you a favor in the store today, but we got sidetracked."

"What favor?"

"Well . . . you know quite a bit about ghosts, so Maggie and I thought we'd ask your advice about Robbie. She's a very bored and frustrated ghost, it seems to me, and lately she's been an awful pest. It would be bad enough if only Maggie and I were living at the house, but with nightly guests, Robbie banging around the place can get very awkward."

"Does Maggie still have conversations with her?"

Catherine grimaced. "Their communications aren't really civil enough to be called conversations. Argument is a better word. Maggie has demanded that Robbie leave her alone, but Robbie is having none of it."

"Fascinating."

"Fascinating," she echoed with a smile. "You sound just like Mr. Spock on the old *Star Trek* show."

"You're not old enough to be an original Trekkie."

"Reruns. And tapes. I have a complete set of tapes."

"You don't say! We should sit down and watch those sometime."

"Anytime you want." Every night of the week if he wished, Catherine thought. And if he liked old movies, she could keep him occupied for at least a year. Maybe by that time he would realize she was a woman.

"But back to the subject." He looked thoughtful. "I assume you'd want to send the lady on her way with the least fuss possible."

"That would be good."

"You'd probably be doing her a favor, you know. Most ghosts I've read about stick around simply because they're confused about their status. Somehow they didn't get the message when they died."

"Robbie doesn't really strike me as confused . . ."

His brow furrowed. "Let me think a while, and—"

"Tom!" came Martha's call from the front of the group. "Do you know the name of this tree? It's not labeled, and our ranger isn't sure."

Tom excused himself and went to help Martha. Catherine didn't follow. She should have, because as a biology teacher she probably could have identified most of the plants on the hillside for the group, but she wanted a few moments alone. Far below the ruins, the valley stretched away in shades of muted green and dusty brown. Tuzigoot was not as high as Jerome, but the view was just as good. How she loved this area. It seemed more like home than the desert around Chandler. Perhaps that was why she was so attracted to Tom. He represented the small-town, peaceful atmosphere of the Verde Valley. She didn't love him; she merely envied him.

It wasn't the first time love had entered her thoughts hand in hand with Tom Matthews. All in all, it was a startling, scary concept. Romance was something she had pursued since she'd first been old enough to understand what it was. She'd always believed in love at first sight, or so she said. But at her age, perhaps it was time to become more sensible and mature. Real, honest-to-goodness love didn't develop overnight. All she felt, Catherine assured herself, was an attraction.

Attraction. Catherine rolled the word around her mind and grimaced. It seemed a puny term for the jolt that went through her every time Tom Matthews looked her way. He was perfect. Smart, independent, friendly, interesting. He had the kindest brown eyes she had ever seen. And he was wonderful with kids. The camper girls obviously adored him, and the boys joshed around with him as if he were just one of the gang. Maybe he didn't really have movie star looks, but in Catherine's eyes he was the handsomest man she'd ever seen.

Not that she was a great catch in the looks department, Catherine admitted. She could lose thirty pounds and be acceptably attractive, but she would never make the cover of *Cosmopolitan*. She didn't want to, though. Life had more important things to worry about than fitting into a size six and spending an hour every morning perfecting makeup and hair. The things she could offer a man were more important than a perfect figure and head-turning appearance. She, just like Tom, was smart, independent, friendly, and kind. Some good man should be able to love her for those qualities. How nice it would be if that good man was Tom Matthews.

Sighing, she increased her pace to catch up with the group. As the campers piled into the van, arguing over seats and begging Martha to stop by McDonald's on the way home, Tom flashed her a private smile. He helped her into the van, and his touch set her nerves to singing.

"I might have something that would work with your Robbie."

"Wonderful."

"I'll tell you about it after we ditch Martha and the kids at McDonald's."

"Hey!" Martha feigned hitting his shoulder. "You're ducking out?" But she gave Catherine a girl-to-girl wink. Apparently she approved of her little brother's date.

Catherine smiled to herself. Date. If only it were true.

Colby sat in Nina Farcourt's living room. In the family room, through a Spanish-style set of archways, a sitcom chatted away on the television. Two small children sitting cross-legged in front of the set giggled along with the laugh track. Beyond French doors leading out of the family room, green-and-blue lights enhanced the sculptured landscaping and a kidney-shaped swimming pool.

Middle-class suburbia in the Valley of the Sun, Colby thought. So different from Virginia, where summer flowed through the windows of his turn-of-the-century brick house carrying the smell of blossoms and the song of crickets. In Phoenix, the summer was shut out—with good reason, since even with the sun long set, the temperature outside still hovered near the century mark. The sound of summer in the desert was the hum of air-conditioning, and the only scent flowing through this house was the smell of pizza.

An attractive young woman with short, permed hair and a two-year-old on her hip walked into the room. "I'm sorry I took so long! My husband's at a baseball game, and with three kids . . ." She left it to his imagination. Setting the toddler down, she patted the well-padded rear and pointed him toward the family room.

"Elsa! Watch your little brother for a while, please."

The request brought a predictable whine of complaint.

"You do have your hands full," Colby commented.

"If I had six sets of hands, they would all be full. Now, Mr. Drake—"

"Colby is fine."

She visibly melted at his affable smile. "Colby . . . You said on the phone that you're doing a story on Maggie Potter?"

"I understand you were her roommate for two years at NAU."

"Yes. We were really good friends. I'm not sure I

should talk to you, you know. I haven't seen Maggie in years, but I still consider us friends. I don't believe all the things the news shows said about her. That isn't the Maggie I know."

"The story I'm doing isn't going to trash Maggie, Mrs. Farcourt. The scandal is old news. I think some of my colleagues got carried away, and I'd like to present a more balanced view without preconceived ideas. I want to hear about who Maggie Potter was before she joined Governor Kilbourne's staff."

"Well . . ." She eased down into a chair across from him. "I guess I could help you there. I guess Maggie wouldn't mind."

Two hours later, Colby sat in his room at the Super 8 and went over his notes. He'd been a busy fellow over the last few days. One of Maggie's former political science professors at NAU had been only too glad to pontificate on Maggiegate and his personal observations of the woman who had almost destroyed Jack Kilbourne's campaign.

"Never thought Maggie Potter would turn out that way," Dr. Tarkin had said. "Oh, she was pretty enough. And men buzzed around her like flies, if you know what I mean. It wasn't just her looks. She has a magnetism, a manner that makes a man comfortable."

Colby knew exactly what he'd meant. The good professor had colored up in a way that revealed he'd felt that magnetism himself. Tarkin had gone on to say that Maggie was smart, a quick study, and a hard worker, but she'd never quite gotten it through her head that politics was down-and-dirty real life, not idealism and the star-spangled banner.

"In a university full of young cynics, Maggie clung to her idealism. I really thought once she saw the muck firsthand, she'd get out of politics," Tarkin had said, rather sadly. "I guess I was wrong."

Colby glanced through the other interviews. Maggie's old high school counselor in Glendale, Arizona. A fellow she'd dated at NAU who'd been only too eager to step forward into the media glare. The manager of a restaurant where Maggie had worked when she was pursuing her master's degree. They'd all presented a slightly different picture of Maggie Potter. The former boyfriend claimed he'd taught Maggie everything she knew in bed. Colby had barely restrained himself from cleaning the guy's clock—not a very objective reaction for an experienced newsman. The restaurant manager wasn't at all surprised at Maggiegate. He'd always known Maggie was a slut. She'd just been saving her favors for some man who offered the right price. Obviously, the manager hadn't offered the right price, and he was still miffed about missing out. Colby had wanted to put a fist in his face, too.

This material would make good copy—a new angle on an old story. Politics takes a bright, naive idealist, drags her down into corruption and debauchery, then turns her into a national scandal. He could rennovate the whole dirty mess with a new twist.

Closing his notebook, Colby recalled Nina Farcourt's comment. Maggie wouldn't mind, she'd said hopefully. But Maggie would mind. Colby was counting on it. Not because the story he would write was trash, or untrue, but because Maggie Potter never wanted to see her name in print again. And just what would Maggie do to keep this story from hitting the presses at *America Today*?

Ten

The Red Room was now the Green Room—almost.
One wall had yet to be papered with the ivory, green,
and yellow flowered paper that Maggie had chosen.
The curtains—gauzy things that would let in a maximum of light—were on the bed, waiting to be hung.
Tom had done an admirable job of laying a rather non-
descript beige carpet, and now he nailed the saddle
over the threshold. Catherine was painting the two
walls that would be left unpapered. She wore enough
forest green paint herself to cover half another wall.

Maggie looked up from scrubbing the baseboard of
the wall she'd just papered. Another couple of hours
and they would be through, and the room looked
great. Conservative, ordinary, a bit dull, and just great.
Robbie was going to hate it. In fact, Robbie already
hated it. She'd expressed her displeasure in a number of
ways since they'd started work early that morning.

"You think you've seen enough of a real live ghost
today, Tom?" Maggie asked with a wicked grin.

Tom sat back and looked around the room. His face

wore the dazed, delighted expression of a man whose
dream has just come true. He'd looked that way since
Robbie's first intrusion into their remodeling effort.
"This day has been unbelievable," he said. "Absolutely
unbelievable."

"You were right," Catherine granted. "We've certainly made Robbie mad. I wish you could have seen
your face, Tom, when she rolled that carpet back up
after you unrolled it."

He grinned. "It couldn't have been anything like
your expression when she slapped you in the face with
a paintbrush."

"I wouldn't have minded so much if there hadn't
been paint in it."

"Do you think it was Robbie who cut the electricity
when we were trying to use the power drill?"

"Of course it was," Maggie said. "And it was her
that sent that hurricane through the window just as I
was trying to put up the curtains. And her who's been
yo-yoing the temperature from freezing to fricassee."

"Fascinating," Tom said.

"There speaks Mr. Spock," Catherine teased.

Maggie smiled to herself. The teasing had been back
and forth between Tom and Cat all day. Between the
smudges of paint, Catherine glowed. She seemed more
at ease around Tom Matthews than any man Maggie
had seen her with. Tom was a very nice guy, she admitted. A bit of an oddball—but then, weren't they all?
And he did seem to genuinely like Catherine, when he
wasn't staring openmouthed at Robbie's displays of
temper. It had been his idea to chase Robbie from the
premises by altering her favorite refuge.

"Should we try to hang the curtains again?" Catherine asked in a near-whisper, as if Robbie might not

hear. "She hasn't been around for a bit. Maybe she's taking a rest or something."

Maggie was willing, but she tied her hair more tightly into its ponytail in case they were treated to a private hurricane again.

They had just set the curtain rod on its brackets when the rod lifted up and floated away. For a few seconds it twirled like a majorette's baton, then it smashed into the new lamp that sat on the bedside table.

"Robbie! Damn you!" The distinct sound of a rude raspberry answered Maggie's curse. She turned in a circle, searching, but the raspberry-maker was nowhere to be seen. "You don't like your new room, Madam Rowe? Then just leave!"

Tom's mouth hung open. His eyes looked slightly glazed. Catherine jumped as overbalanced shards of broken glass tinkled from the bedside table to the floor. "I'll . . . I'll just clean this up," she whispered furtively.

Maggie sighed. "You're certainly seeing Robbie at her worst, Tom."

His mouth snapped shut. "Interesting."

"It's a shame she's not showing you her better side."

Through all the pranks she'd thrown at them, Robbie hadn't deigned to actually appear. Either she didn't want to grant them the entertainment of her appearance, or she was using all her energy to stir up trouble.

"She has a better side?" Tom asked dubiously.

Maggie speculated that he might be a little less fond of ghosts after this day's experience. "Most of the time she's argumentative, nosy, bossy, and stubborn, but this is the first time she's actually been destructive. I guess you were right about this remodeling making her really, really uncomfortable."

"Poor Robbie," Catherine said.

"Poor Robbie, my foot! Most people," Maggie announced to the thin air, just in case Robbie was listening, "have the good sense to leave when they die. They don't hang about and make trouble for people who still have their lives to live."

A great clatter of kitchen pots rocked the downstairs.

"I think she's answering you," Tom ventured.

Thumps from the direction of the living room sounded like books being thrown across the room.

"A genuine temper tantrum," Maggie agreed.

"I hope she doesn't break anything." Catherine grimaced. "We have reservations for tonight, and check-in starts in a half hour."

"Let's get finished, then, while Robbie's busy venting." Maggie grabbed the curtain rod and curtains.

With a sigh, Catherine went back to painting. Maggie wondered if the hopelessness in her sigh was for Robbie or for Tom, who knelt at the door threshold, hammer in hand, looking longingly toward the downstairs, where Robbie was currently expressing her outrage. If he would ever look at Catherine with that expression on his face, Cat would be in heaven. Maggie sympathized with her sister. Just how did a woman compete for a man when the competition was a ghost?

Next morning, at 7:00 A.M., Maggie woke to the buzz of her alarm. Fumbling woozily, she switched off the offensive thing and opened one eye, shutting it promptly against the bright morning light that poured in through the basement window.

"Oohhhhh, geez!" She groaned at the necessity of waking. Her head still pounded from spending the pre-

vious day amid fumes of paint and wallpaper paste.
Her shoulders ached from wallpapering. After scrubbing baseboards and helping Tom lay carpet, she felt
her knees might never be the same. But the room was
done. Robbie had given up her ghostly guerrilla campaign before the first of the evening guests checked in,
much to Maggie's relief. In fact, the miffed madam had
been very quiet the rest of the evening and night. Maggie entertained hopes that she'd gotten the message. A
tiny bit of guilt nibbled at her conscience, but she told
herself she was being silly. This was not like evicting a
helpless old pensioner from her home. Robbie was far
from helpless, and surely there were better things for a
spirit to do in the afterlife than hang about in her former abode making a pest of herself. By giving Roberta
Rowe's spirit a shove on her way, they were doing her
a favor. Or so Maggie told herself.

From the kitchen upstairs came a crash, then a muf-
fled string of unintelligible words. Catherine must be
feeling even worse than Maggie this morning—not surprising, since she had worked just as hard and then
gone with Tom for a hamburger. Poor Cat. Probably
Tom had wanted to do nothing more interesting than
talk about Robbie. And from the sounds of things upstairs, Catherine's usual cheerfulness was out the window. Maggie decided she should at least try to help,
even if her presence in the kitchen was mostly hindrance.

She dragged herself from bed and trundled into the
bathroom to splash water on her face. Not until she
looked into the mirror did she come fully, startlingly
awake.

"What's this? Cripes!"

Scrawled across the mirror in her Bronze Frost lip-
stick was the message: *Homewrecker!*

"Oh, very funny, Robbie. I'm shaking in my boots."

A few minutes later, Maggie wished she had those boots—or at least shoes with no laces—when she opened her closet to discover her joggers and high tops sitting in neat pairs, laces tied together in a Gordian knot that would take a pair of sharp scissors to free.

"Infantile, Robbie. Extremely infantile."

She slammed the closet shut and trekked up the stairs in stocking feet and a scowl.

Robbie had not limited her tricks to the basement. When Maggie got upstairs, she found Catherine muttering curses in the middle of a mess. Maggie's eyes grew wide as she looked around. "What happened here?"

A black mess on the griddle might once have been one of Catherine's famous omelets. Whatever it was, though, now stunk up the kitchen with the odor of scorched protein. The floor was littered with splattered eggs, and the room had apparently been bombarded with blueberry muffins. One was smashed against the wall. Another decorated a window, stuck to the glass in a brown-and-blue smear.

Catherine grimaced. "Food fight. Robbie won. As soon as I started breakfast, things started flying around the room. I had to take cover beneath the table. And when it stopped, the eggs were . . . well . . ." She waved a hand toward the burned omelet.

"That ghost is a damned menace! This time she's gone way too far!"

"Now, Maggie! She's put out, is all. She'll calm down."

"Well, I won't! Shit! We have to get this cleaned up before the guests come downstairs. Dump those eggs. I'll get another skillet out and some more eggs, and—"

"Don't open the fridge!"

The warning came to late. Maggie stared into a refrigerator dripping with greenish slime. Jars of jam, bottles of milk, cartons of eggs, wine bottles, the water pitcher, the plastic container of leftover spaghetti—all of it looked like props from the movie *Ghostbusters*.

"Uk!" Maggie slammed the door shut. "That ghost is history. I swear it."

"We're in trouble. Breakfast is supposed to be served in an hour."

"Takeout seems like an excellent idea. Hop in the car, go down to the English Kitchen, and see what they can do for us." She surveyed the kitchen in disgust. "This is the last time this will happen. I'm not going to let Robin screw up Robin's Nest Inn. After everyone is checked out, give Tom a call. We're going to roll out the nukes. No more Ms. Nice Guy. This is war!"

The nuke they employed was a man named Mick Simmons. Tom had assured them that Mick was the equivalent of at least a fifty-megaton blast as far as ghosts were concerned. In any case, that was what Mick claimed. It was difficult to quantify firepower in the realm of the paranormal.

"Does paranormal mean abnormal?" Maggie had asked Tom facetiously when she and Catherine had solicited his strategic advice.

He'd chuckled. "You can make up your own mind when you meet Mick."

At Maggie's invitation, Mick appeared at the house the very evening of the day Maggie had declared war. It was midweek, and the inn had no reservations for that night, so Maggie and Catherine had decided to hang a No Vacancy sign on the door for that evening. They wanted to expel their resident ghost without involving innocent bystanders. The ceremony would include Maggie, Catherine, Tom, and, of course, Mick, and they wouldn't need to worry about guests bumbling into the middle of it.

"They might run off and report us to the sanity police," Maggie muttered to Catherine as Mick familiarized himself with the house and its "aura."

"Sssshhh!" Catherine cautioned her. "Mick will hear you."

"If Robbie has an ounce of sense, she'll take one gander at Mick and laugh herself into the next dimension. The man is a fright."

Catherine gave her a poke in the ribs. "Be good, Mags. Remember this morning."

Maggie sat in the living room along with Catherine and Tom, twiddling her thumbs while Mick absorbed the atmosphere in Robin's Nest. She had meant it this morning when she'd vowed to roll out the nukes, but the nuke she had gotten looked more like a popgun than an armed missile. Mick Simmons truly was a caricature. He smelled of incense. His waist-long hair was plaited into numerous tiny braids that were woven with beads and feathers. They cascaded over his shoulders and back like an unattractive, hairy veil. His clothing looked like a mishmash of sixties hand-me-downs and Salvation Army thrift store. The jeans were split at the knees and several places higher up that revealed more of Mick than Maggie wanted to see. A faded T-shirt lauding the Grateful Dead peeked from beneath a serape-style blanket draped across his shoulders. And to top off the ensemble, a beaded headband kept his decorative braids from swinging into his face.

On a teenager the getup might have been understandable, if laughable. On a forty-something businessman who ran his own jeep tours and owned a Sedona curio shop, the look inspired laughter. Maggie tried her best to keep a straight face as he came down the staircase, but she had to bite her lip to do it.

"Did you tell me that one room in particular is the spirit's favorite haunt?"

"The Green Room," Catherine answered. "It used to be the Red Room until we did a facelift on it yesterday."

"Ah!" he proclaimed in a pontifical manner. "Tom mentioned that. And it made our ghost very angry, did it?"

Maggie didn't care for the way he appropriated her ghost. Robbie might be a pain in the tush, but she was Maggie's pain in the tush. This puffed-up ghostbuster owned no part of her.

"Perhaps," he continued, "it would be wise to conduct our séance in a more neutral room, one that doesn't make the spirit so mad. I felt her anger as I opened the door to that room. She's a very powerful presence there, our Madam Rowe."

"She goes all over the house," Catherine told him. "Everywhere. Outside, too, and into town."

"Ah. A well-traveled ghost. Very unusual. Most spirits manifest in only one place."

"Robbie doesn't believe in following rules," Maggie said dryly.

"I see. Let's set up a table here in the living room, where we're all comfortable."

Maggie gave the spiritualist a jaundiced look. "How many ghosts have you put to rest?"

"Hundreds," he claimed. "Don't worry, Maggie. Ghosts are really very biddable if you know how to handle them. Mostly they're confused, unfortunate creatures who were losers in life and continue to be losers in death. Most of them just need a little soothing and a push on their way, and even the stubborn ones aren't that hard to outsmart. Just sit back and let me handle her. You've come to the right man."

Maggie had difficulty holding back a cynical comment. It would have been a waste of sarcasm, because Mick probably wouldn't have noticed it. He was too busy enjoying the prospect of adding another notch to his popgun. She shrugged off Catherine's restraining hand on her arm and ignored her sister's silent plea to behave.

"Is this guy for real?" Maggie asked Tom while Mick went to his car for ghostbusting supplies.

Tom pushed his glasses up the bridge of his nose and gave her a sheepish look. "I just said I knew about him. I didn't claim to know him personally. He's supposed to be good. Really."

Catherine grimaced. "I feel sorry for Robbie."

Maggie was feeling a bit sorry for Robbie herself until she invoked the memory of that morning. The mischief with her shoes, the slimed fridge and ruined breakfast—all that hadn't been enough for their resident poltergeist. One of the guests—a nitpicking elderly lady who had complained about everything from the water pressure to the noisy birds outside her window—found a spider in her juice glass. And a lawyer from Pennsylvania complained that the shower water had turned bright red—Robbie's favorite color. The lawyer had demanded and received a refund, the grandmother had threatened them with the board of health.

Robbie was well and truly annoyed. She had to go, and the sooner the better.

Mick spent ten minutes setting up his paraphernalia and arranging everything just so—candles all around them, crystals set at the corners of the card table, and, of all things, Native American dream-catchers hung in the doors to the hallway and the sunroom. He sat them in chairs around the card table, thought for a moment, then had Tom and Catherine switch positions. "Is there anything else I should know about Robin Rowe before we begin?" The question was intoned with the same gravity as the opening to the Mass.

"Let's just get this over with," Maggie said.

"I hear anger in your voice," Mick told her in a soothing, annoying voice. "You mustn't be angry with the spirit. She is like a confused child, not knowing where to turn, striking out in fear and helplessness.

Maggie had never known anything less childlike or helpless than Robbie, but she decided to let Mick do his thing.

Incense burned, making her want to sneeze. Candles flickered on the mantel, the occasional tables, and in a circle on the card table. They joined hands, breathed deeply, as Mick instructed them, and cleared their minds of all negative energy. For Maggie, the last task was impossible.

"Red Robin Rowe," Mick intoned. "Roberta Rowe. We call you from the spirit world. Hear us. Come to us."

Maggie had never needed candles and incense to get a visit from Robbie. All she'd ever had to do was turn around. But maybe Mick knew what he was doing.

"We are your friends. We want to help you from your quandary. Come to us in trust. Tell us what you need. Share your burden and let us help you progress to a higher plane."

Maggie could feel Robbie's ghostly glee.

"I don't think this is a good idea," she muttered to Tom, who sat next to her.

"Silence!" Mick scolded. "I feel a Presence."

If he felt what Maggie felt, then he should have called it a night then and there. Apparently he didn't have that much sense, because he started to sway. His eyes closed, opened, then rolled back in his head as if he were going into a trance. Maggie didn't believe his grandstanding for a moment, especially when Robbie herself popped into sight behind him and began imitating his swaying, eye-rolling dramatics.

On one side of her, Catherine started and gasped. On Maggie's other side, Tom's mouth fell open. He squeezed Maggie's hand so hard she thought the bones might crack.

"She is trying to speak to me," Mick groaned. He gasped theatrically and shuddered. Behind him, Robbie shuddered with him, pointed a finger down her throat in the universal gesture for a gag, and blinked out of sight. At the same moment, a book disengaged itself from the bookshelf by the fireplace and floated across the room toward the medium.

It occurred to Maggie that someone should warn the the poor man. Tom and Catherine both seemed spellbound. If anyone was going to warn him, it would be her. But at this point, she wasn't sure whose side she was really on, despite Robbie's offenses.

So Maggie sat in silence, wondering what Robbie was up to, while the book sashayed across the room, floating on air. It hesitated a mere moment, as if for dramatic effect, then whopped Mick Simmons on the back of his head. The medium grunted out a loud "Ooof!" His braids swung wildly as he shot up and whirled about, wide-eyed and openmouthed.

"Ouch!" Maggie sympathized. "Lucky that wasn't a hardcover!"

"What . . . ? Who . . . ?"

"You've just met our ghost," she explained.

Mick's face lost what little color it had, and he dropped back into his chair as if his legs had turned to rubber. Furtively he glanced around the room to discover evidence of a trick being played upon him.

Tom retrieved the offending volume from the floor where it had fallen. "*The IQ Booster,* by Erwin Brecher."

Maggie had to bite her lip to keep a straight face.

With visible effort, Mick gathered his composure, straightened his serape, and drew himself up in an attempt at dignity. "As I said, she was trying to communicate with me."

"Creative way of communicating," Maggie said.

Mick gave her a stern look, and Maggie tried hard to hide her smirk. "She has come to my summons," he declared dramatically. "I will now help her realize her situation and send her on her way, at peace." He closed his eyes again, starting to sway. "You are here with us, Roberta Rowe, known as Red Robin. We are your friends. You can trust us. Hear what I say to you."

He slit one eye open to make sure no books were flying his way.

"Hear me now, Roberta Rowe. Your soul is tortured by shame for the life you led. But that life is over, and no one here condemns you for what you were. You can be at peace now. Everyone in this house wishes you well. You can go on your way knowing that we here on earth have only good thoughts for you."

Maggie thought that was piling it on a bit thick, and apparently Robbie did also. The drawer of an occasional table whipped open, and out came a deck of cards. They landed on the table in front of Maggie, where they were expertly shuffled by a pair of invisible hands. Tom looked like he was going to hyperventilate.

Catherine grasped Maggie's hand beneath the table, and Mick stared in white-faced fascination.

A woman's happy humming came out of thin air as the cards were neatly cut and presented to Tom. Gingerly, Tom reassembled the deck. It was promptly whipped from his hands by an invisible dealer, who dealt them each one card with the speed and expertise of a Las Vegas pro.

"She's up to no good," Maggie warned.

No one disagreed, but no one could resist turning over their card. Maggie was dealt a queen, Catherine a ten, Mick a five, and Tom a deuce.

"I'm low man," Tom said uncertainly.

Laughter sounded behind his chair. Tom jumped up with a "Yeow!" then turned red and pulled at his Dockers. "Wedgie," he explained with a weak smile.

Maggie had just about had enough. "Robbie! Cut it out. We're here to help you. Stop acting like a five-year-old!"

Tom managed to get his underwear back where it belonged, but Robbie's happy humming continued, circling the table twice, then stopping behind Catherine's chair. Catherine squirmed, ready to bolt, but she was too late to save herself. She shot out of the chair with a surprised cry, then stood stone-still. Gradually her features acquired a heavy-lidded sensuality, her mouth a sultry curve very unlike her characteristic sunny smile.

"Catherine?" Tom ventured.

Catherine shot him a look that would have simmered water in January. She sauntered around the table, ignoring both Maggie and Mick, stalking Tom like a sinuous lioness on the prowl.

"Catherine . . . uh . . ." Tom's voice rose on a note of alarm. He pushed his chair backwards with such force it toppled as he got up. "Catherine? What are you doing?"

"Don't run away," she admonished. Her voice was low and husky, laced with promise.

Tom threw Maggie a look of desperate question. She searched her mind for something to do and came up blank.

"Now, Tom," Catherine crooned. "Don't be shy. You've been a very bad boy, ignoring me like I wasn't worth a man's notice."

As the others watched, wide-eyed, Tom retreated, giving ground as Catherine gained it. Soon he found himself backed against a bookcase. There was no escape. Catherine smiled and walked her fingers up his chest.

"What to you think, Tommy boy? Am I worth a man's notice?"

"Uh . . . sure . . . Catherine. You're . . . you're . . ." His tongue lost the gift of speech as Catherine posed in front of him. She no longer looked plump—just voluptuous. The persona who wore her body was a natural-born siren. Every stance and attitude was a come-hither with a definite R rating.

Maggie had seen enough. Actually, she'd seen too much. "Robbie! Stop it this minute, you hear? This is going too far!" She reached out for Catherine's arm, but Cat shrugged her off, sending her a playful look over her shoulder.

"Go find your own man, honey. This one's all mine."

Tom choked and stammered out a lame "Wait a minute! Maggie! Do something!"

Maggie threw up her hands in frustration.

Mick regarded them all with an unbelieving stare. "This is . . . this is incredible! This is an act, right?

It's got to be an act. How did you do the book, you guys?"

They all ignored him as Catherine herded Tom into the corner where the bookcase met the wall, then along the wall until his knees hit the arm of the loveseat. In his flustered state, one dainty finger against his chest easily toppled him onto the cushions, and Catherine landed neatly in his lap.

"See how easy it can be to fall for the right woman?" With that, Catherine wound her arms around his neck and planted a quick but thorough kiss on his mouth. She grinned tauntingly. "What do you know, folks. Mr. Bookworm does have some juice in him after all. Who would've guessed it, hm?"

She bounced up from a dazed Tom's lap, twirled a graceful pirouette of victory, blew kisses to everyone in the room, and collapsed into a dead faint. At least, Catherine collapsed. Robbie flew off to who knew where. Her disembodied laughter faded to a whisper, and then there was silence.

Eleven

Tom was the first to reach Catherine's side. He knelt beside her, chafed her limp hands and brushed strands of hair from her face. "Catherine? Catherine!" When she didn't respond, his mouth pulled into a tight line. "For God's sake turn the lights on! What's that damned ghost done to her?"

"I'll call an ambulance," Maggie said.

"Wait. She's coming around." Brushing off Maggie's offered help, Tom carried Catherine to the couch. "Get some water," he commanded. "And a cool cloth."

Though concerned for her sister, Maggie noted with interest Tom's transformation from amiable, accommodating nerd to commander in charge of the crisis, the change provoked by his worry for Catherine. She wondered if there had been some design to the ghostly madam's prank other than pure mischief.

"You don't think we need a doctor?" she asked.

Sitting beside Catherine's prostrate form, Tom sent her an anxious look. "I don't know. She's getting some color back."

"She does look better."

Catherine groaned, and a look from Tom sent Maggie after water and a wet cloth. When she returned, Cat's eyes were open and she was groggily trying to push herself up on one elbow.

Tom gently eased her back down to the cushions. "Just stay down for a minute or two." He took the cloth from Maggie and gently bathed Catherine's face and wrists. "Do you remember anything?"

With a groan, she brought an arm up to cover her face. Obviously she did remember and wished she didn't.

Mick had been wandering around the living room, examining walls and bookcases, no doubt looking for a trapdoor, hidden speakers, or anything else that might indicate that the incident was staged. Nodding and muttering to himself, he finally joined the group around Catherine.

"This was real, wasn't it?" he asked, his voice still unbelieving. "This is fantastic. You know, we should get the newspapers up here, or even better, the television people. Maybe Oprah would be interested, do you think?"

Maggie sighed.

"Is she okay?" Mick asked. "She could probably get rich from just this one possession, you know. There aren't that many possessions with eyewitness verification. We could all hit the talk-show circuit."

Maggie took his arm and ushered him toward the door. "I think we've done enough damage here."

"This could be really big," he assured her. "Really big. I wasn't prepared for something this strong, you know? It's knocked me way off center. Made me lose control. I'm going to have to talk to my spirit guide about all this."

"You do that," Maggie said. "But your spirit guide is the only one you talk to, Mick. We had an agreement about confidentiality, if you remember. Not a word. I'm going to hold you to that."

Mick's face fell as he saw his chance for fame disappear. "I need to get my stuff." He looked longingly back toward the living room, hopeful, no doubt, that Robbie would come flying out of the fireplace or waft through a wall.

"I'll box it up and you can pick it up later. My sister needs some peace and quiet. I know a sensitive person like you understands that."

He was still groping for a reason to stay as Maggie gave him a less-than-subtle push out the front door. She locked it—something she almost never did in the peaceful town of Jerome—and looked back to where Catherine was still supine on the couch, one arm covering her face, Tom sitting beside her on the edge of the cushions. He engulfed one of Catherine's hands with both of his.

Maggie decided that three was definitely a crowd, and it wasn't Tom who was the interloper.

"Can you take care of her?" she asked Tom.

His hands tightened on Catherine's. "You can depend on it." If he thought it odd Maggie would leave her sister in his care, he didn't comment on it. In fact, his attention was so focused on Catherine that he scarcely spared Maggie a glance.

"I'll be in the Blue Room if you need me, then."

When she left, he didn't seem to notice.

Looking out the window upon the sparse lights of Jerome and the valley below, Maggie permitted herself to feel a bit of envy for Robin's Inn guests. The upstairs bedrooms were certainly a different world than the little basement apartment where Catherine and she slept. Since there were no guests that night, Maggie had decided to sleep upstairs. She'd left the bigger front bedroom, the Master Suite, for Catherine—just in case she and her Tom needed the privacy. If tonight's little drama had opened his eyes to Catherine, then Robbie had done a good deed, whether or not that had been her intention.

The double bed, with its homey handmade quilt and brass bedstead, beckoned her to sleep, even as a swarm of questions buzzed around her mind like so many mosquitoes. What would she do if Mick Simmons decided to talk to the press? And what was she going to do about Robbie? Close the inn? Pack away her hopes of a new career, a new, peaceful life? She wouldn't do that. Robin's Nest had become important to her—both as a home and a business. She had more than money invested in this place; she had hard work, small victories, a few defeats, and a rapidly building tapestry of memories, both good and bad. She wasn't going to call it quits and leave. If only there was some bargain she could strike that would persuade Robbie to quiet down—short of letting the madam run her life and fix her up with a man like Colby.

Colby. His name always lurked just around the corner of her mind, waiting to jump out at her. Maggie's hands curled into fists. She didn't want to go there. Or rather, part of her really did want to go there. But Maggie knew better.

After a half hour staring into the dark, Maggie gave up on sleep and got a book from the upstairs bookcase. She chose Cooper's *Last of the Mohicans*, figuring if that wouldn't make her doze off, nothing would.

James Fenimore Cooper's tortured prose was not

enough to keep Colby's image at bay, however, now that it had been called up. Like Robbie, he was a phantom that was hard to discourage. What was he up to? she wondered. Had he given up on her, or had he meant his threat about getting tough? And why was her mind so determined to become mush where Colby was concerned? Or perhaps it wasn't her mind that was the problem, but her heart. Her heart always had been a troublemaker. She knew better than to listen to it. Or at least, she ought to know better.

The soft murmur of voices floated upstairs from the living room—Tom's, then Catherine's. The front door clicked shut, then Catherine's soft footsteps sounded in the kitchen.

Maggie poked her head out the bedroom door and called down the stairs. "Are you okay?"

"I'm fine."

"You could sleep upstairs tonight. That's what I'm doing. Wallowing in luxury while there are no guests around."

"I don't think so. G'night."

Catherine certainly wasn't her usual talkative self, Maggie noted. Small wonder. And Tom, the fool, had apparently gone home. If tonight hadn't opened his eyes to her sister, then the man was beyond hope. The dolt didn't deserve someone like Cat.

She set her book aside and turned out the light, determined to sleep. Sleep came reluctantly, however, drifting in on uneasy dreams. Robbie was in the room, tossing flamboyant, elaborate curls and striking an indignant pose.

"You're a disrespectful woman, Maggie Potter. Trying to kick me out of my own home—the beautiful house I built when everything else in this town was no better than boards and canvas! You're a stubborn,

*thickheaded idiot who doesn't appreciate what you
have, and you're long overdue for a lesson in manners."*

Maggie didn't like this dream. She flopped over,
punched her pillow, and tried to put the image from
her mind. She felt strange—probably the night's excitement piled on the frozen pizza she'd had for dinner.
Maybe a dose of antacid was in order.

Somewhere in Maggie's mind, someone hummed a
merry tune. She didn't feel right at all. Floating. She
was floating. Whirling about . . .

By the time Maggie realized what was happening, it
was too late. She was shunted somewhere to the back
of her own brain, suddenly a passenger instead of the
driver.

*The ghost business was getting more and more fun.
Waltzing around in Catherine was a hoot. I just
couldn't resist, and I don't think you can blame me
much. Look what those girls were trying to do. And
that Simmons toad treated me as if I was some kind of
idiot. He's lucky I didn't find a brick instead of a pa-
perback book to knock him over the head with.*

*Besides, I didn't do Catherine any harm with her
young man. He's a quality piece, I'll grant you, but he
needs a lesson in courting about as much as any man
I've ever met. Lordy! Was he surprised. We knocked
some of the starch out of Tom Matthews's spine, Cat
and I. I really don't think she minded too much, even
though she was beet-red embarrassed. Such a sweet little gal. She just needs a little push in the right direction
to get her man.*

Maggie, however, needed a bigger push. Actually,

Maggie needed a kick in the rumpus, and I was just the gal to deliver it.

Now, don't you start feeling sorry for Maggie. She deserved to get her tail twisted a bit. Besides, I had the best of intentions, here. You see, unlike Mags, I knew who was speeding along the highway towards Jerome. Maggie was going to get another shot at Mr. Right, and this time, she was going to have help from an expert, whether she wanted it or not. Yesirree. My intentions were as sterling as intentions can get. Pure altruism. But that didn't stop me from enjoying myself a bit.

It felt so damned good to be back in the flesh! To feel the breeze come through the window and brush against my skin. To feel muscles stretch and pull when I raised my arms. To scratch an itch, to smell the night air, to feel the soft tickle of hair on my cheek. You can't possibly appreciate your body until suddenly you no longer have it. Believe me. Being a disembodied spirit has its limitations.

Having some time to kill before the main event, I trotted Maggie and me down to the kitchen. Such delights awaited us there! Bread, cheese, doughnuts, yogurt—I'd never tasted yogurt before. The stuff with the strawberries on the bottom is great! You should try it. I'd never tasted pretzels, either. They don't mix too well with the yogurt, I discovered, but I enjoyed them all the same. What a joy to be able to taste, to savor texture on my tongue, juice running down my chin. I couldn't get enough.

A plate of cheese, a box of chocolates, and a bottle of wine went upstairs with us, where we preened once more in front of the mirror. The wine was heavenly. It set me to dancing—all in front of the mirror, of course. When you're only borrowing a body, you have to make the most of every minute. I could hear Maggie scolding like a starchy schoolmarm. I told her to relax and have a good time. With any luck she might learn a thing or two. With the help of the looking glass, I showed her how to make the most of her appearance. Her curling iron was used so little it had dust on it. I fixed that! Curled and pinned up, her hair looked almost as good as mine once had.

Then I dug into the little makeup case she'd left in the bathroom. A little blusher, eyeshadow, powder, and presto! Instant beauty. Modern cosmetics are much better than the stuff we had to work with a hundred years ago. So are the fabrics. Modern synthetics— wonderful! The girl didn't own a suitable negligee, but I did find a very sexy teddy in her underwear drawer in the basement. It made her look, well, very hot. Maggie should learn to enjoy what she had, I told her. Someday she would be dead, and only memories would be left. Of course I couldn't say for sure that other dead folks didn't live in the lap of luxury somewhere that I never got to, but memories were sure the only things left to me.

Not that they aren't powerfully good memories. After a hundred years, I can still pull them out and get a kick from watching them. I was Queen of Jerome. If you don't believe me, just look at some old newspapers. Why, once a Salvation Army lady came all the way from Phoenix just to stand in the streets of Jerome and declare what a wicked town it was. And who do you think made the town wicked? I wasn't bad wicked, you understand. More like delightfully wicked.

Jerome loved me, and not just in the way you're thinking. Every once in a while the town fathers got a hair up their butts and tried to "clean up the town." Once they outlawed whoring on Sundays. I didn't mind. I just gussied up all my ladies every Sunday and took them out to dinner at the fancy Connor Hotel. Right out there in the open with the regular folks so everyone could see us. Especially the gents. Advertising pays, you know. Even in my business.

Yes indeedy! Some mighty fine memories. I was the prettiest gal in the Verde Valley. The eyes of every man I met told me so. You can't believe what comes out of a man's mouth, you know, but you can believe his eyes. If those eyes are hot with desire, it's the truth, sister. And an admiring look means ten times more than any fancy words a man can spout.

Once I even saw love in a man's eye. It was such a startlement that it made me go all soft—in the head as well as the heart. He was a good man, Horton Tolliver. Handsome, too—handsome enough and good enough to make me willing to dump my glamorous life for a shoestring cattle operation outside of Albuquerque. He died in 1884, kicked in the head by a crazy-loco horse. I wonder sometimes how my life would have turned out if Horton had never climbed aboard that damned horse. Love went a long way toward making up for the lack of money and pretty dresses and little luxuries. That's why I believed in it and wanted it for Maggie. My goals here weren't completely selfish, you know. Only partly.

The thought of love made me remember that someone important was headed our way. Colby Drake was bound for Jerome, and he was almost here.

I shifted my attention to Maggie, who still seethed. She was being a very poor sport about sharing her body. "Tonight is your lucky night, honey," I told her. "Mr. Right is back in town, and this time I'm in charge."

•   •   •

Night in rural Arizona was a whole world different from night in Virginia, New York, Washington, D.C., and the other places Colby usually spent his time. Here there was no softness to the night. The occasional twinkle of light from a small town or roadside service stop did nothing to relieve the hard-edged finality of darkness. Neither did the far-off crystalline gleam of stars, even though the clear, dry air made them so much more brilliant than in the softer climes of the East.

The headlights of Colby's Taurus seemed a futile weapon against the utter blackness as he cautiously found his way along the winding road above Cottonwood. It was late. There were no other cars on the road. Above him, the lights of Jerome were wan and sparse.

On another night, Colby might have found such a quiet night enjoyable. But tonight the stark blackness was too close to his own mood. City lights and bustle can draw a man outside himself and lay a buffer between him and his thoughts, but the isolation of a night such as this one left a man alone with his soul—sometimes a painful companionship, and not one that Colby particularly liked.

Colby had spent the drive from Phoenix arguing with his better self. Now he was nearly worn down, almost convinced that he didn't really want to present Maggie Potter with his completed commentary for *America Today*. It was a good column, a timely piece on what a corrupt and immoral political milieu could do to innocent young idealists. It was a new twist on an old scandal and a thoughtful portrait of Maggie drawn from the people who had known her as a friend, a student, an employee. He owed his friend George Masters much more than the promised lobster dinner for supplying the names of Maggie's old associates.

The column would make Jack Kilbourne uncomfortable, which was a good thing. And it would make Maggie seethe. Her distaste for such things had led her to boot him out of her inn and her life, and Colby thought it might very well persuade her to let him back in—the price for his ripping the column into small pieces and erasing the electronic version from his laptop computer.

It was a low strategy, and thinking about it made him weary. Colby didn't know quite why his conscience was giving him so much trouble on the subject. He'd always had the ability to cold-bloodedly assess what it would take to achieve a necessary end. Oh sure, he had his limits. He didn't write trash. He didn't grab onto rumors and pass them off as truth. But he also didn't let sentiment cloud his perspective and get in the way of a worthwhile story.

Sentiment could destroy a reporter, turn his mind to mush. But where Maggie Potter was concerned, Colby's mind had already turned to mush. He could tell himself a hundred times that he was doing her a favor. He was giving her the chance to expurgate her bitterness by helping to bring down Kilbourne. He was doing this partly for Maggie's own good.

But his conscience gave such rationalizations the credit they deserved, which was none. Maggie was too smart to be taken in by such self-serving drivel. Colby couldn't even fool himself.

Colby muttered a curse. He'd always known this could be a dirty business, but he'd thought himself tough enough to play hardball when hardball was needed. Until now.

When Colby rounded the final hairpin curve into Jerome, the headlight-swallowing blackness was unrelieved, both in the night and in his mind. The shops were closed and dark. Only Paul and Jerry's saloon and the bar in the old Connor Hotel showed signs of life. A single light shone on the front porch of the little Jerome Inn, where the proprietor had promised to leave the door open for him. He didn't stop. Two streets above him was Robin's Nest. He wanted to drive by it. There was no reason. At this late hour, everyone would be asleep. No solution to his dilemma would be painted across the front window or on a banner hanging from the porch railing. It was simply something he wanted to do.

The inn was dark and still, just as he'd known it would be. Not so much as the glow from a night-light gave an indication of life. Still, he pulled into an empty parking spot in front of the garage. All five parking slots were vacant, which made him wonder. Was the inn empty in the middle of tourist season? Had something happened to Maggie or Catherine that made them shut down?

Colby got out of the car, walked to the front of the house, and looked up, not sure what he expected to see. He was so damned tired. He was almost tempted to sit on the front steps and sleep right there. In the morning, he could talk with Maggie. Maggie. Maggie. The name seemed to echo in his weary brain. Almost as if someone else willed him to move, he tried the front door. It was unlocked. The staircase leading to the second floor was in front of him. He felt compelled to go up. There was just no way to resist. At the top, he turned and passed the door to the Yellow Room, the door to the infamous Red Room, and found himself in front of the closed door to the Blue Room.

The door opened, and Maggie stood there in a filmy,

lacy piece of underwear. Every curve, every beautiful inch of skin seemed to glow at his startled perusal.

"Hello, Colby," she purred. "Do come in."

You should've seen the look on the man's face! Confusion, lust, suspicion, amazement, desire. He knew something wasn't right. You can bet on it. But he came on in anyway. Of course he did. He was a man, after all.

And oh heavenly days, did it feel good to have a man look at me that way again, as if he could eat me whole. I'd been a hundred years without that look, and it didn't make a bit of difference that he was looking at Maggie Potter, not Roberta Rowe. The real Maggie was gasping with horror in the back of my head, but I ignored her. Someday she would appreciate the little push I was delivering.

"I knew you'd come back," I told him softly.

"Maggie." Colby was breathless. Helpless as a babe. I could tell. A hundred years, and I hadn't lost the touch. "What the . . . what the hell are you up to, Maggie?"

My smile was irresistible. "What do you think I'm up to, Colby?"

"I don't have a clue."

"Yes, you do."

Colby Drake was no green boy. He knew good and well what was in the works. I brushed his cheek with one finger and sent him an unmistakable invitation with Maggie's pretty hazel eyes—eyes so like my own. "I have a lot to make up for with you." I hooked a finger in his waistband, pulled him into the room, and closed the door.

"Uh . . . Maggie?"

"Yes?" I began to unbutton his shirt.

He sounded as if he was going to choke. "Have you been drinking?"

"Just a teensy-tiny drop." I took my time with the buttons, then peeled off his shirt and tossed it aside. "I'm so sorry I've been cranky and rude. Sometimes I'm just impossible."

"This isn't like you, Maggie." His eyes narrowed suspiciously, and I suspected I was taking the humble act too far. So I gave him one of Maggie's bright, sassy smiles. "A woman's entitled to a change of heart now and then. Just relax, Colby. I don't bite. Usually."

I ran a finger down his bare chest, then slid my hand behind his neck and pulled him toward me for a kiss. He might have been confused, but his kiss wasn't. No indeed.

You didn't expect him to resist, did you? He is a man, after all. I'll admit I was tempted to stick around when I felt Maggie's young, healthy body respond to the opportunity I was giving her, but my better side— yes, I do have one—won out. I'd lured Colby up here, swept away Maggie's silly inhibitions, and put them both in the mood. If Maggie couldn't take it from there, she was worse off than I thought.

After a hundred years of celibacy, I think I should be sainted for resisting such temptation.

Maggie drowned in sensation. She had no governance over her actions, and little over her feelings. Maggie Potter wasn't the one who pulled Colby Drake into her room, unbuttoned his shirt, and melted when his lips touched hers. It wasn't her, really, and yet it was. She didn't start this, didn't want this, but her senses, like turncoats joining the winning side, enjoyed themselves enormously.

Suddenly, Robbie was gone. Maggie once again controlled her arms, legs, fingers, mouth. Yet for the time being, as Colby's kiss deepened, Maggie left all those things right where they were—until her anger rose up and washed over her like a splash of cold water.

At the first sign of struggle, Colby released her. Cool air washed between them. Maggie tensed herself for a comeback attempt by Robbie, but it didn't happen. Apparently, Robbie had had enough. Maggie was on her own.

"What the hell is going on here?" Colby demanded. Arousal pulsed from him—the heat in his eyes, the tension in his body, the taut set of his mouth. Maggie looked away and took a deep, calming breath.

"Well?" he demanded.

"Just stay away from me, please."

"That's not what you wanted two minutes ago."

How was she going to explain the situation to a man who didn't believe in ghosts? She picked up his shirt and threw it at him. It bounced off his bare chest and landed on the floor. "Get dressed."

"You are insane. Do you know that? You're either insane or the flakiest female I've ever had the misfortune to know."

"I am not insane," she insisted in a cold, clear voice. "I am not a flake. And you have very little room to complain. What were you doing knocking at my bedroom door at this time of night?"

That gave him pause. He frowned, apparently puzzled at just how that came about. Maggie gave him no time to think. Her temper rose in a cold flood. Exhausted, furious, she had been used one too many times—by Jack Kilbourne, by Colby Drake, and now by a dead woman who managed to walk all over her even from the grave. It was too much. The flood of anger overflowed and spurted in all directions.

"Get out of my way!"

She brushed Colby aside and marched to the closet, her temper wrapped about her in a shield of fierce armor. Colby's gaze went from irate to bemused as she pulled on a chaste terry-cloth bathrobe that covered her from neck to ankles. She shot him a glare designed to wither an oak tree.

But the blast of fury wasn't entirely for him.

"I know you're still in this room, you body-snatching sneak. I hope you're proud of yourself. You've made a fool out of an unsuspecting man and trespassed in a way that would make Hugh Hefner blush."

A sultry silence permeated the air.

"Show yourself, you floozy! Own up to your mischief. What happened to honor, huh? To respect, consideration, privacy, live and let live? You had your chance at life. You were allowed to make your own mistakes. Why won't you let me live my life and make my own damned mistakes, you nosy, manipulating, sorry-assed strumpet?"

Nothing but silence answered her. In pure frustration, Maggie kicked the closet doorframe, then hopped about and cursed the pain in her foot. Damn Robbie! Damn Colby Drake! And damn herself. She was so tired of allowing herself to be a victim, a patsy for other people's plots. She was tired of donning the mask of a cynical bitch, of fighting her own softer side, of fighting Robbie, of trying to make herself despise Colby Drake when deep in her soul she couldn't.

Tears ran down her cheeks, and she impatiently brushed them away. Colby was looking at her as though she'd lost her mind, and she didn't really blame him.

"It wasn't me," she tried to explain. "I told you there's a ghost here. She thinks it's great fun to move into people's heads and take their bodies for a test drive. She started out with poor Catherine. Now she's having her fun with me." She corrected herself bitterly. "With us."

He gave her a blank look.

She shook her head, knowing it was impossible to convince him. "It wasn't me, Colby."

Twelve

Colby felt as though he'd walked into a hornet's nest. Maggie was closer to the edge than he'd suspected. Either that, or she was on something mighty strong.

"Mags, are you taking medication?"

"No!" She turned to the wall, pounded it with a fist, then leaned her forehead against the plaster. "You think I'm on drugs, don't you? Or I'm a few cannolis short of a full plate. God! What a choice. Maybe I am crazy. But if I am, then Catherine is too. And Tom Matthews. Shit!"

Colby didn't really trust himself. He ached for her. His emotions reeled from the roller-coaster ride of desire, confusion, and alarm. But Maggie looked wilted and miserable, and no man could have resisted reaching out to offer comfort.

He touched her, and a spark seemed to shoot from her flesh to his. She turned to him, accepting his arms around her, using his bare chest to hide her face. He was lost, Colby admitted to himself. Totally, utterly lost. Objectivity was a thing of the past, along with rationality and control. Some things were just meant to be, no matter the good reasons not to be.

"I'm telling the truth," she cried into his chest. "I always tell the truth. But you think I'm crazy."

"No," he whispered into her hair. Sweet-smelling, soft-as-silk, seductive hair. "I know you always tell the truth."

She was trying hard not to weep, Colby could tell.

"You think I'm a fruitcake."

"You are a fruitcake," he agreed with a sigh, "and I'm a jerk." He wanted to forget the reason he had come to Jerome in the first place, and even more, he wanted to forget the reason he'd come back tonight, the column about Maggie written specifically to flaunt in her face and frighten her into doing as he wanted.

Even worse, he had taken advantage of her in the worst sort of way. What the hell had he been thinking, surprising her in the middle of the night, taking advantage of her unsettled state of mind? It was almost as if some evil twin had taken control of his body. He was the worst kind of slime.

"I'm a jerk," he repeated, nestling her against him, rubbing her back as if she were an upset child. "And you need a good night's sleep. Things will look better in the morning."

"You think so?" Her arms circled his waist. She leaned against him, pressing closer with each circle of his hands on her back. He inhaled the warm scent of her, the scent of a woman on the edge of passion. Colby gritted his teeth, wondering how he was going to leave.

"Of course things will look better. I'll come back in the morning, and we can talk. Or maybe you don't want me to come. You're right, you know, Mags. I'm a dickhead. Maybe it's just time I stopped bothering you."

With a strength he didn't know he had, Colby gently separated them. He ought to be sainted for that, he told himself. He should get a halo right along with the pitchfork he also deserved. "I'm going now. To tell the truth, I don't know what the hell I was thinking to come up here. I'm sorry."

She gave him a searching look, her hazel eyes dark with emotion. "I know how you got up here, though you wouldn't believe me. Don't worry about it."

Her lashes were wet and spiky, her lips red and swollen. How much temptation could a man endure? "I'm going now."

It took a superhuman effort to move toward the door. Standing there bundled in terry cloth, she looked even more appealing than she had in the filmy thing she'd worn before. He was going to leave, Colby told himself. He had his hand on the doorknob. Then she whispered his name.

"Colby?"

He didn't answer, just turned.

"You forgot your shirt."

"Oh. Yeah." Clenching his jaw, he marched stoically over to the crumpled garment. He didn't bother to put it on. If he didn't get out of the room before his good intentions failed, there would be hell to pay.

She reached out and touched his arm before he could escape. "Colby?"

"What?" His reply was sharp, desperate.

"I'm confused. And I'm sorry. I think maybe I'm not the tough cookie I told you I was."

"Being tough isn't all it's cracked up to be."

"And I think maybe you're not the complete dipshit I said you were."

He gave her a wry smile. "You had it right the first time, Maggie. I'm everything you said I was, and maybe more. It's in the job description these days. When my daddy was a newspaper man, there was room for principles. Not today."

"Maybe you're a better man than you think you are."

"Nope. I'm a shithead."

She planted her fists on her hips. "I'm tired of being argued with."

This whole night, Colby decided, was like a weird *Alice in Wonderland*. Any moment the Queen of Hearts would pound into the room shouting "Off with his head!" Only it wouldn't be his head the old bat would be trying to lop off. He surrendered to the madness.

"Okay, Mags, I'm not arguing. I'm a saint. To prove it, I'm out of here."

At once her fighting stance melted. "Don't go." Warily she reached out a hand and touched his arm. "Don't go, Colby. I need you to stay."

Curiouser and curiouser. "Maggie, I'm not that much of a saint. I'm stretched as tight as a balloon that's about to pop, and my control isn't up to any more comforting embraces."

Her mouth tilted in a half smile of resignation. "Maybe a comforting embrace wasn't what I had in mind."

She untied her sash and let the robe drop to the floor. It draped around her ankles, a terry-cloth pedestal for a flesh-and-blood Venus clad only in scanty lace. She could have made a mummy sweat.

"Shit!" Colby muttered under his breath.

She stepped out of the terry cloth and headed his way. His feet rooted to the floor, Colby felt every noble resolution and good intention melt as fire raced through his veins. A man could be expected to endure just so much. She hooked a finger in the waistband of his trousers, and he was lost.

Maggie surrendered willingly to the arms that enclosed her and the mouth that took hers, robbing her of breath, thought, and reason. They stumbled together to the bed, not wanting to release each other even for a heartbeat of time. Their clothing was gone in an instant, and they tangled together, relishing the slide of skin on heated skin, legs and arms bumping against sensitive, desire-charged places to inspire both laughter for their awkwardness and groans of rapture for the release of pent-up passion.

All Maggie's uncertainty dissolved in the force of her need. She didn't care if this was foolish. Something inside her cried out for this man to touch her. Her need for him at this moment was more alive, more elemental, than anything she'd felt for any other man. She didn't care if Robbie was watching. She didn't care if every spy satellite in orbit was beaming the scene all over the world. She was going to steal one night from the world—forget suspicion, bitterness, fear, and humiliation. She would steal one solid night of loving a man whose smile made her heart turn over and whose touch made her body sing. To hell with caution and good sense.

Their first coming together was an explosion, swift and fierce, but if it suffered from the haste and awkwardness of desire too long denied, they made up for it during the rest of the night. They learned each other's bodies, what provoked laughter, what brought desire to the flash point, what prolonged the slow boil of pas-

sion and drew out pleasure to the extreme. When appe-
tites were fully sated and weary flesh could do no more,
Maggie lay contentedly in Colby's arms, their bodies so
entangled that she could scarcely tell where she ended
and he began. The steady beat of his heart kept the
world at bay. Content in her lover's nearness and the
warmth of his breath in her hair, she drifted to sleep
with no thought of tomorrow.

Maggie woke to a room flooded with sunshine. At first
she didn't know where she was. The most sunshine she
saw in her basement apartment was in the three small
squares of morning light that sneaked through the
basement windows—never this golden deluge of
warmth and cheer. She raised up on her elbows to better appreciate such a gift—and saw the man sleeping
next to her. Maggie smiled, remembering. Even in the
woozy half sleep of first waking, she'd known something more than the sun gave the morning a special
glow.

Colby was still asleep. The bedsheet covered him
from knee to navel. The rest of him was pleasantly
bare. He slept on his side, one nicely muscled arm
tucked beneath the pillow. His broad back was toward
her. She noted with appreciation how wide shoulders
tapered to lean ribs, then narrowed further to trim
hips. The temptation to appreciate the line of his torso
with her hands, to wake him with gently exploring fingers sliding beneath the sheet, was almost irresistible.
But Maggie managed to resist. She had no regrets
about the night, but morning sunlight brought caution.
Darkness was romance's friend, but daylight allied itself with good sense.

She settled back onto the pillows with a feeling of

contentment. Robbie must be beside herself with joy, she mused. She ought to be furious with the sneaky strumpet, but right at the moment she couldn't call up much righteous indignation. The nosy busybody had been right about a few things, Maggie had to admit. Colby Drake was more than just a sleazoid reporter out for a sensationalist story. He was human. He had a heart, and at least a vestige of conscience. And what he'd given her last night had been more than a quick good-time roll between the sheets. He'd given her part of himself. Maggie wasn't sure what defined the difference, but it was there in his smile, in the warm looks, the gentle, loving caresses.

Loving. Love. A highly overrated word, Maggie reflected. Overrated, and overused. Maggie didn't really believe in love any longer. A noble passion that could conquer all belonged in the realm of the Brothers Grimm. She ought to know, because she had learned the hard way that fairy tales don't come true.

Yet something could exist between the right man and the right woman, beyond friendship, beyond fun, beyond simple infatuation. She couldn't deny it. Her father had found it with her stepmother Virginia. She'd seen it in other couples as well—rarely. But it was sometimes there.

She looked over at Colby, sleeping so peacefully. He didn't drool when he slept, she noticed. Nor did he snore, apparently. She smiled wryly. What a catch! It would be so easy to fall for him—head over heels into that something that was beyond friendship, fun, and infatuation. So easy to accept that the feeling for him that pounded through her veins would make everything all right. Colby would suddenly be a knight in shining armor, and together they would make the world a better place. She would give him her heart and her loyalty, and she would be the center of his universe, more important than money, his career, his friends.

Such whimsy! As if such things really happened. They didn't, at least not to Maggie Potter. Her past record of romantic disasters should have convinced her that walking through life alone was the best way to go. Her most notable talent was tumbling head over heels for the wrong man, starting in high school with Kenny Osborn, whom she had worshipped from afar for a year, and who had asked her to the junior prom. She'd been in heaven—until he spent the entire night dancing with the girlfriend who'd just dumped him. Maggie had finally called her father for a ride home.

In college there had been charming Sean Brownley. They'd dated seriously for two years. Maggie had been ready to pick out a wedding ring when he'd called to ask her for bail. He'd been picked up on a drug dealing charge.

Graduate school had brought Danny Olivera. He'd moved in with her, and Maggie had been certain that she'd struck gold. He was everything a girl could want—considerate, sensitive, fastidious, intelligent, easy to get along with. He made her laugh, never made her cry, and was a friend as well as lover—until he revealed that the fellow in the apartment next door turned him on more than she did.

And one couldn't forget Jack Kilbourne, the jewel in her crown of unwise loves. She didn't even want to think about Jack. Not only had she gotten fired, dumped, betrayed, and vilified, but it had all happened on prime time. Not that Jack had had much choice about it, but all the same, such a thing could only happen to the romantically challenged.

There was absolutely no reason to believe that her romantic future was any less flawed—especially if she continued to act on spur-of-the-moment passion. Love was a liar, she reminded herself. Colby Drake might make her heart do flipflops. They might have connected in a very special way in the darkness of a most unusual night. And perhaps, against all odds, Colby Drake and Maggie Potter together was The Real Thing.

But probably not. She would step cautiously into this minefield.

Resolve thus strengthened, Maggie started to climb from the bed and make for the shower. A hand on her thigh stopped her.

"Good morning, sunshine." Colby's voice was husky with sleep, but those daylight blue eyes were definitely awake.

"Morning." She smiled at his touseled, well-tumbled appearance. Slightly too long black hair sprouted from his head in all directions. His left cheek was creased where the pillow was wrinkled. And a morning stubble of beard darkened his jaw.

All in all, Maggie thought he was the most magnificent man she'd ever seen.

With a groan, he covered his eyes. "Do we have to turn on the sun quite so early?"

"It's an Arizona specialty."

He grunted, then peeked out from between his fingers. She thought his eyes—what little she could see of them—had a suspicious cast. No doubt he was a bit hesitant about her sanity after the night before. "How are you this morning?"

She couldn't resist a bit of needling. "How should I be?"

"Uh . . . ecstatic? Awestruck? Happier than you've been in years?"

"Bingo."

He grinned. The hand fell away from his eyes.

"Same here. Actually, I feel as if I've been run over by one of those monster machines they have down in the mine museum, but it's a good feeling."

"Well, if you're that bad off, I guess I could feed you breakfast."

"Or," he suggested tactfully, "we could wait for Catherine's breakfast."

"Oh? You want to wait for the fancy stuff? You don't think I can cook?"

"I didn't say it. Catherine—"

"Isn't cooking this morning. We didn't have guests last night. And for your information, I can cook well enough to pour milk on cornflakes."

"That's hard to believe."

She took a swipe at him. "What do you think I am? A moron?"

"What? Oh, no. Of course you can pour milk on cereal, Mags. I meant that it's hard to believe you were empty last night. Robin's Nest is the talk of the Verde Valley."

"We needed some privacy last evening, so we put up a No Vacancy sign." She read the question in his eyes. "We indulged in a séance, if you must know, and we didn't want any innocent bystanders in the way."

The laugh lines around his eyes smoothed out, leaving his expression blank. A moment passed before he commented. Maggie fiddled with the bedsheet, not conscious until now that it didn't cover several strategic parts of her anatomy. Suddenly, she felt exposed.

"A séance," he said slowly.

"A friend of Tom Matthews's fancies himself a medium. Well, he's not really Tom's friend. Actually, he's a bit of a loon. But Robbie has been driving us crazy, and we hoped maybe this would help."

Again he waited, considering, looking at her as if she

were some kind of spring-loaded trap. Push the wrong button and she would snap. "You really do believe in this ghost stuff," he concluded.

"When a Mack truck flattens you on the highway, you believe in Mack trucks." At his skeptical expression, she objected. "Come on, Colby! A reporter, of all people, should have an open mind—though maybe I should know better after the last few months. Don't you believe in anything out of the ordinary? Can't your imagination conjure something beyond the physical world? What about last night?"

He arched a brow. "I'd be the first to admit that last night went way beyond the physical."

"That's not what I mean!" She refused to be side-tracked, though she did store away the comment for future pondering. "I told you Robbie moved into my head and made a play for you last night. If you truly can't believe in ghosts, you must either think I'm lying or I'm a crazy woman. Is that what you think?"

"I think . . . you've been under a lot of stress. I think I've added to it, and that I owe you an apology."

"You *do* think I'm crazy." She prepared to flounce out of bed, but he caught her arm.

"Maggie, let's not fight. I know you believe what you're saying, and I promise to keep an open mind, okay? And I do owe you an apology."

She softened. He pulled her gently backward, an invitation too tempting to refuse. "I'm sorry to be so touchy. Believe in them or not, ghosts can get on your nerves."

"Worse than I get on your nerves?" His eyes crinkled once more with good humor.

"It's a toss-up." She flopped back against the pillows, and he shifted so that he looked down on her. Lord, but he was handsome, even with his explosion of uncombed hair and early-morning stubble. Having him loom above her—all muscle, lean flesh, and warm eyes—made that ache start. After last night, she would have thought that particular ache was plumb worn out for a while.

She raised her hand and ran a finger over his raspy cheek. "I know I mentioned this last night, Colby, but we were so busy, I doubt you paid attention."

"We were very busy," he agreed with a manly smirk that made her smile.

"I am sorry for treating you like slime."

"And I'm sorry for acting like slime."

"And for throwing you out of the inn on your booty."

"No big deal. My booty is used to rejection."

"And for letting my ghost lure you into decadent behavior."

He chuckled. "Thank the ghost for me. I owe her one. Actually, I owe her several, I think."

Maggie rolled her eyes. "Don't make fun of her. She'll make you sorry."

He moved so that he was fully on top of her, a position that was tantalizing with possibilities. "I wouldn't make fun of anything about last night—or this morning." He kissed her—a quick, test-the-waters sort of kiss—then followed it with a more thorough effort.

"What about your cornflakes and milk?" she teased, her smile an invitation to much more than cold cereal.

"Breakfast can wait." Another kiss. "Breakfast can wait until dinnertime, if this is how we spend the day."

Maggie voiced no objections.

Catherine dumped half a pound of bacon into the cast-iron skillet and turned the gas burner down to medium.

Even though no guests were there to appreciate her efforts, she intended to cook a good breakfast. Habits were hard to break. Besides, she enjoyed working in the kitchen. She opened the fridge—clean now of Robbie's slime treatment—to look for eggs. Maggie had put away the groceries after shopping the day before and hadn't arranged the shelves in Catherine's usual systematic order. She finally located a carton of eggs in the vegetable drawer and took out three, smiling. She dearly loved her sister, but she wouldn't wish her running loose in anyone's kitchen—especially hers. Catherine had decided that somehow she would manage to stay in Jerome come fall—even if she had to live on a very tight budget until the inn started to show a good profit. Obviously, Maggie couldn't run this place without her, and giving up public school teaching would certainly be no sacrifice. She'd rather deal with a dozen troublemaking ghosts than some of the high school students in her classes.

"Chirp!"

Catherine rolled her eyes upward toward Attila the Bird, who perched on her head. Since there were no guests for the bird to mangle, Cat was giving her time out of her cage. The tiny lovebird peered down at her inquisitively.

"Is that your opinion on the subject, Attie?"

The bird's next chirp was even more assertive.

"I totally agree," Catherine replied with a smile. "I'm not afraid of ghosts, either, but high school students are something else altogether."

And speaking of ghosts . . . Sooner or later, Catherine told herself sternly, she needed to confront last night's very weird, very confusing experience. All night, alone in her bed, her mind had shied away from the subject. Touching on the memory made her hot with embarrassment, and perhaps something else as well. Kissing Tom Matthews had been . . . had been—

"Damn!" She cursed aloud when the egg she'd just cracked landed on the counter instead of in the bowl. "A little distracted, Catherine?" she asked herself. "Stupid idiot."

Attila squawked in agreement, climbed down Cat's hair and hopped onto her shoulder. She nibbled at her cheek in a bird version of a kiss.

"Yes," Catherine told the bird. "It's nice that you love me anyway."

She didn't know quite which she was calling an idiot, herself or Tom. The night before, Catherine had thought he was actually going to make a move on her. She remembered his startled response when Robbie had made her kiss him. He'd shattered, like a stone set too close to a fire. Catherine's own response had jumped through every nerve like an electric shock. She was only too aware that Robbie was doing what Catherine herself had longed to do.

Afterward, back in control of herself, she hadn't known what to think. More than anything she had longed to hide and never come out, but Tom hadn't seemed angry at her, or repulsed. He'd held her hand as if she were some fragile princess who'd been given into his care, and his eyes, fixed on her face, had been hungry for her.

But he'd turned shy at the last minute—stammering, squeezing her hand but afraid to touch her anywhere else. Finally, when she'd convinced him she was still in one piece—even if it was a frazzled piece—he'd made his excuses and left. Every movement, every glance, every accidental touch, said he wanted to stay. But he hadn't.

If she were really the siren Robbie had made her into, would Tom have stayed? Catherine wondered morosely. Is that what it took to get a man interested? She didn't know if she could be so uninhibited and sensual, or even if she wanted to be.

"Be glad you're not human, Attie. Especially single-female human."

Attila rocked back and forth on her shoulder, then climbed headfirst through the neckline of Catherine's tank top.

"Hey! Watch what you're climbing on down there!"

"Chirp!" The bright green-and-apricot head poked out beneath her arm, then ducked back under cover.

Catherine shook her head and grinned. A girl couldn't take herself too seriously with a bird hanging off her bra.

"You'd better throw another pound of bacon in the skillet and a half dozen eggs in the bowl," said a voice out of nowhere.

Catherine jumped so violently that Attila lost her purchase and had to cling upside down from the tank top's armhole, vocalizing a very indignant objection. Feeling as if she might do her own bit of screeching, Catherine carefully rescued the lovebird and set it on her shoulder. "You shouldn't sneak up on a person like that!"

"Ha! Scare you?" Robbie slowly materialized, lounging in the chair by the worktable. As Catherine watched, wide-eyed, the figure grew more and more solid. Every elaborate red curl was in place. The rose in her hair was as fresh and bright as if it had just been plucked from the stem. *"Boo!"*

When Catherine jumped again, Robbie chuckled. *"What's the matter, sweetie? Jumpy this morning? I figured after our adventure together last night, we should be friends."* When Catherine simply stared, she continued. *"I thought I'd let you know that the puny breakfast you're cooking won't do by a long shot. Mr. Newshound is going to come down those stairs in a minute or two, and your sweet sister will be right behind him. Those two worked up an appetite last night that could go through at least a henhouse full of eggs and a side of bacon."*

"Colby?" Cat's eyes grew even wider. "Colby's upstairs with Maggie? Is he still alive?"

Robbie smirked. *"Let me tell you, honey. That man is alive. Alive and kicking. Mmm!"*

Catherine almost forgot she was talking to a ghost. "You're kidding! They . . . they . . . slept together?"

"They did a hell of a lot more than sleep."

On cue, voices drifted down the stairway. Before Colby and Maggie appeared, Robbie gave Catherine a saucy wave and blinked out.

"Good morning!"

Catherine hadn't heard her sister's voice so lighthearted since Maggie had moved back to Arizona.

"Good morning," Catherine replied. "And to you too," she said to Colby, who grinned at her in unabashed satisfaction from behind Maggie.

"We're going on a picnic!" Maggie declared. "Do you mind?"

"No. Of course not."

"I'll be back in time to get ready for check-in this afternoon."

"You don't have to. I can do it. Do you want some breakfast?"

"Got cornflakes?" Colby asked. He shared a private look with Maggie that was part laughter, part intimacy.

Catherine longed to hustle her sister into another room and grill her about what had happened. The day before, Maggie would have cheerfully staked out Colby Drake on ground zero of a nuclear test site. This morning her sister gazed at the man as if he walked on water. But Maggie obviously wasn't going to be pried from Colby's side by anything less than a crowbar. Catherine would be forced to wait until later for the story.

Unless Robbie . . . Cat discarded the horrible thought before it fully formed. Gossiping about Maggie with that wicked ghost would be a dreadful thing to do.

"I've got bacon and eggs," Cat offered uncertainly.

"Nah!" Maggie and Colby said together, then laughed.

"We're going to stop by the grocery store for sandwich fixings anyway. Thanks, though."

Colby echoed Maggie's thanks as they went out the front door. Before they disappeared, he looked back and gave Catherine a surreptitious wink. Maggie's hand was clasped lightly in his, and she seemed to be enjoying every minute of it.

Catherine stared after them long after they were gone. On her shoulder, Attila cheeped questioningly.

"My feelings exactly," Catherine agreed. "How do you suppose that came about?"

"Honey, you're pretty hard up if you don't have anyone better to talk to than a bird."

"Chirp!"

"A bird that talks back, at that."

"Attila doesn't like ghosts," Catherine said. She turned to see Robbie reclining seductively on the stainless steel worktable.

"That little feathered fiend doesn't like anyone, from what I can see."

"Leave her alone, Robbie."

"Ooooooh!" Robbie feigned alarm at Catherine's sharp tone. *"Cranky this morning, aren't we?"*

"Did you do something to Maggie?"

"Why would you ask that?"

"You know why. You've been trying to match her up with Colby for days and days, and suddenly she waltzes down the stairs with him like Ginger Rogers on Fred Astaire's arm."

The apparition shrugged and waggled artfully penciled brows. *"I might have just a little, teensy-tiny bit to do with Maggie's coming to her senses, but she did the important stuff herself. That girl is a corker once she gets started. Just ask Colby."*

"Why are you doing this, Robbie?"

"I have my reasons." The ghost examined her fingernails for some imagined flaw. *"And I'll tell you when I'm good and ready. Trust me. I'm not doing anything I don't have a right to do."*

"Hmmph!" Catherine marched back to the counter, picked up a fork, and whipped the eggs into submission. "I think you should leave Maggie alone. You don't have any right to come barging into her life and making her miserable."

"Mags sure didn't look miserable to me. What's wrong, honey? Jealous?"

"Jealous? What do I have to be jealous of?"

Robbie snorted. *"What gets under any gal's skin, that's what. Your sister's walking off with a premium cut of man, and you're stuck here alone with a bad-tempered bird."*

"Chirp!"

"Same to you, featherhead. What about it, sweetie? Want me to work a miracle for you, too?"

Catherine's heart jumped in a leap of undisciplined insanity. Then she realized to whom she was talking. "Don't be ridiculous." She pointedly turned her back on the ghost as she fished crisp bacon from the skillet and poured eggs into the hot bacon fat. "Maggie doesn't need your nosing into her life, and neither do I."

"Suit yourself."

Catherine refused to turn around and look at Robbie, but she could hear the smile in her voice—the smile of a temptress. When Robbie was alive she had tempted men. Now she was reduced to tempting lonely spinsters with promises of miracles. Catherine almost felt sorry for the one-time toast of Jerome.

"From what I can see," Robbie continued enticingly, *"you're in a sad way of needing some help with the fellows. I'll admit Maggie's my big interest here, but that doesn't mean I can't spare a little time for you."*

"Please don't," Catherine said curtly. She slammed the plate of bacon into the pass-through window to the dining room. "I don't need help with men."

Robbie chuckled knowingly. *"How about our friend with the glasses? He's a pretty good kisser."*

The reminder of last night's humiliation snapped Catherine's temper. "You had no right to do that, Robbie! I was totally, totally embarrassed! I wanted to die!"

"From a simple kiss?"

"From you making me act like a . . . like a . . ."

"Woman?"

"One doesn't have to be a slut to be a woman!"

Robbie sat up and regarded Catherine with narrowed eyes. *"I might have been a whore, honey, but I was never, ever a slut!"* With a flip of her finger, she snuffed the gas flame under the skillet. *"You're burning the eggs."*

"Ooooh!" Catherine growled. Attila danced from side to side on her shoulder, regarding her with open beak, either amazed or alarmed at the vehemence in her exclamation.

Feeling out of control, Catherine struggled to curb her temper. She managed only to divert the swell of emotion into despair. "In case you haven't noticed," she snapped at Robbie, "I am not exactly the sort of woman who turns men to quivering jelly at the first glance, or who even rates a first glance. And I don't care. I don't want to have Maggie's problems, or Maggie's figure, or Maggie's looks. Why don't you just go away?"

"Now, why would you say that?"

"Because I want you to go away!"

"No. Why would you say that you can't turn a man to quivering jelly? Believe me, honey. Men are easy that way. Any woman can turn a man to quivering jelly without hardly trying."

Catherine responded with a skeptical snort.

"Besides, sweetie. Like they say on those TV shows, you're a babe."

"Right." Catherine dumped the charred eggs onto a plate and yanked open the fridge for a carton of juice. "I'm a babe, all right."

Robbie turned palms up and spread her arms. *"What do you want Maggie's figure for? Look at yourself in the mirror."*

"I don't want Maggie's figure, and I have looked at myself in the mirror." Brushing by Robbie, careful not to touch her, she carried her breakfast to the dining room table. "May I eat in peace, please? You're giving me indigestion."

Robbie followed her into the dining room, hopped onto the table, and sat cross-legged, elbows propped on her knees and hands cupped to cradle her chin. She gave Catherine a frankly appreciative once-over. *"You've got what it takes, gal. A man likes a little cushioning on a woman, you know?"*

"A hundred years ago, maybe."

"Hell! Men don't change. Trust me. I know. All you need is a few lessons on how to use what you've got, and you'll knock that good-looking bookworm right out of his boots."

Catherine tried to be not interested. She tried to concentrate on her bacon and eggs and not listen to the temptation of Robbie's voice. Her effort failed.

Robbie gave her a wicked smile, as if looking into her mind and reading her weakness. *"Now, Catherine, dear, I just happen to be an expert on the art of using womanly assets. I don't generally offer to share my secrets. But since we're such close friends, and since you're dear Maggie's sister . . . well, hell. I can't really consider you competition—can I?—seeing that I'm dead and all."*

Catherine looked into Robbie's eyes and knew that she was putty in the madam's hands. Silly Putty, at that.

Thirteen

Oak Creek Canyon is spectacular any time of the year, but in June, when the cottonwoods wear the fresh new green of early summer, it is close to paradise. Oak Creek has carved a deep gash in the Mogollon Rim— the great escarpment that separates northern Arizona's high country from the deserts in the south. Pine forests carpet the dark volcanic basalt of the canyon's rim, and from those heights the land tumbles downward through lighter colored limestone and sandstone to the great red desert buttes of Sedona. The entire canyon echoes with the music of rustling cottonwood leaves and the merry sound of clear, cold water rushing over boulders. Quiet, shady pools beckon swimmers and trout fishermen. Sun-warmed shelves of sandstone are made for sunbathing, and grassy little rock-rimmed alcoves lure picnickers with a promise of privacy.

In one of these alcoves, Colby and Maggie spread a picnic blanket and laid out a feast of prepackaged deli sandwiches, fruit, bottled iced tea, and Hostess Twinkies. The Twinkies were Colby's.

"I can't believe you actually eat those," Maggie said.

"No picnic is complete without them."

"Uk."

They lay prone on a sandstone ledge overhanging a quiet pool, trailing their fingers in the cold water and watching trout dart here and there like silent gray shadows. Maggie had donned her swimming suit—a two-piece that showed off just enough to invite men's eyes, but not enough to draw women's disapproving glares. Colby had simply stripped down to his BVDs.

"Twinkies are pure sugar. Useless sugar at that."

"Yeah. Ain't it great?"

She laughed. "Did you ever grow up?"

"Nope. At least, my taste buds didn't."

They lay together in companionable silence for a few moments. Maggie hadn't felt so relaxed in a long time. A pleasant breeze played across her bare back, relieving the heat of the sun. The chortle of the creek might have lulled her to sleep, but sleep wouldn't be as enjoyable as staying awake to enjoy Colby's company. Too soon this precious sliver of time—when they were able to put the real world aside—would end.

"God," Colby groaned. "I wish I had a fishing pole. Look at that monster trout. He must be sixteen inches long."

"You're a fisherman?"

"An addict," he admitted. "My big sister taught me to fly-fish when I was eleven."

The statement called up a picture that was difficult for Maggie to imagine: a skinny eleven-year-old kid standing in hip boots three sizes too large, listening patiently to his big sister while the waters of a river rushed around them and fish lurked safely beneath the riverbanks, laughing at their efforts. The imaginary scene made her smile.

"What's that about?" he asked.

Maggie chuckled. "I was just picturing you learning how to fish from your sister. I guess my concept of Colby Drake has been limited. Either you were the handsome photographer come from nowhere to sweep me off my feet, or the sleazeball reporter who was going straight to hell for . . . well . . . just for being a reporter. I never thought of you as a real person with family and hobbies and . . . you know"—she chortled—"a skinny kid cleaning a big fish."

"My sister cleaned them. The sight of guts made me want to puke."

Maggie laughed. "You made your sister clean the fish?"

"She was fifteen at the time and much tougher than I was."

"And now?"

"Now she has two kids, a civil engineer husband, and an interior design business she works from her home. She's still much tougher than I am."

"You've toughened up enough to rip out someone's guts with the printed word."

"Hm. I thought we were past that," he said quietly.

Maggie rolled onto her side, propped her head upon her elbow, and regarded Colby with a somber expression. Maybe there was no way to put aside the real world, after all. He made circles in the water with his index finger, his expression thoughtful beneath a lifted brow.

"Colby, I . . . uh . . ."

"Yes?"

"I apologized last night for going overboard in casting you as a villain. And I meant it."

"I'm glad you finally realize what a sterling character I am."

She smiled wryly. "I have a bad habit of creating heroes for myself, then overreacting when those heroes don't live up to the impossible standards I set for them."

He rolled so he was facing her, pillowed his head on a folded arm, and gave her a smile. "So I was a hero, then a villain, and now . . . ?"

"Now you're an unbelievably hunky, mildly villainous, very entertaining man who has an incredible sister who doesn't mind cleaning fish."

He chuckled. "Okay. I can live with that. But what are you, Maggie Potter?"

"I am—"

"No, no. You got to define me, so I get to do you." His eyes sparkled with a good-humored wickedness that told Maggie she was in for it. "What you are . . . hm. What you are is a smart, sexy, endearingly crazy, beautiful lady who makes me question what I do and how I live. And who also makes me feel like a teenage boy always on the edge of lust."

She laughed. "Really? The last part, I mean. Do I?"

He reached out and began to play with the top hem of her swimsuit bra, then slipped a seeking finger beneath. "Want me to demonstrate?"

"You're bad!" she scolded, and abruptly got up. Otherwise she was going to say yes, she did want a demonstration. The magic of the night had not worn off.

"Yeah," he admitted with a lazy, sensuous smile. "I'm bad. We already settled that."

He followed her to their picnic blanket, still smiling, still looking at her as a hungry man might look at a juicy steak. She intended to feed his hunger with deli sandwiches, though. Before anything more serious passed between them, she wanted to make sure Colby understood the rules. Getting hurt, she had decided, was generally a result of someone not comprehending the rules.

"It's lunchtime!" she declared. "We have turkey, ham, and egg salad sandwiches, apples, pretzels, fruit salad, and"—she pulled a face—"Twinkies."

He accepted the sandwich she handed him and sat down on the blanket, lounging with his back against a log. But Maggie knew from the way his gaze still rested on her face, her breasts, her legs, that the sandwich was not what he really wanted.

"This is good," she commented on the egg salad sandwich.

"This is very good," he replied, but he hadn't yet tasted his food.

"You know, Colby? The conversation so far this morning hasn't gone quite the way I intended it to go."

He didn't look surprised. "How did you intend it to go?"

"Well, I had some time to think this morning." She smiled warmly. "That was before you woke up."

His smile was more than warm, threatening to distract her. She couldn't go there right now.

"The point is, that I did some thinking. About you and me, and . . . us. And I don't want you to get the wrong idea. That wouldn't be fair."

"What would be the wrong idea?"

"The wrong idea would be that, because we're suddenly on friendly terms—"

"Very friendly terms," he interjected with a wicked grin.

"Okay," she conceded, "very friendly terms. Obviously I'm attracted to you—a lot. And I'm willing to forget you're a reporter as long as you're willing to forget I'm a news item. But Colby, this doesn't mean I'm going to fall in line with any of your plans."

"What you're saying is that you don't exactly trust me." He didn't look hurt, just interested.

"Trust? Come on, Colby! You're a reporter!"

"Ah! Okay. No-brainer there."

"Don't use that tone! You know what I mean."

He reached for the pretzels. "What about love?"

"Love?" Maggie almost choked on her bite of sandwich. "Love? You don't seriously mean to imply you're in love with me!"

He shrugged, and his eyes studied her carefully, as if gauging her reaction. "I wouldn't say that I'm not in love with you."

She rolled her eyes. "Whatever that means! Colby, I've thought I was in love with every man my perverse imagination made into a hero, and love always turned out to be something else. Fascination, hero-worship, lust, insecurity, status-seeking—you name it! I don't believe in love anymore."

He shook his head sadly. "That's much worse than me declaring I don't believe in your ghost."

"Oh, for heaven's sake!" She brushed crumbs from her lap and got up. "This is a ridiculous conversation!"

"You started it," he accused with a boyish grin.

"Did not!"

"Did too."

"Did not!"

"Did not!"

"Did t—! Oh, shit!" She laughed, and Colby joined in. The sudden release of tension made her laugh so hard that tears rolled down her cheeks. Colby came to her aid, patting her back and laughing with her. "Damn, Colby! I love a man who can make me laugh. Why can't you be one of the good guys?"

"I am a good guy."

"Then why are you a reporter?"

"A man's got to earn a living."

The laughter within her faded, and she sighed. "This thing I have for you is just pure insanity. But since you already think I'm insane, you shouldn't have a problem with that."

He slipped one hand around the back of her neck and held her for a slow, gentle kiss, taking her back to that place where only the two of them mattered. He tasted of ham sandwich and pretzels, smelled of sunshine, fresh air, and passion. With one simple kiss he knocked the real world from beneath her and sent her spinning into that world they created together. By the time he released her, she was dizzy with the feel and taste of him. She struggled to catch her breath, and then his eyes caught hers, making the task impossible.

He seemed to be having trouble breathing as well, Maggie noted with some satisfaction. For a moment they just looked at each other, waiting for the world to settle back into place. Slowly, a cat-in-the-cream-pitcher smile grew on Colby's face, and a sparkle of mischief lit his eye. "Come on," he said. "This way."

Before Maggie could object, Colby had her arm in a viselike grip and was hauling her toward the creek. The next instant she was treading air, and then the cold water swallowed her. She surfaced, sputtering her indignation and laughing at the same time. Colby bobbed in the water beside her, grinning from ear to ear.

"You're a menace, Colby Drake!"

"We've already established that, haven't we?"

She struck out toward the ledge, and he objected. "Come back here! Don't be a spoilsport!"

"I don't like swimming in the creek. It's too cold.

Besides, I'm always afraid a fish is going to swim into my suit."

He guffawed. "You're kidding!"

"No."

But she no sooner grabbed the ledge and angled herself to jump up than his arm wrapped about her waist and pulled her back.

"Colby! Quit!"

"I know how to make sure a fish doesn't swim up your suit."

"Don't be—yike!" She squealed as his deft hands peeled down her suit bottom and pulled it over her ankles. It flew through the air to land on a bush near their blanket. The top followed soon after. "What are you . . . ? Colby!"

His BVDs joined her suit. "Haven't you ever gone skinny-dipping?"

"This is . . . this is public!"

"No it's not. We're secluded as can be. And if some nosy person should poke a head into our private place, we'll just give a friendly wave and smile until he goes on his way."

With a naughty slant to her smile, she asked: "What if he's a she?"

"Oh. Well, in that case, we'll ask her to join us."

She sent a fountain of creekwater into his face, then fled with a laugh. He caught her ankle and pulled her under. When she bobbed up, sputtering, he was still there to grab her.

"Never try dirty tricks on the master of dirty tricks," he warned.

"You're admitting it, are you?"

He dunked her again and grinned wickedly when she surfaced. "Say hello to the fish."

She swiped at him, but he held her attack at bay

with one long arm. "Cheat!" she cried. "You can stand up."

He was tall enough to stand on the rocky bottom that was just beyond the reach of Maggie's toes. Colby didn't hesitate to take advantage.

"Now to your second complaint," he said as he reached out and pulled her through the water toward him.

"What complaint?"

"You said the water's cold."

"The water is cold."

"I know how to make it warm," he offered. "Absolutely steaming, in fact." He wrapped her naked legs around his waist, bringing them into intimate contact, and Maggie pretended shock.

"Why, Colby Drake! You billy goat. You're stiff as a crowbar!"

"No small accomplishment in this cold water."

She laughed, then put on a prim face. But when he thrust toward her, she obligingly moved against him. It would have been impossible not to, for having him against her, flesh to flesh, seemed so right.

"Lord, woman! You are a wonder." Colby's expression lost its boyishness and became all man, intense and aroused. He cradled her bottom with his hands, bringing them into even more exquisite contact.

Just as Colby had promised, Maggie was no longer cold. The creek water's cool caress was a sensual contrast to the heated rush of her blood. It caressed with cold fingers every nook and crevice of her body, making her want Colby's touch in those same places, making her even hotter. She was surprised that the water didn't steam as it flowed around them.

Abruptly, Colby released her, holding her lightly as

she tread water. "Blanket," he said in a husky voice. "Now."

Aching with need, she followed him to their sandstone ledge, where he jumped up and then pulled her from the water. The remains of their picnic was pushed hastily aside to make room for them on the old wool blanket, where they took turns dishing out sweet torment until they could no longer stay apart.

Once again Colby proved his claim that he was a very good man. And Maggie discovered that Oak Creek Canyon was indeed paradise.

When she could breathe again, Maggie propped herself on one elbow and looked down at the long masculine body that lay beside her. Colby wore only a sated smile and a gleaming sheen of sweat. Wickedly, she touched her finger to his breastbone and ran it slowly, tantalizingly in a line down to his navel, where he caught it in his hand and stopped its progress.

"We need another swim," she told him. "We're both sweathogs."

He didn't open his eyes, but his smile grew wider. "Is it going to end the same as the last swim?"

She chuckled. "You *are* a billy goat!"

"Not usually. It must be you." His eyes slitted open, and he perused her nakedness with appreciation. "Let's just stay here for the next two weeks, okay?"

She leaned over and kissed him, but shied away when he reached for her breast. "It's getting late, and I have to get back. The real world awaits, Romeo."

"I prefer this world."

Maggie didn't say it aloud, but so did she.

They rinsed themselves in the stream, then dressed, wrapped the blanket around the leftovers and trash, and prepared to make the long climb up to the car, which was parked a hundred feet above them on a pull-out beside the highway. Maggie paused for one more look at their grassy bower.

"I don't want to go back to the real world," she admitted. "The real world is infected with sleaze."

Colby came up beside her and put a hand to the back of her neck, massaging away the tension that suddenly tightened her muscles.

"Sometimes," she continued, "I think the sleaze is in me. That's why I see it everywhere I look. It didn't used to be that way."

"The sleaze is not in you, Maggie." Colby put down the blanket and its contents and urged her over to a log, where they sat.

"We should go," she objected.

He ignored her. "The sleaze is not in you."

She sighed and accepted the comfort he offered. If she could stay in the shelter of his arms for the rest of her life, the sleaze would go away. But of course, that wasn't true, because he was part of the sleaze.

"Maggie, why don't you tell me what happened with you and Kilbourne?"

She exhaled in a rush. "So you can write about it?"

"Because Jack Kilbourne is the Typhoid Mary of sleaze. He's a carrier, infected to the gills, yet he presents the picture of wholesomeness to the world. And the goddamned dipshit is running for president."

Maggie sighed and pulled away, staring out at the stream, unable to look at Colby—though she couldn't quite muster the antagonism that she should. "Why do you think Jack is such a monster?"

"You don't?"

"No."

"After what he did to you?"

She didn't want to remember—not in this place where she and Colby had just made love. She was creating a new world, discovering a new Maggie, and learning that joy was still possible—thanks to Colby, of all people. And yet maybe Jack Kilbourne needed to be hauled out of the locked closet in her mind. Perhaps if she dusted off those memories and examined them, they would lose the power to dim her days and cloud her future.

"You have the wrong idea about Jack Kilbourne," she said quietly.

"Do I? Then tell me. I don't want to print your story, Mags. I wouldn't do anything to hurt you. I just want to pick your brain."

She shook her head. "It wouldn't do you any good."

He took her chin and turned her face toward him, forcing her to look into those clear blue eyes that seemed so honest and caring. "How can you know it wouldn't do any good? Try me."

Maggie sank into his eyes, just as she'd earlier melted into his arms. She took a deep breath, then let it slowly out. "All right," she said. "I'll tell you."

Colby watched Maggie's expression darken as she stared into the distance. He should have been exultant, but he wasn't. Instead, he ached for the pain on Maggie's face as she sorted through memories of another man. He really was getting soft, Colby told himself.

"I went to work for Jack right out of graduate school. The ink on my master's degree was still wet," Maggie said with a rueful smile. "He represented everything I believed in—state's rights, less government, simpler tax codes, honesty in politics."

Colby snorted, then promptly shut up when she glared.

"Do you want to hear this or not?"

"I'm sorry," he said meekly. "Go on. Please."

"Anyway, I worked on his reelection campaign for governor of Ohio, and when he won, he made me an aide. We got along, like friends. He was in the process of a messy divorce, and he'd been separated from his wife quite a while. Jack never went out, never had fun. He worked all hours, and I worked with him. I didn't mind. I thought he was important not only to the state, but to the country. Everyone knew he had great things ahead of him. Even before I went to work for him there were rumors that he'd be a candidate for president. And Jack taught me so much. It was like being in college all over again, only this time in the real world."

Colby bit down on his lip to keep from blurting out an ill-considered comment. He could imagine the things Jack Kilbourne might teach a pretty, naive young aide, and none of those things were things one learned in college, at least not in the classroom.

Maggie stared at the creek, as if she saw her life in Ohio passing with the current. "We spent a lot of time together, and one thing just led to another. We never so much as kissed before Jack's divorce, though, in spite of the lurid speculation of the press. Jack and Trudy were fighting like cats and dogs long before I came upon the scene." Her mouth twisted ruefully. "I thought I was in love. Jack is . . . well, Jack is Jack. He could charm a nun right out of her habit if he put his mind to it. It didn't matter that he was twenty years older than me and had a future as one of the nation's most important men. To me he was just Jack. We talked about marriage, but things were so up in the air with what would happen with the presidential campaign . . . Besides, after his divorce, I don't think he was too keen on marrying again. In any case, it was much too soon."

She trailed off, biting her lip. Colby wanted to reach out and comfort her, but he didn't dare interrupt. This catharsis was important, he told himself. He was not being totally selfish in asking her to go through this. Selfish, yes, but not totally.

"Anyway," she continued with a grimace. "You know what happened. It didn't seem so morally reprehensible to us that we were lovers, but once the media got hold of the story, they just blew everything out of proportion—as though Jack were some lecherous pervert indulging in sexual harassment, and I were a scheming slut planning to bring down the nation's moral code—as if the nation has a moral code. When there's a campaign going on, the news people will grab at anything to create a scandal." She gave him a jaundiced look. "Of course, you wouldn't know anything about that!"

"Ouch!" He winced. "I'll have you know I didn't do one column about Maggiegate. Well, one—but it was a call to rationality. I thought we should get back to slamming the man's political record and lay the bedroom stories to rest."

"Should I believe you?" she asked, unsmiling.

"Have I ever lied to—oops! Belay that. Yes, I have lied to you. Lies of omission, maybe, but still lies. This time I'm not. We're way past lying to each other, aren't we, Maggie?"

She broke eye contact, fastening her gaze once more on Oak Creek. "I've never lied to you. I never will."

"And I'll never lie to you again."

The look she gave him wasn't completely trusting.

"How long were you . . . uh . . . with Jack?"

"I worked for him for a little over three years. We were lovers for less than one." She bit her lip again. "Jack was very kind to me, and I was so happy. Delirious, really. Maybe I didn't really know him as well as I thought. There was a lot about him that was private, that he didn't share. But he was my hero. At the time, I thought he could do no wrong, had no weaknesses. Of course I knew that was silly, but that's still how I felt in my heart. Sometimes the brain and the heart don't always connect."

"Been there," Colby agreed. In fact, he admitted silently, he was there right at that very moment.

"I kept my own apartment, but we were together all the time. When we weren't working, we'd go somewhere private where Jack could just relax and get away from the press. I remember one great trip on Jim Sweeney's sailboat. It was heaven. Blue sky, bright water, sunburn and salty hair, the rocking of the waves to put you to sleep at night. Someday I'd like to have a sailboat."

Colby sat bolt upright. He almost couldn't believe he'd heard right. He couldn't be that lucky.

"Jim Sweeney?"

"Yes, Jim Sweeney. He was a good friend of Jack's from North Carolina. I think they were frat brothers in college. Nice guy. His wife is nice, too."

Colby's heart picked up its pace. He had a whiff of victory, and it was very, very sweet. Almost as sweet as Maggie Potter. "Did Sweeney ever come to Kilbourne's office?"

"Yes, sure. Jim was in Columbus a lot on business. Every once in a while they'd go to lunch, or Jim would just drop by and they'd chat in Jack's office. Why?"

Here came the big one. Colby's gut knotted. "Is Sweeney in your logs?"

"Probably."

"Dates and times?"

"I always entered dates and times. Colby, what is it? I thought you wanted to hear about Jack."

Now they were at the sticking point. Colby couldn't spin a tale to entice Maggie into handing over those logs. He'd promised her he would never lie to her again. He had to do this by the front door, and that was going to be difficult. "Maggie, I really need to see those logs."

"You've seen them," she said, a chill in her voice.

"I need to really see them. Read them. Make some copies. Kilbourne's relationship with Jim Sweeney might not mean anything to you, but it might be the key to bringing out the truth of Kilbourne's true character."

Her frown grew deeper. "Colby, I don't think you know anything about Jack's true character."

"And perhaps you don't, either," he replied with a flash of exasperation. That wasn't the tack to use, but he suffered a sudden stab of jealousy for her loyalty to a man who didn't deserve it and her refusal to trust Colby Drake. Granted, he wasn't a saint, and his record with Maggie was a far cry from pristine, but after a night and day spent in each other's arms, Colby thought he might expect to be cut some slack.

"Colby . . ." Her tone shifted from annoyed to placating. "Vengeance is a poor excuse for turning on someone who's been a friend. If I gave you those logs, the press would pick them apart, piece by piece, trying to find dirt to smear on Jack. They would take things out of context, they would read things in that weren't there. I have no desire to bring Jack Kilbourne down. He's a good man. I still believe that. He never meant to hurt me. What happened was not Jack's fault."

Colby sighed, got up from the log, walked to the edge of their little ledge, and stared at the creek. "I wish to God that I could inspire that kind of loyalty in a woman—the kind of loyalty that survives even after you save yourself by throwing her to the wolves."

She was silent for a moment. When he didn't turn back to face her, she said, "Loyalty dies hard, even after it gets knocked in the head."

"And trust, apparently, is something that's born hard."

He heard her quiet sigh. "Yes. I suppose so."

He turned then. No sense hiding the disappointment on his face; it was reflected in hers. She was disappointed, Colby assumed, that he'd even asked for the logs.

"What makes you think Jack Kilbourne deserves such unshakable loyalty?"

She shook her head. "It's something I feel, not something I think. You can't just turn off feelings."

He was tempted to ask if she still loved the louse, but that would be revealing the petty jealousy that was making it impossible for him to remain objective. "You haven't read many newspapers lately, have you?"

"No."

"Or watched the TV news."

"I try to avoid the pronouncements of the press these days. I suppose it's petty, but every time I see a newspaper or hear some suave oh-so-knowledgeable anchorperson, I want to throw up."

"Then you haven't heard the latest piece of dirt that our friend Jack is trying to dodge."

Her eyes flickered. Was there a bit of interest there? Colby hoped.

"What piece of dirt?"

"That Kilbourne scammed the Ohio taxpayers on the new Toledo airport."

"The governor's office didn't have anything to do

with the Toledo airport. The mayor and city council ran that show. Except . . ." She gave him an uncertain look.

"Except what?"

"Except nothing. Jack came out heavily in favor of the airport during the bond election. He thought it was in the best interests of both the city and state."

"According to some disgruntled bidders, Kilbourne made sure that airport was in the best interests of some of his good buddies, too. They accuse him of making sure the contracts were awarded to his friends."

She was silent.

"That airport turned out to be very costly to the taxpayers, and it's coming to light now that some of the work isn't up to standard. Jim Sweeney just happens to be a partner in the firm that oversaw construction—a very silent, in-the-closet kind of partner. They somehow underbid everyone for the job and then overran the budget in everything from A to Z."

"Jack couldn't have rigged the bidding. That's ridiculous. The bids went to an independent consulting firm who then made recommendations to the city about the contracts."

"Are you saying that the consultants wouldn't have discussed the bids with the governor if he asked?"

"Well—"

"And that Jim Sweeney wasn't in a position to hear about his competition sometime when he and the guv were having lunch or sailing the deep blue sea?"

She folded her arms across her chest and glared at him. "Jack wouldn't have done that."

Colby allowed himself some sarcasm. "No, of course not. Not the saintly Jack."

If she weren't sitting on a log ten feet away, she might have pushed him into the stream. Or he might have pushed her. He was beginning to get very tired of the shadow of saintly Jack drifting between them. Especially since he knew that Jack Kilbourne was anything but a saint. "No one," Colby conceded, "has come up with any concrete evidence to pin charges of tampering on Kilbourne."

"Of course they haven't," Maggie said.

He thought she looked relieved, and it was with a perverse satisfaction he continued. "The guv was very up front with the press and the city council. He even released all the daily logs of his office during the entire time the airport was an issue, just to prove he was clean."

The beginnings of a frown puckered her face. "Why would he release the logs?"

"Probably to prove that no one in the least connected with the bidding was in contact with his office during that time. Does it surprise you that Jim Sweeney's name doesn't appear on those logs even once? Not that Sweeney couldn't have made contact with the guv without calling or coming into his office, of course. But having a record that he *was* in the office, or called the office, during a critical period of bidding would certainly make certain people sit up and take notice."

She sat in thoughtful silence.

"Most of the clerical help and gofers that worked in Kilbourne's office have changed since then—except for a few loyal aides and his personal secretary, and they aren't talking to anyone save to sing Jack's praises."

"That's because he's praiseworthy!" Maggie insisted. But there was a hint of doubt in her voice.

Colby gave her a wolfish grin. "It would be interesting, wouldn't it, to see in what substantive ways your logs differ from the logs he released to the public."

She bit her lip.

"Wouldn't it?" he insisted.

"If I thought the press would be responsible in the matter, I might hand them over. But we both know what a media feeding frenzy would result."

"I don't suppose you would trust me to do the right thing with them."

She laughed harshly, then apologized. "Colby, I'm sorry. I didn't mean that like it sounded."

He picked up their blanket bundle and started up toward the car. "Let's go."

She hastened to follow and stopped him with a hand on his arm. "Don't be mad, Colby. I know it's hard to understand how I can . . . can like you and still hate and distrust what you do. But when someone's been attacked by a pack of dogs, they don't willingly dive back into the kennel." Her eyes pleaded eloquently for understanding. "But that someone might not mind having just one of the dogs around. I mean, when they're not part of a pack, a dog can be very appealing."

"I'm very flattered," he growled. "Should I wag my tail?"

Her sigh was long-suffering. He relented and gave her a wry smile. "Maggie, did you ever consider that those logs of yours might somehow prove that Kilbourne is innocent? If you have so much faith in the man, then put it to the test."

Her gaze dropped. Both physically and metaphorically she took a step away from him. "We're going to have to agree to disagree on this, Colby."

He knew an unscalable wall when he saw one. He put on a charmer of a smile. "Suppose we disagree about agreeing to disagree?"

Maggie picked up his attempt to lighten the mood.

"Then we'll just have to agree to disagree about agreeing to disagree."

They both smiled, pretending things were back the way they were before. But the sun seemed dimmer somehow as they climbed up to the car.

Fourteen

"Guess who's coming up the walk?" Robbie crowed.
"Just the man we want to see."

Catherine jumped up from the dining room table,
where she'd been eating her eggs and indulging in a
bewildering but rather fascinating discourse with Robbie on the feminine arts. "Who's coming? What man?"

*"What other man are you yearning for, honey? Mr.
Bookworm, of course."*

"Tom! Omigod! Tom is coming up the walk?"
Looking at the mess around her, she gave a squeak of
alarm. There were dirty skillets on the stove, mixing
bowls soaking in the sink, biscuit crumbs littering the
table, and a smear of strawberry jam on the centerpiece
doily. Of all times for Tom to pay a visit! Turning first
one way and then another, she couldn't decide where
to start.

With a shrill chirp, Attila let Catherine know that
she did not appreciate the sudden movements—and
also reminded her that she had a bird on her head.

"Oh, lord! Attila! I've got to do something with Attila. She'll eat poor Tom alive."

"Lovebird pie," Robbie suggested.

"Aaaagh!"

"Leave that egg platter where it is, girl! The man's a bachelor, so he needs a decent meal. You're a hell of a cook. Show it off."

"Everything's such a mess!" Catherine's voice rose in panic.

"Men don't care about such things, as long as you fill their stomachs." She winked. *"And then give them the dessert they want afterwards."*

"Robbie! Don't!"

"Oh, look at her blush! Honey, you're a treasure. If Tom Matthews doesn't snap you up like a dog grabbing a ham bone, then he's a pea-brain."

The doorbell chimed. Catherine's emotions were as scrambled as the eggs. What was Tom doing here? After the night before, Catherine would have thought he'd avoid Robin's Nest like a plague house and eschew any further interest in ghosts.

The doorbell chimed again.

"Well, are you going to open the door, or am I?"

Wouldn't Tom just love that—being greeted at the front door by Robbie in full regalia! Yesterday it would have made his day. Today . . . ? Catherine didn't think so. "Stay away from the door," she warned the ghost. "I'll get it." She raced downstairs, stuffed an indignant Attila in the cage with Hannibal, and raced back upstairs in record time. By the time she yanked open the door, she was gasping for breath.

"Uh . . . hi," Tom said, giving her a concerned look. "Are you all right?"

"Fine! . . . Just fine! . . ." She managed to answer between puffs. " Attila was out. Had to run down and stuff her in her cage so she wouldn't make bird eyes at you."

"Bird eyes?" He looked a bit uncertain of her sanity. After the night before, Catherine didn't blame him.

"She does that to men. Bats her cute little bird eyes and then turns into a lethal weapon when the guys come close to admire her."

"Oh. Well, in that case, thanks. She would have snookered me for sure. I've always been a sucker for animals. Uh . . . I brought over some more books."

"Books?" For a moment Catherine simply stood in the doorway, overwhelmed by a confusing mix of feelings at the sight of him.

"Books on Jerome history. A couple of them include some pretty interesting stuff about Robbie. May I come in?" His smile was endearingly lopsided. "As long as the coast is clear of birds?"

"Oh! Of course! Come in!"

"You were eating breakfast?"

"Uh . . . brunch. I slept in."

"Offer the poor man some food!"

Robbie was nowhere to be seen, but her voice rang in Catherine's head.

"Are you hungry? There's plenty. Maggie and . . . uh, well, Maggie didn't eat this morning. She's already gone out."

Tom sniffed. "Smells really good."

"Just bacon, eggs, and biscuits."

"Biscuits? Homemade biscuits?" He headed toward the table like a bloodhound on a hot trail.

"Of course they're homemade."

"Good," Robbie said. *"Let him know that this is the real stuff."*

"If you don't eat it, it'll just be thrown to the squirrels."

Tom grinned. "We can't allow that."

Tom made up for Maggie's and Colby's absence at the table. He was lavish with his compliments to the cook, which put a smile on Catherine's face. The fact that every once in a while he slipped a piece of bacon or biscuit to George, who had stationed herself beside his chair, made the smile grow even wider. It was all well and good for a man to be handsome, intelligent, charming, and well-read. But if he was fond of animals as well, then he was a keeper.

"More eggs?" she offered.

"Gosh no! I'm about to bust. I'll bet you made that jam, too, didn't you."

"Well, yes."

"Enough food talk. Take the man into the living room."

Catherine jumped.

"Something wrong?" Tom inquired.

"No!" If Tom knew Robbie was about, Catherine thought, he'd be out of the house in a flash. He wouldn't want a repeat of last night.

"Go, girl. You've played the food angle to the hilt. Now's the time to move on to the next step."

"Uh . . . let's go into the living room and look at those books you brought."

He hesitated, probably remembering their last encounter in the living room, but the dining room table was too strewn with breakfast leavings to be of use. "The living room." His jaw firmed into a staunch line, as if he were preparing to brave a lion's den. "Sure. Let's."

Catherine hung behind, ostensibly to carry some dishes into the kitchen. "What do I do? What do I do?" she whispered frantically.

"Just do what I tell you to do. You'll be fine."

"You're not going to show up, are you?"

"Don't worry, sugar. I'm not going to distract your man. He's all yours."

Tom was standing at the big front window when she walked in. Catherine gave him a wan smile, feeling more nervous than when she'd stood up before the Chandler PTA and talked about sex education in the schools.

"Are these the books you brought?" She picked up the well-worn volume on top—a softbound book that was little more than a pamphlet. *Verde Valley Vivantes* was the title. *Tom must have really dug through the store to find this one,* Cat thought. Was he looking for an excuse to come back?

"That one is more like a tourist circular. It does have a paragraph about Roberta Rowe, though. The one under it has more. Did you know that Robbie had a daughter?"

"Really?" Catherine looked up in surprise. "Are you sure?"

Their eyes met, and Catherine forgot all about Robbie's daughter. She put the book down.

"Get down to work," Robbie whispered in her head. *"Remember what I told you."*

"Uh . . . it was nice of you to bring these by."

"Soft," Robbie reminded her. *"Your words are a soft breeze tickling his senses."*

Catherine lowered her voice and felt like an idiot. "We could . . . uh . . . look at them over here."

"Sure." Tom, poor unsuspecting innocent, picked up the books and took them to where Catherine indicated.

Catherine sat beside him. The sofa cushions were soft and deep. They sat shoulder to shoulder, hip to hip, thigh to thigh, the books piled around them and covering them like a weighty blanket.

"Now in this one"—Tom opened the thickest of the volumes—"a whole section of a chapter is devoted to our girl."

Catherine leaned close, inspired by the push of an invisible hand. Her lips nearly brushed Tom's ear as she leaned over to look at the book. Tom's voice started to quaver.

"And this one has a . . . uh . . . a great photo."

"Oh, it does!" Her breathy words caressed his chin. And such a strong, square chin it was, flowing into a noble jaw. She longed to trace the line of that jaw with her fingers, and soothe the muscle that jumped just in front of his ear.

Something caught in Tom's throat, or at least his choking sputter gave that impression. He rose abruptly. "Uh . . . uh . . . wow! It's really warm in here, isn't it?"

Catherine sighed. "I'll turn on a fan." She gave her invisible conspirator a discouraged moue as she got up to plug in the table fan.

"Coward!"

"This isn't working," she said under her breath. She wasn't exactly a star pupil in the art of seduction. "Just go, Robbie. Leave me be!"

"Fine! I know when I'm not wanted! I'll just leave you to bungle things on your own!"

Catherine sighed as Robbie flounced out of her mind. She obviously never would have made it as one of Robbie's girls.

Tom watched Catherine with mixed and confusing emotions. She was acting damned peculiar. Not like herself at all. Something was up, and it probably involved Robbie. The thought excited and alarmed him at the same time. He didn't want a repeat of last night—or did he? Last night had been enough to flip his mind several times over.

Actually, since the morning he'd showed up to help Catherine and Maggie remodel Robbie's private hangout, his emotions had been batting back and forth like a tennis ball at Wimbledon. Theory and conjecture had become mischievous, prank-playing reality—sometimes a bit too real. He'd known the sisters only a short time, but he felt as if they'd been through a war together, or at least a battle. They were comrades exploring unknown and possibly dangerous territory, and the shared adventure brought them closer than mere casual friends.

In Catherine's case, Robbie had brought them a good deal closer—uncomfortably so. Since last night, Tom had been having trouble regarding pretty Catherine Potter with simple comradeship. When she had fainted, he'd suffered an alarming jolt of concern, and when he'd finally left the house some hours later, he hadn't wanted to leave at all. His feelings at the time had been downright ungentlemanly, to tell the truth. And they'd stuck with him through the night and morning, goading him to dig out these histories, which at first he'd intended to give to Catherine next time she was in the store. Then he'd thought to phone her and tell her he had them. And finally he'd needled himself into showing up at Robin's Nest, unannounced, only hours after he'd left.

Catherine's odd behavior wasn't helping his unsettled feelings. She wasn't possessed. Tom was quite sure of that. He thought after last night he could recognize Robbie peering out through Catherine's usually diffident blue eyes. But she wasn't quite herself, either.

He decided the simplest thing to do would be to ask

her. Just a simple question. Yet, looking into her some-what anxious, wonderfully bright blue eyes, he stammered several times before he managed to get the words out of his mouth. "Uh . . . uh . . . Catherine? Are you feeling yourself this morning?"

She spread her hands in mute apology. "I'm sorry, Tom. Robbie was whispering in my ear."

He gave Catherine a wary look. "What was she whispering?"

"You don't want to know," she told him with a grimace.

"I don't?" Somehow the subject of ghosts seemed less fascinating than simply watching the play of expressions on Catherine's face. She was disturbed about something. This might be the time to tactfully broach the idea that had come to him in the night—not the rather lurid ideas involving him and Catherine alone between the bookstacks of his store, but the one involving Robbie. He sat back down and tried to look composed. "You know, Catherine, maybe if we discovered more about Robbie and her history, we might find a clue about why she sticks around with such tenacity. If we knew that, we might be able to persuade her to leave."

Catherine looked dejected as she dropped down beside him. The sultry manner she'd affected earlier was gone, but the magnetism of her nearness was not. "I've grown to like Robbie, I think. I know that sounds loony. But she grows on you after a while. I'm not sure I want to see her tossed out of her place."

Tom started to put a hand on her arm, but stopped himself. The gesture seemed very natural, but after last night, Catherine was sure to interpret it wrong. "We wouldn't be tossing her out. In helping her to move on, we'd be doing her a favor."

"What if she really wants to stay?"

"If she really wants to stay, no power short of heaven will make her go, Catherine. It wouldn't hurt to do some in-depth research and then decide."

"I guess not," she sighed.

"I thought I might go down to Phoenix, to the state archives and genealogical library. I might be able to find out something about Miss Roberta Rowe that would help us—and her."

"You're going to Phoenix?" Catherine sounded rather plaintive.

"Only for a couple of days."

"Oh."

"Actually, I've been thinking that Robbie would be excellent as the subject of a paper for the *Journal of the American Society for Psychical Research*. If you and Maggie don't mind."

Catherine's face went blank.

"I realize Maggie doesn't want that kind of publicity for the inn. But publishing in the *Journal* is hardly the same thing as trumpeting the news in the *New York Times*. Or even the *Arizona Republic*."

Catherine merely bit her lip.

"Actually, Catherine, why don't you come with me to Phoenix?" The thought had leapt to his lips almost without passing through his brain. Was he insane? Tom asked himself, but his mouth went on talking. "You could help me with the research, and depending on what we find, you can decide for yourself what we should do."

Catherine's eyes were wide, her full lips parted in surprise. Tom didn't know where the invitation had come from—some imp that was playing havoc with his good sense. But wherever it had come from, it was suddenly very important. He held his breath, willing her to say yes at the same time he feared she would say yes.

"Come with you to Phoenix?" she breathed.

His heart pounded. "How about it? Can Maggie spare you from the inn for a couple of days?"

"I don't know. The weekend's coming up. Still . . ."

Hope climbed a notch.

"It's about time Maggie learned to cook. Don't you think? There's a time in every woman's life where she needs to become domestic. After all, what's she going to do if I go back to teaching this fall?"

Hope soared. "That's right. Besides, we'll be back Saturday evening or Sunday."

"I'll go! It'll be fun."

Tom almost keeled over at the prospect.

Catherine did a jig around the kitchen. "He's coming back at three!" she told George. "Do you believe it? Phoenix with Tom! I don't believe it! Do you believe it?"

Robbie blinked into sight lounging on the counter. *"Nice work in there, honey. You didn't bungle it as bad as I thought you would. But then, he's an easy mark."*

"He's not a mark." She gave the ghost a beatific smile. "Maggie will be back by opening time. I've got to pack. And write Maggie a note. Be nice to Maggie while I'm gone. I won't be here to defend her against you."

Still smiling, she waltzed out of the kitchen and down the basement stairs.

Robbie snorted to herself as Catherine deserted her. *"Be nice to Maggie,"* she mimicked in a vexed tone. *"Why isn't anyone around here nice to me?"*

•   •   •

When Maggie and Colby returned from their picnic, they found a sparkling clean house, a pile of books, stamped "Matthews," on the living room couch, and a note on the dining room table. When Maggie read the note, her brows jumped upward in surprise.

"Catherine's gone to Phoenix with Tom Matthews!"

"Good for Catherine." Colby put the sack of picnic garbage on the kitchen counter. "Who exactly is Tom Matthews? You mentioned him before once or twice."

"He's a guy who owns a bookstore in Cottonwood. A ghost addict, you might say."

Colby gave her a bemused glance. "A ghost addict?"

"Yes. He reads about them, thinks about them, probably even dreams about them, knowing Tom. And you don't need to look at me that way, Colby Drake. You might think ghosts are a bunch of hooey, but a lot of very educated, intelligent folks think they're real."

"I'm sure they do," he said mildly.

"But I don't know what got into Catherine. She has a crush on Tom, but it's not like her to throw caution to the wind and trot off with some guy."

Colby handed her one of the iced teas he'd poured. "You think he has nefarious designs?"

She had to chuckle, trying to picture Tom Matthews in the role of lecher. "Nothing like that. Tom's about as harmless as men come, I think. But poor Catherine falls in love at the drop of a hat—usually with the hero of a novel or movie, but this time she's got her heart set on a flesh-and-blood man."

"How unwise of her. Flesh-and-blood men are sometimes less than heroic."

Maggie gave Colby a look, but he just grinned.

"I don't want Cat setting herself up to get hurt. And

I'll bet Robbie had something to do with this." She raised her voice, as if volume made any difference to a ghost's hearing. "Didn't you, Madam Busybody."

She sent Colby an arch glance that challenged him to comment. Instead, he dodged around her glass of iced tea to plant a fast kiss on her mouth.

The swift, gentle attack of his lips, so unexpected and so quickly over, made her feel as if her eyes might cross. She struggled to project casual composure. "That was nice, but what was it for?"

For an instant fire flickered in his eyes, gone as quickly as the kiss. "Just for being you, Mags. For worrying about your sister. For still believing that any man under ninety-nine is harmless after what you've been through."

A blush warmed her cheeks, as much for what she'd seen in his eyes as for what she heard. "Catherine's more innocent than I am. She can still be hurt."

"And you can't, I suppose?"

Maggie didn't answer. She could be hurt—especially if she forgot the lessons of the past and let herself go ape over a certain charming reporter who took her breath away.

"But of course you can be hurt. And you think your only defense is to slam the door on me when you think I'm laying siege to your heart. It's less scary surrendering your body than your soul, isn't it, love?"

The endearment made Maggie's heart jump. It was, she told herelf, just a casual slip of Colby's tongue—as much nonsense as the rest of his prattle, as evidenced by the puckish grin that took the weight from his words.

"But someday you'll realize what a harmless, true-blue sort of guy I really am." He gave her an innocent smile. "I'll bet you have an empty room or two available tonight, don't you? That is, if I'm back in your good graces, O Silent One."

Maggie had let herself sink into a near-trance just looking at him, but his inquiry shook her free. "Sorry. You seemed to be providing your own answers. I didn't want to break in."

"That's one of the things we reporters do best, in case you hadn't noticed—make up our own answers."

"I have noticed." She gave him a comic grimace. It was the first time that she'd been able to refer with any lightness at all to what had happened to her.

"And your good graces? Am I back in them?"

"As if you didn't already know, you're in and into just about anything of mine that you please, Mr. Drake."

"Now, that sounds promising."

"Take any room you want."

"Thanks." He gave her a smile that could turn an iron maiden into a molten puddle and slid his arms around her middle. His hands landed in strategic positions on her rear end. "And about those other things of yours that I'm into. You'd better put down the tea."

"Why?" she asked with mock innocence.

"You'll spill it when I kiss you."

"You're asking a lot."

"I'll ask more a little later, if you're lucky."

She couldn't hit him because one hand held the tea glass and the other was trapped against his chest. The devil had planned it that way, Maggie was sure.

"The luck would be all yours," she declared archly, "and don't count on it."

But she put down the glass anyway, and laughed with him as they melted together. The kiss was warm rather than hot, more comfortable than lustful. All in all, it fit her mood perfectly. Did he have a talent for reading people, Maggie wondered, or was it just her he knew so well? Maybe there was indeed something truly special between them.

The kiss might have grown into something more if the doorbell hadn't chimed. They broke apart, and Maggie looked ruefully at her watch.

"Showtime. You'd better go claim your room before the tourists beat you to it."

Robin's Nest had had no reservations for that night, but they ended up entertaining two parties of guests anyway. A middle-aged lady from Pennsylvania took the Blue Room, and a young couple from Prescott—both teachers on summer vacation—fell in love with the newly decorated Green Room, formerly the notorious Red Room. Maggie was very nervous about renting out Robbie's favorite haunt, and she tried to discourage them, saying there had been some trouble with the bathroom and that the room was frequently chilly at night. They were absolutely enamored of the view from the window, however, and assured her she'd hear no complaints from them. Short of telling them the ghost of a nineteenth-century madam might join them in bed, there was no way to discourage them, and Maggie wondered if even that would do it. As she left them to unpack and settle in, she sent a silent plea to Robbie for a bit of ghostly tolerance and consideration.

The evening went smoothly. Catherine had left enough fresh-baked cookies and pretzel-nut-cereal snack mix to last several days. Maggie had breakfast all planned. She was even eager to stretch her talents and discover what she could do in this arena, where before she had regarded kitchen duties as drudgery. In fact, Maggie was feeling quite positive about a number of things that evening. Her whole attitude was up. Searching for the reason, she reflected, would likely ruin the mood, but very little self-examination was required to know part of the reason was staying in the Yellow Room tonight—and for several nights to come, Maggie assumed.

She took a pound of bacon from the freezer and put it in the refrigerator to thaw overnight. A suspicious study of the shelves and drawers proved that for now, at least, no ghost tricks sullied the fridge. They had three dozen eggs, more than enough for a couple of days. Fresh mushrooms, tomatoes, and red bell peppers were clean and crisp, waiting to be cut for an omelet. The guests would have to do without Catherine's special breakfast soups—Maggie wasn't going to even attempt cold raspberry soup with a hint of almond liqueur that her sister prepared to perfection. Catherine's fresh baked bread with homemade marmalade and strawberry preserves would make up for it.

Next chore on Maggie's agenda was watering the various flowerpots and the garden. The guests were occupied entertaining themselves—watching television in the sunroom and playing checkers in the living room. They didn't require her attention. Colby was in his room doing something or other. He'd offered to take her to dinner after the guests had checked in, but she'd had too much to do at the house. She hadn't seen him since, but the anticipation of a late night get-together brought a smile to her face. Warning bells went off in her heart, but she ignored them.

Watering took a good hour, and it had to be done daily. Compared to much of Arizona—the desert to the south and the high rim country to the north—Jerome had a mild climate, but the dry heat of summer could suck the life from flowers and a struggling vegetable garden. Every evening Maggie dragged the hose and sprayer to every flowerpot, vine, and tree. This evening, however, was the first time she'd felt like humming as she did it. She even sang under her breath and did a little twirl in between the big flower barrels by the garage.

When she got to the yard, George meowed at her from a branch of the big ash tree.

"Looking for a handsome reporter to fetch you down?" Maggie asked the cat.

"Meow!" George replied indignantly.

"Yes, I know. He was yours first. But to be honest, puss, I think he was using you to get to me."

"Meeeehhhr!"

An evening breeze ruffled the leaves of the trees and played across the yard in little whirlwinds that hinted of otherworldly mischief. Maggie scrutinized the yard suspiciously. "If you're lurking in the bushes somewhere, Robbie, just behave yourself. I've had enough of your hijinks to last a whole lifetime."

Robbie was there, Maggie suspected. She felt her in the air, the breeze, the itchy feeling between her shoulder blades that told her someone was watching.

"I'm still very angry with you for last night," she told the unseen ghost. "That was unforgivable. You have no right to go dancing around in someone else's body. I can manage my own love life, thank you very much!"

She felt just a bit guilty about that remark. Would she have ever connected with Colby without Robbie's rude push?

"I know you were mad about the séance," she told the ghost in a more conciliatory tone. "But is it any wonder that no one wants you around? You sing in the middle of the night, turn both me and Cat into puppets, run amuck in the kitchen—of course we want to get rid of you! And this moving into people's heads has to stop."

She moved the sprayer to the flowering pomegranate tree. The evening had grown darker in more ways than just the approach of night. Some of the brightness of her own mood had dimmed. Robbie was hurt. Maggie could feel it. She shouldn't give a damn, but she did.

Maggie lugged the hose to the artichoke plant, soaked it good, then sent the spray over the bed of poppies.

"I tell you what, Robbie," she said after a few minutes of thought. "We can do a deal, you and I. You've pretty much got what you wanted, right? Colby is still here. He and I are . . . well . . . together for a little while. If you can just mind your own business, stay out of my hair—and my head—and keep away from the guests, I'll stop trying to give you the boot. You want to stick around? Fine. Stick around. Have a ball spying on everyone and anyone. But keep to yourself. You did it for a hundred years. You can do it again."

There was no answer, but that certain heaviness in the air didn't depart.

"Think about it," Maggie urged. "Peaceful coexistence. It worked for the U.S. and Soviets. It can work for us."

Of course, the U.S. and Soviets together had several times brought the world to the brink of annihilation. Maggie could imagine Robin's Nest going up in a spectral mushroom cloud, taking Jerome and the Verde Valley with it.

By eleven o'clock that night, the lady from Pennsylvania was fast asleep in her room. The schoolteachers were prowling the late-night haunts in town, and everything in the kitchen was ready for breakfast to be prepared the next morning. Maggie made sure the back door was unlocked for her wandering guests, then headed for the basement apartment and bed. She hesitated on the first stair, however. Temptation beckoned her upward—up the hall stairway to the bedrooms on the second floor. Specifically, the Yellow Room and Colby Drake's bed. She hadn't seen him all evening, and she was trying very hard to not be miffed about it.

What odd twists and turns a human heart could take. A few days ago, Maggie would have sworn she wanted to never lay eyes on Colby Drake until Judgment Day, when presumably he would be sucked straight to hell with the rest of the news media and gossipmongers. Yet tonight she felt deprived after not seeing him, talking to him, touching him for only a few hours. She was a moron, Maggie told herself. Besides, odds were he'd steal down to her apartment later tonight. He knew Catherine was gone and Maggie had the apartment to herself. There was no need for her to go knocking at his door, pleading for attention like a dog.

Besides, she didn't really care all that much if he came or not. This thing with Colby was a fling, a casual friendship with a bit of spice added. It was nothing to brood over, nothing to worry about, wonder about, chew her nails about. Nothing like that. She would get in bed and go peacefully to sleep. If he came, fine. If he didn't, fine.

So Maggie went to bed. She wore her usual oversized T-shirt, but soon got up and changed into a short, lacy nightgown. Back in bed, she lay there, staring into the dark, trying to think about Catherine and Tom, Robbie, the account books, the water heater, which was still making noises—anything that didn't have to do with Colby Drake. Attila and Hannibal chattered to each other in bird talk. George jumped onto the bed and curled into a ball at her feet. The schoolteachers came in quietly and climbed up to their room. The hall clock upstairs chimed midnight, then one. If Maggie listened hard enough she could even hear the ticking. But no footsteps sounded on the basement stairs.

He was waiting long enough, Maggie complained to herself. What was he doing in his room that was more important than being with her? Sleeping?

Fifteen

Colby woke to bright morning sun pouring into the Yellow Room and spreading across the floor, the walls, and the bed with buttery warmth. It was a good day to be alive, he decided—something that didn't usually occur to him first thing upon awakening. But this morning was different. He'd spent the day before with a lovely, beguiling woman, he'd spent the evening brainstorming some fine journalism, and the night had brought one of the best, most restful sleeps he'd had in months. Better still, the aroma of sizzling bacon was drifting upstairs and making his mouth water.

He got out of bed and stretched elaborately, looked out the window at the hillside that climbed up to the mountains, and grinned. Life was good, and it looked as if it was only going to get better.

By the time he'd showered and descended the stairs, the aroma of sizzling bacon had acquired a hint of char. And when he poked his head in the kitchen, the look Maggie threw him seemed a bit on the burned side as well.

"Good morning," he said cheerily.

The answer he got was an indistinct grunt.

"Breakfast smells good," he lied. Maggie looked as though her morning needed a bit of sugarcoating.

"Breakfast!" she grumbled. "Half the bacon is burned. The other half is limp. Tell me how I did that when it was all cooked in the very same skillet!"

Colby didn't have the foggiest.

"The eggs are watery."

"A lot of people like them that way," he said tactfully.

"The sausage is crisp all the way through, and the muffins are . . . oh damn! The muffins!" She dashed to the other side of the kitchen and pulled open the oven door. Colby fanned aside some of the smoke and looked inside. "They're just nice and dark brown. Isn't that how muffins are supposed to be cooked?"

She gave him a sour look as she pulled on a mitt to take the muffin pan from the rack. "You're very cheerful this morning."

"I am, aren't I?" He grinned.

"Is that what getting a good night's sleep does for you?"

The edge in her voice had sharpened on more than a chaotic morning in the kitchen, and Colby was unsure just how to respond. "I did get a good night's sleep—among other things."

"Wonderful."

Oops. He recognized that tone. Something was definitely bothering the lady, Colby decided. What had he done now? Yesterday they'd spent a wonderful day together. They'd laughed a bit, made love a lot, argued a little—but the arguing had made them even more intimate with each other, or so he'd believed. Each had bared a bit of soul to the other.

Colby thought that was what women liked—intimacy, sharing traumas, fears, emotions, talking openly about feelings. But then, Maggie wasn't like most women he knew. And Colby would be the first to admit that he understood women about as well as he understood quantum physics. Both were equally complex, as far as he was concerned.

Maggie slammed the muffin pan down upon the metal worktable, yanked open the fridge, and grabbed the juice pitcher so abruptly that the juice threatened to slosh over the lip.

"Uh . . . could I help with something?"

"Do I look as if I need help with something?"

A loaded question if Colby had ever heard one. "I could set the table, or maybe make toast."

The look in her eyes let him know he *was* toast. Since he was apparently already in deep trouble, Colby decided to make a departure from his usual approach and try honesty.

"Are you angry with me, Maggie?"

"No. Should I be?"

"You sound angry."

Maggie sent him a look, then wilted and sighed. She plopped down in the chair beside the worktable. "I'm sorry, Colby. I've had a rotten morning, as you can probably tell. And . . ." She looked sheepish. "I guess I sort of expected to see you last night."

Now there was a piece of honesty for you, Colby reflected. Maggie was indeed an unusual woman. And here he'd thought when she'd declined dinner, she'd been sending a signal that she needed a bit of space.

He grimaced. "Miscue on my part. And to think I spent last night working!"

"Working?"

"I do still work for a living—occasionally. Some of

the things you said yesterday got the wheels in my mind turning. I put together an outline for a column on Sweeney and Kilbourne." He grinned. "I haven't been so inspired in quite a while."

This announcement didn't meet with much enthusiasm. In fact, the tightening around her eyes and the sudden tension of her mouth signaled even more trouble.

"Colby, none of what I told you yesterday was on the record. How could you think that it was?"

"I knew that. I'm not going to quote you, or even mention you. But you gave me some leads that I can follow up. I have to do some research. I'm going to take off today, as a matter of fact. I managed to get plane reservations to D.C. this afternoon. Four o'clock."

She stared at him for a moment, and in that stare he could see the gathering storm clouds, complete with lightning and thunder. Apparently he'd put his foot in it. Again.

"You're leaving."

"Well, not forever."

"To do research on Jim Sweeney based on what I said yesterday."

"You expect me to ignore an opportunity like that?"

She got up, marched to the buffet in the dining room, and started grabbing plates from the shelf. He hoped it wasn't expensive china, because the way she banged them onto the table was going to reduce her inventory of dishes if she wasn't careful.

"You have no ethics at all, you know that?"

"What?" He grabbed a plate out of her hand and set it on the table—just so she wouldn't throw it at him. "I have no ethics? Compared to what? Jack Kilbourne, the saintly paragon of expediency and kickbacks from his friends' construction companies?"

"You're just assuming the worst."

"That's my job. I'm a reporter." He grabbed a handful of silverware from the drawer and banged it onto the table. "I'm certainly not assuming the worst about what he did to you. I know what he did, and so do you."

"There's enough been written about that. Too much."

"I agree, but there's not nearly enough been written about the more germane subjects of his crooked nest-feathering at Toledo's expense."

She made a rude sound and flounced back into the kitchen. Colby followed, shaking a fork in her direction. "Don't you think the public has a right to know something about the character and ethics of a man who wants to hold this country's highest elected position? Maggie? Don't you?"

She whirled on him, her back to the counter and her knuckles white as she gripped the edge. "What about *your* character and ethics?"

Colby lowered his fork. "Maggie," he began in a less argumentative tone, "we're not talking about me. Or you."

"Yes we are. Don't you see? I thought we were friends. More than friends. But you're still using me to get Jack Kilbourne."

She was right in a way. He was torn between placating Maggie and being honest. Thwarting Jack Kilbourne's presidential goals was, as far as Colby was concerned, a worthwhile public service project—his little contribution to making the world a more decent place to live. He couldn't understand why Maggie was still loyal to a man who had caused her so much pain.

His crusade against Kilbourne had acquired a personal flavor, Colby realized. Part of his fervor to nail the bastard was jealousy. Kilbourne had possessed Maggie. As if that wasn't enough reason for a man to be jealous, Jack still had Maggie's admiration and loyalty. And Colby didn't—at least not in the way that the governor did. What's more, the sonovabitch had taken Maggie's admiration and loyalty and flushed it down the toilet. For that he not only deserved to be hung by his toenails—or other parts more picturesque—but he ought to be inducted into the fool's hall of fame. But how did Colby communicate that to a pigheaded woman who wouldn't listen?

"Maggie . . ." He let a long-suffering sigh escape as he regarded the stony set of her face. "Jack Kilbourne is a man who deserves to be revealed for what he is. Of all the people in the world, you should know best what he is—an ambitious, self-seeking, unethical shithead."

Her chin tilted up and locked into firing attitude. "You're a fine one to call Kilbourne unethical! You have the ethics of a tabloid dirt-peddler."

"Jesus Mary Lord have mercy! You are unreasonable, you know that! You think everything the press does is wrong and everyone they go after is an innocent victim. Get real, Maggie. The world isn't black and white, you know? Most of us are shades in between."

She turned, giving him her back, dismissing him in favor of a box of biscuit mix she took from the cupboard.

"You want ethics?" he shot at her back. "I'll give you ethics. Wait here."

Muttering to himself with every step, he shot up the stairs and into his room. There he dug through his briefcase for the hard copy of the column he had intended to use to blackmail Maggie. No, not blackmail. Blackmail was such an ugly word, and it fit too well with Maggie's accusation. He hadn't intended blackmail. He'd just wanted a little leverage to budge her from stubbornness. And after their night together, he'd scarcely even remembered that he'd written it.

The column was buried beneath the notes he'd made the previous night. Colby pulled it out, headed for the door, then on second thought went back to grab his laptop as well. Might as well be thorough. The lady wanted a knight in pristine armor. That's what he would give her, by damn!

Back in the kitchen, Maggie had a rolling pin in one hand and a biscuit cutter in the other. Colby figured he'd better make this good. She could do as much damage to him with those things as she'd done to the biscuit dough.

He set the laptop on the worktable and waved the printed pages in front of her. "Look!"

She regarded him warily. "What's that?"

"Read." He took the potential weapons from her hands and gave her the column. She scanned down the first page and started to go red. He took it from her before she could reach the boiling point.

"Observe!" he commanded, then flamboyantly ripped the pages in two, and then ripped again, and again, until all that was left was confetti. "And more!" he declared, gesturing to the laptop. "First we open it, then we turn it on." He demonstrated with a flourish. "Now we call up the file named Mpotter. See? There it is. The same thing that you just read."

She gave him a look people reserve for the mentally deranged, but at his insistent gesture, she read.

"Same article?" he asked.

"Yes."

"Okay. Now we do Control Delete. Like this. And presto? The machine asks if we really, really want to delete this file. And I say yes." He punched the key with grim finality. "Gone. Kaput! That was an excellent column. My editor would have loved it, and loved me because I wrote it. It was accurate, well researched, well written, and just oozed professionalism. But it's gone. I never was going to print it, really. When I drove back to Jerome, I was going to show it to you in hopes you might give me something more relevant to write about."

Maggie started to open her mouth, no doubt to fire off a scathing reply, but Colby didn't give her the chance. He took a breath and plunged on. "I ended up not even doing that, as it turned out, because I realized you would be hurt that I'd done it. So I didn't use it. And now it's gone. Days worth of work. Because I'm not after you, Maggie. I'm after Kilbourne. And if you want to cling to your illusions that he's Saint Jack, then that's what you'll do. But don't accuse me of being the villain here, because I'm not."

Her jaw fell open, but she closed it again.

"I am not a sensationalist. I do not use my friends—or my lovers—to their detriment and my gain. And I am not going to apologize for my profession or my manner of pursuing it just because you think everything the press does is crap. If you think about it, you're doing the very same thing to the press—and to me—that you accuse them of doing to you. 'I've made up my mind, so don't bother me with the truth.' Does that sound familiar?"

"I don't—"

"You do!" he snapped. "Now, I'm going to pack my things and go back to Virginia for a while. But I'll be back, because I think we've made a special connection between us—in spite of the fact that the fireworks haven't all been good. I promise you two things. Whatever I write about Kilbourne, I'll keep your name out of print. And when the job is done, I'll come back to Jerome. Then maybe we'll be able to decide what's really between us."

Her eyes had grown big, but her face had lost none of its rigid set. "If you decide to come back, Mr. Drake, feel free to call for a reservation."

He shook his head. "I'm not giving up on you, love. Don't you give up on me. You never can tell—I could be the best thing that's happened to you since sliced bread." He grinned. "And vice versa."

He saw her swallow hard as he headed toward the hall stairs. Her voice stopped him on the first step.

"Colby?"

"Yes, Maggie?"

"Go stick your swollen head in a printing press."

Yes indeed, Maggie thought to herself as she piled the dirty breakfast dishes into a sink full of sudsy hot water, that had certainly been an intelligent, thoughtful, mature way to say good-bye. Colby Drake brought out the worst in her—and the best. He made her carp like a fishwife and then inspired her to laugh, love, and live life in the manner that it should be lived. Damn, but he was a frustrating man!

Frustrating, and gone. Very gone. And Maggie felt very alone. Catherine was away. After a very lackluster breakfast, the guests had checked out. And Colby was gone. Gone, gone, gone. What possessed her to be sorry the worm was gone? He was hopeless, another entry on Maggie's list of losers. He wanted Jack Kilbourne's head on a platter, and to achieve that end, he would lie, snoop, blackmail, and pretend to be smitten with a lady gorilla if need be.

"Damn it all!" She wadded the wet dishrag into a ball and threw it against the wall. It connected with a satisfying splat. She wished Colby had been standing against the wall as a target. Wouldn't he be surprised to get a soapy, greasy rag right between the eyes?

The image made her laugh. There he went again, moving her from wrath to laughter, and he wasn't even there. She had to admit that her pique was as much inspired by his neglect as his journalism. First he'd been plotting against Kilbourne all night instead of making love to her—a much more worthy pursuit. Then he breezily announced he was going back to Virginia when just the day before he'd been prattling on about believing in love and the special connection they had. The creep. She'd expected him to stick around a few days at least. A love affair wasn't much fun with only one of the lovers present.

Maybe he would be back, and maybe he wouldn't. After the way she regularly lost her temper with him, called him names, and generally behaved like a snotty, spoiled child, she wouldn't blame him if he never darkened her door again. And she shouldn't care, because he was a reporter, and a cheeky one at that. But reporter or not, frustrating or not, he'd gotten under her skin—and into a few other places as well.

Maggie smiled wryly and looked around. "It's just you and me today, Robbie. The place is empty. No guests for you to annoy, no man for you to throw in my face."

The silence of emptiness answered her.

"Well, maybe you're gone as well." She gave the emptiness an injured pout. "You didn't have to take my little lecture in the yard so seriously."

She listened hard, both with her ears and her mind, but there was no reply.

"Well, damn!" She went back to scubbing the pots. "No lover, no sister, no guests, and not even a ghost to talk to. Damn!"

The state archives in Phoenix was an unlikely place for romance. In fact, much to Catherine's disappointment, there wasn't much romance going on between the stacks of dusty records, the file cabinets, the microfilm and microfiche, and the computer stations. Ninety-nine percent of the men in the world, when they ask a woman to accompany them on an overnight outing that involves a hotel, have but one thing in mind. But Catherine wasn't with a man included in that ninety-nine percent of the male population. She was with Tom Matthews, who was hot on the trail of a ghost mystery and hadn't taken his attention from the files since they'd walked through the door. And when they weren't physically in the building, he was still there in spirit. He talked of nothing but of birth records, census records, death certificates, marriage certificates—anything he could find to trace the history of Roberta Rowe and her descendants.

They had arrived late the afternoon before and checked into the Radisson in Tempe—a thirty-minute drive from the capitol building that housed the archives. The Radisson was a good deal fancier—not to mention more exorbitant—than what Catherine was used to, but Tom had insisted on paying their expenses. It had been too late to go to the archives when they arrived, so they had enjoyed the pool and the lounge, then a good dinner at the hotel restaurant.

The whole evening was so aboveboard and innocent

that Catherine could have cried from absolute frustration. Not only had Tom registered them in separate rooms, but during their time together he'd not made one move on her. In the pool they had talked of the inn and his bookstore, his sister and her little day-campers, Catherine's mother Virginia and her penchant for trying to run Catherine's and Maggie's lives. During dinner they had talked of ghosts. Surprise! Catherine should have known, she chided herself glumly. She was trying to put Robbie's good advice to use—applying makeup with a freer hand, wearing cologne, dressing in cotton slacks and a knit top rather than her usual jeans and T-shirt. She'd batted her eyelashes until her eyelids were sore, brushed subtly against Tom until it was no longer subtle, showed interest in his store, his family, his likes and dislikes. And in spite of feeling like a tramp, she'd thrown back her shoulders (*"Be proud of your breasts,"* Robbie had said. *"There's nothing that gets a man's attention like a nice set of bosoms"*), let her hips sway when she walked, and taken a curling iron to her hair. And while she did catch Tom giving her some curious looks during dinner, they weren't the enamored, lustful looks she was hoping for.

And today, for all that they were working together on the same project, in the same building, and spoke frequently about the research, they could have been on different planets for all the notice Tom took of how she looked or smelled or acted. He had his nose buried in the microfiche and his heart focused on the past.

Catherine sighed and rubbed eyes tired from staring at microfilm, remembering too late that she'd applied mascara that morning. She cursed under her breath and peered at her indistinct reflection in the reader screen to discover if she now had raccoon eyes. If she did, they didn't show up on the screen.

Something else showed up on the screen, however—
something she had missed in the torpor of viewing page
after page of boring records from the past. Laura Tolliver Pilford's name jumped out at her.

"Tom!" she whispered in as loud a voice as she
dared in this librarylike setting. "Tom, I found something."

He came up beside her, put a friendly hand on her
shoulder, and looked at the screen. How Catherine
wished his touch were more than just friendly.

"Laura Tolliver Pilford," he read cheerfully. "That's
Robbie's daughter. Divorced! Oh my! Back then, that
was very serious stuff."

"I understand it's no lark these days, either. That's
why it's important to recognize the right person when
he or she comes along."

He refused to be distracted from the subject at hand.
"Look at the date."

"What about it?"

"Just six months before this date, Laura's second
daughter was born. Imagine divorcing your husband
when you have a six-month-old baby. Especially back
then. Must have been pretty grim."

"At least she had her children. That's important."

"Those daughters of hers weren't real lucky, either.
The older girl died birthing an illegitimate baby, and
the younger had a husband run off with another
woman after she'd borne him three children."

"You found record of that in the archives?"

"Old newspaper article about a property dispute between husband and wife. Newspapers were interested
in the racy stuff back then, just as they are now."

"Quite a string of descendants our Robbie had.
They could qualify for one of those melodramatic family sagas that are so popular."

"A pretty sad saga these ladies had, if you ask me," Tom said quietly. "Why don't we get some lunch? I'm starving."

Well, what do you know? Catherine thought. He's human after all. Too bad his hormones weren't as human as his stomach.

Lunch was on a park bench, eating tacos from a Mexican food vendor whose place of business—a little cart with an umbrella attached—rolled along the sidewalk. The food wasn't bad. Homemade, Catherine thought, because no one prepared green chile sauce quite so spicy as a Hispanic matron who still fixed the traditional recipes. The teenage boy who'd sold them the food had been all impish smiles, no doubt wishing he could see the gringos' faces when they bit into his mother's jalapeno-laced sauce.

"Steam is going to blow from my ears any minute," Catherine told Tom.

"Mm! Good, though." Sauce ran down Tom's chin and fingers. He mopped the mess with a napkin and smiled that heartstopping, boyish smile of his. So unaffected. So cheerful. So oblivious, Catherine grumbled silently.

"What do you think of what we've found so far?" he asked. "You know Robbie a lot better than I do. Has any pattern jumped out at you? Anything ring a bell that Robbie might have mentioned? Something that she might be really worried about, or feel guilty about, or think she had to stick around to fix?"

Was Robbie all he could think about? Was Catherine totally uninteresting, or was Tom Matthews just a numbskull?

When she didn't answer him, Tom continued. "The whole family seems cursed, don't they? All Robbie's descendants are female—have you noticed? They all had wretched marriages and wretched lives, if you can read such a thing into dry archives records."

Catherine felt a bit cursed herself. Why did she care for this man? He had a one-track mind, and the track definitely was not set on romance. To Tom Matthews, she was the person who'd given him his first acquaintance with a real ghost, not a woman who was offering her heart.

Catherine wondered if shedding forty or so pounds would get his attention but she doubted it. A man noticed a woman because of her looks, but he stayed with her because of who she was. Tom had noticed her because of her ghost, but a knock over the head with a two-by-four wouldn't make him notice who she was, or love who she was—the nitwit. This was certainly not the kind of love story she concocted in her imagination in the dark loneliness of her bed, or a heart-thumping romance of the sort played on the screen by Bogie and Bacall, or Hepburn and Tracy. So far, in fact, Potter and Matthews were not a romantic item at all.

Back at the archives, Tom once again buried himself in the files and left Catherine at a microfiche reader. By then she was almost as steamed at herself as she was at Tom. She had the moxie of limp spaghetti, Catherine decided with disgust. How did she expect to be noticed when she let people take advantage of her, when she accepted with such puppyish gratitude any morsel of attention thrown her way, when her repertoire of feminine wiles came from the ghost of a long-dead whore, for pity's sake? Was that pathetic? Was she pathetic?

Here in the archives she felt surrounded by the dead. Dead children of dead parents. People who had lived their lives, who grew up, married, loved, had children, enjoyed triumphs, endured heartaches, and then moved on. Catherine felt as dead as the records she searched through, as dried-out as the musty files that held Tom's attention.

But that was going to end. The sad fate of Robbie's descendants made Catherine realize how precious were the few short years of a person's life, and how easily happiness could evade a the best efforts to possess it. It was a lesson she took to heart. Catherine Potter would be a doormat no longer. She was going to live life to the fullest, and no opportunity would slip through her fingers. She was going to live, by God, even if she had to make an ass out of herself to do it. Just see if she didn't!

Tom Matthews had earned straight A's in both high school and college, not because he possessed genius, but because he learned early in life to focus intensely on whatever work was at hand. His concentration was sharp as a stiletto. Distraction seldom penetrated his mental defenses.

Some distractions, however, were more insidious than others. Some distractions snuck up on a man to dull concentration and dissolve focus. It was happening to him. For the first time in memory Tom Matthews couldn't keep his mind on what he was doing. Fascinated as he was by Robbie Rowe, his thoughts still insisted upon wandering. Fantasies popped into his mind uninvited. He caught himself staring into space, or worse still, staring with unheeding eyes at a document while his mind's eye traveled to the microfiche cubicles where Catherine Potter sat.

There was the source of his confusion. Catherine Potter. The night of the séance had opened his eyes to her appeal as something more than just a likable, interesting person. Suddenly she was a woman, a beautiful, warm, funny woman who seemed at the same time fragile as a dandelion and strong as an oak. Ever since that night, his awareness had grown. He noticed new charms every time he looked at her. The sheen of her hair occupied his mind for a whole day. The softness of her skin distracted him for more than an hour. Her smile could light up a whole room. Her laughter was finer music that the New York Philharmonic. And in a less platonic vein, the curve of her neck made him want to taste the spot right between her collarbones, and then run his mouth up to just beneath her ear—and then down . . . Oh, no! He wouldn't let his mind go there. If he started thinking in that direction, he'd never get his mental faculties back together.

Tom didn't have a great deal of experience with women. It wasn't that they didn't attract him. He was as interested as any other man. But the modern singles game was more of a chore than a delight. Dating was hardly worth it, considering the nuances, the unspoken rules, the complex give and take of a relationship. His mother had raised him to be a gentleman, but he wasn't sure that women expected gentlemanly behavior anymore. He wasn't sure what they expected.

One thing he knew for sure. Catherine trusted him to be a friend. Why else would she have agreed to come with him on this trip? He was trying very hard to be that friend, to not reveal the more serious interest he had conceived. He didn't want to scare her away. Let her be secure in his friendship, he thought. Let her know that his affection was for the whole person, not just the gleaming blond hair, the bright green eyes, the curves that promised paradise. Women needed that sort of assurance, didn't they?

Tom closed the file he was perusing and glanced

toward the microfilm cubicles. He could see Catherine's foot beneath the cubicle partition. She had delicate feet. Beautifully shaped feet. Feet with toes he would like to—damn! He stopped himself with a silent curse.

A clerk set another pile of files and record books on the table in front of him. "I thought these might have some bearing on the family line you're tracing."

"Thanks," Tom said with a sigh.

For the next half hour he forced himself to knuckle down to work. He added to his notes, stared at a couple of birth records, found a death certificate that he'd been looking for, then added more to his notes. Scratching his head, he went over his notes again. Then again. Finally, he smiled. The smile became a grin, and it was all he could do to keep himself from shouting in triumph. Instead, he sprang to his feet and headed toward the cubicles to let Catherine know of his discovery.

"Catherine! Look at this!"

She looked up from her work, but the momentary brightness in her smile faded when he waved his open notebook for her attention. "Look what I've found! What I've deduced, actually, from putting together a couple of different lines of research. This is amazing."

"What's so amazing?"

"I think I know why Robbie . . . Catherine? Why are you looking at me like that?"

She rose from her chair and faced him with the air of Teddy Roosevelt about to charge up San Juan Hill. "You know what, Tom? I don't really care what you've discovered or what you've deduced."

"Uh . . . you don't?"

"I have something to say, Tom." She glanced around

and lowered her voice. But the intensity of emotion stayed the same. "And I think you should listen."

Something in her eyes made him want to sit down. He pulled over a chair from the adjacent cubicle. "Okay."

Catherine squared her shoulders and stiffened her jaw. "All right. Here goes. You're a very nice man, Tom Matthews, but let me tell you this. You are also a narrow-minded, tunnel-visioned idiot with upside-down priorities. You turn your hobby into an obsession, and it's downright unnatural for you to be so absorbed in a string of dead women that you can't see the very alive woman in front of you—the woman who . . . who has tons more to offer than those who've already lived out their lives and exist in this world only in microfilm and dusty files!"

Tom was speechless. He had to clench his jaw to keep it from dropping. And here he'd been thinking that Catherine was a shy flower who needed protection from his ungentlemanly lust.

"And I'll tell you something more, Tom Matthews! You're going to waste away to a shell of a man before you realize what's really important in life. You have so much potential to be an extraordinary human being, but you'll never realize that potential as long as your mind is stuck in the netherworld day in and day out— reading about ghosts, thinking about ghosts, hunting for ghosts. How can an educated, intelligent man like you allow an obsession to ruin your life? Don't you want a real life, with friends, a wife, family? Don't you think those things are more important than something you'll never really know the truth of until you're a ghost yourself? Don't you?"

He got up, looked down at her flushed face, and then blocked whatever else she was going to say with a kiss. Her lips were warm, parted in surprise, and tasted every bit as sweet as Tom had imagined. At first she stood perfectly still, stiff with the remnants of her anger, but she softened quickly. Tom didn't care if the other people in the room stared at them. Catherine felt so good in his arms that he might never let her go.

When he did finally draw back, her head swayed woozily. Her eyes were fuzzed with passion.

"I think I've found out what's important," he whispered in her ear. "Why don't we call it quits for the day and take ourselves a holiday."

Sixteen

Tom's room at the Radisson was identical to Catherine's, except of course there was a shaving kit beside the sink instead of her makeup case and lotions. He was neat, she noted as they walked in. There was no underwear on the floor, no pop cans or beer bottles scattered around. On the desk was a short stack of issues of the *Journal of the American Society for Psychical Research*. A laptop computer sat beside the journals. Tom's suitcase—one of those very efficient kinds with the built-in handle and wheels—was closed and stored out of the way beside the TV stand.

It was a very male room. Businesslike, focused—like Tom. Catherine's room had two romance novels on the bedside table and an open suitcase piled high with clothes, and the bathroom was littered with bottles of shampoo, conditioner, a curling iron, and the double set of towels she had requested from housekeeping. How different they were. Man and woman, male and female, Tom and Catherine.

And all these nonsense thoughts and observations,

Catherine admitted to herself, were simply her cowardly way of avoiding thinking about the reason she was in this room, with this man, shaking like a leaf inside and trying to look composed and sophisticated on the outside. She longed to be cool as Ingrid Bergman, spirited as Katharine Hepburn, romantic and passionate as Ava Gardner. Instead, she was awkward and bumbling as plain little Catherine Potter. Her earlier verve had dissipated the moment her challenge was accepted.

Feeling a bit weak in the knees, she sat down upon one of the queen-size beds, then immediately sprang up when she realized it might look as if she was anxious to be there—in his bed, in his arms. The thought made her dizzy with both anticipation and panic.

"This is nice," she said lamely, gesturing to the room and its impersonal hotel accouterments.

Tom cocked his head her way. "Same as yours, isn't it?"

"Well, yes, but, well, you know, the carpet is different. And the bedspreads." She wanted to kick herself for the inanity.

But he smiled in understanding. "It is a nice place, isn't it."

"Do you . . . do you want dinner?"

"I'm not hungry. You?"

"No," Catherine admitted.

"Should I call room service for some wine?"

The coward's way out, Catherine told herself. Where was the brave, centered woman who decided to stop tiptoeing around life? "I don't need wine," she lied.

Tom put his arms loosely about her waist and looked down at her with a smile. He did have the most winning smile, Catherine decided. "You were right," he confessed. "I've been a moron, acting like a tree stump with no eyes or ears. But, Catherine, believe me, it wasn't because I didn't notice you."

Catherine could feel herself relaxing in his arms. His touch made all her nervousness go away.

"How could any man help but notice you," he continued. Leaving one arm about her, he brought the other hand to her cheek, gently cupping her jaw and running a thumb back and forth over her cheek. The caress made her smile. "I noticed you, all right, but I thought it might scare you, having a rather odd sort of nerd panting after you."

Catherine's smile grew wider. "I like the idea of you panting after me. But I'm flattered that you were considerate of my feelings."

"I didn't want you to think I was a hound dog out on a prowl."

She laughed. "A hound dog?"

He shrugged and released her with a self deprecatory grimace. "Sorry. I've never had the silver tongue. In fact, I've never known what to do with women. Books and ghosts are much easier to deal with. Even my sister's little campers are easier to deal with."

She took his hands and placed them once again at her waist. "I'm easy to deal with," she told him softly.

He chuckled. "No, no. You're much too beautiful to be easy to deal with. And I'm a man who's always going to be a blockhead half the time and a bumbling idiot the rest of the time."

"I don't think you're either of those things, Tom Matthews. And I'm sorry I got so cranky with you."

"It's a good thing you were. I might have waited a decade to make my move, and by then, for sure you would have found someone else."

She gave him a beatific smile. "I don't think I'm going to need anyone else, do you?"

"I'm almost sure you're not."

They kissed—a sweet, undemanding, mutual caress that left Catherine breathless and aching for more.

"Do we know what we're doing?" Tom asked.

"I know." Suddenly all her reservations and shyness were gone.

"You're very sure you want to do this? I'm not taking advantage of the situation, am I?"

"If you don't start taking advantage soon, Mr. Matthews, I'm going to be very, very disappointed."

They kissed again, and this time she felt the heat of his desire. There was no mistaking the rise of his passion as he pressed close. They got so entangled that they stumbled back onto the bed—a convenient happenstance, since they were headed there anyway. They rolled so that he was on top with one leg between hers. Catherine closed her eyes from the sheer delight of it.

"I've got to tell you," he said between kisses, "I'm not a one-night-stand kinda guy."

She worked to unfasten the buttons of his shirt, fumbling with trembling fingers. "Isn't that supposed to be my line?"

"Yeah. But it's mine too."

He shrugged the shirt off his shoulders—nicely broad shoulders, Catherine noticed—while she pulled the tails out of his waistband.

"You take me, woman, and you take all of me. I'm talking commitment, Cat."

"You've got a deal, Tom."

His belt proved difficult, and he helped her unfasten it so that her seeking fingers could caress him. His breath caught, held, then came out in a groan. "Jehosephat! You're going to give me a heart attack."

Catherine just smiled.

He practically ripped off her shirt, but was almost reverent when he unhooked her bra. For a moment he only looked, then he touched, first with his hand, then his mouth. Catherine thought she would die of ecstasy.

"Oh, God!" he groaned. "You are beautiful. You look beautiful, you feel beautiful, you taste beautiful."

The only answer she could give him was a sigh, which shortened to a series of pants and little mewls of encouragement as he proceeded to taste every exposed inch of her flesh, and then worked to expose more. Then, abruptly, he stopped.

"Oh, no."

"What?" she demanded.

"I don't believe it. Stupid idiot."

"What?" Her voice was near frenzy.

"I didn't bring . . . anything."

"Anything?"

"You know!" He gestured helplessly. "Anything!"

"Oh!" She felt her face heat. "I brought something."

"You did?"

"Just in case."

He pressed a fervent kiss in the vicinity of her navel. "Thank you, thank you, thank you."

"Now . . ." She shimmied out of her panties, which was the last remnant of her clothing. "Can we get back with the program here?"

They did, with great enthusiasm. And if they fumbled like a pair of awkward teenagers, laughed as often as they sighed in rapture, and didn't quite dance a ballet of love from a scene in Cat's favorite romance novel, none of that mattered. Catherine had never known such happiness, and she saw the same joy reflected in Tom's eyes. They took each other to a place they made their own. Then, in the wonder of discovery, traveled there again, and yet again.

When they had worn each other out and lay peaceful and naked, locked together in sated intimacy, Tom breathed out a satisfied sigh, gave Catherine a wicked smile, and said, "Now can I tell you what I found?"

It was early Saturday when Catherine returned to the inn. Maggie was in the kitchen mixing waffle batter. Waffles, she had discovered, were somewhat easier than omelets, and when she burned one or two, the job of making up a new batch was fast and simple. That's the kind of cooking she liked—fast and simple.

"Hellllooooo!" Catherine sang as she came through the front door. "Maggie?"

"In the kitchen," Maggie called out in a disgusted voice.

Catherine all but bounced into the room. Maggie gave her a narrow-eyed look. "You must have gotten on the road long before the crack of dawn to get up here this early."

"We did."

"There are circles beneath your eyes," Maggie noted with sisterly concern. "Did our local ghost expert work you all hours of the night?"

Catherine's grin was very un-Catherine-like, Maggie thought. "Yes, in a manner of speaking."

"Well, throw your bag into the basement and put on an apron. I'm going to be a slave driver, too. We've had almost a full house both nights you were gone. This place is popular even with me doing the cooking. And you go off and leave me with guests banging down the door and a busybody ghost poised to wreak merry havoc.

"For a while I thought Robbie had left us, but she hasn't. You don't want to know what she did with the vacuum cleaner yesterday. And last night she waltzed into the living room and regaled everyone with stories of old Jerome, making out Red Robin to be some sort of heroine-celebrity, of course. They all thought she was a local entertainer, and I didn't disabuse them of the notion. And worse than Robbie was the guest—a twenty-five-year-old guy, would you believe?—who wanted a vegetarian breakfast. He was allergic to citrus, egg yolks, milk, didn't do well with bleached flour products, and coffee upset his stomach. You try making a breakfast for someone like that."

Catherine grabbed an apron. "I'm so sorry, Mags. But I just had to go."

"That's okay." Now that her sister was back, Maggie was feeling more generous about her absence. "It didn't hurt me to discover how hard you work and just how much this place needs you. We really do have to talk about you making this a permanent job. We're doing better than we ever anticipated."

Catherine laughed—a weak, peculiar sort of laugh. Maggie frowned at her. "What?"

"Uh . . ."

"Come on! I recognize that laugh. You only laugh like that when you've gotten into some sort of trouble."

"I'm not in trouble. Quite the opposite." She took a deep breath, her eyes glowing. "Tom and I are getting married."

Maggie's mouth dropped open, but no sound came out.

Catherine smiled at her reaction. "Wonderful, isn't it?"

Wonderful wasn't the description that came to Maggie's mind. "You and Tom are getting married," she echoed in amazement. "Catherine!"

Catherine couldn't contain herself. She danced around the kitchen, ending with an elaborate pirouette and an ungraceful collapse into the chair beside the worktable. The grin on her beaming face spread from ear to ear. "Do you believe it?" she asked breathlessly. "We're getting married. I'm going to be Mrs. Thomas Matthews. Oh, that has music in it! Mrs. Thomas Matthews! Mrs. Thomas Matthews!"

"You're getting married?" Maggie was still incredulous. "Catherine! Tom seems to be a very nice guy, but you've known him for what? A few weeks. And you haven't really known him. I mean really *known* him. Acquainted is more like it. And now you're getting married?"

"Isn't it romantic?" Catherine took the bowl of waffle batter from Maggie's hands. "Here, let me do that. You didn't put any blueberries in it. Shame on you."

"To hell with blueberries. Catherine, this is unreal! Don't you think you're being a bit hasty?"

"Yes," Catherine admitted. "But it doesn't matter. Sometimes you just know. And I know. About Tom. About me. We're meant to be together. It's simply fate."

"Bullshit. Fate is the lazy man's excuse for not thinking. Think about it, Cat. What are you doing? Marriage is a big deal. If it's not right, divorce is a heartbreak, and expensive to boot."

Catherine whipped the waffle batter with energetic strokes. "Don't worry," she said cheerfully. "I know it's right. Tom and I both knew it was right the moment we . . . uh . . ." She broke off and blushed brightly. "The moment we . . . you know."

Maggie threw up her hands in frustration. "Yeah, I

know. Catherine, believe me, I've known it was right, too. And it was never right."

"What about Colby?" Catherine put the batter bowl on the counter and opened the fridge. "What did you do with the blueberries? Oops! Never mind. Here they are."

Maggie sighed. Her sister was impossible to budge when she got into a romantic mood. "Colby's gone."

Catherine was immediately crestfallen. "Oh, Mags. I'm sorry. Did you two have another fight?"

"No. Yes. Sort of. He packed off to finish his job and I just realized that, attractive as he is, he and I have priorities that don't match."

"Like what?"

"Like honesty, integrity, and ethics."

"Oh." She grimaced sympathetically. "The reporter thing again, huh?"

"Something like that."

"I'm sorry, Mags."

"Cat, don't change the subject. We're talking about you and Tom, not me and Colby."

Catherine took Maggie's hands and squeezed. "I just want you to be happy for me, Mags."

Maggie gave her a fond, exasperated smile. "And I just want you to be happy. A couple of weeks' acquaintance and a night or two in bed is hardly something to base a lifetime on."

"You're a cynic, Maggie. You don't believe in love."

Maggie pulled away. "You're the second person this week who has accused me of that."

"Colby?"

Maggie made a face.

"You know, Mags—just because you've fallen for a few bad apples doesn't mean that love isn't real, that some people aren't positively made for each other. Tom and I are made for each other. Honest."

"I think you and Tom—or you, at least—are stuck in a nineteen-forties movie with Bogie and Bacall."

"Unbeliever!" Catherine accused affectionately. "True romance isn't dead, you know. Some of us still have faith in love." She smiled wickedly. "I'll bet Robbie would be on my side. Are you listening in, Robbie?"

"Of course she is," Maggie said sourly. "She's always listening in, looking over your shoulder, preparing to jump out at you when you least suspect it."

"And you'd be damned lonely without me, too!" A familiar voice chimed in.

Maggie groaned. "Did I tell you?"

"Welcome back, Cat. I'm proud of you." Robbie was suddenly sitting in the chair beside the worktable. *"Just one lesson from me, and you caught your man. Good work, honey. You could teach your sister a thing or two. She won't listen to me."*

"Robbie, you stay out of this," Maggie warned.

"Well, someone's got to congratulate Catherine and wish her well, since you're being such a cranky old poop. She went out and got herself a good man. That's what young women are supposed to do, or hadn't you noticed, Mags honey?"

"Oh, look who's talking! What would you know about good men and marriage, Madam Red Robin?"

"I know the most important thing, missy, and that's how it is to live without those things."

Catherine faded back and listened as her half sister and Robbie sniped at each other. She had to regard Robbie in a new light, knowing what Tom had discovered about her relationship to Maggie. She should have told Maggie the news first thing when she had come home, instead of blabbing on about her engagement—which she should have known would lead to a major discussion. But she certainly couldn't tell her now, with Robbie hovering about. If the ghost had wanted Maggie to know who she was, she would have said something before now.

Suddenly, Maggie was talking to empty air. "Come back here!" she demanded. "You can't call me a curmudgeon and just blink out like that!"

"Good morning?" came Tom's hesitant greeting from the front hallway.

Catherine looked at the spot where Robbie had disappeared. "You don't have to pop out for him, Robbie dear. He's practically part of the family, you know."

Nevertheless, the ghost was gone. Tom came into the kitchen as if he were treading on eggshells and caught the full brunt of Maggie's glare.

"Ouch!" He winced from the impact of accusation in her eyes. "You broke the news, huh?"

"Well . . ." Catherine assumed he meant the news about Robbie and Maggie. Tom, being a man, would naturally think that bit of information would take precedence over a mere engagement. "Not exact—"

"Yes, she did," Maggie interrupted. She regarded Tom with a penetrating stare, as if she wanted to peel away his skin and look right down to his soul and motives. "I guess we're going to be one big happy family."

Tom brightened. "Really? You're taking it awfully well."

"Actually, I told Catherine that I think a few weeks' acquaintance is scarcely enough basis for a lifetime's relationship."

Tom frowned in confusion. "You hardly have a

choice about what kind of family relations you get stuck with."

"What do you mean?" Maggie asked.

"What do *you* mean?" Tom asked back suspiciously.

"Wait a minute!" Catherine broke in. The misunderstanding was perilously close to revealing something that should be said only in private, away from Robbie's sharp if currently invisible ears. Catherine could sense the ghost listening in even though she couldn't see her. "Tom, I told Maggie about us getting married, and she thinks we haven't known each other long enough. That's all."

Sudden understanding brightened his face. "Oh. I get it."

"You get what?" It was Maggie's turn to sound suspicious.

"He gets that you're thinking like an overprotective big sister who hasn't admitted that I'm a grown woman able to make mature decisions."

Maggie relented with a wry smile. "Okay." She flashed Tom a reluctantly apologetic glance. "Not that I don't think you're first-rate, Tom. It's just that Catherine is the only sister I have."

"And Maggie thinks love is a crock."

Tom chuckled ruefully. "Love isn't a crock. It's a Sherman tank waiting around some corner of your life to rumble out and flatten you before you can so much as blink."

Catherine laughed. "Only a man would describe love as a Sherman tank." She grabbed his arms and wrapped them around her. "Do you feel flattened?"

"Thoroughly."

"We can fix that," Maggie said prosaically. "Help

us fix breakfast, and we'll feed you. That ought to make you three-dimensional again."

"I can do that," he replied, giving Catherine a hug. "I'm quite a hand in the kitchen, if I do say so myself."

"You see?" Catherine teased Maggie. "I told you we're a perfect match."

Gilbert Meineke slammed the latest issue of *America Today* onto his desk, overturning the photograph of the love of his life—the thirty-two-foot sailboat that awaited him even now in the Chesapeake Bay, where he'd planned to fly for a three-day weekend. But this storm that had blown up was likely to keep the sailboat in dock, and the storm wasn't of Mother Nature's making.

"Have you read this, Governor?"

Jack Kilbourne, perched casually on the corner of his senior aide's deck, smiled ruefully. "I've read it."

Meineke picked up the newspaper, snapped it open, and read in a contemptuous voice: " 'Jim Sweeney is at no loss for excuses when the substandard concrete work at Toledo's new state-of-the-art airport is laid at his feet, but as yet he has had nothing to say about the fact that a reliable source places him in Governor Kilbourne's offices several times prior to the final contract being let for the airport—a very lucrative contract which was awarded to his firm for general oversight. Nor has the governor's office commented on the fact that Sweeney's visits do not appear on the daily logs released to the public for the time period in question."

"I said I read it, Gil," Kilbourne snapped.

" '. . . embarrassment to the governor . . . public should demand' . . . hm. Shit! Listen to this! 'Another set of independent logs exist for this time period.

If the courts of Ohio wish to bring this matter to an official investigation, which public duty demands, these logs should be subpoenaed to substantiate any alteration and erasures of information in the public logs.' " He snorted. "This Drake is the proverbial jawbone of an ass. Can't we put out a contract on him, or something?"

Kilbourne grimaced. "Don't I wish."

From the leather upholstered couch by the window, Sylvester "Sly" Traveterri grumbled agreement.

"Who does this guy think he is, anyway? Don Quixote?" Gilbert got up and started to pace out his frustration. "Why us, I mean? Why doesn't he pick on Clint Dugan? Does he think Dugan's record is squeaky clean, that he's never helped a buddy or found a way to get around the damned bureaucrats? And how about Didi Buckman—Miss Independent Party herself. How about those photos that the *Voice* printed of her playing footsie in the Jacuzzi with her political handler? Handler, indeed! Why doesn't Mr. Bloodhound Drake go after her?"

"You're just jealous that you don't have a boss who wears a 36D and likes Jacuzzi games," Kilbourne said with a smile.

"Damn right," Gilbert muttered. He picked up his cup of coffee, grimaced at the cold brew, then trained his eyes on his boss. "So what's the straight story, Governor? Is this guy just blowing hot air? Or does another set of logs really exist?"

"No. Of course not. Do I look that stupid?"

Gilbert stared him down.

"Or at least I don't think another set exists. Let me put it this way. I suppose there's a very slight possibility that Maggie Potter kept a duplicate set. She was like that—always backing things up. Very efficient, always." His eyes lost their focus momentarily. "God, I miss her."

"Jesus!" Sly pounded his fist onto the arm of the couch. "You let her get out of the office with something like that?"

"Of course I didn't! If I'd known she had such a thing, I would have asked for it. If I'd known, I wouldn't have gone public with our logs."

"You didn't have her check out with anyone, have her stuff inspected before she left?"

"How could I do that, guys? You know how it was between me and Maggie."

"Yeah, we know," Gilbert cracked. "And the rest of the country knows, too. Fuck it, Jack. Didn't it occur to you that Maggie Potter might try to get back at you?"

"No, Gilbert! Not for one minute did I think that. And I still don't. I don't know what this fellow Drake is up to, but Maggie has nothing to do with it. Even if she did keep an independent log, even if she took it with her, and even if Jim Sweeney's visits are mentioned in them, she would never show those logs to someone like Colby Drake. The media treated her like dirt, and she'd have no truck with them, even if she was angry with me."

Gilbert and Sly looked askance at each other. Gilbert gave his colleague a subtle shake of the head. "Governor, do you know where Maggie is?"

"Yes. She's in Arizona, where her family lives."

"Since we're taking the campaign out west anyway, it would be easy to modify our itinerary so we could take in Arizona."

"That's not a bad idea. Good, solid Republican state, Arizona. Hear the whole state went into mourning when Barry Goldwater died a couple of years ago.

It wouldn't hurt to stop by and bolster our support there. Try to schedule something in Flagstaff as well as Phoenix."

Gilbert gave Sly a knowing smile. "Is that where Maggie is?" he asked Kilbourne.

"No. But she's close by. Since you fellows are so jumpy about this fellow Drake, I'll pay Maggie a visit and quiz her on it. She should be warned about the fellow, in any case."

"Oh yeah." Sly leered. "We've got to warn the lady."

A look from Kilbourne wiped the leer from his face.

Gilbert stepped into the tension between the two men. "Governor, this thing with the airport could potentially be far more damaging than your divorce or Maggiegate, and it comes at a very bad time. It's not something to take lightly. Candidates who suffer embarrassment right before the convention generally do not get nominated. It's not as if there aren't other contenders."

"I know that, Gilbert. I've been playing this game far longer than you have. But we don't need to worry about Maggie Potter. The woman adores me, and she would never do anything that would damage the campaign."

"Yes sir," both men said promptly. When the governor started using his "statesman" tone, there was no arguing with him.

But once Kilbourne had gone back to his own office, his aides shook their heads in long-suffering disgust. Both had joined Kilbourne's campaign after Maggie Potter had left. They were professional "handlers," taken on board to help the governor create a new, fresh, positive image in the last months before the national convention. The only thing they knew about

Maggie Potter was that she and Governor Kilbourne had been having themselves a high old time and were caught out by the media's arbiters of moral purity. Potter had been cut loose and made the sacrificial lamb—a smart move on the governor's part. But it had definitely not been smart to let the bimbo get out of the office with anything more important than a paper clip.

Gilbert snorted contemptuously and sat back down. "I guess Kilbourne hasn't read the old axiom about a woman scorned, huh?"

"Hell hath no fury," Sly supplied. "Jesus! He says she'd have no truck with the media because they treated her like dirt. How does he think *he* treated her? If she's like every other woman on the planet, Maggie Potter will crater him the first chance she gets."

Gilbert picked up a pencil and tapped it thoughtfully on the desk. "No matter what the governor thinks about this, we have to take the threat seriously. I have a friend at *America Today*, and I asked him about Drake. He says Drake's been out of town. Somewhere out West. He doesn't know where exactly."

"Arizona's out West," Sly rumbled ominously.

"Exactly. And Maggie Potter is in Arizona. Quite a coincidence. Let's put our heads together, Traveterri. We need to devise some contingency plans."

Seventeen

The wedding was slated for a Sunday in mid-July. So short a time from proposal to perpetuity, Catherine teased her intended. Maggie kept a tactful silence. She liked Tom more and more as the days passed, and recognized finally that her initial alarm at Catherine's announcement was mostly due to envy—envy and the terrifying prospect of no longer having Catherine as helper and partner at Robin's Nest. She was disappointed to recognize such selfishness in herself, but there it was. Catherine deserved a wonderful husband and children, and Tom's devotion became more obvious every day. Maggie couldn't help but be happy for them both.

She had to battle the temptation to feel sorry for herself, though. Tom practically lived at the inn, and the couple's mooning over each other only accentuated Maggie's loneliness. Robbie didn't help matters, floating about, rhapsodizing about weddings, brides, true love, and all that garbage. For a woman who'd lived her life outside marriage, she seemed curiously eager to embrace it now that she was dead. What's more, she really knew how to rub salt into Maggie's wounds. Maggie could learn a thing or two from her sister, Robbie kept reminding her. Didn't she want to be happy and secure as Catherine was? Didn't she think it was time to settle down and get serious about life and love? The refrain went on and on. Robbie was nothing if not persistent.

Life became even more chaotic a few days before the wedding. On Wednesday, Tom's parents came from Cottonwood to meet and confer with Catherine's parents, Roger and Virginia, who were spending these last days before the wedding in Jerome, in the Master Suite at Robin's Nest. Tom's sister, Martha of day-camp fame, was in the mix as well. Roger Potter grumbled about weddings being "women's business" and spent the day in the sunroom talking via E-mail to his office in Phoenix. Whatever was going on around him, Maggie's father always found an excuse to ignore it in favor of business. Maggie didn't know how her stepmother put up with the man.

The rest of the group merrily dominated the living room, dining room, and kitchen, sometimes in a large group, sometimes split into pairs and trios, to plan and speculate about "the children's" wedding. It was to be a very simple affair, with only family and closest friends attending a ceremony held outdoors in Sedona. The reception would be a combination of potluck donations and refreshments that Catherine herself insisted on preparing. For the wedding day and the day before, Robin's Nest would hang out the No Vacancy sign.

Everything was already arranged, actually. But the families enjoyed the friendly debates, mutual backslapping, and opportunity to get acquainted with soon-to-be in-laws. Maggie felt somehow separated from the celebration. She was the daughter not getting married, and silly as it seemed in this day and age, the position was an awkward one. Tom's parents were sweet, polite, and very complimentary of the inn, but Maggie could feel their curious looks now and then. Her infamy had spread even to their retirement village in little Cottonwood. Would it never end?

Thursday, after breakfast was finished and the paying guests had checked out, Catherine asked Maggie to take a walk with her before Tom and his family descended upon them once again. The morning was still very pleasant, the heat of midday having been deflected by an early buildup of thunderstorms over the rim to the east. They strolled down the stairways that connected street levels until a spectacular view through a stand of paradise trees beckoned them to stop and take a long look.

"Beautiful, isn't it?" Maggie commented.

"Truly beautiful. I'm so grateful that you persuaded me to come up here this summer. My whole life has changed. I feel like a new person. And I'm *so* glad I don't have to go back to school this fall."

"You aren't going to apply for a teaching job in Cottonwood?"

"I haven't quite decided." She gave her sister an impish smile. "I know a bed-and-breakfast inn that could probably use my help."

Maggie sighed with relief. "I was afraid I was going to be stuck with all that work by myself."

"You could have hired someone."

Maggie gave Catherine a big-sisterly thump. "It wouldn't have been the same."

"Well, that's true. Who else would put up with someone as grumpy as the slave driver who runs Robin's Nest?"

"Who else but that slave driver would put up with all those late-night ancient movies that have you mopping your eyes?"

"I don't need Bogie and Cary Grant anymore. I have Tom."

"Yes, you have Tom." Sentimentality swelled in her throat. "I'm sorry about what I said when you first told me about the wedding, Cat. I was wrong. Any dolt can see that you and Tom are made for each other."

Catherine sighed. "We are, aren't we? But Mags, in all the debate of that morning, I didn't tell you something I should have told you. And I haven't had a chance to get you private since then—until now."

"What didn't you tell me?"

"Hold on to the railing, there, kiddo, because this might send you over the edge."

"What?" Maggie's curiosity was burning now. "Tell me, Cat."

"When Tom and I were in Phoenix, we spent hours sifting through the files at the state archives, trying to trace Robbie's line of descent. Tom's doing a paper for the *Journal of the American Society for Psychical Research*."

"Yes," Maggie sighed. "I know. I guess it was too much to hope that Robbie could be kept a secret."

"He'll 'change the names to protect the inn' if you want, but the paper would be more effective with real times, places, identities, and stuff like that. I don't think we need to worry about becoming a sensation. This isn't the *National Enquirer* he's publishing in, you know."

"We can talk about that later. Go on."

"Yes. Well, Tom was hoping to find a hint of why Robbie stuck around when she died, and specifically why she decided to pop out and say hello when we bought the place."

Maggie tapped her fingers on the sidewalk railing. "Yes?"

"Well . . ." She glanced about, as if fearing ghostly ears might be in the vicinity. "The point is, Mags, is that you are Robbie's great-great- I don't know how many times great-granddaughter on your mother's side. Roberta Rowe is your dear old granny."

Maggie's mouth fell open. For a moment she couldn't say anything. Finally, she managed to choke out, "I don't believe it."

"Believe it."

"It couldn't be!"

"Tom can show you your pedigree, Mags. It's true."

"I . . . I would have known."

"Really? Name all your ancestors on your mom's side. Quick now."

"I . . . I . . ."

"You don't know, do you? Scarcely anyone cares about that sort of thing except people who are into genealogies. But we've got this documented by records all the way from Robbie to you. We're being haunted by your granny, kiddo. No doubt that's why she's so interested in running your life. You're the last relative she has on this earth."

Emotionally, Maggie couldn't accept it. But intellectually, she had to. Catherine claimed the proof was there, and Catherine wouldn't lie. Tom had the evidence in black and white.

They walked on, Maggie stunned and simply wandering wherever Catherine led, Catherine chatting about Tom's family, the wedding, their plans for the honeymoon—anything to divert Maggie from the disturbing revelation. They ended up at the English

Kitchen, their old standby for escaping work and wasting time. As the threatening storm clouds were now spouting lightning and thunder, they slid into one of the three indoor booths instead of sitting on the big porch. They both ordered diet Cokes.

"I'm being so good I can't stand myself," Catherine commented. "That piece of pie called to me when we walked in, but I resisted. Do you know I've lost five pounds since Tom proposed?"

Maggie smiled. "I'd noticed. You look great."

"Well, I'm going to look greater a few months down the line. It's so much easier to lose weight when you have a specific somebody you want to look good for, you know?" Catherine indulged in a soupy sigh. "Love makes everything easier."

"Only for some people," Maggie reminded her.

As if on cue, Colby Drake walked into the restaurant. The day could not get any weirder, Maggie thought. The famous line from the movie *Casablanca* came to mind: "Of all the gin joints . . ." She was getting as bad as Catherine, thinking of everything in terms of celluloid melodrama.

"I don't believe it!" Catherine whispered frantically when she saw Colby. "Do you see who—"

"I see all right." This very restaurant was the first place she'd ever seen Colby Drake. On that day Cat had classed him right up there with the movie studs and had assured Maggie he was ogling her. He had been ogling, in fact, but not for the reason Catherine had thought. He'd had his damned newspaper column on his mind, not romance.

And who knew what was on Colby's mind today. He didn't bother to claim a table of his own, but walked right over to theirs.

"Ladies," he greeted them with a grin. "Catherine, I

hear felicitations are in order. Tom Matthews was at the inn when I dropped by and was crowing like a rooster over his fortunate conquest."

"Colby Drake!" Catherine smiled up at him. "How nice that you're back in time for my wedding! Tom is already at the inn? Oh dear! I'd better get up there, then." She vacated her seat with a half-apologetic, half-encouraging waggle of the fingers at Maggie. "Bye now, you two. See you later."

Not waiting for an invitation, Colby slid into the vacant seat. "What a great sister you have. Smart, tactful, understanding. However, you're the woman I'm looking for."

"Is that so?" Maggie put as much coolness into her tone as she could manage. Those blue eyes and wicked smile threatened her equanimity, and she didn't want to fall under their spell again. Dredging up old anger was her best defense.

In the seat opposite, Colby looked quite insouciant, but Maggie noted a hint of caution in his eyes. He was treading his way cautiously for a change. After all, the last time he'd seen Maggie, she'd invited him to stick his head in a printing press. She supposed a man didn't forget that kind of sendoff.

"Why do you look so surprised?" he asked her. "I said I'd come back. You didn't believe me?"

"It's been one of those mornings," she said cryptically. "And here you are—back in Jerome. Are you finished throwing mud at Jack Kilbourne?"

"I'm not throwing mud at good old Jack. I'm just trying to scrape away the whitewash to show the rotten stuff beneath." He signaled the waitress, who promptly hurried to their table—certainly faster than she ever had for Maggie.

Once the waitress had left with Colby's order of a

beer and sandwich, Maggie regarded him coolly. "Does that smile of yours always work like that? On women, I mean. Liza's never been so eager to take *my* order."

He grinned wickedly. "It's a gift."

Maggie made a rude sound.

"And no, it doesn't always work. There's one woman in particular I can't get it to work on." His steady look made the identity of that woman obvious.

It worked well enough, Maggie thought ruefully.

"Did you read my columns?" he asked eagerly.

"I did happen to glance at one of them. Only because a guest dumped the paper in my living room. I certainly didn't go out and buy it."

He was transparently crestfallen at her disdain, though with Colby, one could never know if it was real or some kind of calculated manipulation.

"I suppose I should thank you for keeping my name out of it."

"I promised that I would."

"So you did." She gave him a thoughtful look. "You really do believe all that garbage, don't you, Colby?"

"You bet I do."

Liza came with his club sandwich and Moosehead. "Anything else?" she asked hopefully, and Maggie sourly wondered just how much else she was willing to give.

Colby declined, and Liza left them in peace.

"I wouldn't be writing about this if I didn't believe it, Maggie. Damn it, you worked with the man for three years. How could you not know what he was? How could you not see it."

Maggie pinched her lips together in silence and looked down at her diet Coke, as if she might find the answer in one of the bubbles fizzing there. "People see what they want to see," she finally said.

"People?"

"Okay. I saw what I wanted to see. I was idealistic. I thought I was in love." She snorted at the very concept. "I wanted Jack to be everything I thought he should have been." She signaled Liza. If they were going to endure a session of soul-baring, then she needed sustenance. Liza was at the table in three seconds flat, looking inquiringly at Colby, not Maggie.

"It's me this time, Liza. Not him."

Liza looked Maggie's way in surprise, almost as if she hadn't noticed her sitting there. "Oh. Hi, Maggie."

"Bring me another diet Coke and a BLT, please."

"Coming right up," she said with a smile at Colby.

For a moment they sat staring at each other in silence, Maggie's reluctant confession hanging between them. When Maggie's sandwich came, at least she had an excuse not to talk, but she couldn't escape the weight of Colby's measuring stare.

"You know," he finally said, "I had a couple of reasons for coming back here."

"Really?"

"Really. Both involve you."

"How flattering."

He ignored the barb in her voice. "Kilbourne's planned a campaign swing through the West for quite some time. Now he's changed his itinerary to include a couple of stops in Arizona. The change was announced shortly after my columns appeared."

"I don't care what Jack is doing. It's nothing to me."

"Does he know where you are?"

"Yes. I'm not hiding from him. He's even written me a couple of times, believe it or not." She had to smile at Colby's grim look. "I know what you're thinking, Mr.

I-See-a-Plot-Everywhere-I-Look. And you're wrong. I'm sure Jack's coming to Arizona has nothing to do with either me or your column. He has much more important things to worry about than an ex-girlfriend and a tabloid reporter."

Colby looked hurt. "*America Today* isn't a tabloid. Close, but we still have some trappings of respectability—such as at least one damned fine columnist."

Maggie laughed. "Of course. Erudite, articulate, and sharp as the keen edge of a knife. And obviously modest."

"Thank you," he said dryly. "I am indeed."

A spark of warmth flashed between them.

"And now," he continued, taking a deep breath, "we get to the more important reason I came back."

"And that would be?"

"You, of course."

Maggie opened her mouth for a skeptical reply, but he forestalled her with a raised hand. "Don't say something smartass, Mags, because I'm talking serious, here. We have something between us, something we should explore. We set off fireworks in each other—both good and bad, but that's good, really, because we can fight and disagree and still feel the connection that pulls us together. There aren't many people who can do that. So that's the more important reason I'm here. I came back for you."

He threw out the statement like a challenge, daring her to throw it back in his face. He was good, Maggie thought. Persuasive, sincere, heartfelt. Too bad she couldn't believe him. It was tough being a cynic, Maggie reflected sadly. Life would be more fun if she were still naive.

"You came back for me?"

The edge in her voice merely made him stiffen his jaw. "I did."

"For me, Colby? Or for a certain set of business logs I have in my possession?"

He took a bite of his sandwich and chewed thoughtfully. "Good question," he admitted finally. "It's true I can't go much further without the actual logs, but I'm willing to hang the damned things. If you don't want me to use them, so be it. It's you I'm after, and I don't mean for any kind of a story. For me. Just for me." His eyes grabbed hers and held on, and she couldn't disbelieve the emotion coming her way. "Maggie Potter, if I don't love you, then this is the closest thing to love I've ever felt."

Maggie struggled to escape the spell of those blue, blue eyes on fire with truth, sincerity, and the promise of the L word. Love.

"Colby, let me tell you what Catherine said to me when I very rudely reamed her out for wanting to marry Tom Matthews. She accused me of not believing in love. You said the same thing to me not long ago. 'You don't believe in love,' like if I could just bring myself to believe in it, I would find love and it would find me and every little thing would be just hunky-dory.

"But it's not that I don't believe in love, Colby. I admit love exists. Some people find it. It appears that Catherine has—knock on wood. But other people are missing a gene or something. They're allergic to love, and every time they take a taste, they break out in a nasty rash. That's me. I've had more rashes than a kid with drippy diapers."

Undeterred, Colby smiled. "Haven't you ever heard of people outgrowing allergies?"

She snorted. "No."

"Okay, okay. So you don't love me, and won't accept that I might love you." He'd put on his game face, and Maggie couldn't tell what he was thinking. "What do you feel for me, Mags? Contempt? Friendship? Liking? Camaraderie?" His smile turned deliberately wicked. "Lust, perhaps?"

Maggie couldn't help but laugh. "No wonder you're a good reporter. You never give up, do you?"

"Ah ha!" He leaped upon the slip of her tongue. "You think I'm a good reporter. This is progress."

"Stubborn," she added to her evaluation. "Unreasonable. Doesn't know when to back off."

"All true."

She sighed, serious again. "Colby, I don't know what I feel for you. You irritate the hell out of me one minute and make me want to get naked the next. You're Mr. Nice Guy one day, and a sneaky sleaze the next day, and I never know what it's going to be. When you're around, you occupy the biggest part of my attention. I'll admit that. And when you're gone, even if I was the one who booted you down the road, I miss you."

His eyebrows jumped at her honesty. "Well, that's a start, don't you think?"

"It won't work," she said flatly. "I don't trust you."

"I can earn your trust, Maggie."

"Sometimes I don't even like you."

He gave her a lopsided smile. "Sometimes I'm not all that likable. I admit it. And I haven't exactly earned good marks for straightforwardness and honesty. I'll admit that too. But trust me, I'm a hell of a guy. I'm worth a second chance, or a third."

Again he forced her to smile. "Your modesty overwhelms me."

"See there? I made you smile. If you weren't so determined to be a sobersides this morning, you'd laugh. How many people in your life make you smile?"

"Colby . . . this is ridiculous."

"No, it's not. We have lots to build on."

"Like what?"

"I'll be a gentleman and not even mention how good we are in bed."

"You just mentioned it," she noted dryly.

"But more important than that"—he lifted one wicked brow—"and there are things more important than that—as long as there are moments that you think of me for no reason at all . . ."

All the time, Maggie admitted to herself.

". . . dream of me when your bed is empty . . ."

Every night.

". . . laugh at some memory I gave you, well then, there's definitely something to work with. Don't you think?"

Maggie felt her defenses begin to erode. The Great Wall of China couldn't stand up to Colby Drake.

"Maybe," she admitted dubiously.

"No maybe about it. I intend to stick around a while and harass you until you give me a another chance. No work this time. I have vacation coming and I'm taking it." He counted on his fingers then grinned. "You think I can win you in two weeks?"

"Was Rome built in a day?"

"Ah, good! A challenge. That's another reason why I'm a great reporter. I love a challenge."

Liza walked up and laid the checks on the table. Colby reached out and grabbed Maggie's before she could take it. "I'll start out my campaign by being a big spender. Diet Coke and a BLT—peanuts, my dear."

"You have peanuts for brains," Maggie told him as he handed both checks to the cashier.

As they walked out the door and turned up the street together, Colby took her arm. She couldn't bring herself to take it back. Sunlight on his hair made black a beautiful color. His eyes were too blue, too sparkling with his own arrogant humor, to resist. His touch felt too right on her skin. He cocked his head toward her in inquiry, his look full of mischief. "I don't suppose you'd like to make your life more interesting by letting me stay at Robin's Nest."

"I wouldn't have you stay anyplace else," she replied with a mocking smile. "I want you where I can keep an eye on you."

Two weeks. Surely she could keep good sense about her for two short weeks.

After the confusion of the day before the wedding, the night seemed strangely quiet. All were settled into their rooms for the night. The bride's family was in the Master Suite. The groom's family had settled into the Blue Room after taking the entire crowd out to dinner at an expensive restaurant in Sedona. Tom's brother Duane, from Casa Grande, was in the Yellow Room. Colby was in the Wicker Room. Tom Matthews was thought by most to be in his apartment in Cottonwood, but in reality, he was in the basement with Catherine. Their late-night leavetaking had been so heartfelt that Maggie had told him he might as well stay and save the drama. She suggested they take the Green Room and keep Robbie company. Catherine had balked at the idea, so it was Maggie who ended up in the Green Room, while Catherine and Tom took the basement apartment. Catherine and Tom had shared conspiratorial smiles, and Maggie had accused them both of manipulation. The exchange had been good-natured and ended in laughter, and as she towed Tom to the basement stairs, Catherine had reminded Maggie that Colby was in the room directly across from the Green Room.

"Don't push," she'd warned her sister with a tolerant smile. "And tell Tom to watch out for Attila if he wants to have all his fingers intact on his wedding day."

So now Maggie was stuck in the Green Room with Robbie, who had declared—just to get her goat, Maggie was sure—that she actually liked the new decor and that she, being a ghost who was smart enough to change with the times and keep her fashion sense modern, would be just as happy housed in conservative green and beige as her customary scarlet and tassels.

Maggie supposed she was lucky that there was even one room available for the odd-woman-out in this little family ensemble, then she gave herself a mental rap for feeling sorry for herself. After all, Colby was right across the hallway. She was sure that he would gladly keep her company all night. She had managed to keep him at arm's length in the two days since he'd come back, but it hadn't been easy. There was a war going on in her heart, and the outcome—victory for good sense or triumph for romance—was still, for Maggie, undecided. Alone in the Green Room, chewing on her own loneliness, the thought of knocking on Colby's door was a powerfully seductive temptation. But if she did, her life would become complicated beyond all reason, more complicated than it was even now, with a ghostly great-great-grandmother for a roommate.

"Hey, Robbie, you want to go for an evening stroll?"

"Well, isn't this nice! You're being polite for a change."

"I'm always polite to people who are polite to me."

"The mark of a real lady, honey, is that she's polite to all, whether or not they deserve it. If you have to be nasty, do it behind people's backs."

"That's not a lady, Robbie. That's a politician. Do you want to keep me company or not? I don't have all night."

She did have all night, though. That was the trouble. All night to sit alone in the Green Room thinking about going across the hallway.

The evening was pleasantly warm, the air so clear that the few lights on the rim, fifty miles away, twinkled as if they were just next door. Robbie kept her invisible company. It was just as well the ghost didn't flaunt her presence, since Maggie wasn't the only late-night stroller. But Maggie could almost hear the rustle of her silk skirt, smell the eternally fresh rose in her hair. For a change, she was actually glad Robbie was near. They had a thing or two to talk about.

"So, grandmother dear, were you ever going to tell me that we're family?"

A hint of surprise charged the air. *"Well, aren't you the smart one? Of course I was going to let you know. Sometime."*

"Why didn't you tell me?"

"You haven't been the friendliest gal around, honey."

Maggie shrugged. "Making friends with a ghost is a lot to ask. Especially when that ghost is trying to run your life and ruin your business."

"I never tried to ruin your business. As a matter of fact, having all these people in the house is downright entertaining."

Maggie snorted. "Entertaining, are we? You must

have known all along that I was your granddaughter many-times-great."

"Of course, dear. Why did you think I came out of the closet after all this time? Why do you think I lured you into buying the place?"

"You did that?"

"You don't think such a grand idea was yours, do you?"

They passed the darkened post office and proceeded down the street where Maggie and Robbie had walked together on a day that now seemed so long ago, although it wasn't. Maggie recalled how alarmed she'd been, how convinced that insanity was stalking her. It seemed much more likely than a ghost.

They strolled in a silence that was almost companionable.

"Why don't I just lay my cards on the table, now that the hand's been played?" Robbie materialized, flamboyant as ever with the never-wilting rose in her hair and her gown dripping in lace and silk. *"I figure it's easier to talk about these things in person."*

"Someone might see you."

"Right now, honey, only you can see me. It's a ghost trick, okay?"

They took a seat on the steps that led up to the next street level. "Okay, Robbie. Lay your cards on the table, then. I would appreciate it."

Robbie arranged her skirts about her and settled herself, looking for all the world as if she were seated on a velveteen loveseat in a fancy nineteenth-century drawing room. She might have been a madam in a cathouse, Maggie mused, but no one could say her granny didn't have class.

"I had a daughter," she began.

"So Tom told me. Her name was Laura?"

"Yes. I sent her to the best schools. Kept her in the best clothes. Saw she never lacked for one damned thing. Didn't even let her know where I got the money that kept her in style. She thought I ran a hotel."

Maggie shrugged. "In a manner of speaking, you did."

Robbie chuckled appreciatively. "That's right. I did. Anyway, when Jackass Jake shot me dead and Laura found out what I was, the ungrateful little twit actually ripped my name right out of the family Bible and never mentioned me again. Never to her daughters, or grand-daughters. Thought she could erase me just like that, and she pretty much did."

"She was shocked, huh?"

"She was so prim and starched she crackled when she walked. I don't know how I birthed a gal like that. But anyway, she up and married Homer Pilford, who only wanted her for the money she inherited, and she was pretty miserable for most of her life. She had a couple of daughters, and they didn't have much better luck finding good menfolk. And so on down the line until we get to you. Do you know you're the last rela-tive I've got on this earth? Just you. The last of my blood. Can you blame me for wanting to be a part of your life when you showed up in Jerome, looking at my house and not even knowing who I was?"

Maggie chuckled and shook her head. "Come on, Robbie. You expect me to believe that you just wanted to get to know me? No dice. I've worked for and with some of the best liars in the country. You don't hold a candle to them."

Robbie smiled. "Cards-on-the-table time?"

"Cards on the table. What's it going to take to make you happy?"

"I want the recognition I deserve from my family."

"According to you, I'm the only family you have left, and I recognize you just fine."

"Well, that's another thing. I want more family—another generation of Roberta Rowe great-grandkids."

"Another generation?" Maggie laughed. "Like, from me?"

"Who else?"

"Is that why you've been playing matchmaker?"

"Well, honey, you haven't had a lot of success on your own."

Maggie got up and dusted off her jeans. "Sorry, Robbie. I can't offer you much hope. As far as a love life goes, I was born under an unlucky star—in case you haven't noticed."

"Stars don't have anything to do with it. The entire family is cursed. But now that I'm taking a hand to help out, things are going to be better. Though things might go more smoothly if you weren't so headstrong."

Maggie laughed. "Don't count on it. I've just recently learned that I came by that honestly—by direct line of descent."

They walked back up the hill, bantering mutual insults, but the exchange lacked the sharpness of their earlier set-tos. Maggie felt almost congenial toward the apparition. How could she be annoyed with her own grandmother? Nor was she afraid. There were a lot of things in this world scarier than a ghost.

She found herself thinking the same thing a half hour later as she stood in front of Colby's door. The prompt manner in which he opened it told her he hadn't been asleep.

"Don't jump to conclusions," she warned him when his eyes lit up at the sight of her. "This is not love."

That was hard to remember when he took her hand and urged her inside. No more words were spoken.

None were needed. What they had to say was more effectively expressed in other ways. In spite of an almost painful urgency to come together, they took their time with the preliminaries, tasting, savoring, enjoying each touch, smile, and expression, drawing out each moment to make the inevitable end that much more rapturous. Reclining near-naked upon Colby's sheets, Maggie admitted to herself that cool good sense was impossible with Colby's intoxicating smile filling her with warmth, not to mention his tanned and utterly glorious body igniting the flames of desire.

"No strings," she insisted. "I have not surrendered. I already admitted that you make me want to get naked. This is nothing more than . . . than a romp."

He looked close to laughing, but he didn't, which was a good thing, because she might have hit him.

"At least you're not telling me to put my head, or any of my other parts, in a printing press. That's progress of a sort, you must admit."

She gave him a severe look. "I admit nothing, Colby Drake. Now, are you going to loom over me like a cover model on one of Catherine's romance novels, or are you going to give some of those 'other parts' that you mentioned some exercise?"

He took her up on her invitation with a vengeance, and sweet vengeance it was. At the height of it, Maggie wondered if such rapture could be experienced without that elusive quality of love she was so determined to discount.

It was the weakness of the moment, Maggie decided later. One couldn't be responsible for one's thoughts at such a time.

Eighteen

Sunday's dawn found them all in a picturesque little wash just outside of Sedona, on national forest land of juniper, sage, red soil, and redder rock. The backdrop for the wedding was one of nature's most spectacular works of art. The rising sun turned the cliffs blood red against the deep blue morning sky. Songbirds provided the wedding music. Maggie and two curious squirrels were Catherine's attendants, and Tom's brother Duane stood as best man.

After the ceremony, everyone repaired to Robin's Nest for a wedding breakfast prepared by the bride herself. Catherine had insisted, laughingly turning down Maggie's offer to do the cooking.

"Not that your cooking isn't improving," she had told Maggie. "But—"

"I know, I know. Burned toast, doughy waffles, and rubber omelets are my specialties. No need to say more."

Tom was allowed to help, though. He'd claimed earlier to be a fair hand in the kitchen, and the claim was justified. Roger and Virginia Potter, George and Stephanie Matthews, Duane, Martha, Maggie, Colby, and the Reverend Timothy Sharpe of the Red Rocks Congregational Church sat and stood about the living room and dining room, drinking fresh-squeezed orange juice and chatting about the wedding.

Robbie was there, too. She wasn't visible, but Maggie could feel her. She'd been at the wedding as well. Maggie had halfway expected her to materialize beside the bride, white lace handkerchief dabbing at spectral tears of wedding joy. She hadn't, thank heaven. For Robbie, she was being very discreet, a point Maggie mentioned quietly to the invisible presence after she escaped the crowd to take a breather on the front porch.

"Thank you for not making a sideshow of Catherine's wedding," she said, knowing Robbie would hear.

The presence didn't remain invisible for long. Robbie blinked in, winked, and smiled widely. *"I wouldn't dream of embarrassing dear Catherine. A wedding is the most special occasion in every girl's life. But then, I guess you wouldn't know, would you, honey."*

With that, she blinked out. An automatic sharp retort came to Maggie's lips, but she bit it back. She'd been about to snipe that Robbie wouldn't know either, but that wasn't true. Tom's search had shown that Roberta Rowe had once been married to a young rancher by the name of Horton Tolliver—Laura's father. The man had died before Laura was born. Laura's legal name was Tolliver, but Robbie had used her maiden name after Tolliver's death had forced her to resume her former profession. Maggie suspected she had done that to protect Laura from the consequences of her mother's reputation.

"You're right, Robbie," she conceded. "Weddings

are very special events. The most special event in a girl's life."

"What was that?" came a question from behind her in Colby's voice.

Maggie smiled tauntingly. "I was talking to the ghost."

He sauntered into view, his mouth twitching in amusement. "Do tell."

"Turns out she's my great-great-granny. Or great-great-great. I can't keep it straight. Have a seat." She swung her long legs off the porch swing to make room.

He sat, leaned back, and gazed appreciatively at the bright blue sky with its puffs of cottony clouds. "Nice that granny could be here to see her granddaughter married."

"She's not Cat's granny. Just mine. On my mother's side. But she's very big on weddings, so I imagine she enjoyed herself just the same."

He smiled. "You're pulling my leg, right?"

She smiled innocently back. "What do you think?"

"Think? You know I can't think straight when I'm around you."

"Do you think straight when you're not around me?"

"Ouch!" He winced theatrically. "And here I thought we were making progress."

"I told you not to jump to conclusions from last night."

"After last night, I doubt I could summon up the energy to jump anywhere."

Maggie was a bit tired herself, and she felt a flush come to her cheeks when she thought about the reason why.

"So . . ." She cast about for a safer subject. "I guess this is going to be a busy summer for you with the political conventions coming up soon. Lots of politicians to pummel."

He didn't rise to the bait, just smiled. "If I didn't get after a few, they'd think I was neglecting them."

"Don't you have any ambition to work for something . . . well . . . a little higher class than *America Today*?"

"Is there a difference? I thought all reporters were slime."

"Give me a break here," she said archly. "I'm trying to be reasonable."

"And a fine job you're doing. Yes, actually, I have ambition coming out the ears. But for right now, *America Today* is fine. They let me do what I want for the most part. I'll admit they would be happier with a good juicy sex scandal mixed in or"—he grinned—"maybe a nice ghost story from Jerome."

"You still don't believe in my ghost." She sighed dramatically. "You want me to trust *you*, but you won't trust me. You're a contrary man, Colby Drake."

"More than you know." He stood and leaned on the porch railing for a moment, looking out over the valley. Then he turned, a half smile on his face and a resolute look in his eyes. He propped his backside against the porch railing and folded arms across his chest in a deceptively casual pose, but his intent gaze seemed to create a high voltage charge in the air.

"Maggie Potter, what would you say to marrying me and coming back to Virginia? If you're determined to run a haunted inn, I'm sure we could find you one back there."

Maggie's mouth fell open. In her head, Robbie shrieked loud enough to fry her brain cells.

"You go, girl! Jump on it! Jump on him!"

"Be quiet!" Maggie groaned.

"What?"

"Not you. Damn it, never mind! Colby, you're pulling my leg, right?"

"I've never been more serious."

"We've known each other—"

"As long as Catherine and Tom have known each other."

"I'm not Catherine, and you're not Tom."

A wild, insane tidal wave washed up from the pit of Maggie's stomach and threatened to crumble the bastion of her reason, careening around her mind with the crazy urge to say yes, to challenge fate, to take the leap and damn the rocks below—because she thought of Colby nearly every minute of the day, because he made her smile at odd moments, and even when they fought, they were bonded somehow. Because she loved—no, she did not love him! All this wedding nonsense had demolished her hard-won realism.

"I can't marry you, Colby." She hoped her tone didn't hint of the insane beating of her heart. Through all the disastrous romances she'd suffered, no one had ever proposed marriage. Men had proposed bedroom arrangements, committed relationships, uncommitted relationships, live-in agreements, but never marriage.

Colby was unruffled. "Give me one good reason why not."

She looked at him as if he were crazy. "I'll give you a dozen good reasons."

"Start with just one. A good one. Really good."

"I hate what you do for a living."

"That's extraneous. We could work on that."

"We scarcely know each other."

"Now that's just not true. Time isn't always a measure of how well two people know each other. We know each other very well, Maggie."

"I don't trust you."

"As I said earlier, I can earn your trust."

"I don't love you." She emphasized each word, hoping they would make an impression—on herself as well as him.

He leaned back, shook his head, and regarded her with a tolerant, long-suffering smile. "The crux of the problem. You don't love me." He sighed. "That would be a good reason, I suppose, except that you don't really know that you don't love me."

"What?"

"How many times have you said that you're allergic to love? Obviously you've never experienced real love, or you'd know it doesn't really cause rashes. It's not a disease or a thicket of poison ivy. Consider that you might not recognize love when you find it. It might be something totally different from what you'd think."

She was awestruck by his twisted reasoning. "You are so full of bullshit! If there were a Pulitzer prize for bullshit, you'd win it, hands down."

"No bullshit, Mags. I wouldn't play around with such an important part of your life—and mine. I think you do love me."

"When I warned you not to jump to conclusions the other night, I didn't know I was speaking to an Olympic class conclusion-jumper. I told you at the time—that, and every other time we've been together, was a romp."

He smiled with infuriating confidence. "Nope. I've known a lot of women, Maggie. There are women who enjoy a good romp and have a lot of fun in bed, and there are women who can turn what should be uncomplicated lust into a giving, soul-shattering, loving, absolutely complicated experience. And you're one of the latter."

She shook her head in denial. "You don't know what you're talking about."

"The problem here"—he stabbed his words home with a finger pointed in her direction—"is that you want to be completely, totally safe for the rest of your life. You want to be swaddled in certainty. You refuse to take any chances with your life and your heart. Love and marriage are the biggest chances a person can dare. They can screw up your whole existence, or they can add a dimension that makes everything else in life worthwhile.

"Take a chance, Maggie. Push your way out of that cocoon you've retreated into. Otherwise your life is going to be gray and mediocre."

Inside Maggie's heart, a battle raged. The words she should throw back in his face, the words of denial and reason and logic, were caught up in the melee. She could only stare at him in silent agony.

"Marry me, Maggie. I promise your life won't be mediocre."

She took a deep breath and said simply, "I can't," and fled to the safety of the house.

Now you can see what I had to deal with. It's a good thing I was already dead, because Maggie could drive a person to suicide. Really she could.

Girls today have too many options, if you ask me, and it confuses them. Take Maggie, for instance. She went into politics, of all things. Not a thought for marriage, children, or stuff like that. Politics! Now, is that a suitable line of work for a young woman? She gets burned, as I could have told you she would, and runs back home to do what? Settle down to a normal, productive life? No. She casts about for something just as

stupid to do. I probably saved her from God knows
what when I sucked her into buying my house. At least
keeping a boarding house is a pretty sane way for a
woman to make her way in the world.

In my day, a girl didn't get confused. She didn't have
a million lines of work to choose from. Be a wife, be a
schoolmarm, a seamstress, a laundress, or a whore.
Not a whole lot of choice. It kept things simple. Of
course, there were those pioneers who didn't fit the
mold and bucked tradition, but mostly not. The safest
of the choices was marriage. If a good-looking fellow
like Colby Drake got down on one knee, a smart girl
said yes before he had a chance to have second
thoughts. In those days, girls knew up from down and
the butter side from the dry side. You know what I
mean?

And then there's modern Maggie. Enough to give a
ghost heartburn, or worse. I listened in on the whole
exchange, of course, and couldn't believe my ears. And
if I had real ears, they would have turned red with rage
long before Maggie stormed into the house like the pitiful coward she was.

I confronted her in the kitchen, where she stomped
around in a pretense of cleaning up the breakfast mess.
From the sound of her mutterings I was surprised that
she dumped the dirty plates into the sink instead of
throwing them against the wall. Although what she
had to be miffed about, I don't know. I was the one
who'd been betrayed. Me and Colby Drake. Colby had
rejoined the party and was trying hard to look as if
everything was hunky-dory. Not me. I'm not so good-
natured. I was determined to give my stubborn twit of
a granddaughter a sharp piece of my mind.

"You blew it!" I scolded. "You had it all in your
hands, you dimwit, and you blew it!" If I were really

good at this ghost stuff, I would have made flames shoot from my eyes, or something equally scary, but I had to settle for folding my arms and tapping my toe like a stern old grandmother—something I never got to be, by the way, because of my untimely demise.

"Get lost!" she snapped. "I don't feel like talking."

"Well, I do, missy! As hard as I worked to get you two together, as much as is riding on this—and you blow it off like some kid kicking a rusty can out of his way. How can you do this to me? Your own kin! Your own grandmother who has only you to save her from being consigned to oblivion!"

She slapped a handful of sudsy water toward me. Of course it sailed right through me to land with a splat on the tile floor. This seemed to make Mags even more downcast. In fact, she looked so down in the mouth I almost felt sorry for her. But not sorry enough to let her off the hook.

"You know what this meant to me, Maggie. I feel absolutely betrayed."

She snorted—very unattractive. The girl never learns. "I haven't done anything to you, Robbie. This isn't about you. It's about me. My life. You're dead, remember?"

"You don't need to remind me. And just because I'm dead, that's no reason not to consider my needs. Just wait until you're dead and see how you like everyone ignoring your advice. Why do I even try to help you?"

Maggie's sympathy is what I aimed for. The girl has a soft heart, for all that she tries to hide it. If she felt sorry enough for my plight, her heart might lean a little bit my way, and Colby's way. It's not as if I was asking her to jump across the Grand Canyon, after all. I was asking her to say yes to an incredibly hunky man who

*had already proven willing to put up with all her non-
sense. Would that be so hard to take?*

*She refused to look at me, attacking the dishes as if
they were the enemy instead of her own stubborn stupidity.* "Go away, Robbie," *she ordered.*

"I'll go when I'm well and good ready to go," *I
snapped.* "You are a spoiled, selfish, thoughtless little
brat," *I told her.* "It's no use talking to you. I don't
know why I bother. So just see how you like being
ignored for a change!"

*A dose of her own medicine might set her straight. I
popped out with dramatic flair, smarting with genuine
hurt. After all this time, I had thought she understood.*

"Come back here!" *she called after me.*

I ignored her. Let the baggage see how it feels.

"Be that way, then!" *She grabbed a dirty skillet and
slammed it into the dishwater—on top of a plate, apparently, because the sound of breaking china was loud
and clear. Served her right. She should learn some control. Men don't appreciate temper in a woman.*

*I drifted on to more entertaining things—such as
Catherine's wedding party—as Mags quietly turned the
kitchen air blue. My blockhead granddaughter was not
having a good day.*

Maggie cleaned the kitchen until it sparkled—a chore
that was preferable to going into the living room and
being social with Colby Drake. She was angry and embarrassed at the same time, guilty and confused,
ashamed of having been rude to a man she'd come to
like—and like was all there was to it, she insisted to
herself. And against all reason she was flattered by his
proposal—and ashamed of being flattered.

She might be ready to face Colby in, say, a decade or

so. Not now. Maggie was contemplating spilling a carton of milk on the floor to give herself an excuse for more cleaning, but an excited Virginia, clad in her mother-of-the-bride sequined dress, dithered through the kitchen door and interrupted her plot.

"There you are! Maggie! Maggie! You'll never guess who's here."

"About twenty people, more or less," Maggie said.

Virginia ignored Maggie's sour face. "Don't be a smartmouth. For that I'll let you be surprised. Mercy! He is so handsome in person. I fully understand how he could turn a girl's head."

For a confused moment, Maggie assumed her stepmother was referring to Colby. But that didn't make sense. "Virginia, who are you talking about?"

"Jack Kilbourne! That's who! My word! If the society reporters were here, we'd be the talk of the state. Imagine Jack Kilbourne coming to my little girl's wedding reception."

Maggie was stunned. "Why is Jack here?"

"To see you, of course! Come on, Maggie! You're a sight, of course, after spending the last hour cleaning up this mess, but I'm sure he's used to seeing you casual." Virginia had the grace to redden when she realized the implication of her words. But in the long tradition of mothers, she tried to cover up her slip by dithering. "Come on! Come on! Everyone's just holding their breath to hear why he's here."

"I'll bet," Maggie said sourly.

Jack Kilbourne was indeed in her living room, in all his glory. No wonder Virginia was agog, for the Ohio governor was an impressive figure of a man. He'd lost none of his luster since Maggie last saw him. Of course, when she last saw Jack he was apologizing for having to cashier her, explaining that politics sometimes required injustice so the greater good could be accomplished. She hadn't considered him particularly appealing right then.

Maggie shrugged off Virginia's eager hand and took a moment to watch her former boss. As always, he couldn't be in a room full of people without working the crowd. To Jack Kilbourne, working a crowd was like breathing. And he was very good at it. She'd once told a fellow aide that Jack could walk into a den of wolves and walk out the pack leader. He was that slick. People might disagree with his politics, envy his power and success, or just plain believe that he was an ass, but almost everyone liked him when they met him in person. Even her own family seemed charmed.

An anxious glance about showed that Colby wasn't in the room. Maggie guessed that he was one of the few who couldn't be charmed, and she was glad he wasn't there to create a scene.

"Maggie!" A grin spread across Kilbourne's face when he spied her. "Maggie! There you are. What a splendid family you have! I understand today's your sister's wedding day! If I'd known, I wouldn't have intruded."

"Oh! You're not intruding, Governor!" Virginia gushed. "Not at all!"

"So this is where you took yourself off to! It's beautiful! Absolutely beautiful! I understand you're doing very well!"

"She'll give you a tour, won't you, Maggie!"

If she didn't get the man away from Virginia, her stepmother would probably kiss his feet. Maggie put on a smile. "One tour, coming up."

The minute they were away from the others, Kilbourne's facade of bonhomie faded. For an awkward moment, they both were ominously silent. The silence lasted all the way up the stairs and into the upstairs hall, where Kilbourne put a hand on her shoulder and turned her to face him.

"It seems like forever, Mags. How have you been?"

"How do you think I've been? Why are you here, Jack?"

He grimaced, but didn't remove his hand. "Same old Maggie. Cut to the chase. I was in Arizona doing some campaigning, and I couldn't resist a visit. Don't worry. The press doesn't know anything about it. I've really missed you, sweetheart."

He looked at her expectantly, no doubt anticipating that she'd say the same. She didn't. Though she had missed him, she wasn't about to admit it to his face. In fact, she suspected it had been her exciting job that she'd missed rather than Jack.

So she simply smiled, not wanting to hurt his feelings. Kilbourne and she had parted friends, with his apologies and her understanding. Maggie had reserved her bitterness for the press. Jack had simply done what he had to do, salvaging his campaign with a human sacrifice thrown into the maw of the media. Just Maggie's bad luck that she was the sacrifice.

The house tour led to a dinner invitation. "What's that restaurant up here that everyone talks about?" Kilbourne asked. "The really exclusive one."

"The House of Joy. It's booked a year ahead of time, Jack, and it only has four tables. We'd never get in."

He wagged a finger at her. "You're forgetting what a little political pull can do."

Several hours later, they sat in the Haunted Hamburger, across from Robin's Nest. Jack hadn't been able to get them into the House of Joy, and Maggie wondered if he had even tried. He still had his eye on the nomination, after all, and being seen with Maggie Potter in an exclusive restaurant couldn't be something he'd want to chance. Maggie was glad, actually. At the Haunted Hamburger she knew the people well enough to be confident no one would place a call to the press.

"Are you enjoying Arizona?" she asked once they'd ordered.

"Beautiful state," he replied.

"I've always thought so. But I like the greenery of the Midwest and East, too."

"I suppose after a while, the aridness of this area could get to you."

Maggie sipped her margarita as they lapsed into uncomfortable silence. Why was Jack really here? she wondered. Colby would have told her the governor was worried about his hide and had come to Jerome to make sure that Maggie was still in his corner. But she hadn't been required to endure Colby's opinion. She hadn't seen him since his proposal on the porch that morning.

And how strange, Maggie thought, that her mind was still full of Colby after she'd spent the day visiting with Jack Kilbourne, the man she'd been mad for and heartbroken over. Proposal or not, Colby Drake should be the farthest thing from her mind.

"*You're thinking of him because he's your man,*" said a voice in her head. With sinking heart, Maggie realized they were a threesome—her, Jack, and Robbie. She couldn't see the spectral intruder, but she could hear her well enough. "*Colby is a real man. This guy's a walking dick. Damn, Maggie girl! I expected you to have better taste than this!*"

Maggie suddenly realized that Jack had asked her a question and was looking at her for a reply. "I'm sorry, Jack. What was that?"

"I asked if you've been following the polls. The president's numbers have slipped badly over this tax bill. Wouldn't you think the man would have enough sense not to address such a sensitive issue in an election year? Even if he isn't running, he should have some consideration for the vice president, who almost certainly will be running. He has no sense of timing. Straightforwardness is all very well and good—I know you were always nagging me about that—but the voters want to hear what the voters want to hear. If you're going to talk about raising taxes, do it long enough before an election for the voters to forget. Of course, it's good ammunition for me, so I shouldn't complain."

"I haven't been reading the paper much lately," Maggie explained. "And I'm too busy to watch TV."

"Poor Maggie," Jack sympathized. "Banished to the boondocks when you should be helping me with this campaign. You have no idea how much I miss your advice."

"Did the jackass ever take your advice?"

"Once I'm in office, I intend to reward you for the sacrifice you made."

"Like it was voluntary?" Robbie snickered.

Unaware of the commentary, Kilbourne continued smugly. "As long as it's not a high-profile job, I don't see any reason why there should be trouble over it. The press won't catch on. They're mostly a bunch of morons, anyway. If we're lucky, we might even manage to see each other from time to time."

"Actually, Jack, I don't think it would be such a good idea."

The waitress set their food on the table, then nervously presented Jack with a napkin to sign. "Could I have your autograph, Mr. Kilbourne? I'm such an admirer."

"Certainly you can. What's your name, dear?"

"Sarah."

He signed his name with a flourish. "There you go. I hope I can count on your vote in November."

"Oh, you bet!"

Sarah left with a glow on her face. Maggie sighed. "You'll be lucky if the press doesn't get hold of this little private dinner."

He smiled fondly and reached across the table to touch her hand. "Always thinking of my good, aren't you, Maggie?"

"He's the one always thinking of his good, the jerk. Does he kiss himself in the mirror every morning?" Robbie made a wet, smacking sound that made Maggie's mouth twitch in the beginnings of a smile.

"And would you get a load of his clothes? Where's he think he is? Nooo Yawrk City?"

She sounded so much like a certain salsa commercial that Maggie had to bite her lips to keep from laughing. "Stop," she whispered.

"His nose has been done. I swear it has! It's been fixed up right pretty. Ask him! I'll bet you wouldn't have fallen for him if you'd known he was a sissy boy who paid out good money to make himself prettier. Sheeesh!"

While Kilbourne droned on about the hardships of the campaign trail, Maggie tried to look as if she were paying attention. She wasn't about to ask the man who might be the country's next president if the nose he was wearing was the nose he was born with. But it would be more entertaining than listening to campaign war stories that she'd had no role in and anecdotes about former friends whom she would probably never see again.

The thought didn't bring the pain it might have a

month ago. She didn't really want to see those people again—all her fair-weather buddies who had disavowed friendship when the press had started their pursuit. And Jack's war stories of campaign pranks and pratfalls didn't seem funny, merely the actions of childish, self-indulgent, self-appointed elitists who believed they were somehow above Joe Schmoe who had to work at an everyday job, pay everyday taxes, and obey the law.

"And speaking of our friends in the press," Jack said, jumping onto a tangent from the story he'd just finished, "do you know anything about a reporter fellow by the name of Colby Drake?"

That caught Maggie's attention. "Colby Drake?"

"He works for *America Today*. You know it. A rag, mostly. They're the ones who went after Senator Grosmeyer when he had that little fling with his stepson. Nasty business. They really raked the guy over the coals."

"He deserved it."

"Yes, of course. But the point is, the publication's a questionable one. This Colby Drake has been a thorn in my paw for a while, and now he's mouthing off again. When you're in the public life, you get no peace. No privacy. Sometimes I think we need legislation to curb some of these people."

Maggie knew all about the excesses of the press, but the idea of curbing them made her laugh. "The Constitution might have something to say about that, Jack."

He pulled a face, then smiled. "I suppose so. Anyway, Drake's made some fairly lurid accusations in his column, and he's been out this way recently. He hasn't been pestering you, has he?"

Maggie took a long sip of her margarita. "He interviewed me a couple of times." If Colby and she had

merely "interviewed," Maggie thought dryly, then An-
tony and Cleopatra had indulged in nothing more than
a political summit meeting.

Jack shook his head sympathetically. "The nerve of
the guy. These go-for-the-throat reporters just never
give up." He gave her the smile of a kindred spirit, a
fellow sufferer of the world's injustice. Jack Kilbourne
was good at that smile. Maggie had watched him use it
on labor leaders, lobbyists, legislators, factory workers,
and DAR members with similar effect. It didn't work
on Maggie. She knew Jack too well.

"And they twist perfectly innocent statements into
earth-shaking scandals to sell their newspapers or up
the ratings on their news shows." The smile became
rueful. "But then, I don't have to tell you that."

"No, you don't."

His look of inquiry was unmistakable, but she didn't
give him the reassurance he wanted. At one time she
would have laughed and sworn that the villain Colby
Drake would never get a thing from her, but tonight
she didn't. Tonight, Jack Kilbourne's luster was peeling
off like old paint, and Colby Drake was looking very
good in comparison.

Maggie's mind was still full of Colby when Jack Kilbourne walked her across the street to her front porch
and planted a kiss on her lips. She stood absolutely
rigid as he pressed against her and demonstrated his
readiness to graduate from a kiss to something more
interesting. Maggie realized that nothing Jack Kilbourne might offer would be very interesting. His body
was too soft, his aftershave too sweet, his face too
smooth, his hints too subtle, and his hand too uncertain when it tentatively inched toward her breast. He
wasn't sufficiently brash, mocking, overconfident, and
rashy arrogant. In short, he wasn't Colby Drake.

"I have to go in, Jack. Long day tomorrow."

He instantly moved back, giving up without an argument—something that Colby would never have done.

"Thanks for dropping by, and good luck in the rest of the campaign. Say hello to the crew for me, those who are still with you."

She went inside without a backward glance, and finally let herself laugh as Robbie called after her retreating date. *Nice nose job, honey. But you need some rouge to bring out those lovely cheekbones!*

Nineteen

In a motel room in Cottonwood, the phone rang. Gilbert Meineke muted the television and reached across the bed to pick up the receiver. In the process, he rolled over the bag of Doritos he'd purchased at the vending machine. They surrendered with a pathetic crunch.

"Goddamn it!" Lifting his backside, he saw that the only survivors were crumbs.

"What?" Sly Traveterri asked from the room's one chair.

Gilbert motioned him silent as he brought the receiver to his ear and cautiously said hello. The only calls so far this evening had been from the press.

"Gilbert?" the phone said. "What's going on?"

"Nothing, Governor. I was just cussing out my corn chips."

"You've been out West too long, man."

"Yessir." Gilbert rolled his eyes at Sly, who'd relaxed back into his chair. "How's your evening going, sir?"

"Oh, fine. I had dinner with Maggie Potter, and I

was right. She's not a threat, Gilbert. We had a long talk, and I'm sure she's not a problem."

"That's excellent, Governor. Did you ask her about the logs Drake referred to?"

"Not specifically, but we did talk about Drake. She said he interviewed her a couple of times."

Gilbert made a face. "What did he want from her?"

"She didn't go into detail, but I feel confident that Maggie and I are still good friends. She won't do anything that would embarrass me. You boys can stop worrying."

"That's good to know, Governor."

"Is there anything else we need to discuss, Gilbert? I may not be in until late, and we'll be leaving for the fund-raiser in Flagstaff early tomorrow morning."

"Nothing here, Governor Kilbourne. Have a nice evening."

When he hung up, he rolled his eyes again.

"Well?" Sly asked.

"He had dinner with Potter. And it sounds like he's going to shack up with her tonight. Said he wouldn't be back until late."

Sly took a pull from his beer and grinned. "Damn! The governor's getting some and we're stuck in this friggin' motel. Want to go out on the town?"

"What town?"

Sly shrugged. "Sedona? It's—what?—fifteen miles or so up the road. Isn't it supposed to be some sort of a tourist mecca? That means they have a bar or two."

"Yeah. Okay." He switched the television off but continued to look thoughtfully at the screen. "I've still got a bad feeling about this. Just because Potter's still willing to put out for the guv, that doesn't mean she wouldn't roast his ass if some reporter offered her a few bucks. The governor's a smart man, but he's too trusting. Likes women too much. He thinks they're people, just like everybody else."

Sly agreed. "You'd think he'd have learned by now. One woman's already taken him for a chunk of alimony, and Potter almost cost him the election."

"Still could, I'm thinking. There's nothing that can cause more trouble than a riled woman. And just because she's in bed with him doesn't mean she's not riled. Not if she's like most women I know. The governor's at NAU tomorrow and tomorrow night, and he's got enough people to take care of him that he doesn't really need us there. It's just a hick university in a hick town, anyway. I'm thinking we should stay here and do a little investigating on our own. What do you think, Sly?"

"Okay by me."

Gilbert picked up the keys to the rental car, tossed them high, then caught them with a flourish. "That's why the governor hired me—to keep the campaign on track. Now I'm happy. Let's go find ourselves a bar."

Jack Kilbourne wasn't normally a heavy drinker, but tonight he deserved a few stiff ones, or so he told himself when he walked into Paul and Jerry's on Main Street, Jerome. Main Street, he snickered to himself. That was a laugh. The podunk town had only one street, really. Every time the snakelike highway switched back on itself to climb the hill, it acquired a different name. Trying to make the town look bigger and more important, that's what they were doing. But it was still Nowheresville, USA. Historic or not. Artsy-fartsy or not. Maggie Potter still lived in Nowheresville, and she'd turned down his discreet offer of a more exciting life after he was elected.

That wasn't all she'd turned town, he reminded himself gloomily.

The bartender nodded politely to him as he walked through the door, but the man gave no sign of recognition, nor did the five or so other customers look up to acknowledge him. One lone man sat at the long bar that occupied one side of the room. A middle-aged couple were busy in conversation in one of the booths, and a pair of cowboy types laughed and joshed together in a game of pool.

Jack bellied up to the bar, grateful that no one recognized him in the dim lighting. At the same time, he was a bit annoyed. He was Jack Kilbourne, quite possibly the next president of the United States. He got red carpets, security guards, and eager reporters wherever he went. Who the hell were these people to treat him like Joe Nobody?

And who the hell was Maggie Potter to give him the cold shoulder? He still felt the sting of her rejection. He'd been doing her a favor. Probably half the women in the country would jump at a chance to crawl into his bed, and Maggie, who had once declared she would always love him, turned him down.

She was probably still mad about being canned, Jack thought. At the time, she had said she understood, but women seldom said what they really think or feel.

"I'll take a gin," he told the bartender. "On the rocks, please."

"Yes, sir." The man set a glass in front of him. "Enjoying the town?"

Jack was tempted to tell him the truth. No, he wasn't enjoying the damned one-horse, podunk tourist trap. But that wouldn't have been politic. And Jack Kilbourne was always politic. "Sure am," he lied. "Beautiful little place. Historic."

"Can you believe one time Jerome was the largest town in Arizona?" the man asked with pride. "That was when the mines were going, of course. Man, there's some stories here in this town, in these old buildings. You can almost see the ghosts walking the streets."

"Oh, yes indeed. Yes indeed."

If Maggie had had to flee, why couldn't she have gone someplace interesting, like Taos, New Mexico, or Aspen, Colorado? And why hadn't she kept her promise to always love him, damn it? They could have worked something out eventually. Nothing open, of course. Not after the press had made Maggie look like Eve juggling apples. But a man in power could always find the means to indulge his needs.

The whole situation was ridiculous to start with. If the CEO of some big corporation had been fucking his executive assistant, no one in the world would have cared. But let a politician dip his wick with some young honey, the press indulged in a feeding frenzy.

Jack ordered another gin. The more he drank, the more desirable Maggie seemed, the more unfair her rejection. A man in his position didn't get rejected by women.

Jack was well on the way to a good drunk when he noticed that the lone fellow four seats down the bar was looking at him as if he recognized him. At least someone in this town knew who was who. That made him feel marginally better. Jack raised a glass in the stranger's direction. It was only politic.

Colby had ended up at Paul and Jerry's after spending much of the day wandering around Jerome nursing his wounds. Rum and Coke gave more comfort than wandering the streets, however, and for the past two hours, he'd sat in the bar, easing the pain.

It wasn't as if he'd expected Maggie to give him an outright yes. "I'll think about it" would have been a fine answer, an answer that left him hope. And her trotting out every reason why they shouldn't be together hadn't been a surprise. He'd heard them all before. Hell, he'd thought of most of them without Maggie's help. They didn't matter, though. Someday he'd make her see that. He'd plow through a dozen of her rejections in the faith that at the end she would give him a yes.

Still, rejection was hard on the old self-image. Colby wasn't accustomed to woman troubles. The ladies liked him. His mother said it was because he was kind. A lot she knew! His sister said it was because he was a hunk, and laughed when she said it. Colby thought it was because he liked the ladies in return—not just for bed sport, but to be with, laugh with, talk to. He was a charming fellow, he thought cynically. So charming that Maggie Potter all but threw up when he proposed.

That wouldn't last, Colby told himself. She loved him, and deep down, Maggie knew it. Some day she would find the courage to admit it.

When Jack Kilbourne walked through the door, Colby was surprised to see him. Earlier in the day he'd seen the guv come through the door of Robin's Nest. Colby had beat a hasty retreat, not trusting himself to remain civilized in his current mood. He hadn't expected the Great High Pooh-Bah to show up at Paul and Jerry's—and without an entourage, yet. A little down-home tavern was scarcely Jack's style.

But then, Jack didn't seem quite himself, Colby acknowledged. Even the uncertain light couldn't hide the fact that the man looked like hell. Colby watched while

Kilbourne took a seat at the bar, ordered a gin, and downed it faster than any good gin deserved. He ordered another. And then another. His Honor the Governor of Ohio was getting thoroughly soused, and none of his little sucker fish seemed to be around to save him. It was an opportunity that a news shark just couldn't pass up, even if he was a bit tipsy himself. He picked up his drink and moved down the bar.

"Hey, Jack."

Kilbourne gave him a curious look. Colby could tell he was trying to don his political face, but he was too wasted to do it. Smiling wickedly, Colby stuck out his hand to be shook. "Colby Drake."

"Shit."

"Yeah. Life sucks, doesn't it?" It didn't surprise him when Kilbourne declined to take his hand, but he was too mellow on liquor to be truly indignant.

"Life sucks," Kilbourne agreed darkly. "This town sucks. Women . . ." He heaved a sigh. "Women suck."

So that was the problem, Colby thought. He knew of only one woman in Jerome who could have put the great Jack Kilbourne in such a mood, and she was the same one who had turned his own day into a dismal funk. He actually felt some sympathy for the man. "Why don't we sit at a table and talk about it?"

Kilbourne growled. "I'm not that stupid. Or that drunk."

"Off the record," Colby promised. "There's some places where a man is entitled to let it hang out without the world peeking in."

"Thas . . . that's for sure."

Coffee, Colby mouthed at the bartender as he helped Kilbourne to a booth. The bartender nodded.

"Women aren't human," Kilbourne complained into

his drink as Colby sat down. He looked up sharply and glared. "Off the record."

"Off the record," Colby assured him. "Believe me, buddy, I know where you're coming from."

"They aren't human, y'know? Their little minds work in odd ways."

"If they work at all."

"Right. If they work at all. Ya know why God made 'em little and weak?"

"Why?"

"Because He knew he'd made a mistake when He gave 'em so much power over men, ya know? They can rip a man from the inside out and spit him out in li'l pieces. An' laugh. They laugh when they do it. So God made 'em smaller 'n men so they wouldn't have all the advantage. But it doesn' do any good, 'cause we're not supposed to hit 'em."

"Sometimes it's a temptation," Colby grumbled. "Maggie Potter is a walking invitation for a good clout to unscramble her brains."

At Maggie's name, Kilbourne's eyes sparked. "How'd you know I'm talking about Maggie?"

"Who else in this town would you be talking about?"

Jack belched loudly, then took another swallow of gin. "She said you talked to her."

Right then Colby didn't feel like telling the man he'd done a lot more than just talk to her.

"But she didn't give you nothing. She might not fuck me, but she's schtill my friend. She believes in me. Thinks I'm great. She jusht . . . just . . . she just wasn't in the mood tonight."

"She thinks you're great," Colby agreed with a wry smile.

Kilbourne looked at him with a warmth of fellow

feeling in his eyes. "So what're you drowning in drink?"

"A woman," Colby admitted. He didn't bother to explain that she was the same woman Kilbourne was trying to drown.

"Women!" the governor grumbled.

The bartender set a pot of coffee and two cups on the table. "Drink up, gents. Compliments of the house."

"Thanks," Colby said, but Kilbourne pushed his cup aside.

"We men gotta stick together, Drake. If the world had only men, it would be . . . would be . . ."

"A hell of a dull place."

Kilbourne chortled. "Right! A dull place. Dull."

Colby wondered what twist of thinking made the man believe that Maggie should welcome him with open arms after what he had done to her. Was political expediency such an ingrained reaction in him that he didn't realize how much she'd been hurt? Were the brutalities of public life so commonplace that he didn't understand that she'd been sent reeling from his betrayal? Maybe he didn't know. Maybe what had been a nightmare for her had simply been an inconvenience for him—something to be mended when the time was right.

Yet the man could be hurt. That much was plain. Maggie had gotten a certain measure of revenge, if that was what she had intended. Colby couldn't imagine that revenge had been at the root of her rejecting him. Maggie had a temper, heaven knew, with a fuse of microscopic length, but she wasn't a woman who lurked in wait with vengeance on her mind.

He poured himself a cup of coffee. Inebriation no

longer lured him, seeing how bad it looked on Kilbourne. Strange to think of the man as human, vulnerable, subject to the same uncertainties and setbacks that ruled the common man. Such inconvenient revelations made it impossible to really hate him.

It wasn't impossible, however, to still despise him as a politician. "You ought to drink some of that coffee."

"Uk. Think I'd rather be wasted. Right now, feels better'n bein' sober."

"Hm. Yeah, I guess. You know, Jack, you were probably an okay guy once."

"Huh?"

"And as politicians go, you're probably no worse than a lot, better than some. Strictly off the record." Colby grinned.

"Well, thanks, Drake. I guess."

"It wasn't a compliment."

"Oh." Kilbourne looked at both the gin and the coffee, then took a gulp of gin.

"I'm going to nail you for corruption, Jack. I'm going to lose you this election."

Kilbourne snorted. "Ya know, Drake, almost all the press are pricks. But you're worse. You're the world's biggest pain in the ass."

"Thanks."

"It wasn't a compliment."

"From you, Kilbourne, it is. If you want to be president, you'd better get used to us pains in the asses. Because we'll be all over you like maggots on rotten meat." He reached over and poured hot coffee into Kilbourne's cup. "Now drink, man. And I'll drive you back to your motel. It's probably the last favor I'll ever do for you."

Kilbourne propped one elbow on the table and

looked at Colby with woozy hostility. "Don't bother. I huv . . . have friends. They'll get me."

Colby picked up the bill and shook his head. "That's another thing you'd better get used to, Mr. Would-be President. In a position like that, you have no friends."

As Colby walked out the door, Jack sighed heavily and stared into his gin. "Don' I just know it."

• • •

Drunk as a skunk, and just as stinkin',
Hardly worth the lead to plug, I'm thinkin'.

Not bad, eh? Gives new meaning and luster to the term "Dead Poets Society"? Well, okay. Maybe as a poem it's lame, but it was running through my mind when the high and mighty Governor Jack Kilbourne stumbled out of Paul and Jerry's Saloon—which, by the way, used to be the Senate Saloon back in 1899. I like Paul and Jerry's better. It's cleaner.

Back to the point, though. I followed Kilbourne after he left Maggie on her porch, enjoying—I admit it—the sight of him suffering. He did the manly thing, of course—sat in the bar wallowing in self-pity and gin. Too bad I didn't have a camera. I could have snapped a shot that would have sold to the tabloids for big bucks. Not that I needed the cash. I was a ghost, after all, and ghosts don't pay rent or buy groceries. But the satisfaction! Ah, the satisfaction of seeing that puffy, bloated face and those bleary eyes exposed to his adoring public. It would have been sweet. In my former profession, a gal gets lots of chances to see men make fools of themselves. It was an entertainment I never got tired of.

Anyway, I lurked in wait as Kilbourne stumbled out of the saloon. He was morose and thoroughly pickled,

*poor little man, and having a very bad night. First
Maggie gives him the cold shoulder, bruising his delicate feelings, and then he meets his nemesis—dear
Colby—who reminds him what a jerk he is. I decided
to make his evening complete.*

"Hello there, handsome!"

*He jerked like a puppet on a string when I strolled
from around the corner and lounged seductively
against the big cog-wheel displayed in front of the
Mine Museum, which is right next to Paul and Jerry's.*

Jackie boy stared at me, pie-eyed and stupefied.

A cigarette rested between my fingers. "Got a
light?" *I purred. The vamps in Catherine's forties and
fifties flicks couldn't have been smoother.*

*He still looked stupefied. I raised a brow. Sophisti-
cated boredom, an edge of contempt, a lot of invitation. It was all there, guaranteed to drive a man wild.*

"I . . . I don't smoke."

"Neither do I." *I flicked the cigarette away and
walked sinuously forward.*

"Whoa! Uh . . . hi. Nice dress. Really nice."

"I'm an actress," *I explained.* "Local color. I'm
working here to get experience for the legitimate
stage."

"Oh."

"I'm supposed to make the tourists happy."

"Oh."

*His eyes got bigger when I ran a coy finger down his
lapel.* "Real happy," *I explained.* "Real, real happy."

He swallowed hard.

"My shift was over five minutes ago. And I'm
headed home to my lonely little room." *Even a drunk
politician should have been able to pick up on that
hint.*

He did. "R-really? Uh, where's your room?"

"Just up the street." I backed up a step. He followed like a puppy on a leash. Across the street was one of those concrete stairways that climbed up to the next street level, to Clark Street. If I could get the swine up there, I'd see his evening end on a very worthy note—and not the one he was expecting, either.

He tottered across the empty street after me, looking like a donkey with a carrot in front of its nose. But when we got to the stairs, he sat down, or maybe I should say he fell down with his butt hitting the first step. "My car," he slurred. There were only three cars in the little dirt lot next to the stairway, and it wasn't hard to guess the Cadillac with the rental sticker was his. "Gotta go."

"Don't go." I sat down beside him and leaned close. "You can't drive right now, Romeo. Come to my room. I'll give you some coffee." And much, much more my tone implied. My lips were close to his ear. I could feel him shiver. Oooooh! I am good at this!

He didn't resist as I lured him up the stairs. When we reached the top and stopped for breath, he fastened his bleary eyes on my fetchingly displayed bosoms. I motioned him onward, my eyes promising paradise. "This way, lover."

The town of Jerome is conscientious about putting rails on the steep drop-offs beside the switchback road that leads through town. They don't want tourists tumbling down the mountain. In my day, we weren't so careful. Men who made their living working in those mine tunnels weren't squeamish, and neither were their families. I guess they figured that if people didn't have the good sense to keep away from an edge, they deserved what they got. And that's what I think, too. I'm old-fashioned that way.

Just north of that stairway was a nice embankment dropping down to the little parking lot that we'd just passed. At one end of the lot is a stand of those obnoxious green torture chambers called portable toilets. Actually, I guess they were no worse than the outhouses of my day, but as I already told you, outhouses aren't my favorite places, seeing as I met my end in one of them.

It was toward those green outhouses that I led my victim. Trees and bushes hid the embankment, and they were thick enough that the town council hadn't stuck a railing there. I danced up the sidewalk, leading on poor Jackie boy with a not-so-subtle promise of pleasure to come. When I turned into the trees, I beckoned him to follow.

"Right here, honey. Watch your step. It's a bit overgrown."

It was dark. Kilbourne didn't know the layout of the town. I was right in front of him, smiling seductively, one shoulder of my gown drooping so that my bodice was only precariously balanced on the very tips of my breasts. He didn't know I was standing on air. Ghosts can do that.

No man could have resisted, if I do say so myself. With a shit-faced smile, he followed. And the earth dropped out from under him. I heard his curses as he bounced from tree trunk to bush and finally crashed through the top of one of those green things. I hoped his head had landed in a fitting place, like the hole of the shitter. I looked forward to seeing his face when someone got around to rescuing him in the morning.

Of course, the cans were locked at this late hour. No telling what kind of vermin might wander in in the dead of night.

"Bye, bye, Jackie boy," I called after him. "Next

time you feel like screwing over some innocent gal, don't mess with Robin Rowe's great-great-granddaughter, you hear?"

I dusted off my hands and congratulated myself. After a hundred years, I still had the touch.

Twenty

The weekend had seen an explosion of activity, culminating with the wedding on Sunday, Colby's proposal, and Jack Kilbourne's surprise visit. After all that, Monday seemed quiet as a tomb. Since the inn had been closed to guests over the weekend, there was no need for an elaborate breakfast, which was a very good thing, since Catherine was on a weeklong honeymoon at the Grand Canyon. For the rest of the week's meals, Catherine had prepared everything she could ahead of time and left Maggie detailed instructions on how to go about cooking omelets, waffles, and pancakes without turning the kitchen into a disaster area. Maggie appreciated her sister's effort and thanked heaven that Catherine had decided to continue working at the inn.

This quiet Monday, however, she was almost glad that no one else was around. After yesterday, she didn't think she could take any more excitement. Afternoon check-in time had come and gone, and no guests had appeared to disturb her peace. Colby was in the house, but he hadn't stirred from his room all day. Robbie was quiet, and George, Attila, and Hannibal weren't much for conversation, so Maggie was left alone with her thoughts—thoughts that had been blurred for a while and were just now coming into focus.

Such as the thought that Jack Kilbourne really was an ass. It had taken Maggie months to shake free of the magic net the governor cast over his acolytes and see him for the ordinary, flawed, very ambitious man that he was. Last night had done the trick, though. Not that he'd done anything atrocious. He had simply been himself, and she had seen him in a new way, away from his base of power and in the more down-to-earth setting that had become her home.

Now she was free of him. A weight no longer dragged at her heart. She could contemplate reading the morning paper without getting sick to her stomach. She might even watch the six o'clock news on television this evening. In fact, sitting at the kitchen worktable, munching on the bologna sandwich she'd made herself for dinner, the thought was even appealing. She could take her sandwich to the sunroom and watch the TV news. How lovely.

She was just walking out of the kitchen with her sandwich when the sight of Colby Drake coming down the stairs stopped her. He looked so much like the day after the night before that she had to laugh. Hair still wet from a shower, misbuttoned shirt hanging out of his trousers, and feet clad in beach thongs that had seen better days, he was obviously the worse for wear. There were circles beneath his eyes and his face was pasty white.

Still, to Maggie's eyes, he looked good. Since much of her thinking this quiet day had concerned him, she couldn't help but smile at the sight of him. "Well, look what the cat dragged in."

Colby grunted, then sat down on the steps. Standing for any amount of time apparently was beyond him. "What did the cat drag in? Has George been prowling?"

"Looks as if you're the one who was prowling. Want a sandwich?" She held up her bologna sandwich as an example of her culinary expertise.

He groaned. "I don't think so. Thanks anyway."

"Hm. I guess that was you I heard stumble in before breakfast and crash in your room."

"Yeah. I'm afraid I tied one on last night. I obviously haven't been drinking enough lately. My tolerance is down."

She pulled out a chair for him at the dining room table. "Sit. I'll get you some chicken soup. It's canned, so you don't have to worry about me having cooked it."

"Well, in that case . . . I'll take you up on it."

Five minutes later, she came out of the kitchen with a bowl of soup and a plate of buttered toast.

"The toast isn't burned," he noted. "Who made it?"

"Smartass. Eat. You'll feel better."

Maggie sat down opposite Colby and watched him dig in. She enjoyed watching his jaw muscles work. She enjoyed watching warmth and relief color his face as the soup hit his stomach.

"Mmm." He nodded as he swallowed the next spoonful. "Good."

She shook her head. "You really must have tied one on. Aren't you old enough to know better?"

He shook the spoon at her as he swallowed a mouthful, then grinned. "It was worth the hangover, believe me!"

"Really!"

"Yeah, really. You'll never guess who I ran into at Paul and Jerry's Saloon."

She tapped a fingernail on the table. "Let's see. Who could put that wolfish look in your eyes? Could it be Jack Kilbourne?"

"Bingo. He was soused. Absolutely wasted. You drove him straight to drink, sweetheart."

Her heart thumped at the endearment, and she told it sternly to be quiet. "Jack Kilbourne is responsible for his own drunk. Don't pin it on me."

"Heartless woman. Seems poor Jack isn't used to rejection."

"Poor Jack. So you trailed him to the saloon to expose yet another of his vices to the world."

"Nope. I was already in the saloon getting snockered on rum and Coke." He gave her a quick, searching glance. "For much the same reason Jack was."

She bit her lip. What could she say?

"Jack and I managed to have a comradely conversation as we drank our way to oblivion. The woes of being a man in a woman's world, and all that. But it gets better. Early this morning, the dawn patrol extracted poor Jack from one of those porta-cans in the lot across from the Nellie Bly shop. It was locked from the outside. Seems he entered the hard way—through the roof. He must have stumbled down the embankment."

"Omigod! Was he hurt?"

"Just his pride, was all. And if I were him, I'd throw that suit of clothes away. He upset the thing when he fell in. It was lying on its side."

"Shit!"

Colby grinned. "Exactly. Kilbourne claimed a woman in historic costume deliberately suckered him into falling off the embankment. She wore a red silk

dress and had feathers in her hair, or flowers, or something. Similar creature to a pink elephant, probably. He
was drunker than I thought."

Maggie groaned. So that was why Robbie had been
so quiet last night. Poor Jack hadn't seen a pink elephant; he'd been set upon by a ghost with a twisted
sense of humor. She was glad that Robbie wasn't
about, because she didn't know whether to scold her or
give her an "attagirl."

"When I stumbled in this morning," Colby continued around mouthfuls of toast, "I spent an hour setting
the whole thing down on paper. Couldn't resist."

"Oh, Colby! You wouldn't print that! Would you?"

"Probably not. I have to cut the jerk a small amount
of slack in this case. Every man can relate to a fellow
getting snockered after being dumped by a beautiful
woman."

Maggie slumped in her chair and sighed repentently.
"Colby, I didn't dump you."

He looked up quickly. "Gee, Mags. That's the way
it sounded to me. But don't worry. It's only a temporary setback."

She chuckled and shook her head. "You're impossible, you know?"

"I've been told that a time or two. Most lately by
you."

"Well, you are. That's one of the things I like about
you."

"That's encouraging."

"I don't want to lose you, Colby. As a friend.
And . . . and more. But I'm just too confused about
what I feel to commit to something big like marriage."

He pushed his plate aside, giving her his unwavering
attention. Suddenly Maggie remembered just how dis-
concerting was the full power of those intense blue

eyes. "Confused," he said thoughtfully. "We can ex-
trapolate confused to vulnerable. I think I can take advantage of that. Fair warning."

She grimaced. "Consider me warned. But perhaps
you won't need to take advantage when I tell you that
I'm going to make you a happy man."

His gaze grew sharper. "You're going to marry me?"

"Better."

Suspicion knit his brows. "There is no better. But I
suppose the next-best thing would be going upstairs to
get even better acquainted. I warn you, my room's a
mess."

"We're not going upstairs." A corner of her mouth
twitched upwards. "Downstairs, to my office, where
I'm going to give you the complete set of daily logs I
kept when I worked for Jack Kilbourne."

She didn't get quite the reaction she expected. Could
it be that the logs weren't really what he was after?
There was a definite glow in his eyes, though. "Can we
still go upstairs? Please."

Maggie's pulse quickened, but she wagged an ad-
monitory finger at the scoundrel. "Work first. Then
play."

They ended up in Colby's bedroom, of course.
Colby set his booty—two boxes of files—on the dresser
and then moved directly for Maggie. He took her face
in both hands and kissed her thoroughly.

"That was a thank-you," he said when they came up
for air. Then he kissed her again. "And that was an
invitation."

"Invitation?" she asked in a daze. Colby's kisses had
an effect more powerful than liquor.

"Invitation to play."

"Aren't you going to look at the logs?"

"Later. First things first." He unbuttoned her shirt

as he spoke. She didn't try to stop him. "Do you know how beautiful you are?"

"Oh, sure."

"Inside beautiful, not just outside. I've missed you."

"I've missed you too. I'm sorry that sometimes I'm such a witch."

"You're worth it."

By now they were on the bed. Clothes came between them, but it didn't matter. Maggie loved the feel of him so close, the look he gave her when she put her hand on him. The heat of him melted the chill in her soul—the chill that had settled in the day she realized she was an expendable pawn in a world where she thought she mattered. Colby healed her soul. Maggie didn't know how he did it, but every time she was close to him she felt the wound close a little more.

The urge to say something stupid was almost irresistible. Something stupid as in a declaration of love. That wouldn't do at all. No matter how close she felt to the man, she still didn't really believe in love. Not for her.

"I love you," he said quietly. His serene smile seemed to expect nothing from her as he continued. "Someday you're going to say it back to me. 'I love you, Colby.' That's what you're going to say. 'And I was a stubborn moron not to have known it from the first day I met your charming self.' "

She tangled her hands in his hair and pulled him down for a kiss. "Right now you'll have to settle for this."

During the kiss they managed to divest themselves of most of their troublesome clothing. Then, when Maggie thought the time for talk was well past, Colby slowed, kissed her forehead, her nose, and gave her a very serious smile.

"What?" she asked.

"Are you still angry at me?"

She thought a moment, then said, "No."

He looked almost afraid to go on. "Think about this before you say anything. It's important. Are you still in love with Jack Kilbourne?"

She didn't have to think. She'd been thinking all day. "No, Colby. I'm not."

In a tender gesture, he brushed a stray wisp of hair from her face. "What I'm most mad about right now is how he used you."

She closed her eyes, not wanting this to intrude upon the world they made together in this intimacy. But it seemed important to Colby, so she answered.

"Didn't *you* use me also, Colby?"

"Yes, I did. Everyone uses other people, but not everyone uses them dishonestly, and hurtfully, then betrays them when they become inconvenient."

Somehow, that simple statement made something fall into place in Maggie's mind, answered a question she didn't even know she had. She looked up at Colby with a wicked grin.

"Colby, I'd very much appreciate your using me a bit right now. If you don't, I think I just might die of frustration."

He chuckled. "At your service, my lady."

How very cozy. There they were, enjoying youth, life, and passion by making whoopee on the sheets, and as the night drew on, they fell asleep in each other's arms. I told you—didn't I?—that they wouldn't be able to stay apart for long, in spite of Maggie's pigheadedness. And in case you haven't noticed, she comes by that honestly.

What a romantic ending, you say. Catherine got her husband. Colby got his logs, and Maggie—well, Maggie was still whining that love was a sham, even while she was falling right into its arms. Some storytellers would leave you up in the air to figure out for yourself if Maggie finally got smart. I'm not going to do that. The story isn't over yet. Besides, since this isn't something I just made up out of thin air, it has a real ending, and the city-slicker bad guys who were going to bring everything to a head were at that moment creeping into the front hallway.

Did I mention before that Maggie often leaves her front door unlocked for late-night guests? A lot of folks in Jerome don't bother with locks and chains. They prattle on about Jerome being such a peaceful little town. Hah! They should have lived here when I did. A lady couldn't even do her business in the outhouse without getting shot. Peaceful, my foot!

But that's beside the point. Maggie often left her front door unlocked, and tonight that's what she did, even though she didn't have any guests. Of course, she had other things on her mind.

That open door made it easy for a couple of weasels to slip in while she and Colby were sleeping, though by the look of the intruders, they would have found a way to get in even if the door had been locked. They tiptoed through the house, hissing to each other when they didn't find what they were looking for. Then one of them pointed his flashlight at the architectural layout of Robin's Nest displayed in the hallway. The modern use of each room was noted beside the original use, and they homed in on Maggie's office.

"Basement," *one whispered to the other.*

"What if someone's down there?" *asked the other.*

"The only light was upstairs."

The other nodded, and down they went.

And where was our hero while all this skulduggery was taking place? You guessed it, sawing logs in bed, worn out by his efforts with Maggie. And she slept just as deeply as he. The stupid cat was no help. George was curled contentedly at their feet.

So as usual, I had to take a hand. To tell the truth, I was delighted. It stuck in my craw that that Colby didn't believe I was real. After all I'd done to fix him up with Maggie, he thought I was just an eccentric figment of Maggie's imagination. This was my opportunity to give him something to think about.

He slept spoon-fashion on the bed, curled around Maggie like he would protect her from the cruel, cold world. And what a load of bullshit that was, for while he was off in dreamland, the villains were on the prowl. I slapped him on the butt a good sharp smack. A nice tight tush he has, by the way.

He came awake with a start, and so did Gorgeous George, who hissed her displeasure.

"What?" he asked the cat blearily. "I didn't do anything."

I could have materialized right there, told him what was going on, and let him save the day. But that would have been too easy. Instead, I called to him from the hallway.

"Yoo-hoo, handsome. Come out and play!"

"What the hell?" he muttered, then climbed out of bed, pulled on the BVDs and T-shirt he'd so eagerly gotten out of earlier, and stumbled around in the dark until he reached the door. When he looked out, I called from the stairway.

"This way, Colby dear. Come on, you handsome jackass."

His eyes widened. He pinched himself, took a deep

breath, then jumped almost to the ceiling when George curled around his legs. I laughed merrily as he scowled down at the poor cat.

"Come on, lover boy!" I urged. "You're wasting time."

He followed, shaking his head. Poor fellow. He must have wondered if his drinking spree was coming back to haunt him. It wasn't until I'd led him into the downstairs main hallway that he heard the suspicious sounds coming from the basement. The wooziness of sleep seemed to dissolve as he tensed and moved silently to the head of the basement stairs, listening with narrowed eyes.

Then he did something stupid and typically male. Now, I like men as well as anyone. After all, I made a very nice living off them for many years. I ought to like them. But they have this silly need to be tough. Wouldn't you think Colby would have grabbed a weapon before going down those stairs? A skillet? A butcher knife? Something? I would have. But no, he apparently thought he could hold his own with sheer manliness. Men! Gotta love them, but sometimes Gorgeous George had more smarts.

When Colby surprised Gilbert and Sylvester going through Maggie's desk, then it was too late to go back upstairs for a baseball bat. Instead, he got all indignant and confronted the two prowlers. When they wheeled around in a panic, his eyes widened.

"Good God! Kilbourne's Bobbsey twins! What the hell are you doing here?"

What wakened Maggie in the middle of the night she didn't quite know, but as she lay there in Colby's bed, without Colby, she sensed something was wrong.

Colby wasn't beside her. He was probably getting a late-night snack, she mused with a satisfied little smile. She had worked him hard. Not that he hadn't demanded the same of her.

She wondered exactly when in the night she had started believing she might really love Colby Drake. Passion had something to do with her revelation, but not everything. His persistence had something to do with it also. But mostly, her brain had cleared when he'd made that offhand remark about everyone using other people, but not everyone being cruel or dishonest when they did it. The proverbial light bulb had snapped on inside her head, and she realized that she had been afraid of Colby because it was so obvious he was using her. He'd started out being sneaky about it, true, but since they'd become involved, he'd never tried to hide his agenda. He'd been honest about what he wanted from her, and honest about his feelings. She'd been the one confused about what she wanted, making love with him one day, pushing him away the next. And still he loved her. He kept coming back. The man was insane. How could a woman help but fall for a guy like that?

The clock beside the bed kept ticking, and still Colby didn't return. Impatient to finally declare herself, Maggie got up and tiptoed down the stairs in bare feet and one of Colby's shirts. Halfway down she heard the scuffling in the basement.

She detoured into the kitchen to grab a cast-iron skillet, then, suitably armed, hurried down the basement stairs. What met her amazed eyes was a shambles, and in the middle of the shambles was a fighting, punching, writhing ball that seemed to be a tangle of three men. George was backed into a corner for shelter, her spine arched in displeasure, her green eyes spitting alarm. Attila and Hannibal hopped and fluttered about their cage and kept up a running commentary on the action.

Robbie instantly popped into view and waved. *"Isn't it great? Just like the old days!"*

Maggie stood stunned, totally at a loss.

"Well, ninny! Don't just stand there. Your man is getting the shit beat out of him. Do something!" With that piece of advice, she blinked out of sight.

Maggie raised her skillet and prepared to wade into the fray, but before she could intervene, one of the intruders—a beefy, red-faced fellow with a crew cut—grabbed the desk chair and swung it at Colby's head. Colby ducked, only to be tripped by George, who had spotted Maggie and dashed across the room to take shelter behind her. The villain raised the chair for another assault, but the lamp flew from the corner of Maggie's desk and whacked him on the back of the head.

He fell like a toppled tree—right on top of Colby, who struggled in vain to push him off. The fellow's partner in crime fled the scene, stringing curses behind him. Maggie swung her skillet as he went by, but missed.

"No you don't, sucker."

The skillet jerked from Maggie's hands and floated in front of the poor man, who screeched to a halt and stood transfixed. The cast iron bonged when it connected with the skull above his ears. He looked almost grateful as he sank to the floor.

Maggie gave the ghost a thumbs-up. "Thanks, Granny."

"Don't mention it."

Meanwhile, Colby had managed to crawl from beneath Gilbert's limp form. He stood shakily, looking

little better than the fellow who'd been kissed by the
skillet. "Did you see that?" he breathed.

Maggie gave him a half-apologetic, half–I-told-you-
so shrug of her brows.

"He . . . they . . . the lamp . . . Shit! You really
do have a ghost here!"

"Don't worry," Maggie said with a wry smile. "She
likes you."

"That's a relief. Otherwise, I'd be wearing that chair
on my face."

Maggie succumbed to a sudden case of the shakes.
She righted the chair and sat. "Colby! I can't believe
you tackled two intruders by yourself. Why didn't you
just call nine-one-one?"

"Don't you know who these guys are?"

She looked closely at the unconscious villains. "No.
Who are they?"

Colby picked up the skillet from the floor and waved
it at the first assailant like a loaded gun. "The charming
fellow who looks like a gorilla is Gilbert Meineke. He's
the spin doctor who's trying to keep Jack Kilbourne's
rep squeaky clean, and he's a lot smarter than he looks.
The other one is Sly Traveterri. He's sort of Gilbert's
understudy. The press has been calling them 'Gilbert
and Sullivan,' figuring their versions of the guv's character and intentions are about as serious as a comic
operetta."

"They were looking for the logs," Maggie concluded.

"Right. They were looking for the logs. And if the
cops are called on this, you become the star of another
national press frenzy."

Her mouth slanted down in disgust. "At least you'll
get your scoop. Do they still call it that?"

"The only scoop I want is from the ice-cream parlor

down the street. Why do you think I didn't call nine-one-one?"

She went to him and touched his arm gently, almost unbelievingly. "You would give this up? The ideal chance to show the country just how low Jack Kilbourne really is?"

He smiled down at her. "I've got the logs. That's the real story." He tried to look noble, but spoiled the effect with a sidelong glance to assess her reaction. Then he gave it up and just grinned.

Maggie's heart felt light, in spite of the two goons lying at her feet.

"Besides," Colby admitted. "I doubt Jackie boy knew about this. He's a toad, but this isn't his style. I say we just pack these lads back to their boss with the understanding the less said, the better."

Avoiding the skillet, she slipped her arms around him. "I love you, Colby Drake."

He grew still. "Because I'm willing to squelch a story?"

"No. I knew earlier that I love you. But this does seem an appropriate time to tell you, with my enemies strewn at your feet."

"Compliments of your ghost." He cupped her cheek with one hand, caressing it. "Isn't there something we can do to thank her?"

Maggie stood on tiptoe to kiss him. "Yes, there is. And it's going to make us both very happy."

Well, there you have it, all sewn up with a happy ending. Myself, I think I did a bang-up job. Maggie wasn't that easy of a nut to crack, you know. And I even managed to fix up Catherine, who isn't even a blood relative.

This is the part of any spook story where the restless spirit finds peace and toodles off to a higher realm. Right? The curse that plagued my family was ended, and if the look in Colby's eye was any clue, the next generation of Roberta Rowe's descendants wouldn't be long in coming. So should I do the expected and move on?

What do you think?

Epilogue

Washington Post, *October 10, 2000*

The Post is proud to announce that columnist Colby Drake has joined our staff of writers. Mr. Drake's investigative reporting was instrumental in bringing to public notice certain allegations about Jack Kilbourne, who surprised the nation this past summer by withdrawing his name from consideration of his party for the presidential nomination. Up until that time, Kilbourne had been considered the front-runner for the nomination and possibly for the upcoming election. The facts brought to light by Mr. Drake's investigation are currently being looked into by the Ohio courts.

Arizona Republic, *November 20, 2000*

Margaret Potter and Colby Drake were married Saturday at Red Rocks Congregational Church in Sedona. The bride was attended by her sister, Catherine Matthews, as matron of honor, and the groom was attended by Tom Matthews as best man. The groom is a nationally noted columist for the *Washington Post,* and the bride is a partner in the recently renovated historic Robin's Nest Inn in Jerome. The successful inn will remain open with Catherine Matthews as hostess while the bride resides in Arlington, Virginia, with her new husband. She has accepted a position as public liaison in the office of Arizona Congresswoman Jill Schneider.

America Today, *December 6, 2000*

The folks in the Senate Office Building have been a bit spooked lately, and not just by the prospect of a new president taking office next month. Three secretaries and one political assistant have reported seeing a ghostly apparition—one in the Senate cloakroom, two in the ladies' powder room, and one in the cafeteria. The descriptions given by eyewitnesses are similar: the apparition is a buxom woman with red hair, a wicked smile, a rose in her hair, and a silk gown of a fashion worn a century ago. One sighting from the powder room noted black fishnet stockings.

If any of our esteemed senators have seen this vision in silk and fishnet, they're keeping it to themselves.

Well, I couldn't very well let those two go off to the nation's capital on their own, could I? Someone has to keep an eye on them, keep them on track—and there's no sense in not having a little fun while I'm doing it.

ABOUT THE AUTHOR

EMILY CARMICHAEL, award-winning author of nineteen novels and novellas, has won praise for both her historical and contemporary romances. An Arizona native, she currently lives in the Chicago area with her husband and a houseful of dogs.

Jean Stone

First Loves

For every woman there is a first love, the love she never forgets. Now Meg, Zoe, and Alissa have given themselves six months to find the men who got away. But can they recover the magic they left behind?

_____56343-2 $5.99/$6.99

Places by the Sea

In the bestselling tradition of Barbara Delinsky, this is the enthralling, emotionally charged tale of a woman who thought she led a charmed life…until she discovered the real meaning of friendship, betrayal, forgiveness, and love.

_____57424-8 $5.99/$7.99

Birthday Girls

Abigail, Maddie, and Chris were childhood friends who celebrated birthdays together. Now, as they near the age of fifty, they must try to make each others' wishes come true.

_____57785-9 $5.99/$7.99

Tides of the Heart

In an attempt to make peace with her past, a woman goes to Martha's Vineyard to find the daughter she gave up for adoption thirty years ago.

_____57786-7 $5.99/$7.99

Ask for this book at your local bookstore or use this page to order.

Please send me the book I have checked above. I am enclosing $_____ (add $2.50 to cover postage and handling). Send check or money order, no cash or C.O.D.'s, please.

Name _____

Address _____

City/State/Zip _____

Send order to: Bantam Books, Dept. FN 4, 2451 S. Wolf Rd., Des Plaines, IL 60018
Allow four to six weeks for delivery.
Prices and availability subject to change without notice.   FN 4 12/98

Deborah Smith

*"A uniquely significant voice
in contemporary fiction."*
—Romantic Times

Silk and Stone ___29689-2 $6.50/$9.99 in Canada

Blue Willow ___29690-6 $6.50/$9.99

Miracle ___29107-6 $6.99/$9.99

A Place to Call Home ___57813-8 $6.50/$8.99

When Venus Fell ___11143-4 $23.95/$29.95

Ask for these books at your local bookstore or use this page to order.

Please send me the books I have checked above. I am enclosing $____ (add $2.50 to cover postage and handling). Send check or money order, no cash or C.O.D.'s, please.

Name _____

Address _____

City/State/Zip _____

Send order to: Bantam Books, Dept. FN72, 2451 S. Wolf Rd., Des Plaines, IL 60018
Allow four to six weeks for delivery.
Prices and availability subject to change without notice.   FN 72 1/99